1 National Bestseller
Shortlisted for the Man Booker ...e
A *New York Times* Notable Book ...009
A *Publishers Weekly* T p 100 Bo t 2009

International Acc'
The Little Sti

"Waters's masterly novel is a perverse hymn to decay, to the corrosive power of class resentment as well as the damage wrought by the war. . . . Its mood lingers."
– Hilary Mantel

"The best book I read this year. . . . A tale of deepening obsession . . . authentically horrifying."
– Stephen King

"A terrific consideration of the ravages of class in post-war Britain, and a ripping ghost story, too."
– Audrey Niffenegger

"Poignant. . . . Waters is clearly at the top of her game."
– Tracy Chevalier

"A classic ghost story of the haunted house, Edgar Allan Poe variety."
– Fay Weldon

"One of the best ghost stories of the decade."
– David Mitchell

"Completely absorbing. . . . A ghost story full of mystery [by a] gifted storyteller." — *Newsday*

"A stunning haunted house tale whose ghosts are as horrifying as any in Shirley Jackson's *The Haunting of Hill House*."
— *Publishers Weekly* (starred review)

"Sarah Waters has renewed a chilling genre. Just don't read her new book in the house on your own at night." — *Evening Standard*

"Hauntingly good. . . . [Waters has a] Hitchcockian gift for making mundane household occurrences – spots on the wall, a lost pair of cufflinks – turn into intimations of evil." —*Seattle Times*

"Masterly, enthralling. . . . An astonishing performance, right down to the book's mournful and devastating final sentence." — Salon.com

"There are hints of the dark anger that pervades Emily Bronte's *Wuthering Heights* in this latter-day gothic masterpiece."
— *Washington Times*

"A terrific tale. . . . [Waters] tells a story like no one else."
— *NOW* magazine (Toronto)

"An engrossing, highly enjoyable read. . . . A hell of a ride."
— *The Telegraph*

"A marvelous and truly spooky historical novel [written in] precise and chilling prose."   – *Boston Globe*

"Waters writes with great insight about what it means to hold out in an age of progress. For Faraday, it's a cracked window pane that reflects a permanent present and a dusty future. And that may be much worse than the dim hope of a green light."   – *Chicago Sun-Times*

"A stunning ghost story that nurtures *Turn of the Screw*–style ambiguities. . . . Waters waits until the last possible minute to unveil her answers."   – *TimeOut New York*

"Darkly atmospheric. . . . An eerie ghost story mixed with piercing class commentary, Waters' latest is downright haunting."   – *Booklist*

"The beauty of *The Little Stranger* is how deftly Waters has recreated a believable world of the past, with all of its clashes and conflicts."
                                    – *Seattle Post Intelligencer*

The Little Stranger

SARAH WATERS

EMBLEM

McClelland & Stewart

Cloth edition published 2009
Emblem edition published 2010

Emblem is an imprint of McClelland & Stewart Ltd.
Emblem and colophon are registered trademarks of McClelland & Stewart Ltd.

Library and Archives Canada Cataloguing in Publication

Waters, Sarah, 1966-

    The little stranger / Sarah Waters.

ISBN 978-0-7710-8789-9

I. Title.

PR6073.A828L57 2010   823'.914   C2009-905209-1

We acknowledge the financial support of the Government of Canada through the Book
Publishing Industry Development Program and that of the Government of Ontario
through the Ontario Media Development Corporation's Ontario Book Initiative. We
further acknowledge the support of the Canada Council for the Arts and the Ontario
Arts Council for our publishing program.

Typeset in Sabon

Book design by Amanda Dewey

Printed and bound in the United States of America

McClelland & Stewart Ltd.
75 Sherbourne Street
Toronto, Ontario
M5A 2P9
www.mcclelland.com

1   2   3   4   5   14   13   12   11   10

To my parents, Mary and Ron,
and my sister, Deborah.

ONE

I first saw Hundreds Hall when I was ten years old. It was the summer after the war, and the Ayreses still had most of their money then, were still big people in the district. The event was an Empire Day fête: I stood with a line of other village children making a Boy Scout salute while Mrs Ayres and the Colonel went past us, handing out commemorative medals; afterwards we sat to tea with our parents at long tables on what I suppose was the south lawn. Mrs Ayres would have been twenty-four or -five, her husband a few years older; their little girl, Susan, would have been about six. They must have made a very handsome family, but my memory of them is vague. I recall most vividly the house itself, which struck me as an absolute mansion. I remember its lovely ageing details: the worn red brick, the cockled window glass, the weathered sandstone edgings. They made it look blurred and slightly uncertain—like an ice, I thought, just beginning to melt in the sun.

There were no trips inside, of course. The doors and French windows stood open, but each had a rope or a ribbon tied across it; the lavatories set aside for our use were the grooms' and the gardeners', in the stable block. My mother, however, still had friends among the servants, and when the tea was finished and people were given the run of the grounds, she took me quietly into the house by a side door, and we spent a little time with the cook and the kitchen girls. The visit impressed me terribly. The kitchen was a basement one, reached by a cool vaulted corridor with something of the feel of a castle dungeon. An extraordinary number of people seemed to be coming and going along it with hampers and trays. The girls had such a mountain of crockery to wash, my mother rolled up her sleeves to help them; and to my very great delight, as a reward for her labour I was allowed to take my pick of the jellies and 'shapes' that had come back uneaten from the fête. I was put to sit at a deal-topped table, and given a spoon from the family's own drawer—a heavy thing of dulled silver, its bowl almost bigger than my mouth.

But then came an even greater treat. High up on the wall of the vaulted passage was a junction-box of wires and bells, and when one of these bells was set ringing, calling the parlourmaid upstairs, she took me with her, so that I might peep past the green baize curtain that separated the front of the house from the back. I could stand and wait for her there, she said, if I was very good and quiet. I must only be sure to keep behind the curtain, for if the Colonel or the missus were to see me, there'd be a row.

I was an obedient child, as a rule. But the curtain opened onto the corner junction of two marble-floored passages, each one filled with marvellous things; and once she had disappeared softly in one direction, I took a few daring steps in the other. The thrill of it was astonishing. I don't mean the simple thrill of trespass, I mean the thrill of the house itself, which came to me from every surface—from the polish on the floor, the patina on wooden chairs and cabinets, the bevel of a looking-glass, the scroll of a frame. I was drawn to one of the dustless white walls, which had a decorative plaster border, a representation of acorns and leaves. I had never seen anything like it, outside of a church, and after a second of looking it over I did what strikes me now as a dreadful thing: I worked my fingers around one of the acorns and tried to prise it from its setting; and when that failed to release it, I got out my penknife and dug away with that. I didn't do it in a spirit of vandalism. I wasn't a spiteful or destructive boy. It was simply that, in admiring the house, I wanted to possess a piece of it—or rather, as if the admiration itself, which I suspected a more ordinary child would not have felt, entitled me to it. I was like a man, I suppose, wanting a lock of hair from the head of a girl he had suddenly and blindingly become enamoured of.

I'm afraid the acorn gave at last, though less cleanly than I'd been expecting, with a tug of fibre and a fall of white powder and grit; I remember that as disappointing. Possibly I'd imagined it to be made of marble.

But nobody came, nobody caught me. It was, as they say, the work of a moment. I put the acorn in my pocket, and slipped back behind the curtain. The parlourmaid returned a minute later and took me back downstairs; my mother and I said goodbye to the kitchen staff, and rejoined my father in the garden. I felt the hard plaster lump in my pocket, now, with a sort of sick excitement. I'd begun to be anxious that Colonel Ayres, a frightening man, would discover the damage and stop the fête. But the afternoon ran on without incident until the bluish drawing-in of dusk. My parents and I joined other Lidcote people for the long walk home, the bats flitting and wheeling with us along the lanes as if whirled on invisible strings.

My mother found the acorn, of course, eventually. I had been drawing it in and out of my pocket, and it had left a chalky trail on the grey flannel of my shorts. When she understood what the queer little thing in her hand was, she almost wept. She didn't smack me, or tell my father; she never had the heart for arguments. Instead she looked at me, with her tearful eyes, as if baffled and ashamed.

'You ought to know better, a clever lad like you,' I expect she said.

People were always saying things like that to me when I was young. My parents, my uncles, my schoolmasters—all the various adults who interested themselves in my career. The words used to drive me into secret rages, because on the one hand I wanted desperately to live up to my own reputation for cleverness, and on the other it seemed very unfair, that that cleverness, which I had never asked for, could be turned into something with which to cut me down.

The acorn was put on the fire. I found the blackened nub of it among the clinker, next day. That must have been the last grand year for Hundreds Hall, anyway. The following Empire Day fête was given by another family, in one of the neighbouring big houses; Hundreds had started its steady decline. Soon afterwards the Ayreses' daughter died, and Mrs Ayres and the Colonel began to live less publicly. I dimly remember the births of their next two children, Caroline and Roderick— but by then I was at Leamington College, and busy with bitter little battles of my own. My mother died when I was fifteen. She had had miscarriage after miscarriage, it turned out, all through my childhood, and the last one killed her. My father lived just long enough to see me graduate from medical school and return to Lidcote a qualified man. Colonel Ayres died a few years later—an aneurism, I think.

With his death, Hundreds Hall withdrew even further from the world. The gates of the park were kept almost permanently closed. The solid brown stone boundary wall, though not especially high, was high enough to seem forbidding. And for all that the house was such a grand one, there was no spot, on any of the lanes in that part of Warwickshire, from which it could be glimpsed. I sometimes thought of it, tucked away in there, as I passed the wall on my rounds—picturing it always as it had seemed to me that day in 1919, with its handsome brick faces, and its cool marble passages, each one filled with marvellous things.

So when I did see the house again—almost thirty years on from that first visit, and shortly after the end of another war—the changes in it appalled me. It was the purest chance that took me out there, for the Ayreses were registered with my partner, David Graham; but he was busy with an emergency case that day, so when the family sent out for a doctor the request was passed on to me. My heart began to sink almost the moment I let myself into the park. I remembered a long approach to the house through neat rhododendron and laurel, but the park was now so overgrown and untended, my small car had to fight its way down the drive. When I broke free of the bushes at last and found myself on a sweep of lumpy gravel with the Hall directly ahead of me, I put on the brake, and gaped in dismay. The house was smaller than in memory, of course—not quite the mansion I'd been recalling— but I'd been expecting that. What horrified me were the signs of decay. Sections of the lovely weathered edgings seemed to have fallen completely away, so that the house's uncertain Georgian outline was even more tentative than before. Ivy had spread, then patchily died, and hung like tangled rat's-tail hair. The steps leading up to the broad front door were cracked, with weeds growing lushly up through the seams.

I parked my car, climbed out, and almost feared to slam the door. The place, for so large and solid a structure, felt precarious. No one appeared to have heard me arrive, so after a little hesitation I went crunching over the gravel and gingerly climbed the cracked stone steps. It was a hot, still summer's day—so windless that when I tugged on the tarnished old brass and ivory bell-pull I caught the ring of it, pure and clear, but distant, as if in the belly of the house. The ring was immediately followed by the faint, gruff barking of a dog.

The barks were very soon cut off, and for another long minute there was silence. Then, from somewhere to my right, I heard the scrape of an irregular footstep, and a moment later the son of the family, Roderick, appeared around the corner of the house. He squinted over at me with some suspicion, until noticing the bag in my hand. Drawing a collapsed-looking cigarette from his mouth he called, 'You're the doctor, are you? We were expecting Dr Graham.'

His tone was friendly enough, but had a touch of languor to it; as if he were bored by the sight of me already. I left the steps and went over to him, introducing myself as Graham's partner, explaining about Graham's emergency case. He answered blandly, 'Well, it's good of you to come out. On a Sunday, too; and such a filthy hot one. Come this

way, would you? It's quicker than going right through the house. I'm
Roderick Ayres, by the way.'

We had in fact met before, on more than one occasion. But he'd
clearly forgotten that, and as we moved off he gave me his hand for a
perfunctory shake. His fingers felt queer against mine, rough as croco-
dile in some spots, oddly smooth in others: his hands had been burnt,
I knew, in a wartime accident, along with a good part of his face. The
scars aside, he was handsome: taller than me, but, at twenty-four, still
boyish and slender. He was dressed boyishly too, in an open-necked
shirt, summer trousers, and stained canvas shoes. He walked unhur-
riedly, and with a noticeable limp.

He said as we went, 'You know why we called you, I suppose?'

I said, 'I was told, for one of your maids.'

'*One* of our maids! I like that. There's only the one: our girl, Betty.
Some stomach problem, it seems to be.' He looked dubious. 'I don't
know. My mother, my sister, and I tend to manage without doctors as
a rule. We muddle through with colds and headaches. But I gather that
neglecting the servants is a capital offence these days; they're to get
better treatment than us, apparently. So we thought we ought to send
for someone. Watch your step just here, look.'

He had taken me along a gravelled terrace that ran the length of the
north side of the Hall; he indicated a spot where the terrace had subsided, making for treacherous dips and cracks. I picked my way around
them, interested to have been given a chance to see this side of the
house—but aghast, again, at how badly the place had been allowed to
decline. The garden was a chaos of nettle and bindweed. There was a
faint but definite whiff of blocked drains. The windows we passed were
streaked and dusty; all were closed, and most were shuttered, except
for a pair of glass doors that stood open at the top of a set of flying
stone steps wound about with convolvulus. They gave me a view of a
large untidy room, a desk with a mess of papers on it, an edge
of brocade curtain . . . That was all I had time to see. We had reached
a narrow service doorway, and Roderick was standing aside to let
me pass.

'Go on, would you?' he said, gesturing with one of his scarred hands. 'My sister's downstairs. She'll show you to Betty, and fill you in.'

Only later, recalling his injured leg, would I guess that he must not have wanted me to see him struggling with stairs. As it was, I thought his manner rather casual, and I went past him, saying nothing. At once, I heard him crunching quietly away in his rubber-soled shoes.

But I went quietly, myself. This narrow doorway, I had realised, was the one through which my mother had more or less smuggled me, all those years before. I remembered the bare stone stairway it led to, and, following the steps down, I found myself in the dim vaulted passage that had so impressed me then. But here was another disappointment. I had been picturing this passage as something like a crypt or a dungeon; in fact its walls were the glossy cream-and-green of police- and fire-stations, there was a strip of coconut matting on the flagstone floor, and a mop sat sourly in a bucket. Nobody emerged to greet me, but to my right a half-open door offered a glimpse of the kitchen, so I went softly over and looked inside. Yet another damp squib: I found a large lifeless room with Victorian counters and mortuary surfaces, all brutally scoured and scrubbed. Only the old deal table—the very table, by the look of it, where I had eaten my jellies and 'shapes'—recalled the excitement of that first visit. It was also the only thing in the room to bear any sign of activity, for there was a small pile of muddy vegetables put out on it, together with a bowl of water and a knife—the water discoloured, and the knife wet, as if someone had recently started the task and been called away.

I stepped back; and my shoe must have creaked, or scuffed against the coconut matting. There came again the gruff excited barking of a dog—alarmingly close, this time—and a second later an elderly black Labrador burst from somewhere into the passage and began hurtling towards me. I stood still with my bag raised while it barked and pranced around me, and soon a young woman appeared behind it, saying mildly, 'All right, you idiotic creature, that's enough! Gyp! Enough!—I'm so sorry.' She drew nearer, and I recognised Roderick's sister, Caroline. 'I can't bear a leaping dog, and he knows it. *Gyp!*' She reached forward

to give him a swipe upon his haunches with the back of her hand; and
at that he subsided.

'Little imbecile,' she said, tugging his ears with a look of indulgence.
'It's touching really. He thinks every stranger's come to cut our throats
and make off with the family silver. We haven't the heart to tell him the
silver's all been popped. I thought we were getting Dr Graham. You're
Dr Faraday. We've never been properly introduced, have we?'

She smiled as she spoke, and offered me her hand. Her grip was
firmer than her brother's had been, and more sincere.

I'd only ever seen her at a distance before, at county events, or on
the streets of Warwick and Leamington. She was older than Roderick,
twenty-six or twenty-seven, and I'd regularly heard her referred to locally as 'rather hearty', a 'natural spinster', a 'clever girl'—in other
words she was noticeably plain, over-tall for a woman, with thickish
legs and ankles. Her hair was a pale English brown and might, with
proper treatment, have been handsome, but I had never seen it tidy, and
just now it fell drily to her shoulders, as if she had washed it with
kitchen soap and then forgotten to comb it. Added to that, she had the
worst dress-sense of any woman I ever knew. She was wearing boyish
flat sandals and a badly fitting pale summer dress, not at all flattering
to her wide hips and large bosom. Her eyes were hazel, highly set; her
face was long with an angular jaw, her profile flattish. Only her mouth,
I thought, was good: surprisingly large, well-shaped, and mobile.

I explained again about Graham's emergency case and the call having been passed on to me. She said, as her brother had, 'Well, it's good
of you to have come all this way. Betty hasn't been with us very long;
less than a month. Her family live over on the other side of Southam,
just too far for us to think of bothering them. The mother, anyway, is
by all accounts a bit of a bad lot . . . She started complaining about her
stomach last night, and when she seemed no better this morning, well,
I thought we ought to make sure. Will you look at her right away? She's
just up here.'

She turned as she spoke, moving off on her muscular legs; and the
dog and I followed. The room she took me into was right at the end

of the corridor, and might once, I thought, have been a housekeeper's parlour. It was smaller than the kitchen, but like the rest of the basement it had a stone floor and high, stunted windows, and the same drab institutional paint. There was a narrow grate, swept clean, a faded armchair and a table, and a metal-framed bed—the kind which, when not in use, can be folded and tucked out of sight in a cavity in the cupboard behind it. Lying beneath the covers of this bed, dressed in a petticoat or sleeveless nightdress, was a figure so small and slight I took it at first to be that of a child; looking closer, I saw it to be an undergrown teenage girl. She made an attempt to push herself up when she saw me in the doorway, but fell pathetically back against her pillow as I approached. I sat on the bed at her side and said, 'Well, you're Betty, are you? My name's Dr Faraday. Miss Ayres tells me you've had a tummy ache. How are you feeling now?'

She said, in a bad country accent, 'Please, Doctor, I'm awful poorly!'

'Have you been sick at all?'

She shook her head.

'Any diarrhoea? You know what that is?'

She nodded; then shook her head again.

I opened up my bag. 'All right, let's have a look at you.'

She parted her childish lips just far enough to let me slip the bulb of the thermometer under her tongue, and when I drew down the neck of her nightdress and set the chilly stethoscope to her chest, she flinched and groaned. Since she came from a local family, I had probably seen her before, if only to give her her school vaccination; but I had no memory of it now. She was an unmemorable sort of girl. Her colourless hair was bluntly cut, and fastened with a grip at the side of her forehead. Her face was broad, her eyes wide-spaced; the eyes themselves were grey and, like many light eyes, rather depthless. Her cheek was pale, only darkening slightly in a blush of self-consciousness when I put up her nightdress to examine her stomach, exposing her dingy flannel knickers.

As soon as I placed my fingers lightly on the flesh above her navel, she gave a gasp, crying out—almost screaming. I said soothingly, 'All right. Now, where does it hurt most? Here?'

She said, 'Oh! All over!'

'Does the pain come sharply, like a cut? Or is it more like an ache, or a burn?'

'It's like an ache,' she cried, 'with cuts all in it! But it's burning, too! Oh!' She screamed again, opening her mouth wide at last, revealing a healthy tongue and throat and a row of little crooked teeth.

'All right,' I said again, pulling her nightie back down. And after a moment's thought I turned to Caroline—who had been standing in the open doorway with the Labrador beside her, looking anxiously on— and said, 'Could you leave me alone with Betty for a minute, please, Miss Ayres?'

She frowned at the seriousness of my tone. 'Yes, of course.'

She made a gesture to the dog, and took him out into the passage. When the door was closed behind her I put away my stethoscope and thermometer, and closed my bag with a snap. I looked at the pale-faced girl and said quietly, 'Now then, Betty. This puts me in a ticklish position. For there's Miss Ayres out there, who's gone to an awful lot of trouble to try and make you better; and here am I, knowing for a fact that there's nothing at all I can do for you.'

She stared at me. I said more plainly, 'Do you think I don't have more important things to do on my day off than come chasing five miles out of Lidcote to look after naughty little girls? I've a good mind to send you to Leamington to have your appendix out. There's nothing wrong with you.'

Her face turned scarlet. She said, 'Oh, Doctor, there is!'

'You're a good actress, I'll give you that. All that screaming and thrashing about. But if I want play-acting, I'll go to the theatre. Who do you think's going to pay me now, hey? I don't come cheap, you know.'

The mention of money frightened her. She said with genuine anxiety, 'I *am* poorly! I *am*! I *did* feel sick last night. I felt sick horrible. And I thought—'

'What? That you'd like a nice day in bed?'

'No! You in't being fair! I *did* feel poorly. And I just thought—' And here her voice began to thicken, and her grey eyes filled with tears. 'I just thought,' she repeated, unsteadily, 'that if I was as poorly as that, then—then perhaps I ought to go home for a bit. Till I got better.'

She turned her face from me, blinking. The tears rose in her eyes, then ran in two straight lines down her little girl's cheeks. I said, 'Is that what this is all about? You want to go home? Is that it?'—and she put her hands across her face and cried properly.

A doctor sees lots of tears; some more affecting than others. I really did have a heap of chores at home, and was not at all amused to have been dragged away from them for nothing. But she looked so young and pathetic, I let her have the cry out. Then I touched her shoulder and said firmly, 'Come on now, that's enough. Tell me what the trouble is. Don't you like it here?'

She produced a limp blue handkerchief from under her pillow, and blew her nose.

'No,' she said, 'I don't.'

'Why not? Is the work too hard?'

She gave a hopeless shrug. 'The work's all right.'

'You don't do it all by yourself though, surely?'

She shook her head. 'There's Mrs Bazeley comes in, every day till three; every day bar Sunday. She does the washing and the cooking, and I does everything else. A man has a go at the gardens, sometimes. Miss Caroline does a bit . . .'

'That doesn't sound too bad.'

She didn't answer. So I pressed on. Did she miss her parents?—She pulled a face at that idea. Did she miss a boyfriend?—She pulled a worse face at that.

I picked up my bag. 'Well, I can't help you if you won't say.'

And seeing me start to rise, she said at last, 'It's just, this house!'

'This house? Well, what about it?'

'Oh, Doctor, it in't like a proper house at all! It's too big! You have to walk a mile to get anywhere; and it's so quiet, it gives you the creeps.

It's all right in the daytimes, when I'm working, and Mrs Bazeley's here. But at night, I'm all on me own. There in't a sound! I have horrible dreams . . . And it wouldn't be so bad, but they make me go up and down that set of old back stairs. There's so many corners, and you don't know what's round 'em. I think I shall *die* of fright sometimes!'

I said, 'Die of fright? In this lovely house? You're lucky to have the chance to live here. Think of it like that.'

'Lucky!' she said in disbelief. 'All me friends say I'm mad to have gone into service. They laugh at me, at home! I never get to see no one. I never get to go out. Me cousins've all got factory jobs. And I could've had one, too—only, me dad won't let me! He don't like it. He says the factories make the girls too wild. He says I must stop here for a year first, and learn housework and nice ways. A year! I shall be dead of horror, I know I shall. Either that, or dead of shame. You ought to see the awful old dress and cap they makes me wear! Oh, Doctor, it in't fair!'

She had made a sodden ball of her handkerchief, and, as she spoke, threw it to the floor.

I leaned and picked it back up. 'Dear me, what a tantrum . . . A year will pass quickly, you know. When you're older, it'll seem like nothing.'

'Well, I in't old now, am I!'

'How old *are* you?'

'I'm fourteen. I might as well be ninety, stuck here!'

I laughed. 'Don't be silly, come on. Now, what are we going to do about this? I ought to earn my fee somehow, I suppose. Do you want me to say something to the Ayreses? I'm sure they don't want you to be unhappy.'

'Oh, they just want me to do me work.'

'Well, how about if I were to have a word with your parents?'

'That's a laugh! Me mam spends half her time out with other fellers; she don't care where I am. Me dad's useless. All he does is shout his head off. It's just shouting and rowing all day long. Then he turns

round and takes me mam back, every time! He's only put me into service so I won't turn out like her.'

'Well, why on earth do you want to go home? You sound better
off here.'

'I don't want to go *home*,' she said. 'I just— Oh, I'm just *fed up*!'

Her face had darkened, in pure frustration. She looked less like a
child now, and more like some faintly dangerous young animal. But she
saw me watching her, and the trace of temper began to fade. She grew
sorry for herself again—sighing unhappily, and closing her swollen
eyes. We sat for a moment without speaking, and I glanced around me
at that drab, almost underground room. The silence was so pure, it felt
pressurised: she was right, at least, about that. The air was cool, but
curiously weighted; one was aware somehow of the great house above—
aware, even, of the creeping chaos of nettle and weed that lay just beyond it.

I thought of my mother. She was probably younger than Betty when
she first went out to Hundreds Hall.

I got to my feet. 'Well, my dear, I'm afraid we all have to put up with
things we don't much care for, from time to time. That's called life; and
there's no cure for it. But how about this? You stay in bed for the rest
of the day, and we'll think of it as a holiday. I won't tell Miss Ayres that
you've been shamming; and I'll send you out some stomach mixture—
you can look at the bottle and remember how close you came to losing
your appendix. But I *will* ask Miss Ayres if there isn't a way they can
make things a bit more cheerful for you here. And meanwhile, you can
give the place another chance. What do you say?'

She gazed at me for a second with her depthless grey eyes; then nodded. She said, in a pathetic whisper, 'Thank you, Doctor.'

I left her turning over in the bed, exposing the white nape of her
neck and the small sharp blades of her narrow shoulders.

The passage was empty when I stepped into it, but, as before, at the
sound of the closing door the dog started barking; there was a flurry of
paws and claws and he came bowling out of the kitchen. But he came

less frantically this time, and his excitement soon subsided, until he was happy to let me pat him and pull his ears. Caroline appeared in the kitchen doorway, wiping her hands on a tea-cloth—working the cloth between her fingers in a brisk, housewifely way. On the wall beyond her, I noticed, there was still that box of call-bells and wires: the imperious little machine designed to summon a staff of servants to the grander realm above.

'Everything all right?' she asked, as the dog and I moved towards her.

I said without hesitation, 'Some slight gastric trouble, that's all. Nothing serious, but you were quite right to call me in. One can't be too careful with stomach problems, especially in this weather. I'll send you over a prescription, and you might as well go easy on her for a day or two . . . But there's one other thing.' I had reached her side now, and lowered my voice. 'I get the idea she's pretty homesick. That hasn't struck you?'

She frowned. 'She's seemed all right so far. She'll need time to settle in, I suppose.'

'And she sleeps down here at night, I gather, all on her own? That must be lonely for her. She mentioned a set of back stairs, said she finds them creepy—'

Her look cleared, grew almost amused. 'Oh, *that's* the trouble, is it? I thought she was above nonsense like that. She seemed a sensible enough thing when she first came out here. But you can never tell with country girls: they're either hard as nails, wringing chickens' necks and so on; or going off into fits, like Guster. I expect she's seen too many unpleasant films. Hundreds is quiet, but there's nothing queer about it.'

I said, after a second, 'You've lived here all your life, of course. You couldn't find some way to reassure her?'

She folded her arms. 'Start reading her bedtime stories, perhaps?'

'She's awfully young, Miss Ayres.'

'Well, we don't treat her badly, if that's what you're thinking! We pay her more than we can afford. She eats the same food as us. Really, in lots of ways she's better off than we are.'

'Yes,' I answered, 'your brother said something like that.'

I spoke coldly, and she coloured, not very becomingly, the blush rising into her throat and struggling patchily across her dry-looking cheeks. She turned her gaze from mine, as if in an effort to hold on to her patience. When she spoke again, however, her voice had softened a little.

She said, 'We'd do a great deal to keep Betty happy, if you want to know the truth. The fact is, we can't afford to lose her. Our daily woman does what she can, but this house needs more than one servant, and we've found it almost impossible to get girls in the past few years; we're just too far from the bus-routes and things like that. Our last maid stayed three days. That was back in January. Until Betty arrived, I was doing most of the work myself . . . But I'm glad she's all right. Truly.'

The blush was fading from her cheek, but her features had sunk slightly and she looked tired. I glanced over her shoulder, to the kitchen table, and saw the heap of vegetables, now washed and peeled. Then I looked at her hands, and noticed for the first time how spoiled they were, the short nails split and the knuckles reddened. That struck me as something of a shame; for they were rather nice hands, I thought.

She must have seen the direction of my gaze. She moved as if self-conscious, turning away from me, making a ball of the tea-cloth and tossing it neatly into the kitchen so that it landed on the table beside the muddy tray. 'Let me take you back upstairs,' she said, with an air of bringing my visit to a close. And we mounted the stone steps in silence—the dog going with us, getting under our feet, sighing and grunting as he climbed.

But at the turn of the stairs, where the service door led back on to the terrace, we met Roderick, just coming in.

'Mother's looking for you, Caroline,' he said. 'She's wondering about tea.' He nodded to me. 'Hullo, Faraday. Did you reach a diagnosis?'

That 'Faraday' grated on me somewhat, given that he was twenty-four and I was nearly forty; but before I could answer, Caroline had moved towards him and looped her arm through his.

'Dr Faraday thinks we're brutes!' she said, with a little flutter of her eyelids. 'He thinks we've been forcing Betty up the chimneys, things like that.'

He smiled faintly. 'It's an idea, isn't it?'

I said, 'Betty's fine. A touch of gastritis.'

'Nothing infectious?'

'Certainly not.'

'But we're to take her breakfast in bed,' Caroline went on, 'and generally spoil her, for days and days. Isn't it lucky I know my way about the kitchen? Speaking of which—' She looked at me properly now. 'Don't run away from us, Doctor. Not unless you have to. Stay and have some tea with us, will you?'

'Yes, do stay,' said Roderick.

His tone was as limp as ever; but hers seemed genuine enough. I think she wanted to make up for our disagreement over Betty. And partly because I wanted to make up for it too—but mainly, I must admit, because I realised that in staying to tea I'd be able to see more of the house—I said I would. They moved aside for me to go on ahead of them. I went up the last few steps and emerged in a small, bland hallway, and saw the same baize-curtained arch to which I'd been led by the kindly parlourmaid in 1919. Roderick came slowly up the stairs, his sister with her arm still looped through his, but at the top she moved away from him and casually drew the curtain back.

The passages beyond were dim, and seemed unnaturally bare, but apart from that it was just as I remembered, the house opening up like a fan—the ceiling lifting, the flagged floor becoming marble, the bare gloss service walls giving way to silk and stucco. I immediately looked for the decorative border from which I'd prised that acorn; then my eyes grew used to the gloom and I saw with dismay that a horde of schoolboy vandals might have been at work on the plaster since my first attack on it, for chunks of it had fallen away, and what was left was cracked and discoloured. The rest of the wall was not much better. There were several fine pictures and mirrors, but also darker squares and oblongs where pictures had obviously once hung. One panel of watered silk was ripped, and someone had patched and darned it like a sock.

I turned to Caroline and Roderick, expecting embarrassment or even some sort of apology; but they led me past the damage as if quite unbothered by it. We had taken the right-hand passage, a completely interior stretch, lit only by the light of the rooms opening off it on one side; and since most of the doors we passed were shut, even on that bright day there were quite deep pools of shadow. The black Labrador, padding through them, appeared to be winking in and out of life. The passage made another ninety-degree turn—to the left, this time—and here at last a door stood properly ajar, letting out a blurred wedge of sunlight. It led to the room, Caroline told me, in which the family spent most of their time, and which had been known for years and years as 'the little parlour'.

Of course 'little', as I'd already realised, was a relative term at Hundreds Hall. The room was about thirty feet deep and twenty wide, and it was decorated in a rather hectic manner, with more moulded detail on its ceiling and walls, and an imposing marble fireplace. As in the passage, however, much of the detail was chipped or cracked, or had been lost completely. The floorboards, humped and creaking, were covered with overlapping threadbare rugs. A sagging sofa was half hidden by tartan blankets. Two worn velvet wing-backed chairs stood close to the hearth, and sitting on the floor beside one of them was a florid Victorian chamber-pot, filled with water for the dog.

And yet, somehow, the essential loveliness of the room stood out, like the handsome bones behind a ravaged face. The scents were all of summer flowers: sweet-pea, mignonette, and stock. The light was soft and mildly tinted, and seemed held, really embraced and held, by the pale walls and ceiling.

A French window stood open on another set of flying stone steps, leading down to the terrace and the lawn on this, the south, side of the house. Standing at the top of these steps as we went in, just kicking off some outdoor sandals and working her stockinged feet into shoes, was Mrs Ayres. She had a wide-brimmed hat on her head, with a light silk scarf draped over the top, tied loosely under her chin; and when her children caught sight of her, they laughed.

'You look like something from the early days of motoring, Mother,' said Roderick.

'Yes,' said Caroline, 'or a bee-keeper! I wish you were one; wouldn't the honey be nice? Here's Dr Faraday, look—Dr Graham's partner, from Lidcote. He's all finished with Betty already and I said we'd give him tea.'

Mrs Ayres came forward, taking off her hat, letting the scarf fall loosely over her shoulders, and holding out her hand.

'Dr Faraday, how do you do? Such a very great pleasure to meet you properly at last. I've been gardening—or anyway, what passes for gardening, in our wilderness—so I hope you'll excuse my Sundayish appearance. And isn't that strange?' She raised the back of her hand to her forehead, to move aside a strand of hair. 'When I was a child Sundays meant being dressed in one's finest. One had to sit on a sofa in white lace gloves, and hardly dared to breathe. Now Sunday means working like a dustman—and dressing like one, too.'

She smiled, her high cheeks rising higher in her heart-shaped face, giving her handsome dark eyes a mischievous tilt. A figure less like a dustman's, I thought, it would have been hard to imagine, for she looked perfectly well groomed, in a worn linen dress, with her long hair pinned up loosely, showing the elegant line of her neck. She was a good few years over fifty, but her figure was still good, and her hair was still almost as dark as it must have been the day she handed me my Empire Day medal, when she was younger than her daughter was now. Something about her—perhaps the scarf, or the fit of her dress, or the movement of her slender hips inside it—something, anyway, seemed to lend her a Frenchified air, slightly at odds with her children's light brown English looks. She gestured me to one of the chairs beside the hearth, and took the other across from it; and as she sat, I noticed the shoes she had just slipped on. They were dark patent leather with a cream stripe, too well made to be anything other than pre-war, and, like other

well-made women's shoes, to a man's eye absurdly over-engineered—
like clever little nonsense gadgets—and faintly distracting.

On a table beside her chair was a small heap of bulky old-fashioned
rings, which she now began to work on to her fingers, one by one. With
the movement of her arms the silk scarf slid from her shoulders to the
floor, and Roderick, who was still on his feet, leaned forward with an
awkward motion to pick it up and set it back around her neck.

'My mother's like a paper-chase,' he said to me as he did it. 'She
leaves a trail of things behind her wherever she goes.'

Mrs Ayres settled the scarf more securely, her eyes tilting again. 'You
see how my children abuse me, Dr Faraday? I fear I shall end my
days as one of those neglected old women left starving to death in
their beds.'

'Oh, I dare say we'll chuck you a bone now and then, you poor old
thing,' yawned Roderick, going over to the sofa. He lowered himself
down, and this time the awkwardness of his movements was unmistakable. I paid more attention, saw a puckering and whitening appear at
his cheek—and realised at last how much his injured leg still troubled
him, and how carefully he'd been trying to disguise it.

Caroline had gone to fetch our tea, taking the dog off with her. Mrs
Ayres asked after Betty, seeming very relieved to discover that the problem was not a serious one.

'Such a bore for you,' she said, 'having to come out all this way. You
must have far graver cases to deal with.'

I said, 'I'm a family doctor. It's mostly rashes and cut fingers, I'm
afraid.'

'Now I'm sure you're being modest . . . Though why one should
judge the worth of a doctor by the severity of the cases on his books, I
can't imagine. If anything, it ought to be the other way around.'

I smiled. 'Well, every doctor likes a challenge now and then. During
the war I spent a good deal of time on the wards of a military hospital,
up at Rugby. I rather miss it.' I glanced at her son, who had produced
a tin of tobacco and a packet of papers and was rolling himself a ciga-

rette. 'I did a little muscle therapy, as it happens. Electrical work and so on.'

He gave a grunt. 'They wanted to sign me up for some of that, after my smash. I couldn't spare the time away from the estate.'

'A pity.'

Mrs Ayres said, 'Roderick was with the Air Force, Doctor, as I expect you know.'

'Yes. What kind of action did you see? Pretty stiff, I gather?'

He tilted his head and stuck out his jaw, to draw attention to his scars.

'You'd think so, wouldn't you, from the look of these? But I spent most of my flying time on reconnaissance work, so I can't claim too much glory. A bit of bad luck over the south coast brought me down in the end. The other chap got the worst of it, though; him and my navigator, poor devil. I ended up with these lovely beauty spots and a bashed-up knee.'

'I'm sorry.'

'Oh, I expect you saw a lot worse at that hospital of yours.—But look here, forgive my manners. Can I offer you a cig? I smoke so many of these damn things I forget I'm doing it.'

I looked at the cigarette he had rolled—which was pretty wretched, the sort of cigarette we had used, as medical students, to call a 'coffin nail'—and decided I wouldn't take his tobacco. And though I had some decent cigarettes of my own in my pocket, I didn't want to embarrass him by bringing them out. So I shook my head. I had the feeling, anyway, that he had only offered me one as a way of changing the subject.

Perhaps his mother thought that, too. She was gazing at her son with a troubled expression, but turned from him to me to smile and say, 'The war feels far away now, doesn't it? How did that happen, in only two years? We had an army unit billeted with us for part of it, you know. They left odd things about the park, barbed wire, sheets of iron: they're already rusting away, like something from another age. Goodness knows how long this peace will last, of course. I've stopped listening to the news; it's too alarming. The world seems to be run by scientists and generals, all playing with bombs like so many schoolboys.'

Roderick struck a match. 'Oh, we'll be all right, here at Hundreds,' he said, his mouth tight around his cigarette and the paper flaring, alarmingly close to his scarred lips. 'It's the original quiet life, out here at Hundreds.'

As he spoke, there came the sound of Gyp's claws on the marble floor of the passage, like the clicking beads of an abacus, and the slap of Caroline's flat-soled sandals. The dog nosed open the door—something he clearly did often, for the door-frame was darkened from the rub of his coat, and the fine old door itself was quite wrecked, in its lower panels, where he or dogs before him had repeatedly scratched at the wood.

Caroline entered with a heavy-looking tea-tray. Roderick gripped the arm of the sofa and began to push himself up, to help her; but I beat him to it.

'Here, let me.'

She looked gratefully at me—not so much on her own account, I thought, as on her brother's—but she said, 'It's no trouble. I'm used to it, remember.'

'Let me clear a spot for you, at least.'

'No, you must let me do it myself! That way, you see, when I'm obliged to earn my living in a Corner House, I shall know how.—Gyp, get out from under my heels, will you?'

So I moved back, and she set the tray down among the books and papers on a cluttered table, then poured the tea and passed round the cups. The cups were of handsome old bone china, one or two of them with riveted handles; I saw her keep those back for the family. And she followed the tea with plates of cake: a fruit cake, sliced so thinly I guessed she had made the best of a rather meagre store.

'Oh for a scone, and jam, and cream!' said Mrs Ayres, as the plates were handed out. 'Or even a really good biscuit. I say that with you in mind, Dr Faraday, not us. We've never been a sweet-toothed family; and naturally'—she looked mischievous again—'as dairy farmers, one would hardly expect us to have butter. But the worst of rationing is, it has quite killed hospitality. I do think that a pity.'

She sighed, breaking her cake into pieces and dipping them daintily into her milkless tea. Caroline, I noticed, had folded her slice in half and eaten it down in two bites. Roderick had set his plate aside in order to concentrate on his cigarette and now, after idly picking out the peel and the sultanas, he threw the rest of his cake to Gyp.

'Roddie!' said Caroline, reproachfully. I thought she was protesting at the waste of food; it turned out she didn't like the example her brother was setting to the dog. She caught the animal's eye. 'You villain! You know that begging isn't allowed! Look at the sidelong glances he's giving me, Dr Faraday. The old sly boots.' She drew her foot from her sandal, extended a leg—her legs, I saw now, were bare, and tanned, and quite unshaven—and prodded his haunches with her toes.

'Poor old thing,' I said politely, at the dog's forlorn expression.

'Don't be taken in. He's a dreadful ham—aren't you, hey? You Shylock!'

She gave him another nudge with her foot, then turned the nudge into a rough caress. The dog at first rather struggled to keep his balance under the pressure of it; then, with the defeated, slightly bewildered air of a helpless old man, he lay down at her feet, lifting his limbs and showing the grey fur of his chest and his balding belly. Caroline worked her foot harder.

I saw Mrs Ayres glance over at her daughter's downy leg.

'Really, darling, I do wish you would put some stockings on. Dr Faraday will suppose us savages.'

Caroline laughed. 'It's far too warm for stockings. And I should be very surprised indeed if Dr Faraday had never seen a bare leg before!'

But she did, after a moment, draw her leg back and make an effort to sit more demurely. The dog, disappointed, lay with his limbs still raised and crooked. Then he rolled on to his front and began to gnaw wetly at one of his paws.

The smoke of Roderick's cigarette hung bluely in the hot, still air. A bird in the garden gave some distinctive throbbing call, and we turned

our heads to listen to it. I looked around the room again, at all the
lovely faded detail; then, twisting further in my seat, with a shock of
surprise and pleasure I got my first proper view through the open window. An overgrown lawn ran away from the house for what looked
like thirty or forty yards. It was bordered by flower-beds, and ended at
a wrought-iron fence. But the fence gave on to a meadow, which in turn
gave onto the fields of the park; the fields stretched off into the distance
for a good three-quarters of a mile. The Hundreds boundary wall was
just about visible at the end of them, but since the land beyond the wall
was pasture, giving way to tilth and cornfield, the prospect ran on,
uninterrupted, finishing only where its paling colours bled away completely into the haze of the sky.

'You like our view, Dr Faraday?' Mrs Ayres asked me.

'I do,' I said, turning back to her. 'When was this house built? 1720?
1730?'

'How clever you are. It was finished in 1733.'

'Yes.' I nodded. 'I think I can see what the architect must have had
in mind: the shady corridors, with the rooms opening from them, large
and light.'

Mrs Ayres smiled; but it was Caroline who looked over at me as if
pleased.

'I've always liked that, too,' she said. 'Other people seem to think
our gloomy passages a bit of a bore . . . But you should see the place
in winter! We'd happily brick up all the windows then. For two months
last year we more or less lived in this one room. Roddie and I brought
in our mattresses and slept here like squatters. The pipes froze, the
generator broke; outside there were icicles three feet long. We never
dared leave the house, for fear of being harpooned . . . You live above
your surgery, don't you? In old Dr Gill's place?'

I said, 'I do. I moved in there as a junior partner, and have never
moved out. It's a plain enough place. But my patients know it; and it
suits a bachelor, I suppose.'

Roderick tapped ash from his cigarette.

'Dr Gill was a bit of a character, wasn't he? I went into his surgery once or twice when I was a boy. He had a great glass bowl he said he used to keep leeches in. It frightened the pants off me.'

'Oh, everything frightened you,' said his sister, before I could respond. 'You were so easy to scare. Do you remember that giantess of a girl who used to work in the kitchen when we were young? Do you remember her, Mother? What was her name? Was it Mary? She was six foot two-and-a-half; and she had a sister who was six foot three. Daddy once made her try on one of his boots. He'd made a bet with Mr McLeod that the boot would be too small. He was right, too. But her hands were the thing. She could wring clothes better than a mangle. And her fingers were always cold—always freezing, like sausages straight from the meat-safe. I used to tell Roddie that she crept into his room while he was sleeping and put her hands under his blankets, to warm them up; and it used to make him cry.'

'Little beast,' said Roderick.

'What *was* her name?'

'I believe it was Miriam,' said Mrs Ayres, after a moment's consideration. 'Miriam Arnold; and the sister you're thinking of was Margery. But there was another girl, too, less huge: she married a Tapley boy, and the two of them went off to be chauffeur and cook at some house out of the county. Miriam went from us to Mrs Randall, I think. But Mrs Randall didn't take to her, and only kept her for a month or two. I don't know what became of her then.'

'Perhaps she took up garrotting,' said Roderick.

'Perhaps she joined a circus,' said Caroline. 'We really did have a girl once, didn't we, who ran away to join the circus?'

'She certainly married a circus man,' said Mrs Ayres. 'And she broke her mother's heart by doing it. She broke her cousin's heart too, because the cousin—Lavender Hewitt—was also in love with the circus man, and when the other girl went off with him, she gave up eating and would have died. And she was saved, as her mother used to say, by rabbits. For she could resist any dish except her mother's stewed rabbit. And for a time we let her father take a ferret over the park, to get all the rabbits he pleased; and it was the rabbits that saved her . . .'

The story ran on, Caroline and Roderick prompting more of it; they spoke to each other rather than to me, and, shut out of the game, I looked from mother to daughter to son and finally caught the likenesses between them, not just the similarities of feature—the long limbs, the high-set eyes—but the almost clannish little tricks of gesture and speech. And I felt a flicker of impatience with them—the faintest stirring of a dark dislike—and my pleasure in the lovely room was slightly spoiled. Perhaps it was the peasant blood in me, rising. But Hundreds Hall had been made and maintained, I thought, by the very people they were laughing at now. After two hundred years, those people had begun to withdraw their labour, their belief in the house; and the house was collapsing, like a pyramid of cards. Meanwhile, here the family sat, still playing gaily at gentry life, with the chipped stucco on their walls, and their Turkey carpets worn to the weave, and their riveted china . . .

Mrs Ayres had recalled another servant. 'Oh, she was a moron,' Roderick said.

'She wasn't a *moron*,' said Caroline, fairly. 'But it's true she was awfully dim. I remember she once asked me what sealing-wax was, and I told her it was a very special sort of wax for putting on ceilings. I made her stand on a pair of ladders and try some out on the ceiling of Daddy's study. And it made a horrible mess, and the poor girl got into dreadful trouble.'

She shook her head, embarrassed, but laughing again. Then she caught my eye; and my expression must have been chilly. She tried to stifle her smiles.

'I'm sorry, Dr Faraday. I can see you don't approve. Quite right, too. Rod and I were frightful children; but we're much nicer now. You're thinking of poor little Betty, I expect.'

I took a sip of my tea. 'Not at all. As it happens, I was thinking of my mother.'

'Your mother?' she repeated, a trace of laughter still in her voice.

And in the silence that followed, Mrs Ayres said, 'Of course. Your mother was nursery maid here once, wasn't she? I remember hearing that. When was she here? Slightly before my time, I think.'

She spoke so smoothly and so nicely, I was almost ashamed; for my own tone had been pointed. I said, less emphatically, 'My mother was here until about nineteen seven. She met my father here; a grocer's boy. A back-door romance, I suppose you'd call it.'

Caroline said uncertainly, 'What fun.'

'Yes, isn't it?'

Roderick tapped more ash from his cigarette, saying nothing. Mrs Ayres, however, had begun to look thoughtful.

'Do you know,' she said, getting to her feet, 'I do believe— Now, am I right?'

She went across to a table, on which a number of framed family pictures were set out. She drew one from the arrangement, held it at arm's length, peered at it, then shook her head.

'Without my spectacles,' she said, bringing it to me, 'I can't be sure. But I *think*, Dr Faraday, that your mother might be here.'

The picture was a small Edwardian photograph in a tortoiseshell frame. It showed, in crisp sepia detail, what I realised after a moment must be the south face of the Hall, for I could see the long French window of the room we were sitting in, thrown open to the afternoon sunlight just as it was today. Gathered on the lawn before the house was the family of the time, surrounded by a sizeable staff of servants— housekeeper, butler, footman, kitchen-girls, gardeners—they made an informal, almost reluctant group, as if the idea of the picture had occurred belatedly to the photographer, and someone had gone rounding them all up, drawing them away from other tasks. The family itself looked most at ease, the mistress of the house—old Mrs Beatrice Ayres, Caroline and Roderick's grandmother—seated in a deck-chair, her husband standing at her side, one hand on her shoulder, the other tucked loosely into the pocket of his creased white trousers. Lounging with a touch of gaucheness at their feet was the slender fifteen-year-old youth who had grown up and become the Colonel; he looked very like Roderick did now. Seated beside him on a tartan tug were his younger sisters and brothers.

I looked more closely at this group. Most of them were older children, but the smallest, still an infant, was held in the arms of a fair-haired nursemaid. The child had been in the process of wriggling free when the camera shutter had snapped, so that the nursemaid had tilted back her head in fear of flailing elbows. Her gaze, as a consequence, was drawn from the camera, and her features were blurred.

Caroline had left her place on the sofa to come and examine the photograph with me. Standing at my side, bending forward, looping up a lock of dry brown hair, she said quietly, 'Is that your mother, Dr Faraday?'

I said, 'I think it might be. Then again—' Just behind the awkward-looking girl, I noticed now, was another servant, also fair-haired, and in an identical gown and cap. I laughed, embarrassed. 'It might be this one. I'm not sure.'

'Is your mother still alive? Could you show her the picture, perhaps?'

I shook my head. 'My parents are both dead. My mother died while I was still at school. My father had a heart attack a few years later.'

'Oh, I'm sorry.'

'Well, it seems long ago . . .'

'I hope your mother was happy here,' Mrs Ayres said to me, as Caroline returned to the sofa. 'Was she, do you think? Did she ever talk about the house?'

I didn't answer for a second, recalling some of my mother's stories about her time at the Hall—how, for instance, she had had to stand each morning with her hands held out while the housekeeper examined her fingernails; how Mrs Beatrice Ayres would every so often come unannounced to the maids' bedrooms and turn out their boxes, going through their possessions piece by piece . . . I said finally, 'I think my mother made some good friends here, among the other girls.'

Mrs Ayres looked pleased; perhaps relieved. 'I'm glad to hear it. It was a different world for servants then, of course. They had their own entertainments, their own scandals and fun. Their own dinner, on Christmas Day.'

This prompted more reminiscences. I kept my eyes on the picture—

slightly thrown, if I'm honest, by the force of my own feelings, for though I'd spoken lightly, I'd found myself more moved by the unexpected appearance of my mother's face—if it *was* her face—than I would have guessed. At last I put the picture down on the table at the side of my chair. We spoke about the house and its gardens, the grander times that the place had seen.

But I kept glancing over at the photograph as we talked, and my distraction must have been obvious. Our tea was finished. I let a few more minutes pass, then looked at the clock and said I ought to be going. And as I got to my feet, Mrs Ayres said gently, 'You must take that picture with you, Dr Faraday. I should like you to have it.'

'Take it?' I said, startled. 'Oh, no, I couldn't.'

'Yes, you must. You must take it just as it is, frame and all.'

'Yes, do take it,' said Caroline, when I continued to protest. 'I shall be doing the housework, don't forget, while Betty recovers. I shall be awfully glad to have one less thing to dust.'

So, 'Thank you,' I said, blushing and almost stammering. 'It's awfully kind of you. It's— Really, it's far too kind.'

They found me a piece of used brown paper with which to wrap the picture up, and I tucked it safely into my bag. I said goodbye to Mrs Ayres, and patted the dog's warm dark head. Caroline, who was already on her feet, got ready to take me back to my car. But Roderick moved forward, saying, 'It's all right, Caro. I'll see the doctor out.'

He struggled up from the sofa, wincing badly as he did it. His sister watched him, concerned, but he was clearly determined to escort me. So she gave in, and offered me her worn, well-shaped hand for another shake.

'Goodbye, Dr Faraday. I'm so glad we found that picture. Think of us, won't you, when you look at it?'

'I will,' I said.

I followed Roderick from the room, blinking slightly at the plunge back into shade. He led me off to the right, past more shut doors, but soon the passage lightened and widened, and we emerged in what I realised was the entrance hall of the house.

And here I had to pause and look around me; for the hall was very lovely. Its floor was of pink and liver–coloured marble, laid down like a chequerboard. The walls were pale wooden panels, ruddy with reflected colour from the floor. Dominating it all, however, was the mahogany staircase, which rose in an elegant soft square spiral through two more floors, its polished serpent-headed banister climbing in a single unbroken line. It made a stairwell fifteen feet wide, and easily sixty feet high; and it was lit, coolly and kindly, by a dome of milky glass in the roof above.

'A nice effect that, isn't it?' said Roderick, seeing me gazing upwards. 'The dome was a devil, of course, in the black-out.'

He tugged open the broad front door. The door had got damp at some point in the past, and was faintly buckled, and grated horribly against the marble as it moved. I joined him at the top of the steps, and the heat of the day billowed in around us.

He grimaced. 'Still blistering, I'm afraid. I don't envy you the run back to Lidcote . . . What's that you're driving? A Ruby? How do you find her?'

The car was a very basic model, and there wasn't much to admire in her. But he was clearly the sort of boy to be interested in motors for their own sake, so I took him over, and pointed out a couple of features, finally opening up the bonnet to show him the layout of the engine.

I said, as I closed the bonnet again, 'These country roads rather punish her.'

'I'll bet. How far do you take her, day by day?'

'On a light day? Fifteen, twenty calls. A heavy day might have more than thirty. Local, for the most part, though I've a couple of private patients as far out as Banbury.'

'You're a busy man.'

'Too busy, at times.'

'All those rashes and cuts.—Oh, and that reminds me.' He put his hand to his pocket. 'How much do I owe you for seeing to Betty?'

I didn't want to take his money at first, thinking of his mother's generosity with the family photograph. When he pressed me, I said I would send him out a bill. But he laughed and said, 'Look here, if I were you, I'd take the money while it's offered. How much do you charge? Four shillings? More? Come on. We're not at the charity-case stage just yet.'

So I reluctantly said I would take four shillings, for the visit and the prescription. He brought out a warm handful of small coins and counted them into my palm. He changed his pose as he did it, and the movement must have jarred with him somehow: that puckering reappeared at his cheek, and this time I almost commented on it. As with the cigarettes, however, I didn't like to embarrass him; so let it go. He folded his arms and stood as if quite comfortable while I started the car, and as I moved off, he languidly raised his hand to me, then turned and headed back to the house. But I kept my eye on him through my rear-view mirror, and saw him making his painful-looking way up the steps to the front door. I saw the house seem to swallow him up as he limped back into the shadowy hall.

Then the drive made a turn between unclipped bushes, the car began to dip and lurch; and the house was lost to me.

That night, as I often did on a Sunday, I had dinner with David Graham and his wife, Anne. Graham's emergency case had gone well, against some substantial odds, so we spent most of the meal discussing it; and only as we were starting on our baked-apple pudding did I mention that I'd been out to Hundreds Hall that day on his behalf.

He at once looked envious. 'You have? What's it like there now? The family haven't called me out in years. I hear the place has gone badly downhill; that they're rather pigging it, in fact.'

I described what I had seen of the house and gardens. 'It's heartbreaking,' I said, 'to see it all so changed. I don't know if Roderick knows what he's doing. It doesn't look much like it.'

'Poor Roderick,' said Anne. 'He's a nice sort of boy, I've always thought. One can't help but feel sorry for him.'

'Because of his scars, and all that?'

'Oh, partly. But more because he seems so out of his depth. He had to grow up too quickly; all those boys of his age did. But he had Hundreds to think about, as well as the war. And he isn't his father's son, somehow.'

'Well,' I said, 'that might be in his favour. I remember the Colonel as rather a brute of a man, don't you? I saw him once when I was young, going off pop with a motorist whose car he said had startled his horse. In the end he jumped out of his saddle and kicked the car's headlamp in!'

'He had a temper, certainly,' said Graham, spooning up his apple. 'The old-fashioned squire type.'

'Old-fashioned bully, in other words.'

'Well, I shouldn't have liked his job. He must have been out of his mind with money worries half the time. I think that estate was already losing income when he inherited it. I know he sold land all through the 'twenties; I remember my own father saying it was like shovelling water from a sinking boat. I heard that the duties, after he died, were astronomical! How that family keeps going at all beats me.'

I said, 'And what about Roderick's smash? His leg looked bad, I thought. I wondered if a course of electrical therapy would help him— assuming he'd ever let me close enough to try. They seem to pride themselves on living like the Brontës out there, cauterising their own wounds and what not . . . Would you mind?'

Graham shrugged. 'Be my guest. As I said, they haven't called me out in so long, I barely qualify as their doctor. I remember the injury: a nasty break, poorly reset. The burns speak for themselves.' He ate a little more, then grew thoughtful. 'There was a touch of nervous trouble too, I believe, when Roderick first came home.'

This was news to me. 'Really? It can't have been too bad. He's certainly relaxed enough now.'

'Well, it was bad enough for them to want to be a bit hush-hush about it. But then, all those families are touchy like that. I don't think Mrs Ayres even called in a nurse. She looked after Roderick herself, then brought Caroline home to help her at the end of the war. Caroline was doing quite well, wasn't she, with some sort of commission in the Wrens, or the WAAF? Awfully brainy girl, of course.'

He said 'brainy' in the way I had heard other people say it when discussing Caroline Ayres, and I knew that, like them, he was using the word more or less as a euphemism for 'plain'. I didn't answer, and we finished our puddings in silence. Anne put her spoon into her bowl, then rose from her chair to close a window: we were eating late, and had a candle lit on the table; it was just beginning to be twilight and moths were fluttering around the flame. And as she sat back down she said, 'Do you remember the first daughter out at Hundreds? Susan, the little girl that died? Pretty, like her mother. I went to her seventh birthday party. Her parents had given her a silver ring, with a real diamond in it. Oh, how I coveted that ring! And a few weeks later she was dead . . . Was it measles? I know it was something like that.'

Graham was wiping his mouth with his napkin. He said, 'Diph, wasn't it?'

She pulled a face at the thought. 'That's right. Such a nasty way . . . I remember the funeral. The little coffin, and all the flowers. Heaps and heaps of them.'

And I realised then that I remembered the funeral, too. I remembered standing with my parents on Lidcote High Street while the coffin went by. I remembered Mrs Ayres, young, heavily veiled in black, like a ghastly bride. I remembered my mother, quietly weeping; my father with his hand on my shoulder; the stiff new sour-smelling colours of my school blazer and cap.

The thought depressed me, for some reason, more than it ought to have done. Anne and the maid took away the dishes, and Graham and I sat on at the table, discussing various business matters; and that depressed me even more. Graham was younger than me, but was doing rather better: he had entered the practice as a doctor's son, with money and standing behind him. I had come in as a sort of apprentice to his father's partner, Dr Gill—that 'character', as Roderick had quaintly called him; actually the devil of an idle old man, who, under pretence of being my patron, had let me gradually buy out his stake in the business over many long, hard, poorly paid years. Gill had retired before the war, and lived in a pleasant half-timbered house near Stratford-on-Avon. I had only very recently begun to make a profit. Now, with the Health Service looming, private doctoring seemed done for. On top of that, all my poorer patients would soon have the option of leaving my list and attaching themselves to another man, thereby vastly reducing my income. I had had several bad nights over it.

'I shall lose them all,' I told Graham now, putting my elbows on the table and wearily rubbing my face.

'Don't be an idiot,' he answered. 'They've no more reason to leave you than they have to leave me—or Seeley, or Morrison.'

'Morrison gives them any amount of cough mixture and liver salts,' I said. 'They like that. Seeley has his manners, his little ways with the ladies. You're a nice clean handsome sort of family chap; they like that, too. They don't like me. They never have. They've never been able to place me. I don't hunt or play bridge; but I don't play darts or football, either. I'm not grand enough for the gentry—not grand enough for working people, come to that. They want to look up to their doctor. They don't want to think he's one of them.'

'Oh, rubbish. All they want is a man who can do the job! Which you eminently can. If anything, you're too conscientious. You've too much time to fret in. You ought to get married; that'd sort you out.'

I laughed. 'God! I can barely keep myself, let alone a wife and family.'

He had heard it all before, but tolerantly let me grumble on. Anne brought us coffee, and we talked until almost eleven. I should have been happy to stay longer, but, guessing what little time the two of them must get alone together, I at last said good night. Their house is just on the other side of the village from mine, a ten-minute walk away; the evening was still so warm and airless, I went slowly, by a roundabout route, pausing once to light a cigarette, then slipping off my jacket, loosening my tie, and going on in my shirt-sleeves.

The ground floor of my house is given over to a consulting-room, dispensary and waiting-room, with my kitchen and sitting-room on the

floor above, and a bedroom in the attic. It was, as I'd told Caroline
Ayres, a very plain sort of place. I'd never had time or money to
brighten it, so it still had the same dispiriting decorations it had had
when I'd moved in—mustard walls and 'combed' paintwork—and a
cramped, inconvenient kitchen. A daily woman, Mrs Rush, kept things
tidy and cooked my meals. When not actually dealing with patients I
spent most of my time downstairs, making up prescriptions or reading
and writing at my desk. Tonight I went straight through to my consulting-room to look over my notes for the following day, and to put my
bag in order; and it was only as I opened the bag up, and saw the
loosely wrapped brown-paper parcel inside it, that I remembered the
photograph Mrs Ayres had given me out at Hundreds Hall. I undid
the paper and studied the scene again; and then, still unsure about that
fair-haired nursemaid, and wanting to compare the picture with other
photographs, I took it upstairs. In one of my bedroom cupboards there
was an old biscuit-tin, full of papers and family keepsakes, put together
by my parents. I dug it out, carried it over to the bed, and began to go
through it.

I hadn't opened this tin in years, and had forgotten what was in it.
Most of its contents, I saw with surprise, were odd little fragments from
my own past. My birth certificate was there, for example, along with
some sort of christening notice; a furred brown envelope turned out to
hold two of my milk teeth and a lock of my baby hair, unfeasibly soft
and blond; and then came a mess of whiskery Scouting and swimming
badges, school certificates, school reports, and records of prizes—the
sequence of them all mixed up, so that a torn newspaper cutting an-
nouncing my graduation from medical school had snagged itself on a
letter from my first headmaster, 'fervently' recommending me for a
scholarship to Leamington College. There was even, I was astonished
to see, the very Empire Day medal that had been presented to me out
at Hundreds Hall by a youthful Mrs Ayres. It had been carefully
wrapped in tissue paper, and it tumbled heavily into my hand, its
coloured ribbon unfrayed, its bronze surface dulled but untarnished.

But of my parents' own lives, I discovered, there was shockingly little record. I suppose there was simply not much record to be kept. A couple of sentimental wartime postcards, with neat, bland, badly spelled messages; a lucky coin, with a hole for a string hammered through it; a spray of paper violets—that was about it. I had remembered photographs, but there was only one photograph here, a fading postcard-sized thing with curling corners. It had been taken in a photographer's tent at a local Mop Fair, and it showed my mother and father as a courting couple, fantastically posed against an Alpine backdrop, in a roped laundry-hamper meant to be the basket of a hot-air balloon.

I set this picture beside the Hundreds group, and looked from one to the other. The angle at which my balloonist mother was holding her head, however, together with the droop of a sad-looking feather on her hat, meant that I was still no wiser, and finally I gave the thing up. The Mop Fair photograph, too, had begun to look rather poignant to me; and when I gazed again at the scraps and cuttings recording my own achievements, and thought of the care and pride with which my parents had preserved them, I felt ashamed. My father had taken on debt after debt in order to fund my education. The debts had probably ruined his health; they had almost certainly helped weaken my mother. And what had been the result? I was a good, ordinary doctor. In another setting I might have been better than good. But I had started work with debts of my own, and after fifteen years in the same small country practice I was yet to make a decent income.

I have never thought of myself as a discontented man. I have been too busy for discontentment to have had a chance to set in. But I've had occasional dark hours, dreary fits when my life, laid all before me, has seemed bitter and hollow and insignificant as a bad nut; and one of those fits came upon me now. I forgot the many modest successes of my career, and instead saw every failure: the mishandled cases, the missed opportunities, the moments of cowardice and disappointment. I thought of my undistinguished war years—spent here in Warwickshire, while my younger colleagues, Graham and Morrison, enrolled with the RAMC. I felt the empty rooms below me, and remembered a girl with whom, as a medical student, I'd been very much in love: a girl from a good Birmingham family, whose parents hadn't considered me to be a suitable match, and who had finally thrown me over for another man. I had rather turned my back on romance after that disenchantment, and the few affairs I had had since then had been very half-hearted things. Now those passionless embraces came back to me too, in all their dry mechanical detail. I felt a wave of disgust for myself, and a pity for the women involved.

The heat in that attic room was stifling. I switched off my lamp, and lit a cigarette, and lay down among the photographs and fragments on the bed. The window was open and the curtain pulled back. The night was moonless, but the dark was the uneasy dark of summer, fretful with subtle movement and sound. I gazed into it; and what I saw—a sort of curious after-image of my day—was Hundreds Hall. I saw its cool fragrant spaces, the light it held like wine in a glass. And I pictured the people inside it as they must be now: Betty in her room, Mrs Ayres and Caroline in theirs, Roderick in his . . .

I lay like that for a long time, open-eyed and unmoving, the cigarette burning slowly down, turning to ash between my fingers.

Two

The fit of discontentment passed with the night; by the morning I had almost forgotten it. That day was the start of a brief busy phase for Graham and me, for with the hot weather there had come a variety of small epidemics in the district, and now a bad summer fever began to do the rounds of the villages. One already delicate child was severely affected, and I spent a lot of time on him, calling in at the house sometimes two or three times a day until he was better. There was no money in it: he was a 'club' patient, which meant I received only a handful of shillings for treating him and his brothers and sisters over the course of an entire year. But I knew his family well, and was fond of them, and was glad to see him recover; and the parents were touchingly grateful.

I just about remembered, in the midst of all this, to send out Betty's prescription to the Hall, but I had no further contact with her or with the Ayreses. I continued to pass the walls of Hundreds on my regular round, and now and then I'd catch myself thinking with something like wistfulness of the unkempt landscape beyond it, with that poor neglected house at its heart, quietly sliding into decay. But as we turned the high point of summer and the season started to wane, that was as much thought as I began to give it. My visit to the Ayreses soon felt vaguely unreal—like some vivid but improbable dream.

Then, one evening at the end of August—more than a month, in other words, since I had gone out to treat Betty—I was driving along one of the lanes outside Lidcote and caught sight of a large black dog sniffing around in the dust. It must have been half past seven or so. The sun was still quite high in the sky, but the sky itself was beginning to pink; I'd finished my evening surgery and was on my way to visit a patient in one of the neighbouring villages. The dog started barking when he heard my car, and as he put up his head and moved forward I saw the grey in his fur, and recognised him as the elderly Hundreds Labrador, Gyp. A second later I saw Caroline. She was right at the edge of the lane, on the shadowy side. Hatless and bare-legged, she was reaching into one of the hedges—had managed to work her way into the brambles so completely that without Gyp to alert me I would have driven past without spotting her. Drawing closer, I saw her call for the dog to be quiet; she turned her head to my car, narrowing her eyes against what must have been the glare of the windscreen. I noticed then that she had the strap of a satchel over her breast, and was carrying what I took to be an old spotted handkerchief, done up as a bundle like Dick Whittington's. Drawing level with her, I put on the brake and called through my open window.

'Are you running away from home, Miss Ayres?'

She recognised me then, and smiled, and began to back out of the bushes. She did it gingerly, putting up a hand to free her hair from the brambles, then giving a final spring to the dusty surface of the road. Brushing down her skirt—she was dressed in the same badly fitting cotton frock she'd been wearing when I'd seen her last—she said, 'I've been into the village, doing errands for my mother. But then I got tempted from the path. Look.'

She carefully opened the bundle up, and I realised that what I had taken for spots on the handkerchief were actually purple juice-stains: she had lined the cloth with dock leaves, and was filling it with blackberries. She picked out one of the largest berries for me, lightly blowing the dust from it before she handed it over. I put it into my mouth and felt it break against my tongue, warm as blood, and fantastically sweet.

'Aren't they good?' she said, as I swallowed. She gave me another, then took one for herself. 'My brother and I used to come berrying here when we were young. It's the best spot for blackberries in the whole of the county, I don't know why. It can be dry as the Sahara everywhere else, but the fruit here are always good. They must be fed by a spring, or something.'

She put her thumb to the corner of her mouth to catch a trickle of dark juice, and pretended to frown. 'But that was an Ayres family secret, and I shouldn't have blabbed. Now I'm afraid I may have to kill you. Or do you swear to keep the knowledge to yourself?'

'I swear,' I said.

'Honour bright?'

I laughed. 'Honour bright.'

She warily gave me another berry. 'Well, I suppose I shall have to trust you. It must be frightfully bad form to kill a doctor, after all; just a step or two down from shooting an albatross. Also quite hard, I imagine, since you must know all the tricks yourselves.'

She tucked back her hair, seeming happy to talk, standing a yard or so from my window, tall and easy on those thickish legs of hers; and because I was mindful of the engine, idling away and wasting fuel, I switched it off. The car seemed to sink, as if glad to be released, and I became aware of the treacly weight and exhaustion of the summer air. From across the fields, muted by heat and distance, there came the grind and snap of farm machinery, and calling voices. On those light late-August evenings the harvesters worked until gone eleven.

Caroline picked out more fruit. She said, with a tilt of her head, 'You haven't asked after Betty.'

'I was just about to,' I said. 'How has she been? Any more trouble?'

'Not a peep! She spent a day in bed, then made a miraculous recovery. We've been doing our best since then to make her feel more comfortable. We told her she needn't use the back stair any more, if she doesn't like it. And Roddie's got hold of a wireless for her; that's bucked her up no end. Apparently they used to have a wireless at home, but it got broken in some argument. Now one of us has to drive into Lidcote once a week to recharge the battery; but we think it's worth it, if it keeps her happy . . . Tell the truth, though. That medicine you sent over was pure chalk, wasn't it? *Was* there ever anything wrong with her?'

'I couldn't possibly say,' I answered loftily. 'The patient-doctor bond, and all that. Besides, you might sue for malpractice.'

'Ha!' Her expression grew rueful. 'You're on safe ground, there. We couldn't afford the lawyers' fees—'

She turned her head, as Gyp let out two or three sharp barks. While we had been talking he had been nosing his way through the grass at the edge of the lane, but now there was an agitated flapping on the other side of the hedge and he disappeared into a gap in the brambles.

'He's going after a bird,' Caroline said, 'the old fat-head. These used to be our birds once, you know; now they're Mr Milton's. He won't like it if Gyp gets hold of a partridge.—Gyp! Gyppo! Come back! Come *here*, you idiotic thing!'

Hastily thrusting the bundle of blackberries at me, she went off in pursuit. I watched her leaning into the hedge, parting the brambles to reach and call, apparently unafraid of spiders or thorns, her brown hair catching again. It took her a couple of minutes to retrieve the dog, and by the time she had done that and he had trotted back to the car, looking terribly pleased with himself, with his mouth open and his pink tongue loose, I had remembered my patient and said I should be going.

'Well, take some berries with you,' she said good-naturedly, as I restarted the engine. But seeing her begin to separate the fruit it occurred to me that I would be driving more or less towards Hundreds, and, since it was a good two or three miles' journey, I offered her a lift.

I hesitated about doing it, not knowing if she'd care to accept; apart from anything else, she looked very much at home there on the dusty country lane, rather as a tramp or a gypsy would. She seemed to hesitate, too, once I had asked her—but it turned out she was simply thinking the thing over. Glancing at her wrist-watch, she said, 'I'd like that, very much. And if you could bear to drop me at the lane to our farm, instead of at the park gates, I'd be even more grateful. My brother's there. I was going to leave him to it. I expect they'd be glad of some help, though; they usually are.'

I said I'd be happy to. I opened up the passenger door, to let Gyp into the back; and once he had turned and slithered fussily about for a second or two on the rear seat, she moved the front seat back into place and got in beside me.

I felt the weight of her as she sat, in the tilt and creak of the car; and I suddenly wished that the car weren't quite so small and so ancient. She didn't seem to mind it, however. She placed the satchel flat on her knees, and rested the bundle of berries on top, and gave a sigh of pleasure, apparently grateful to be sitting down. She was wearing her flat boyish sandals, and her bare legs were still unshaven; each little hair, I noticed, was laden with dust, like an eye-blacked lash.

Once I'd moved off she offered me another blackberry, but this time I shook my head, not wanting to eat up all her crop. When she had taken one herself I asked after her mother and her brother.

'Mother's fine,' she answered, swallowing. 'Thanks for asking. She was very glad to meet you that time. She does like to know who's who in the county. We go about so much less than we used to, you see, and she's rather proud about visitors, with the house so shabby, so she feels a bit cut off. Roddie is—well, how he usually is, working too hard, eating too little . . . His leg is a nuisance.'

'Yes, I wondered about that.'

'I don't know how much it really troubles him. Quite a lot, I suspect. He says he hasn't time to get it treated. What he means, I think, is that there isn't the money for it.'

This was the second time she had mentioned money, but now there was no trace of ruefulness in her voice, she spoke as if merely stating a fact. Changing gear at a bend in the road, I said, 'Are things as bad as that?' And then, when she didn't answer at once: 'Do you mind my asking?'

'No, I don't mind. I was just thinking what to say . . . They're pretty bad, to be honest with you. I don't know how bad, because Rod does all the book-keeping himself, and he's quite cagey. All he ever says is that he's going to pull things through. We both try and keep the worst of it from Mother, but it must be obvious even to her that things at Hundreds will never be what they were. We've lost too much land, for one thing. The farm's more or less our only income now. And the world's a changed place, isn't it? That's why we've been so keen to hang on to Betty. I can't tell you what a difference it's made to Mother's spirits, our being able to ring for a servant in the old-fashioned way, instead of having to traipse down to the kitchen for a jug of hot water, or something, ourselves. That sort of thing means such a lot. We had servants at Hundreds, you see, right up to the war.'

Again she spoke matter-of-factly; as if to someone of her own class. But she was still for a second, and then she moved as if self-conscious, saying, in quite a different voice, 'God, how shallow you must think us. I'm so sorry.'

I said, 'Not at all.'

But it was clear what she meant, and the obviousness of her embarrassment only served to embarrass me. The road we had taken, too, was one I remembered going up and down as a boy at just about this time of year—carrying out the midday 'snap' of bread and cheese to my mother's brothers as they helped with the Hundreds harvest. No doubt those men would have been very tickled to think that, thirty years on, a qualified doctor, I would be driving up that same road in my own car with the squire's daughter at my side. But I felt overcome suddenly with an absurd sense of gaucheness, and falseness—as if, had my plain labourer uncles actually appeared before me now, they would have seen me for the fraud I was, and laughed at me.

So for a while I said nothing, and neither did Caroline, and all our former ease seemed lost. It was a shame, for the drive was a pleasant one, the hedges colourful and fragrant, thick with dog-rose and red valerian and creamy white keck. Where the bushes gave way to gates one caught glimpses of the fields beyond them, some stripped already to stubble and soil and being picked over by rooks, some still with wheat in them, the pale of the crop streaked scarlet with poppies.

We reached the end of the Hundreds Farm lane, and I slowed the car in preparation for turning into it. But she straightened up as if ready to get out.

'Don't trouble to take me all the way down. It's no distance.'

'Are you sure?'

'Quite sure.'

'Well, all right.'

I supposed she had had enough of me; and couldn't blame her. But when I had put on the brake and let the engine idle she reached to the catch of her door, then paused with her hand upon it. Half turning to me, she said awkwardly, 'Thank you so much for the lift, Dr Faraday. I'm sorry to have gone on, before. I expect you think what most people must think, when they've seen Hundreds as it is nowadays: that we're absolutely mad to go on living there, trying to keep it the way it was; that we ought to just . . . give up. The truth is, you see, we know how lucky we are to have lived there at all. We have to sort of keep the place in order, keep up our side of the bargain. That can feel like an awful pressure, sometimes.'

Her tone was simple and very sincere, and her voice, I realised, was a pleasant one, low and melodious—the voice of a much handsomer woman, so that I was very much struck by it, there in the close warm twilight of the car.

My complicated feelings began to unravel. I said, 'I don't think you're in the least bit mad, Miss Ayres. I only wish there was something I could do to make your family burdens lighter. That's the doctor in me, I suppose. Your brother's leg, for example. I've been thinking, if I could take a good look at it—'

She shook her head. 'That's kind of you. But I really meant it, just now, when I said there wasn't the money for treatments.'

'How about if it were possible to waive the fee?'

'Well, that would be even kinder! But I don't think my brother would see it that way. He has a silly sort of pride when it comes to things like that.'

'Ah,' I said, 'but there might be a way around that, too . . .'

I'd had this idea at the back of my mind ever since my trip to Hundreds; now I put it together properly as I spoke. I told her about the successes I'd had in the past in using electrical therapy to treat muscle injuries very like her brother's. I said that induction coils were rarely seen outside specialist wards, where they tended to be used on very fresh injuries, but that my hunch was their application could be far wider.

'GPs need to be convinced,' I said. 'They need to see the evidence. I've got the equipment, but the right kind of case doesn't always come up. If I had an appropriate patient, and was writing the work up as I went along, making a paper out of it—well, the patient would be doing me a kind of favour. I wouldn't dream of charging a fee.'

She narrowed her eyes. 'I begin to see the misty outline of a beautiful arrangement.'

'Exactly. Your brother wouldn't even have to come to my surgery: the machine's very portable, I could bring it out to the Hall. I couldn't swear it would work, of course. But if I were to get him wired up to it, say, once a week for two or three months, it's just possible he'd feel the benefits enormously . . . What do you think?'

'I think it sounds marvellous!' she said, as if really delighted by the idea. 'But aren't you afraid of wasting your time? Surely there are more deserving cases.'

'Your brother's case seems pretty deserving to me,' I told her. 'And as for wasting time—well, to be quite honest with you, I don't think it'll do my standing at the district hospital any harm, to be seen taking the initiative with a trial of this nature.'

That was perfectly true; though had I been really honest with her,

I would have added that I also had hopes of impressing the local gentry—who, hearing perhaps of my success in treating Roderick Ayres's ailments, might for the first time in twenty years consider sending for me to take a look at their own . . . We talked the matter over for a minute or two, with the car engine idling; and since she grew more excited about it the more she heard, she at last said, 'Look, why not come up to the farm with me right now, and put this to Roddie yourself?'

I glanced at my watch. 'Well, there's the patient I promised to look in on.'

'Oh, but can't they wait a little? Patients must be good at waiting. That's why they're called patients, surely . . . Just five minutes, to explain it to him? Just to tell him what you've told me?'

She spoke, now, like a jolly sort of schoolgirl, and her manner was hard to resist. I said, 'All right,' and turned the car into the lane, and after a short jolting ride we found ourselves in the cobbled yard of the farm. Ahead of us was the Hundreds farmhouse, a gaunt Victorian building. To our left were the cow-pen and milking-shed. We'd clearly arrived near the end of milking-time, for only a small group of cows still waited, fretful and complaining, to be taken in from their pen. The rest—about fifty of them, I guessed—could just be seen in an enclosure on the other side of the yard.

We got out and, with Gyp, began to pick our way over the cobbles. It was hard work: all farm-yards are filthy, but this one was filthier than most, and the mud and slurry had been churned by hooves and then baked solid, in ruts and peaks, by the long dry summer. The shed, when we reached it, turned out to be an old wooden structure in a rather obvious state of dilapidation, reeking of manure and ammonia and giving off heat like a glass hot-house. There were no milking machines, only stools and pails, and in the first two stalls we found the farmer, Makins, and his grown-up son, each at work on a cow. Makins had come in from outside the county a few years before, but I knew him by sight, a harassed-looking lean-faced man in his early fifties, the very image of a struggling dairyman. Caroline called to him, and he gave us a nod, glancing at me in mild curiosity; we walked further and, to my surprise, found Roderick. I'd guessed he was in the farmhouse or busy in some other part of the farm, but here he was, milking along with the others, his face scarlet with heat and exertion, his long lean legs folded up and his forehead pressed into the cow's dusty brown flank.

He looked up and blinked when he saw me—not entirely pleased, I thought, to be caught at work like this, but doing a good job of hiding his feelings, for he called lightly, though without smiling: 'I hope you'll excuse me if I don't get up to shake your hand!' He looked at his sister. 'Everything all right?'

'Everything's fine,' she answered. 'Dr Faraday wants to talk to you about something, that's all.'

'Well, I shan't be long.—Settle down, you great daft thing.'

His cow had started moving fretfully about at the sound of our voices. Caroline drew me back.

'They get skittish around strangers. They know me, though. Do you mind if I help?'

'Of course not,' I said.

She let herself into the cow-pen, slipping on a pair of wellingtons and a filthy canvas apron, moving easily among the waiting animals, then driving one back into the shed and putting it to stand in the stall beside her brother's. Her arms were bare already, so she had no sleeves to roll up, but she washed her hands at a stand-pipe and gave them a swill with disinfectant; she brought over a stool and a zinc pail, put them down beside the cow—giving the cow a shove with her elbow as she did it, to bring it round to the right position—and set to work. I heard the noisy squirt of the milk in the empty bucket, and saw the brisk rhythmic movement of her arms. Taking a step to one side, I could just make out beneath the cow's broad hindquarters the flash of her hands tugging on the pale, impossibly elastic-looking udders.

She had finished that cow and started on another before Roderick finished his. He led the beast out of the shed, emptied his pail of foaming milk into a scrubbed steel vat, then came over to me, wiping his fingers on his apron and jerking up his chin.

'What can I do for you?'

I didn't want to keep him from his work, so told him briefly what I had in mind, phrasing it all as if I were asking a favour, putting it to him that he'd be helping me out with some rather important research . . . The scheme sounded less convincing, somehow, than when I had described it to his sister in the car, and he listened with a very dubious expression, especially when I described the electrical nature of the machine. 'I'm sorry to say we haven't the fuel to run our generator during the day,' he said, shaking his head as if that put an end to it. But I assured him that the coil ran off its own dry cells . . . I could see Caroline watching us, and when she had finished with another cow she came and joined us, adding her arguments to mine. Roderick looked anxiously at the restless waiting cattle as she spoke, and I think he agreed to the scheme in the end purely as a way of shutting us up. As soon as he could, he went limping over to the pen to fetch another beast for milking, and it was Caroline who fixed the date for me to come to the house.

'I'll make sure he's there,' she murmured. 'Don't worry.' And she added, as if just struck by the thought: 'Come long enough to stay for tea again, will you? I know Mother would want you to.'

'Yes,' I said, pleased. 'I'd like to. Thank you, Miss Ayres.'

At that, she put on a comically pained expression. 'Oh, call me Caroline, won't you? Lord knows, I've years and years ahead of me of being dry Miss Ayres . . . But I'll still call you Doctor, if I may. One never quite likes to breach those professional distances, somehow.'

Smiling, she offered me her warm, milk-scented hand; and we shook on it, there in the cowshed, like a couple of farmers sealing a deal.

The date I made with her was for the following Sunday: another warm day, as it turned out, with a parched, languished feel to it, and a sky made heavy and hazy with dust and grain. The square red front of the Hall looked pale and curiously insubstantial as I approached, and only as I drew up on the gravel did it seem to come into proper focus: I saw again all the shabby detail and, even more than on my first visit, I had an impression of the house being held in some sort of balance. One could see so painfully, I thought, both the glorious thing it had recently been, and the ruin it was on the way to becoming.

This time Roderick must have been looking out for me. The front door was drawn gratingly open, and he stood at the top of the cracked steps while I emerged from the car. When I made my way over to him with my doctor's bag in one hand and, in the other, the induction coil in its neat wooden case, he gave a frown.

'This is the gadget you meant? I was picturing something heftier. This looks like something you'd keep sandwiches in.'

I said, 'It's more powerful than you'd think.'

'Well, if you say so . . . Let me show you to my room.'

He spoke as if rather regretting having agreed to the whole thing. But he turned and led me inside, taking me to the right of the staircase this time, and along another cool dim passage. He opened up the last of its doors, saying vaguely, 'I'm afraid it's a bit of a mess in here.'

I followed him in, and set down my things; then looked about me in some surprise. When he had spoken of 'his room' I'd naturally been picturing an ordinary bedroom, but this room was huge—or seemed huge to me then, when I still hadn't quite acclimatised myself to the scale of things at Hundreds—with panelled walls, a lattice-work plaster ceiling, and a wide stone fireplace with a Gothic surround.

'This used to be a billiard room,' Roderick said to me, seeing my face. 'My great-grandfather kitted it up. I think he must have fancied himself as some sort of baron, don't you? But we lost the billiards stuff years ago, and when I came home from the Air Force—home from hospital, I mean—well, it took me a while to be able to manage stairs and so on, so my mother and sister had the idea of putting a bed for me in here. I've grown so used to it, it's never seemed worth going back upstairs. I do all my work in here, too.'

'Yes,' I said, 'so I see.'

This was the room, I realised, that I had glimpsed from the terrace in July. It was even more of a jumble than it had seemed to me then. One corner was given over to a punishing-looking iron-framed bed, with a dressing table close beside it and, next to that, an antique washing stand and mirror. Before the Gothic fireplace stood a couple of old leather armchairs, handsome enough, but both very scuffed and split at their seams. There were two curtained windows, one leading out via those convolvulus-choked stone steps to the terrace; in front of the other, and rather spoiling the lovely long line of it, Roderick had set up a desk and swivel chair. He had obviously put the desk there in order to catch the best of the northern daylight, but this also meant that its illuminated surface—which was almost obscured by a litter of papers, ledgers, folders, technical books, dirty teacups, and overflowing ashtrays—acted as a sort of magnet on the eye, irresistibly drawing one's gaze from every point in the room. The desk was clearly a magnet for Roderick in other ways too, for even while talking to me he had gone across to it and started rooting about for something in the chaos. At last he produced a stub of pencil, then fished in his pocket for a scrap of paper and began copying down what looked like a series of sums into one of the ledgers.

'Sit down, won't you?' he said to me over his shoulder. 'I shan't be a tick. But I've just come back from the farm, and if I don't make a note of these blasted figures right now, I'm sure to forget.'

I did sit, for a minute or two. But as he showed no sign of joining me, I thought I might as well prepare my machine, so I brought it over and set it down between the two scuffed leather chairs, unhooking its latch and drawing off its case. I'd used the apparatus many times before, and it was simple enough, a combination of coil, dry-cell battery, and metal plate electrodes; but it looked rather daunting with its terminals and wires, and when I raised my head again I saw that Roderick had left his desk and was gazing down at it in some dismay.

'Quite a little monster, isn't it,' he said, plucking at his lip. 'You mean to set it going right now?'

'Well,' I said, pausing with the tangled leads in my hands, 'I thought that was the idea. But if you'd rather not—'

'No, no, it's all right. Since you're here, we might as well get on with it. Do I strip off, or how does it work?'

I said I thought we should get away with him simply rolling his baggy trouser leg up, over the knee. He seemed glad not to have to undress in front of me, but once he had taken off his plimsoll and the much-darned sock beneath it and seen to the trousers, he folded his arms, looking awkward.

'I feel like I'm joining the Freemasons! I don't have to swear an oath or anything?'

I laughed. 'In the first place you simply have to sit here and let me examine you, if you don't mind. It won't take long.'

He lowered himself into the armchair, and I squatted before him and gently took hold of the injured leg, drawing it straight. As the muscle tightened he gave a grunt of pain.

'Not too much for you?' I asked. 'I need to move it about a bit, I'm afraid, to get the feel of the injury.'

The leg was slender in my hands, thick with springing dark hair, but the skin had a yellowish, bloodless look, and in various spots on the calf and shin the hair gave way to polished pink dents and ridges. The knee was as pale and bulbous as some queer root, and terribly stiff. The muscle of the calf was shallow and rigid, knotty with indurated tissue. The ankle joint—which Roderick was drastically overusing, in compensation for the lack of movement above—looked puffy and inflamed.

'Pretty foul, isn't it?' he said, in a more subdued tone, as I tried the leg and foot in various positions.

'Well, the circulation's sluggish, and there are a lot of adhesions. That's not good. But I've certainly seen worse . . . How's this?'

'Ouch. Stinking.'

'And this?'

He jerked away. 'Christ! What are you trying to do, twist the damn thing off?'

I gently took hold of the leg again and set it into its natural position, and spent a moment or two simply warming and working the rigid muscle of the calf between my fingers. Then I went through the process

of wiring him up: soaking squares of lint with salt solution, fixing these
to the electrode plates; putting the plates in position on his leg with
elastic bindings. He leaned forward to watch me do it, looking more
interested now. As I made a few final adjustments to the machine he
said, in a simple, boyish way, 'That's the condenser, is it? Yes, I see. And
there's how you interrupt the current, I suppose . . . Look here, do you
have a licence for this? I'm not about to start sparking at the ears or
anything?'

I said, 'I hope not. But let's just say the last patient I hooked up to
this now saves a fortune on permanent waves.'

He blinked, mistaking my tone, taking me seriously for a second.
Then he met my gaze—met it properly for the first time that day, perhaps for the first time ever; finally 'seeing' me—and he smiled. The
smile lifted his features completely, and drew attention from his scars.
One saw the likeness between him and his mother.

I said, 'Are you ready?'

He grimaced, more boyish than ever. 'I suppose so.'

'Right, here goes.'

I threw the switch. He yelped, his leg jumping forward in an invol-
untary twitch. Then he started laughing.

I said, 'Not painful?'

'No. Like pins and needles, that's all. Now it's hotting up! Is that
right?'

'Perfect. Once the heat begins to fade, let me know, and I'll turn it
up a bit.'

We spent five or ten minutes like that, until the sensation of heat in
his leg had reached a constant, which meant that the current had found
its peak. I left the machine to look after itself then, and sat down in the
second leather armchair. Roderick began to feel in his trouser pocket
for his tobacco and packet of papers. But I couldn't bear to see him roll
up one of his wretched little 'coffin nails' again, so I got out my own
case and lighter and we helped ourselves to a cigarette each. He took a
long draw on his, closing his eyes and letting his head grow loose on
his slender neck.

I said sympathetically, 'You look tired.'

At once, he made an effort to sit straighter. 'I'm all right. I was up at six this morning, that's all, for the milking. It isn't so bad in this weather, of course; it's in winter that one feels it . . . Having Makins for a dairyman doesn't help, though.'

'No? Why not?'

He changed his pose again, and spoke as if reluctantly. 'Oh, I oughtn't to complain. He's had it tough, with this bloody heat wave: we've lost milk, we've lost grass, we've already had to start the herd off on next winter's feed. But he wants a thousand impossible things, and doesn't have a clue about how to achieve them. That's left to me, unfortunately.'

I asked, What sort of things? He said, with the same touch of reluctance, 'Well, his big idea is for me to get an extension run out here from the water main. He wants me to bring out electricity while I'm at it. He says that even if the well fills up again, the pump is just about ready to blow. He wants me to replace that; and he's started saying now that he thinks the milking-shed's unsafe. He'd like me to pull it down and build a brick one. With a brick shed and an electric milker we could start turning out accredited milk, and make more of a profit. It's all he talks about.'

He reached to a table at his side for a gun-metal ashtray, already crowded with worm-like stubs. I leaned across and tapped my cigarette into it too, saying, 'Well, I fear he's right about the milk.'

Roderick laughed. 'I know he's right! He's right about it all. The farm's absolutely jiggered. But what the hell am I to do about it? He keeps asking me, Why can't I free up some capital? It's as though he's found the phrase in some magazine. I've told him frankly that Hundreds doesn't have any capital to free. He doesn't believe me. He sees us living here, in this great house; he thinks we're sitting on piles of gold. He doesn't see us blundering around in the night with candles and Tilleys because we've run out of oil for the generator. He doesn't see my sister, scrubbing floors, washing dishes in cold water . . .' He jerked

a hand towards his desk. 'I've been writing letters to the bank, and
putting an application together for a building licence. I spoke to a man
at the district council yesterday about the water main and the electricity. He didn't give me much encouragement; he said we're too isolated
out here to make it worth their while. But of course, the whole thing
has to be put down on paper. They need plans and surveyor's reports,
and God knows what else. That's so it can do the rounds of about ten
different departments, I suppose, before they reject it properly . . .'

He had started speaking almost unwillingly, but it was as if he had
some sort of spring inside him, and his own words wound it: as he went
on I watched the bitter shifting about of his scarred, finely cut features,
the restless dipping and rising of his hands, and suddenly remembered
what David Graham had told me, about his having had that touch of
'nervous trouble' after his smash. I'd been supposing his manner to be
rather casual, all this time. Now I realised that the casualness was actually something else completely: perhaps an exhaustion, perhaps a studied warding off of anxiety; perhaps even a tension, so complete and
habitual it resembled languor.

He became aware of my thoughtful gaze. He fell silent, drawing
deeply on his cigarette again, and taking his time over exhaling. He
said, in a different voice, 'You mustn't let me run on. I can be a frightful bore about it.'

'Not at all,' I answered. 'I'd like to hear more.'

But he was clearly set on turning the subject, and for five or ten
minutes we discussed other things. Every so often as we chatted I moved
forward to check his leg, and to ask him how the muscle was feeling.
'It's fine,' he'd answer each time, but I could see his face growing
flushed, so guessed he was suffering slightly. Soon it was clear that the
skin had started to itch. He began to pick and rub at the edge of the
electrodes. When I finally switched the thing off and removed the elastics, he worked his fingernails vigorously up and down his calf, grateful
to be released.

The treated flesh, as I'd expected, looked hot and moist, almost scarlet. I dried it off, shook powder on it, and spent another couple of minutes working the muscle with my fingers. But it was clearly one thing for him to be wired up to an impersonal machine, and quite another to have me squatting before him going over his leg with quick warm powdered hands: he shifted about impatiently, and at last I let him rise. He saw to his sock and plimsoll and unrolled his trouser leg, all without speaking. But once he had taken a few paces across the room he looked back at me and said, as if pleased and surprised, 'You know, that's not too bad. That's really not too bad at all.'

I realised then how much I had wanted the thing to be a success. I said, 'Walk again, and let me watch you . . . Yes, you're definitely moving more freely. Just don't overdo it. It's a good start, but we must take things slowly. For now, you must keep that muscle warm. You've some liniment, I suppose?'

He glanced doubtfully around the room. 'I think they gave me some lotion or other when they sent me home.'

'Never mind. I'll give you a new prescription.'

'Oh, now, look here. You mustn't trouble any more than you already have.'

'I told you, didn't I? You're doing me the favour.'

'Well—'

I'd anticipated exactly this, and had brought along a bottle in my bag. He took it from me, then stood gazing at the label while I went back to the machine. As I was tidying away the lint there was a knock on the door, which startled me slightly, for I had heard no footsteps: the room had those two great windows, but the wooden panelling on its walls gave it an insulated feel, as if it were the below-decks cabin of an ocean liner. Roderick called out, and the door was opened. Gyp appeared, thrusting his way into the room and trotting straight to me; and behind him, more tentatively, came Caroline. She was wearing an Aertex blouse today, tucked haphazardly into the waistband of a shapeless cotton skirt.

She said, 'Are you cooked, Roddie?'

'Quite fried,' he answered.

'And is that the machine? Crikey. Like something of Dr Franken-stein's, isn't it?'

She watched me lock the thing back in its case, then noticed her brother, who was absently flexing and bending his leg. She must have seen from his pose and expression the relief the treatment had brought him, for she gave me a serious, grateful look, which somehow pleased me almost more than the success of the therapy itself. But then, as if embarrassed by her own emotion, she turned away from me to pick up a stray piece of paper from the floor, and began complaining light-heartedly about Roderick's untidiness.

'If only there were some sort of machine for keeping rooms in order!' she said.

Roderick had unstoppered the bottle of liniment and was lifting it to his nose.

'I thought we had one of those already. It's called Betty. Or else why do we pay her?'

'Don't listen to him, Doctor. He never lets poor Betty in here.'

'I can't keep her out!' he said. 'And she moves things around where I can't find them, and then pretends she hasn't touched them.'

He spoke absently now, already having drifted back to that magnetic desk of his, the bottle put aside and his leg forgotten; and when he had opened up the cover of a dog-eared manila file and was frowning down at it he began, just as automatically, to bring out papers and tobacco in order to roll a cigarette.

I saw Caroline watching him, her expression growing serious again.

'I wish you'd give those filthy things up,' she said. She went to one of the oak-panelled walls and ran her hand across the wood. 'Look at these poor panels. The smoke's ruining them. They ought to be waxed or oiled or something.'

'Oh, the whole house needs *something*,' said Roderick, yawning. 'If you know a way of doing *something* with *nothing*—no money, I mean—

then go ahead, be my guest. Besides'—he had raised his head and caught my eye, and made another obvious effort to speak more brightly—'it's a fellow's duty to smoke in this room, wouldn't you say, Dr Faraday?'

He gestured to the lattice-work ceiling, which I had taken to be ivory-coloured with age, but which I now realised had been stained an irregular nicotine-yellow by half-a-century's worth of cigar-puffing billiard players.

Soon he returned to his papers, and Caroline and I took the hint and left him. He promised, with a touch of vagueness, that he would shortly join us for tea.

His sister shook her head. 'He'll be in there for hours now,' she murmured, as we moved away from his door. 'I wish he'd let me share the work with him, but he never will . . . His leg was really better, though, wasn't it? I can't thank you enough for helping him like this.'

'He could help himself,' I said, 'by doing the right kind of exercises. Or a bit of simple massage every day would make a great deal of difference to the muscle. I've given him some liniment; you might see that he uses it?'

'I'll do my best. But I expect you've noticed how careless of himself he is.' She slowed her step. 'What do you think of him, honestly?'

I said, 'I think he's fundamentally very healthy. I think he's charming, too, by the way. It's a pity he's been allowed to organise his room like that, with the business side of things dominating everything else.'

'Yes, I know. Our father used to run the estate from the library. It's his old desk that Roderick uses, but I never remember it looking so chaotic in the old days, and that was with four farms to manage, not just one. We had an agent to help us then, mind; a Mr McLeod. He had to leave us during the war. He had an office of his own, just back there. This side of the Hall was the 'men's side', if you know what I mean, and always busy. Now, apart from Roderick's room, this whole section of the house might as well not be here at all.'

She spoke casually, but it was novel and curious to me to think of having grown up in a house with so many spare rooms in it they could be shut up and forgotten. When I said this to Caroline, however, she gave that rueful laugh of hers.

'The novelty soon wears off, I assure you! One starts to think of them pretty quickly as something like tiresome poor relations, for one can't abandon them completely, but they have accidents, or fall ill, and finish by using up more money than would have been needed to pension them off. It's a shame, because there are some quite nice features here . . . But I could show you over the house, if you'd like? If you promise to avert your gaze from the worst bits? The sixpenny tour. What do you say?'

She seemed genuinely keen to do it, and I said I'd like it very much, if it wouldn't mean keeping her mother waiting. She said, 'Oh, Mother's a true Edwardian at heart: she thinks it a barbarism to take tea before four o'clock. What time is it now?' It was just after half past three. 'We've plenty of time. Let's start at the front.'

She snapped her fingers for Gyp, who had gone trotting on ahead, and took me back past her brother's door.

'The hall you've seen, of course,' she said, when we reached it and I had set down my therapy machine and bag. 'The floor's Carrara marble, and three inches thick—hence the vaulted ceilings in the rooms underneath. It's a devil to polish. The staircase: considered quite a feat of engineering when it was put in, because of the open second landing; there aren't many others quite like it. My father used to say it was like something from a department store. My grandmother refused to use it; it gave her vertigo . . . Over there's our old morning room, but I won't show you that: it's quite empty, and far too shabby. Let's go in here instead.'

She opened a door on a darkened room which, once she had gone across to the shuttered windows and let in some light, revealed itself as a pleasant largish library. Most of its shelves, however, were hung with dust-sheets, and some of its furniture was obviously gone: she reached into a mesh-fronted case and carefully drew out a couple of what she said were the house's best books, but I could see that the room was not what it had been, and there wasn't much to linger for. She went to the fireplace to peer up the chimney, concerned about a fall of soot in the grate; then she closed the shutter and led me to the neighbouring room—the old estate office she had already mentioned, which was panelled like Roderick's and had similar Gothic touches. Her brother's door was next, and just beyond that was the curtained arch that led to the basement. We went quietly past them both and found the 'boot room', a musty-smelling chamber full of mackintoshes and perished wellingtons and tennis racquets and mallets but really, she told me, a sort of tiring-room from the days when the family still ran a stables. A door inside it led to a quaint delft-tiled lavatory that had been known for over a century, she said, as 'the gentlemen's hoo-hah'.

She snapped her fingers again for Gyp, and we moved on.

'You're not bored?' she asked.

'Not at all.'

'Do I make a good guide?'

'You make a capital guide.'

'But now, oh dear, here's one of those bits from which you must turn your gaze. Oh, and now you're laughing at us! That's unfair.'

I had to explain why I was smiling: the panel she meant was the one from which I'd prised that plaster acorn, all those years before. I told the story rather warily, not quite sure how she would take it. But she widened her eyes as if thrilled.

'Oh, but that's too funny! And Mother really gave you a medal? Like Queen Alexandra? I wonder if she remembers.'

'Please don't mention it to her,' I said. 'I'm sure she doesn't. I was one of about fifty nasty little grubby-kneed boys that day.'

'But you liked the house, even then?'

'Enough to want to vandalise it.'

'Well,' she said kindly, 'I don't blame you for wanting to vandalise these silly mouldings. They were simply asking to be snapped off. What you started I'm afraid Roddie and I, between us, probably finished . . . But isn't that queer? You saw Hundreds before he or I ever did.'

'So I did,' I said, struck by the thought.

We moved away from the broken mouldings, and continued our tour. She drew my attention to a short line of portraits, murky canvases in heavy gold frames. And, just as in some American movie mock-up of a stately home, they turned out to be what she called 'the family album'.

'None of them is terribly good or valuable or anything, I'm afraid,' she said. 'All the valuable ones have been sold, along with the best of the furniture. But they're fun, if you can bear the bad light.'

She pointed to the first. 'Here's William Barber Ayres. He's the man who had the Hall built. A good county chap, like all the Ayreses, but evidently rather near: we have letters to him from the architect, complaining of outstanding fees and more or less threatening to send round the heavies . . . Next is Matthew Ayres, who took troops to Boston. He came back in disgrace, with an American wife, and died three months later; we like to say she poisoned him . . . This is Ralph Billington Ayres, Matthew's nephew—the family gambler, who for a time ran a second estate, in Norfolk, and just like a Georgette Heyer rake lost the whole of it in a single game of cards . . . And this is Catherine Ayres, his daughter-in-law and my great-grandmother. She was an Irish racehorse heiress, and restored the family fortune. It was said that she could never go near a horse herself, for fear of frightening it. Pretty clear where I get my looks from, wouldn't you say?'

She laughed as she spoke, because the woman in the painting was strikingly ugly; but the fact is, Caroline did resemble her, just a little—though it gave me a slight shock to realise it, for I found I had grown as used to her mismatched masculine features as I had to Roderick's scars. I made some gesture of polite demurral, but she had already turned away. She had two more rooms, she said, to show me, but would 'save the best till last'. I thought the one she took me to next was arresting enough: a dining-room, done up in a pale *chinoiserie* theme, with a hand-painted paper on its walls and, on its polished table, two ormolu candelabra with writhing branches and cups. But then she led me back to the centre of the passage and, opening up another door, made me stand just inside the threshold while she crossed through the darkness of the room beyond to unfasten the shutters at one of its windows.

This passage ran from north to south, so all its rooms faced west. The afternoon was bright, the light came in like blades through the seams in the shutters, and even as she lifted the bolt I could see that the space we were in was a large and impressive one, with various sheeted pieces of furniture dotted about. But when she drew the creaking shutters back and details leapt into life around me, I was so astonished, I laughed.

The room was an octagonal saloon, about forty feet across. It had a vivid yellow paper on its walls and a greenish patterned carpet; the fireplace was unblemished white marble, and from the centre of the heavily moulded ceiling there hung a large gilt-and-crystal chandelier.

'Pretty crazy, isn't it?' said Caroline, laughing too.

'It's incredible!' I said. 'One would never guess at it from the rest of the house—which is all so relatively sober.'

'Ah, well. I dare say the original architect would have wept if he'd known what was coming. It was Ralph Billington Ayres—you remember him? the family blade?—who had this room added, in the 1820s, when he still had most of his money. Apparently they were all madly keen on yellow in those days; God knows why. The paper's original, which is why we've hung on to it. As you can see'—she pointed out various spots where the ancient paper was drooping from the walls—'it seems less interested in hanging on to us. I can't show you the chandelier in all its glory, unfortunately, with the generator off; it's quite something when it's blazing. That's original too, but my parents had it electrified when they were first married. They used to throw lots of parties in those days, when the house was still grand enough to bear it. The carpet's in strips, of course. You can roll them back for dancing.'

She pointed out one or two other features, lifting off dust-sheets to expose the fine low Regency chair or cabinet or sofa underneath.

'What's this?' I asked, of one irregular-looking item. 'Piano?'

She put back a corner of its quilted cover. 'Flemish harpsichord, older than the house. I don't suppose you play?'

'Good heavens, no.'

'No, nor I. A pity. It ought really to be used, poor thing.'

But she spoke without much emotion, running her hand in a business-like way over the instrument's decorated case, then letting the cover fall again and going over to the unshuttered window. I joined her there. The window was actually a pair of long glass doors and, like the ones in Roderick's room and the little parlour, it opened on to a set of flying stone steps leading down to the terrace. As I saw when I drew closer, these particular steps had collapsed: the top one still jutted from the sill, but the rest lay scattered on the gravel four feet below, dark and weathered as if they had lain there some time. Undeterred, Caroline seized the handle of the doors and opened them up, and we stood on the little precipice in the soft, warm, fragrant air, looking over the west lawn. The lawn must once, I thought, have been trimmed and level: perhaps a space for croquet. Now the ground was lumpy with molehills and thistles, and the grass in places was knee-high. The straggling shrubs all around it gave way to clumps of purple beech, beautifully vivid in colour but quite out of control; and the two huge unlopped English elms beyond them would, I saw, once the sun sank lower, cast the whole of the scene in shadow.

Away to the right was a clutch of outbuildings, the garage and disused stables. Over the stable door was a great white clock.

'Twenty to nine,' I said, smiling, looking at the stuck ornamental hands.

Caroline nodded. 'Roddie and I did that when the clock first broke.' And then, seeing my puzzled expression: 'Twenty to nine is the time Miss Havisham's clocks are stopped at in *Great Expectations*. We thought it awfully funny, then. It seems a bit less funny now, I must admit . . . Beyond the stables are the old gardens—the kitchen gardens, and so on.'

I could just see the wall of them. It was made of the same uneven mellow red brick as the house; an arched opening in it gave a glimpse of cinder paths and overgrown borders and what I thought might be a quince or a medlar and, since I am fond of walled gardens, I said without thinking that I'd like to take a look at them.

Caroline glanced at her watch and said gamely, 'Well, we still have almost ten minutes. It's quickest to go this way.'

'This way?'

She put her hand to the door-frame, leaning forward and bending her legs. 'I mean, jump.'

I drew her back. 'Oh, no. I'm too old for that sort of thing. Take me some other time, would you?'

'You're sure?'

'Quite sure.'

'Well, all right.'

She seemed sorry. I think our tour had made her restless; or else she was simply showing her youth. She stayed at my side for a few minutes more, but then went around the room again, making sure that the furniture was properly wrapped, and lifting one or two corners of carpet to check for silver-fish and moth.

'Goodbye, poor neglected saloon,' she said, when she had closed the window and fastened the shutter and we had made our way, half blind, back out to the passage. And because she had spoken with something like a sigh, as she turned the key on the room I said, 'I'm so glad to have seen the house. It's lovely.'

'You think so?'

'Well, don't you?'

'Oh, it's not such a bad old pile, I suppose.'

For once, her jolly fifth-form manner grated on me. I said, 'Come on, Caroline, be serious.'

It was the first time I had used her Christian name, and perhaps that, combined with my slightly chiding tone, made her self-conscious. She coloured in that unbecoming way of hers, and the jolliness faded. Meeting my gaze she said, as if in honest surrender, 'You're right. Hundreds is lovely. But it's a sort of lovely monster! It needs to be fed all the time, with money and hard work. And when one feels *them*'—she nodded to the row of sombre portraits—'at one's shoulder, looking on, it can begin to seem like a frightful burden . . . It's hardest on Rod, because he has the extra responsibility of being master. He doesn't want to let people down, you see.'

She had a sort of trick, I realised, of turning the talk away from herself. I said, 'I'm sure your brother's doing all he can. You, too.' But over my words there came, from one of the clocks of the house, the quick, bright striking of four, and she touched my arm, her look clearing.

'Come on. My mother's waiting. The sixpenny tour includes refreshments, don't forget!'

So we continued along that passage to the start of the next, and went into the little parlour.

We found Mrs Ayres at her writing-desk, putting paste to a fragment of paper. She looked up almost guiltily as we appeared, though I couldn't imagine why; then I saw that the fragment was actually an unfranked stamp that had rather obviously already been through the post.

'Now, I fear,' she said, as she attached the stamp to an envelope, 'that this may not be quite legal. But heaven knows, we live in very lawless times. You won't give me away, Dr Faraday?'

I said, 'Not only that, I'll be happy to abet the crime. I'll take the letter to the post at Lidcote, if you like.'

'You will? How kind of you. The postmen are so careless nowadays. Before the war Wills the postman would come right to the door, twice a day. The man who has the round now complains about the extra distance. We're lucky if he doesn't leave our post at the end of the drive.'

She moved across the room as she spoke, making a small, elegant gesture with one of her slim, ringed hands, and I followed her to the chairs beside the fireplace. She was dressed more or less as she had been on my first visit, in creased dark linen with a knotted silk scarf at her throat, and in another pair of mildly distracting polished shoes.

Looking warmly into my face, she said, 'Caroline has told me what you're doing for Roderick. I'm so very grateful to you for taking an interest in him. You really think this treatment will make a difference?'

I said, 'Well, the signs so far are good.'

'They're better than good,' said Caroline, lowering herself with a thump on to the sofa. 'Dr Faraday's just being modest. It really is helping, Mother.'

'But that's marvellous! Roderick works so terribly hard, you know, Doctor. Poor boy. I'm afraid he hasn't the way his father had, with the estate. He hasn't the feel for the land and so on.'

I suspected she was right. But I said, politely, that I wasn't sure a feel for the land counted for much any more, given how difficult things were being made for the farmers; and with that readiness to please that characterises very charming people, she answered at once, 'Yes, indeed. I expect you know far more about it than I do . . . Now, Caroline's been showing you over the house, I think.'

'She has, yes.'

'And do you like it?'

'Very much.'

'I'm glad. Naturally, it's the shadow of what it once was. But then, as my children keep reminding me, we're lucky to have held on to it at all . . . I do think eighteenth-century houses the nicest. Such a civilised century. The house I grew up in was a great Victorian eyesore of a place. It's a Roman Catholic boarding-school now, and I must say, the nuns are very welcome to it. I do worry about the poor little girls, however. So many very gloomy corridors and turns of stair. We used to say it was haunted, when I was a child; I don't think it was. It might be now. My father died there, and he hated Roman Catholics with a passion . . . You've heard about all the changes at Standish, of course?'

I nodded. 'Yes. Well, bits and pieces, from my patients mainly.'

Standish was a neighbouring 'big house', an Elizabethan manor house whose family, the Randalls, had left the county to start a new life in South Africa. The place had been empty for two years, but had recently been sold: the buyer was a London man, named Peter Baker-Hyde, an architect working on Coventry, who had been drawn to Standish as a country retreat by what he considered to be its 'out-of-the-way charm'.

I said, 'I gather there's a wife and a young daughter, and two expensive motor cars; but no horses or dogs. And I hear the man has a good war-record—was quite the hero, out in Italy. He clearly did all right out of it: it sounds like he's already spent a lot of money on renovations to the house.'

I spoke a shade sourly, for none of the new wealth at Standish was headed my way: I'd learned just that week that Mr Baker-Hyde and his wife had registered with one of my local rivals, Dr Seeley.

Caroline laughed. 'He's a town planner, isn't he? He'll probably knock Standish down and build a roller-skating rink. Or maybe they'll sell the house to the Americans. They'll ship it over and have it rebuilt, like they did with Warwick Priory. They say you can get an American to buy any old bit of black timber, just by telling him it comes from the Forest of Arden, or was sneezed on by Shakespeare, or something.'

'How cynical you are!' said her mother. 'I think the Baker-Hydes sound charming. There are so few really nice people left in the county these days, we ought to be grateful for them for taking Standish on. When I think of all the great houses and what's become of them, I feel almost marooned. There's Umberslade Hall, where the Colonel's father used to go shooting: filled with secretaries now. Woodcote stands empty; I believe Meriden Hall is the same. Charlecote and Coughton have both been turned over to the public . . .'

She spoke with a sigh, her tone growing serious and almost plangent; and just for a second she looked her age. Then she turned her head, her expression changing. She had caught, as I had, the faint echoey rattle of china and teaspoons, out in the passage. Putting a hand to her breast, she leaned towards me and said in a mock-anxious murmur, 'Here comes what my son calls "the skeletons' polka". Betty has a positive genius, you know, for dropping cups. And we simply haven't the china—' The rattle grew louder, and she closed her eyes. 'Oh, the suspense!' She called through the open door, 'Do watch your step, Betty!'

'I'm watching it, madam!' came the indignant reply; and in another moment the girl appeared in the doorway, frowning and blushing as she manoeuvred in the large mahogany tray.

I got up to help her, but Caroline rose at the same time. She took the tray capably from Betty's hands, set it down, and looked it over.

'Not a single drop spilled! That must be in your honour, Doctor. You see we have Dr Faraday with us, Betty? He sorted you out with a miracle cure that time, you remember?'

Betty put down her head. 'Yes, miss.'

I said, smiling, 'How are you, Betty?'

'I'm all right, thank you, sir.'

'I'm glad to hear it, and to see you looking so well. So smart, too!'

I spoke guilelessly, but her expression slightly darkened, as if she suspected me of teasing; and then I remembered her having complained to me about the 'awful dress and hat' that the Ayreses made her wear. The fact is, she *was* rather quaintly dressed, in a black frock with a white apron, and with starched cuffs and a collar dwarfing her childish wrists and throat; and on her head was a fussy frilled cap, the kind of thing I couldn't remember having seen in a Warwickshire drawing-room since before the war. But in that old-fashioned, shabby-elegant setting, it was somehow hard to imagine her dressed any other way.

And she looked healthy enough, and took trouble over handing out the cups and the slices of cake, as if she were settling down all right. When she had finished she even made us a dip, like an unformed curt-sey. Mrs Ayres said, 'Thank you, Betty, that will do,' and she turned and left us. We heard the fading slap and squeak of her stout-soled shoes as she made her way back to the basement.

Caroline, setting down a bowl of tea for Gyp to lap at, said, 'Poor Betty. Not a natural parlourmaid.'

But her mother spoke indulgently. 'Oh, we must give her more time. I always remember my great-aunt saying that a well-run house was like an oyster. Girls come to one as specks of grit, you see; ten years later, they leave one as pearls.'

'   She was addressing me as well as Caroline—clearly forgetting, for the moment, that my own mother had once been one of the specks of grit her great-aunt had meant. I think even Caroline had forgotten it. They both sat comfortably in their chairs, enjoying the tea and the cake that Betty had prepared for them, then awkwardly carried for them, then cut and served for them, from plates and cups which, at the ring of a bell, she would soon remove and wash . . . I said nothing this time, however. I sat enjoying the tea and cake, too. For if the house, like an oyster, was at work on Betty, fining and disguising her with layer after minuscule layer of its own particular charm, then I suppose it had already begun a similar process with me.

Just as Caroline had predicted, her brother failed to join us that day: it was she who, a little later, walked with me out to my car. She asked if I was driving straight back to Lidcote; I told her I was planning to call on someone in another village. And when I named the village in question, she said, 'Oh, then you should carry on across the park and go out by the other gates. It's much quicker than going back the way you came and driving round. That drive's as bad as this one, mind, so watch out for your tyres.' Then she was struck by an idea. 'But, listen here. Would it help you to use the park more often? As a short-cut between patients, I mean?'

'Well,' I answered, thinking it over, 'yes, I suppose it would, very much.'

'Then you must use it whenever you like! I'm only sorry we never thought of it before. You'll find the gates are kept shut with wire, but that's simply because since the war we've begun to have problems with ramblers wandering in. Just fasten them behind you, they're never actually locked.'

I said, 'You really won't mind? Nor your mother, or your brother? I'll take you at your word, you know, and be out here every day.'

She smiled. 'We'd like it. Wouldn't we, Gyp?'

She moved back, putting her hands on her hips to watch me start the car and turn it. Then she snapped her fingers for the dog, and they headed off across the gravel.

I picked my way around the north side of the house, looking for the entrance to the other drive: going slowly, not quite certain of the way, and incidentally getting a view of the windows of Roderick's room. He didn't notice my car, but I saw him there, as I passed, very clearly: he was sitting at his desk, with his cheek on his hand, gazing at the papers and open books before him as if impossibly baffled and weary.

THREE

It became a part of my routine, after that, to call in at the Hall on a Sunday to treat Rod's leg, and then to stay on to tea with his mother and sister. And once I'd started to use Hundreds on my trips between cases, I was out there often. I looked forward to the visits; they made such a contrast with the rest of my rather workaday existence. I never let myself into the park and closed the gates behind me, then made my way along the overgrown drive, without a small, adventurous thrill. Arriving at that crumbling red house, I'd have the sense, every time, that ordinary life had fractionally tilted, and that I had slipped into some other, odder, rather rarer realm.

I'd begun to like the Ayreses for their own sake, too. It was Caroline I saw most. I discovered that she walked in the park almost daily, so I'd often catch sight of her unmistakable long-legged, broad-hipped figure, with Gyp cutting a way through the long grass at her side. If she was close enough I would stop the car and wind down my window, and we'd chat, as we had that time in the lane. She seemed to be always in the middle of some chore, always had a bag or a basket with her, filled with fruit, or mushrooms, or sticks for kindling. She might as well, I thought, have been a farmer's daughter; the more I saw of things at Hundreds, the sorrier I was that her life, like that of her brother, had so much work in it and so few pleasures. One day a neighbour of mine presented me with a couple of jars of honey from his hives, for having seen his son safely through a bad dose of whooping cough. I remembered Caroline's having longed for honey on my very first visit to the house, so I gave one of the jars to her. I did it casually, but she seemed amazed and delighted by the gift, holding up the jar to catch the sunlight, showing her mother.

'Oh, you shouldn't have!'

'Why not?' I said. 'An old bachelor like me.'

And Mrs Ayres said softly, with a shade almost of reproach, 'You're really too kind to us, Dr Faraday.'

But the fact is, my kindnesses were very small things; it was simply that the family lived in so isolated and precarious a way, they felt with extra force the impact of any chance nudge of fortune, good or bad. In the middle of September, for example, when I had been treating Roderick for nearly a month, the long summer finally broke. A day of thunderstorms led to a drop in temperature and two or three spells of heavy rain: the Hundreds well was saved, the milking ran smoothly for the first time in months; and Rod's relief was so palpable, it was almost painful to observe it. His whole mood lightened. He spent more time away from his desk, and began to talk almost brightly about making improvements at the farm. He brought in a couple of labourers to help in the fields. And because the house's already overgrown lawns had sprung into life with the shift in season, he set the estate's odd-jobber, Barrett, to go over them with a scythe. They emerged lush and trimly textured as a newly shorn sheep, making the house look more impressive—more, I thought, as it was meant to look; more as I remembered it having looked on that childhood visit of mine, thirty years before.

. . .

Meanwhile, at that neighbouring manor house, Standish, Mr and Mrs Baker-Hyde were now quite settled in. They began to be seen more in the neighbourhood; Mrs Ayres ran into the wife, Diana, on one of her rare shopping trips to Leamington, and found her to be just as charming as she had hoped. On the strength of that encounter, in fact, she began to think of hosting a 'little gathering' at Hundreds, as a way of welcoming the newcomers to the district.

This must have been in late September. She told me all about it while I was sitting with her and Caroline after treating Rod's leg. The thought of the Hall being opened up to strangers unsettled me slightly, and the feeling must have shown in my expression.

'Oh, we used to throw two or three parties a year here, you know, in the old days,' she said. 'Even during the war I managed to put together a regular supper for the officers billeted with us. It's true that one's points went further then. I couldn't manage a supper now. But we have Betty, after all. A servant makes all the difference at that sort of thing, and she can just about be trusted to go around with a decanter. I thought, a quiet sort of drinks party, no more than ten people. Perhaps the Desmonds, and the Rossiters . . .'

'You must come too, of course, Dr Faraday,' said Caroline, as her mother's voice tailed away.

And, 'Yes,' said Mrs Ayres. 'Yes, of course you must.'

She said it warmly enough, but with the briefest of hesitations; and I couldn't blame her for that, for though I was now such a regular at the house, I was hardly a family friend. Having invited me, however, she gamely saw the thing through. My only free evening was a Sunday; I usually spent it with the Grahams. But she said Sunday evenings were as good as any other, and she promptly brought out her engagement book and suggested some dates.

That was as far as we got with it, that day; and when there was no further mention of the party on my next visit I wondered if, after all, the idea had fizzled out. But a few days later, taking my short-cut across the park, I saw Caroline. She told me that, after a flurry of correspondence between her mother and Diana Baker-Hyde, an evening had finally been settled on, three Sundays ahead.

She spoke without much enthusiasm. I said, 'You don't sound very excited.'

She turned up the collar of her jacket, drawing the tips of it across her chin.

'Oh, I'm simply bowing to the inevitable,' she said. 'Most people think Mother's awfully dreamy, you know, but once she has an idea about something it's no use trying to talk her out of it. Rod says throwing a party with the house in the state it's in now will be like Sarah Bernhardt playing Juliet with one leg; and I must say, he has a point. I might just stay in the little parlour on the night, with Gyp and the wireless. That sounds much more fun to me than getting all glamoured up for people we don't even know, and probably won't much like.'

She seemed self-conscious as she spoke, and her tone did not ring quite true to me; and though she continued to grumble, it was clear that she was looking forward to the party to some extent, for over the next couple of weeks she threw herself into cleaning and tidying the Hall, often tucking up her hair in a turban and getting down on her hands and knees alongside Betty and the daily woman, Mrs Bazeley. Every time I visited the house I found carpets being hoisted up and beaten, pictures appearing on empty walls, and various bits of furniture emerging from storage.

'You'd think His Majesty were coming!' Mrs Bazeley said to me, when I went down to the kitchen one Sunday to make up some salt water for Rod's treatment. She had come in for the extra day. 'All this fuss, I dunno. Poor Betty's got calluses! Show Doctor your fingers, Betty.'

Betty was sitting at the table, cleaning various pieces of silver with metal polish and a piece of white scrim, but at Mrs Bazeley's words she readily put the scrim down and turned up her palms for me—liking the attention, I think. After three months at Hundreds her childlike hands had become thickened and stained, but I caught hold of the tip of one of her fingers and gave it a shake.

'Go on,' I said. 'That's no worse than you'd get in the fields—or in a factory, for that matter. They're good country hands, they are.'

'Country hands!' said Mrs Bazeley, as Betty, with a wounded air, went back to her polishing. 'Her got the worst of that from doing over the glass chandeliers. Every blasted drop, Miss Caroline's put her to, this last week.—Excuse my language, Doctor. But them chandeliers, they ought to be brought right down. In years gone by men would come and take 'em off to Brummagem, and dip 'em. All this throwing us in a flummox,' she said again, 'for a couple o' drinks; not even a dinner. And they're only London folks as are coming, in't they?'

But the preparations continued; and Mrs Bazeley, I noticed, worked as hard as anyone. It was difficult, after all, not to be seduced by the novelty of the thing, for in that year of strict rationing even a small private party was something to relish. I hadn't yet met the Baker-Hydes, so I was curious to see them—curious, too, to see the Hall decked out in the style of its grander days. I was also, I discovered to my own surprise and annoyance, a little nervous. I felt I had to live up to the occasion, and wasn't quite sure I knew how. On the Friday of the weekend in question I had my hair cut. On the Saturday I asked my housekeeper, Mrs Rush, to dig out my evening clothes. She found the jacket with moths in its seams, and the shirt so worn in places she had to cut off its own tail in order to patch it. When I finally looked myself over in the cloudy strip of mirror on my wardrobe door, my make-do-and-mend appearance was not very heartening. My hair had recently started to thin, and, freshly barbered, I seemed bald at the temples. I had been out with a patient in the night, and was bleary with lack of sleep. I looked like my father, I realised in dismay; or, like my father would have looked if he had ever worn evening dress: as if I'd be happier in a brown shopkeeper's coat and an apron.

Graham and Anne, tickled by the thought of me hobnobbing with the Ayreses instead of having a Sunday supper with them, had asked me to call in for a drink on my way to the party. I went in sheepishly, and, as I'd expected, Graham laughed out loud at the sight of me. Anne, more kindly, took a clothes-brush to my shoulders, then had me undo my tie so that she could re-knot it herself.

'There. You look perfectly handsome,' she told me when she'd finished, in that voice nice women use for complimenting unhandsome men.

Graham said, 'I hope you put a vest on! Morrison went up to some evening do at the Hall a few years ago. He said it was the coldest night of his life.'

As it happened, the hot summer had given way to a very mixed autumn, and the day had been cool and damp. The rain set in in earnest as I left Lidcote, transforming the dusty country lanes into streams of mud. I had to run from the car with a blanket over my head to open up the gates of the park, and when I emerged from the clinging wet drive and drew up on the sweep of gravel, I gazed at the Hall in some fascination: I'd never been out there so late in the day before and, with its uneven outline, it looked as though it were bleeding itself into the rapidly darkening sky. I hurried up the steps and tugged on the doorbell—the rain tumbling down, now, like water from a pail. No one came in answer to my ring. My hat began to sag about my ears. So finally, in fear of drowning, I opened up the unlocked door and let myself in.

It was one of the tricks of the house, to have distinctly different atmospheres inside and out. The sound of the rain faded as I pushed the door closed behind me, and I found the hall with soft electric lights on, just bright enough to bring out the gleam of the newly polished marble floor. There were bowls of flowers on every table, late-summer roses and bronze chrysanthemums. The floor above was dimly lit, the floor above that even dimmer, so the staircase ascended into shadows; the glass dome in the roof held the last of the evening twilight, and seemed suspended in the darkness, a great translucent disc. The silence was perfect. When I had removed my sodden hat and brushed the water from my shoulders I stepped softly forward, and just stood looking upwards for a minute in the centre of the shining floor.

Then I moved on, along the south passage. The little parlour proved to be warm, and lit, but empty; going further, I saw a stronger light at the open doorway of the saloon, so headed for that. At the sound of my step, Gyp started barking; a second later he came prancing out to me, wanting fuss. He was followed by Caroline's voice: 'Roddie, is that you?'

The words had a note of strain to them. Moving closer, I called back diffidently, 'It's only me, I'm afraid! Dr Faraday. I let myself in, I hope you don't mind. Am I hopelessly early?'

I heard her laugh. 'Not at all. It's we who are hopelessly late. Come and find me! I can't come to you.'

She was speaking, it turned out, from the top of a small step-ladder, at one of the saloon's far walls. I couldn't tell why, at first; I was too dazzled by the saloon itself. The room had been striking enough when I had seen it in a half-light with its furniture sheeted, but now its delicate sofas and chairs were all uncovered, and its chandelier—one of those chandeliers, presumably, that had given Betty her blisters—was blazing like a furnace. Several other smaller lamps were also burning, and the light was caught and returned by touches of gold on various ornaments and mirrors, and above all by the still-bright Regency yellow of the walls.

Caroline saw me blinking. 'Your eyes will soon stop watering, don't worry. Take off your coat, won't you, and help yourself to a drink? Mother's still dressing, and Rod has got himself stuck sorting out some problem at the farm. But I've almost finished here.'

Then I realised what she was doing: she was working her way around the room with a handful of drawing-pins, fixing down the edges of yellow paper that were drooping or bulging from the walls. I went across to help her, but she pressed in the final pin as I reached her side; so then I held the wooden ladders, and offered my hand, to steady her as she came down. She had to do it carefully, lifting up the hem of her skirt: she was wearing a blue chiffon evening gown and silver shoes and gloves; her hair was pinned up at one side with a diamanté clasp. The gown was an old one and, to be honest, not quite becoming. The low neckline showed her prominent collarbones and the tendons of her throat, and the bodice was too tight for the swell of her bust. She had a touch of colour on her eyelids, and rouge on her cheeks, and her mouth, red with lipstick, was almost startlingly full and large. I thought, actually, how much nicer and more like herself she would have looked with a scrubbed face, and in one of her shapeless old skirts and an Aertex blouse; and how much I would rather have seen her in them. But I was conscious of my own deficiencies, in that hard light. As I handed her safely to the floor I said, 'You look lovely, Caroline.'

Her rouged cheeks grew a shade pinker. Avoiding my eye, she spoke to the dog.

'And he hasn't even had a drink yet! Think how good I'll look through the bottom of a cocktail, eh Gyp?'

She was ill at ease, I realised, and not quite herself. I imagined she was simply anxious about the night ahead. She tugged the bell for Betty; there came the stifled creak of the wire, shifting invisibly in the wall. Then she took me over to the sideboard, where she had set out a range of handsome old cut crystal glasses and what, for the times, was a quite impressive selection of drinks: sherry, gin, Italian vermouth, bitters, and lemonade. I had brought along a half-bottle of Navy rum as a contribution to the party; we had just poured out two small glasses of it when Betty appeared, in answer to the bell. She had been spruced up along with everything else in the house: her cuffs, collar, and apron were blindingly white, and her cap was fancier than usual, with a stiff vertical frill like the wafer on an ice-cream sundae. But she had been putting plates of sandwiches together downstairs, and looked warm and slightly harassed. Caroline had called her to take away the step-ladder, so she went quickly and not very gracefully over to pick it up. She must have done it too hastily, however, or had underestimated its weight: she took a couple of steps with it and it went crashing to the floor.

Caroline and I both started, and the dog began to bark.

'Gyp, you idiot, be quiet!' Caroline said. Then, in the same voice, to Betty: 'What on earth are you doing?'

'I in't doing nothin'!' the girl answered, tossing her head, her cap slipping. 'Them ladders is jumpy, that's all. Everything's jumpy, in this house!'

'Oh, don't be so stupid.'

'I in't being stupid!'

'All right,' I said quietly, helping Betty pick up the step-ladder and find a firmer grip on it. 'It's all right. Nothing's broken. Now, can you manage?'

She gazed balefully at Caroline, but carried the ladders away in silence—narrowly avoiding Mrs Ayres, who had just arrived at the doorway and had caught the end of the fuss.

'What a commotion!' she said, coming into the room. 'Good heavens!' Then she saw me. 'Dr Faraday, here you are already. How nice you look, too. What on earth must you think of us?'

She smoothed out her manner and her expression as she came forward, and offered me her hand. She was dressed like an elegant French widow, in a dark silk gown. On her head she had a black lace shawl, a sort of fine mantilla, fastened at the throat with a cameo brooch. As she passed beneath the chandelier she squinted upwards, her high cheeks lifting.

'How very fierce these lights seem, don't they! Surely they were never so bright in the old days? I suppose one's eyes were younger then . . . Caroline, darling, let me look at you.'

Caroline seemed less at ease than ever after the row over the ladder. She struck a mannequin's pose and said, in a mannequin's voice, rather brittle: 'Will I do? Not quite up to your high standard, I know.'

'Oh, what nonsense,' said her mother. Her tone reminded me of Anne's. 'You look very well indeed. Just straighten your gloves, that's right . . . No sign of Roderick yet? I do hope he isn't dragging his heels. This afternoon he was grumbling about his evening clothes, saying they were all too loose. I told him, really, he's lucky to have any at all.— Thank you, Dr Faraday. Yes, a sherry, please.'

I handed her the drink; she took the glass, smiling distractedly into my face.

'Can you imagine?' she said. 'It's been so long since the house was opened up, I feel almost nervous.'

I said, 'Well, no one would guess it.'

She wasn't listening. 'I would be calmer with my son at my side. Sometimes, you know, I think he forgets he's master of Hundreds.'

From what I had seen of Roderick in the past few weeks I thought it very unlikely indeed that he ever did that; and I looked at Caroline, and saw her plainly thinking the same thing. But Mrs Ayres continued to gaze restlessly about. She took a single sip of her drink, then set down her glass and went over to the sideboard, concerned that not enough bottles of sherry had been put out. After that she checked the boxes of cigarettes, and tried the flames of the table lighters, one by one. Then a sudden gust of smoke from the fireplace took her over to the hearth, to fret about the unswept chimney and the basket of damp wood.

But there wasn't time to fetch new logs. As she straightened up we heard the echo of voices out in the passage, and the first of the real guests appeared: Bill and Helen Desmond, a Lidcote couple I knew slightly; a Mr and Mrs Rossiter I knew only by sight; and an elderly spinster, Miss Dabney. They had come all together, squashed into the Desmonds' car to save fuel. They were complaining about the weather, and Betty was loaded with their wet coats and hats. She showed them into the saloon, her own cap straight again; the touch of temper seemed to have passed. I caught her eye, and gave her a wink. She looked startled for a second, then tucked in her chin and smiled like a child.

None of the newcomers knew me, in my evening clothes. Rossiter was a retired magistrate, Bill Desmond owned a great deal of land, and they weren't the sort of people I usually mixed with. Desmond's wife was the first to recognise me.

'Oh!' she said anxiously. 'No one's unwell, I hope?'

'Unwell?' said Mrs Ayres. Then, with a light society laugh, 'Ah, no. The doctor's our guest tonight! Mr and Mrs Rossiter, you know Dr Faraday, I expect? And you, Miss Dabney?'

Miss Dabney, as it happened, I had treated once or twice. She was something of a hypochondriac, the sort of a patient a doctor could make quite a decent living out of. But she was old-fashioned 'quality', with rather a high-handed way with GPs, and I think she was surprised to find me there at Hundreds with a glass of rum in my hand. The surprise, however, was swallowed up in the general stir of arrival, for everyone had something to say about the room; there were drinks to be poured and handed out; and there was Gyp, amiable Gyp, who went nosing his way from person to person, to be fussed over and petted.

Then Caroline offered cigarettes, and the guests got a proper look at her.

'My word!' said Mr Rossiter, with heavy gallantry. 'And who is this young beauty?'

Caroline tilted her head. 'Only plain old Caroline underneath the lipstick, I'm afraid.'

'Now don't be silly, my dear,' said Mrs Rossiter, taking a cigarette from the box. 'You look charming. You are your father's daughter, and he was a very handsome man.' She spoke to Mrs Ayres. 'The Colonel would have liked to see the room like this, wouldn't he, Angela? He so enjoyed a party. A tremendous dancer; tremendous poise. I remember seeing you dancing together once at Warwick. It was a pleasure to watch you; you were like thistledown. The young people today don't seem to know the old dances, and as for the modern dances—well, now I dare say I'm showing my age, but the modern dances always seem to me so vulgar. So much hopping about; like a scene from a mental ward! It can't be good for one. What do you say, Dr Faraday?'

I made some anodyne response, and we talked the matter over for a time; but the conversation soon returned to the great parties and balls that the county had hosted in the past, and I had less to contribute. 'That must have been nineteen twenty-eight or 'twenty-nine,' I heard Miss Dabney say, of some particularly glittering event; and I was just wryly picturing my life in those years, as a medical student in Birmingham, dead on my feet through overwork, permanently hungry, and living in a Dickensian garret with a hole in its roof, when Gyp began to bark. Caroline caught hold of his collar to keep him from racing from the room. We became aware of voices in the passage, one of them apparently a child's—'Is there a dog?'—and our own voices died away. A group of people appeared in the doorway: two men in lounge suits, a good-looking woman in a vivid cocktail gown, and a pretty little girl of eight or nine.

The girl took us all by surprise. She turned out to be the Baker-Hydes' daughter, Gillian. But the second man had clearly been expected, at least by Mrs Ayres; I'd heard nothing about him myself. He was introduced as Mrs Baker-Hyde's younger brother, Mr Morley.

'I'm generally up here with Diana and Peter for the week-ends, you see,' he said, as he shook people's hands, 'so I thought I'd tag along. Not got off to a great start, have we?' He called to his brother-in-law: 'Peter! You're going to get thrown out of the county, old man!'

He meant, because of their lounge suits; for Bill Desmond, Mr Rossiter, and I were dressed in old-style evening clothes, and Mrs Ayres and the other ladies were all in floor-length gowns. But the Baker-Hyde party seemed ready to laugh off its embarrassment over that; somehow, in fact, it was the rest of us who ended up feeling badly dressed. Not that Mr and Mrs Baker-Hyde were in any way condescending. On the contrary, I have to say I found them perfectly pleasant and polite that night—though with an extraordinary sort of finish to them, so that I could well understand why some local people might have felt them to be out of touch with rural ways. The little girl had some of their poise, clearly ready to chat with the grown-ups on equal terms, but she was still essentially a child. She seemed tickled, for example, by the sight of Betty in her apron and cap, and she made something of a show of being frightened by Gyp. When the drinks were handed round she was given lemonade, but she clamoured so much to be given wine her father finally tipped some from his glass into hers. The Warwickshire adults looked on in fascinated dismay as the sherry disappeared into her tumbler.

Mrs Baker-Hyde's brother, Mr Morley, I rather took against from the start. He was, I guessed, about twenty-seven; he had smarmed-down hair and rimless American glasses, and he managed to let us all know quite quickly that he worked for a London advertising agency, but was just beginning to make a name for himself in the film industry by 'writing treatments'. He didn't, for our benefit, elaborate on what a treatment was, and Mr Rossiter, mishearing the end of the conversation, supposed that he must, like me, be a medical man, which led to a confused few minutes. Mr Morley laughed tolerantly at the mistake. I saw him, as he sipped at his cocktail, looking me over and dismissing me; I saw him dismiss the whole bunch of us, before ten minutes had passed. Mrs Ayres, however, as hostess, seemed determined to make him welcome. 'You must meet the Desmonds, Mr Morley,' I heard her say, as she drew him from one small group to another. And then, when he had drifted back to stand at the fireplace with Mr Rossiter and me: 'You gentlemen over here must sit down . . . You too, Mr Morley.'

She took his arm, and stood for a moment as if uncertain where to place him; finally, and apparently casually, she led him to the sofa. Caroline was sitting there with Mrs Rossiter, but the sofa was a long one. Mr Morley hesitated for a second, then lowered himself with an air of surrender into the space at Caroline's side. Caroline moved forward as he did it, to make some adjustment to Gyp's collar; the movement had such a look of falseness to it, I thought to myself, 'Poor Caroline!'—thinking she was wondering how to make her escape. But then she moved back, and I saw her face, and she looked oddly self-conscious, raising a hand to her hair in an uncharacteristic, feminine gesture. I gazed from her to Mr Morley, whose own pose seemed rather forced. I remembered all the work and preparation that had gone into the night; I remembered Caroline's earlier brittleness. And with a curiously dark and cheated feeling I suddenly understood why the party had been thrown, and what Mrs Ayres, and evidently Caroline herself, hoped to achieve with it.

Even as the realisation struck me, Mrs Rossiter got to her feet.

'We must let the young people talk,' she murmured, with a roguish middle-aged look at her husband and me. And then, holding out her empty glass, 'Dr Faraday, would you be a perfect lamb and fetch me a little more sherry?'

I took the glass over to the sideboard and poured out the drink. I caught sight of myself as I did it, in one of the room's many mirrors: in the unforgiving light, with the bottle in my hand, I looked more than ever like a balding grocer. When I returned the glass to Mrs Rossiter, she spoke extravagantly: 'Thank you *so* much.' But she smiled as Mrs Ayres had, when I had done the same favour for her, her gaze sliding away from me even as she spoke. And then she resumed her conversation with her husband.

Perhaps it was my own sinking mood that did it; perhaps it was the Baker-Hyde polish, against which nothing could compete; but the party, which had barely got going, seemed somehow to lose its lustre. Even the saloon was strangely diminished, I thought, now that the Standish crowd were in it. As the evening went on I saw them do their best to admire it, praising the Regency decorations, the chandelier, the paper, the ceiling, and Mrs Baker-Hyde in particular went slowly and appreciatively about, looking from one thing to another. But the room was a large one, and had long gone unheated: a decent fire was kept going in the grate, but there was a creeping chill and dampness in the air, which once or twice made her shiver and rub her bare arms. Finally she drew nearer to the fireplace, saying she wanted to look more closely at a pair of delicate gilded chairs that stood to either side of it; and on being told that the chairs' tapestry seats were the original 1820s ones, commissioned with the building of the octagonal room, she said, 'I thought they must be. How lucky that they've survived! There were wonderful tapestries at Standish when we moved in, but they were practically eaten up by moth; we had to get rid of them. I did think it a shame.'

'Oh, that *is* a shame,' said Mrs Ayres. 'Those tapestries were marvellous things.'

Mrs Baker-Hyde turned casually to her. 'You saw them?'

'Yes, of course,' Mrs Ayres answered; for she and the Colonel must have been regular visitors to Standish in the old days. I had been to the house once myself, to treat one of the servants, and I knew she was thinking now, as the rest of us were, of the fine dark rooms and passageways there, with their ancient carpets and hangings, and of the lovely linenfold panelling that covered virtually every wall, almost half of which—as Peter Baker-Hyde now proceeded to tell us—had proved on close inspection to be infested with beetle, and would have to be removed.

'It's awful to have to let things go,' said his wife, perhaps in response to our grave faces, 'but one can't hang on to things for ever, and we saved what we could.'

'Well,' he said, 'a few more years and the whole place would have been completely beyond repair. The Randalls seemed to think they were doing their bit for the nation by sitting tight and letting the modernising slide; but in my opinion, if they hadn't the money to maintain the house they should have packed up ages ago, let it go to an hotel or a golf club.' He nodded, pleasantly enough, to Mrs Ayres. 'You're managing here all right, though? I'm told you sold off most of your farmland. I don't blame you; we're thinking of doing the same with ours. We like our park, though.' He called to his daughter. 'Don't we, kitten?'

She was sitting beside her mother. 'I'm going to have a white pony!' she told us brightly. 'I'm going to learn to jump it.'

Her mother laughed. 'And so am I.' She reached to stroke the little girl's hair. There were silver slave bracelets on her wrist, which rang like bells. 'We're to learn together, aren't we?'

'You don't ride already?' asked Helen Desmond.

'Not at all, I'm afraid.'

'Unless you count motor bikes,' piped up Mr Morley, from his place on the sofa. He had just given Caroline a cigarette, but now twisted away from her with the lighter in his hand. 'We've a friend with one of those. You should see Diana tear about on it! She's like one of the Valkyries.'

'Don't, Tony!'

They laughed together at what was clearly a private joke. Caroline put her hand to her hair, slightly dislodging her diamanté comb. Peter Baker-Hyde said, to Mrs Ayres, 'You keep horses, I suppose? Everyone seems to, up here.'

Mrs Ayres shook her head. 'I'm far too old to ride. Caroline hires a horse from old Patmore, in Lidcote, from time to time; though his stable isn't what it was. When my husband was alive we ran a stable of our own.'

'A very fine one,' put in Mr Rossiter.

'But then, with the war, that sort of thing grew harder. And once my son was injured, we let the whole thing go . . . Roderick was with the RAF, you know.'

'Ah,' said Mr Baker-Hyde. 'Well, we won't hold that against him, will we, Tony? What did he fly? Mosquitoes? Good for him! A pal took me up in one of those once and I couldn't get out of it quick enough. It was like being hurled around in a sardine tin. Bit of paddling at Anzio, that was more my line. Hurt his leg, I gather. I'm sorry to hear it. How does he manage?'

'Oh, well enough.'

'It's keeping a sense of humour that's the great thing, of course . . . I'd like to meet him.'

'Yes, well,' said Mrs Ayres uneasily, 'I know he'd like to meet you.' She peered at the face of her bracelet wrist-watch. 'Really, I can't apologise enough for his not being here to greet you. That's the worst of running one's own farm, I'm afraid: the unpredictability of it . . .' She lifted her head, and looked around; I thought for a second she might be about to gesture to me. But she called, instead, to Betty.

'Betty, just run to Mr Roderick's room, will you, and see what's keeping him? Be sure to tell him we're all waiting for him.'

Betty pinked with the importance of the task, and slipped away. She returned a few minutes later to say that Roderick was dressing, and would join us as soon as he could.

The evening lengthened, however, and still Rod did not appear. Our glasses were refilled, and the little girl grew livelier, clamouring for another taste of wine. Someone suggested she might be tired, and what a great treat it must be to be allowed up past her bedtime; at which her mother stroked her hair again and said indulgently, 'Oh, we more or less let her run about till she drops. I don't see the point of sending them to bed just for the sake of it. It breeds all sorts of neuroses.'

The girl herself confirmed, in a high, hectic voice, that she never went to bed before midnight—and, what's more, that she was regularly allowed to drink brandy after her supper, and had once smoked half a cigarette.

'Well, you had better not have brandy or cigarettes here,' said Mrs Rossiter, 'for I hardly think Dr Faraday would approve of children doing that.'

I said with mock sternness that I wouldn't, most certainly not. Caroline put in, quietly but distinctly, 'And neither would I. It's bad enough the little wretches getting their hands on all the oranges'—at which Mr Morley turned his head to her with an astonished expression, and there was a second's disconcerted silence, broken by Gillian's declaring that if she wanted to smoke a cigarette, we would not be able to stop her; and if she really cared to, she would jolly well smoke cigars!

Poor little girl. She was not what my mother would have called a 'taking' child. But I think we were all glad to have her there, for, like a kitten with a ball of wool, she gave us something at which to gaze and smile when the conversation lagged. Only Mrs Ayres, I noticed, remained distracted—thinking of Roderick, clearly. When, after another fifteen minutes, there was still no sign of him, she again sent Betty to his room; and this time the girl returned almost at once. She came back looking flustered, I thought, walking swiftly to Mrs Ayres to whisper something in her ear. I had been buttonholed by Miss Dabney by now— she wanted advice on one of her ailments—and couldn't politely have made an escape, otherwise I might have gone over. As it was, I had to watch as Mrs Ayres apologised to the company and went off to see to Roderick herself.

After that, even with the little girl to entertain us, the party floundered. Someone noticed that it was still raining, and we all turned our heads gratefully to the patter of rain on the windows, to discuss the weather, and the farming, and the state of the land. Diana Baker-Hyde saw a gramophone and a cabinet of records and asked if we mightn't have some music. But the records evidently didn't appeal to her, for she gave the idea up, disappointed, after briefly leafing through them.

How about the piano? she asked then.

'That isn't a piano, you philistine,' said her brother, looking round. 'It's a spinet. Isn't it?'

Discovering that it was in fact a Flemish harpsichord, Mrs Baker-Hyde said, 'Not really? How marvellous! And, may one play it, Miss Ayres? It isn't too awfully old and fragile? Tony can play any sort of piano. Don't look like that, Tony, you know you can!'

Without a look or a word for Caroline, her brother left the sofa, went over to the harpsichord, and pressed a key. The sound was quaint, but wildly out of tune; delighted by it, he settled himself on the stool and started up a burst of crazy jazz. Caroline sat alone for a moment, pulling at a thread that had worked its way loose from one of the fingers of her silver gloves. Then, abruptly, she rose, and went to the fireplace, to add more wood to the smoking hearth.

Presently Mrs Ayres returned. She glanced in surprise and dismay at Mr Morley at the keyboard, then shook her head as Mrs Rossiter and Helen Desmond asked hopefully, 'No sign of Roderick?'

'I'm afraid Roderick isn't quite well,' she said, turning the rings on her fingers, 'and won't be joining us tonight after all. He's so very sorry.'

'Oh, what a pity!'

Caroline looked up. 'Anything I can do for him, Mother?' she asked. And I stepped forward, to ask the same thing. But Mrs Ayres said only, 'No, no, he's quite all right. I've given him some aspirin. He's slightly overdone it at the farm, that's all.'

She picked up her glass and rejoined Mrs Baker-Hyde, who looked feelingly up at her and said, 'His injury, I suppose?'

Mrs Ayres hesitated, then nodded—at which point I knew that there was something definitely wrong, for Roderick's leg could be a nuisance, but, largely thanks to my treatments, it was many weeks now since it had given him serious trouble. But at that moment Mr Rossiter looked around the company and said: 'Poor Roderick. And in his youth he was such an active boy. Do you remember the time he and Michael Martin made off with the schoolmaster's motor?'

This proved to be something of an inspiration, and in a sense saved the party: the story took a minute or two to tell, and was immediately followed by another. Everyone, it seemed, had fond memories of Roderick, and I suppose the poignancy, first of his accident, then of his having come so early into the responsibilities of modern landed life, made them fonder. But again, there was little that I could contribute to the conversation; nor was there much to interest the Standish group. Mr Morley kept up his discordant plinkety-plunking at the harpsichord. The Baker-Hydes listened to the anecdotes politely enough, but with rather fixed expressions; soon Gillian whispered noisily to her mother about a lavatory, and Mrs Baker-Hyde, after speaking to Caroline, led her away. Her husband took the opportunity to detach himself from the group and drift a little around the room. Betty was going about at the same time with a tray of anchovy toast, and eventually they met.

'Hello,' I heard him say to her. I was making my way over to the sideboard, to fetch some lemonade for Miss Dabney. 'You're working hard, aren't you? First you take our coats; now you bring the sandwiches. Don't you have a butler to help you, or somebody like that?'

I suppose it was the casual modern way, to chat with servants. But it wasn't the way Mrs Ayres was training Betty, and I saw her look at him blankly for a moment, as if uncertain whether he really wanted an answer. Finally she said, 'No, sir.'

He laughed. 'Well, that's too bad. If I were you I'd join a trade union. I tell you what, though: I like the fancy headgear.' He reached to flick the frill on her cap. 'I'd like to see the look on our maid's face, if we tried one of those on her!'

He said this last more to me than to Betty, having looked up and caught my eye. Betty put down her head and moved on, and as I poured out the lemonade he wandered over to my side.

'Extraordinary place this, isn't it?' he murmured, with a glance at the others. 'I don't mind admitting, I was glad to be invited, simply for the chance to have a bit of a look around. You're the family doctor, I gather. They like to keep you on hand, do they, for the sake of the son? I hadn't realised he was in such poor shape.'

I said, 'He isn't, as it happens. I'm here on a social call tonight, just like you.'

'You are? Oh, I had the impression you were here for the son, I don't know why . . . Rotten do, that, by the sound of it. Scars and so on. Doesn't care for company, I suppose?'

I told him that, as far as I knew, Roderick had been looking forward to the party, but that he tended to take on too much farm work, and must have overtaxed himself. Mr Baker-Hyde nodded, not really interested. He drew back his cuff to look at his wrist-watch, and spoke through the end of a stifled yawn.

'Well, I think it's time I was getting my gang back to Standish— always assuming, of course, that I can prise my brother-in-law away from that lunatic piano.' He gazed over at Mr Morley, narrowing his eyes. 'Did you ever see such a grade-one ass? And he's the reason we're here! My wife, God bless her, is determined to see him married. She and our hostess cooked up this whole do, as a way of introducing him to the daughter of the house. Well, I saw in two minutes how that would turn out. Tony's an ugly little brute, but he does like a pretty face . . .'

He spoke entirely without malice, simply as one chap to another. He didn't see Caroline, looking our way from her place beside the hearth; he gave no thought to the acoustics of that queerly shaped room, which meant that murmurs could sometimes carry across it while louder comments were lost. He swallowed the rest of his drink and put down his glass, and then he nodded to his wife, who had just returned with Gillian. I could see that he was only waiting for the right kind of break in the conversation, now, to make his excuses and take his family home.

And so there came one of those moments—there were to be several, in the months that followed—that I would forever look back on with a sense of desperate regret—almost with guilt. For I could so easily have done something to ease his departure and speed him on his way; but if anything, I did just the opposite. Mr and Mrs Rossiter finished their latest account of one of Roderick's youthful adventures, and though I'd barely exchanged a word with them all evening, as I made my way back to Miss Dabney I called over to them something—something perfectly inconsequential like, 'And what did the Colonel make of that?'—which started them straight off on another long reminiscence. Mr Baker-Hyde's face fell, and I was childishly glad to see it. I'd had a pointless, almost spiteful urge to make life difficult for him.

But I wish to God I had acted differently; for now something terrible happened to his little girl, Gillian.

Ever since her arrival she'd been keeping up a rather monotonous show of being frightened of Gyp, ducking ostentatiously behind her mother's skirts whenever his friendly wanderings around the room took him near her. Just recently, though, she had changed her tack and begun to make small advances towards him. Mr Morley's plucking at the harpsichord had, I think, begun to bother the dog; he had taken himself to one of the windows and had settled down behind a curtain. Pursuing him there now, Gillian drew up a footstool and began gingerly petting and stroking his head, chattering nonsense to him: '*Good* dog. You're a *very* good dog. You're a *brave* dog'—and so on, like that. She was partly out of our view, being over by the window. Her mother, I noticed, kept turning round to her, as if nervous that Gyp might snap at her, and once she called, 'Gillie, be careful, darling!'—making Caroline snort slightly, for Gyp had the gentlest temperament imaginable, the only risk was that the child would tire him with her chatter and her constant dabbings at his head. So Caroline kept turning to Gillian, just as Mrs Baker-Hyde did; and now and then Helen Desmond or Miss Dabney, or one of the Rossiters, would glance over, attracted by the little girl's voice; and I also found myself looking. In fact, I'd say that probably the only person who wasn't watching Gillian was Betty. After going around with the toast, she had put herself over by the door, and had been standing there with her gaze lowered, just as she had been trained. And yet—it was an extraordinary thing, but none of us could afterwards say that we had been looking at Gillian exactly when the incident occurred.

We all heard the sounds of it, however—horrible sounds, I can hear them even now—a sort of tearing yelp from Gyp, with, laid across it, Gillian's shriek, a single piercing note that sank at once to a thin, low, liquid wail. I think the dog, poor thing, was as startled as any of us: he came rushing away from the window, sending the curtain billowing, and distracting us, for a moment, from the child herself. Then one of the women, I don't know which, saw what had happened and let up a cry. Mr Baker-Hyde, or perhaps his brother-in-law, gave a shout: '*Christ! Gillian!*' The two men sprang forward, one of them catching his foot on a loose seam of carpet and almost falling. A glass was set hurriedly down on the mantelpiece and went crashing into the hearth. The little girl was hidden from me for a moment by a confusion of bodies: I looked and saw only her bare arm and hand, with blood running down it. Even then—I suppose the sound of the shattering glass must have put the idea in my head—even then I thought only that a window had broken, and cut her arm, and perhaps cut Gyp. But Diana Baker-Hyde had darted up out of her place and, pushing her way to her daughter, began to scream; and when I moved forward, I saw what she had seen. The blood was coming not from Gillian's arm, but from her face. Her cheek and lip had turned into drooping lobes of flesh—had been practically severed. Gyp had bitten her.

The poor child herself was white and rigid with shock. Her father was beside her and had his trembling hand at her face, was advancing his fingers and drawing them back, not knowing whether to touch the wound or not; not knowing what to do. I found myself at his side without being aware of how I had got there. I suppose my professional instincts had taken over. I helped him lift her; we got her to the sofa and laid her flat; a variety of handkerchiefs were produced, and pressed to her cheek—one, from Helen Desmond, with dainty lace and embroidery, soon sopping scarlet. I did what I could to staunch the bleeding and to clean the injury up, but it was a difficult job. That sort of wound always looks worse than it really is, especially on a child, but I had seen at once that the bite was a bad one.

'Christ!' said Peter Baker-Hyde again. He and his wife were clutching at their daughter's hands; the wife was sobbing. They both had blood on their evening clothes—I think we all did—and the blood was made vivid and ghastly by the brilliant chandelier. 'Christ! Look at the state of her!' He ran his hand across his hair. 'What the hell happened? Why didn't somebody—? What in God's name happened?'

'Never mind that now,' I said quietly. I had the handkerchiefs still pressed hard to the wound, and was rapidly thinking the case over.

'Look at her!'

'She's in shock, but she isn't in danger. But she'll have to be stitched. Stitched quite extensively, I'm afraid; and the sooner the better.'

'Stitched?' His expression was wild. I think he'd forgotten I was a doctor.

I said, 'I've my bag with me, out in the car. Mr Desmond, will you—?'

'Yes, of course,' said Bill Desmond breathlessly, running from the room.

I called to Betty next. She had hung back when everyone else had surged forward, and was looking on as if terrified—almost as pale as Gillian herself. I told her to go down and boil a kettle of water, and fetch blankets and a cushion. And then—gently, and with Mrs Baker-Hyde at my side, holding the bunched handkerchiefs awkwardly to her daughter's face, her hand shaking, so that the silver slave bracelets slithered and rang—I took the little girl in my arms. I could feel the chill of her, even through my shirt and jacket. Her eyes were dark and lifeless, and she was sweating with shock. I said, 'We'll have to get her down to the kitchen.'

'The kitchen?' her father said.

'I'll need water.'

Then he understood. 'You mean to do it here? You're not serious! Surely a hospital—a surgery— Can't we telephone?'

'It's nine miles to the nearest hospital,' I said, 'and a good five to my surgery. Trust me, I shouldn't like to take to the roads with this kind of wound, on a night like tonight. The sooner we tidy her up, the better. There's the loss of blood to think of, too.'

'Let the doctor do it, Peter,' said Mrs Baker-Hyde, beginning to cry again, 'for God's sake!'

'Yes,' said Mrs Ayres, moving forward and touching his arm. 'We must let Dr Faraday see to it now.'

I think I noticed at the time that the man turned his face from Mrs Ayres and roughly shook off her touch, but I was too busy with the little girl to give his gesture much thought. Something else happened, too, which hardly struck me then, but which, when I remembered it later, I realised had set the tone for many of the events in the days that followed. Mrs Baker-Hyde and I had carefully taken Gillian to the threshold of the room, where we were met by Bill Desmond, my bag in his hand. Helen Desmond and Mrs Ayres stood anxiously watching us go, while Mrs Rossiter and Miss Dabney, in their distraction, stooped to pick up the shards of tumbler from the hearth—Miss Dabney incidentally cutting her own finger rather badly, and adding fresh blood-stains to the general gore on the carpet. Peter Baker-Hyde was following me closely, and was in turn being followed by his brother-in-law; but the latter, as he came, must have caught sight of Gyp, who had been cowering all this time beneath a table. Mr Morley stepped rapidly over to the dog and, with a curse, gave him a kick; the kick was a hard one, and made Gyp yelp. To the man's amazement, I suppose, Caroline darted forward and pushed him away.

'What are you doing?' she cried. I remember her voice: shrill and strained and not at all like itself.

He straightened his jacket. 'Didn't you notice? Your damn dog just tore half my niece's face off!'

'But you're making it worse,' she said, getting down on her knees and drawing Gyp to her. 'You've terrified him!'

'I'd like to do more than terrify him! What the hell do you mean by letting him roam about the place when kids are here? He ought to be chained up!'

She said, 'He's perfectly harmless, when he isn't provoked.'

Mr Morley had moved away; but now turned back. 'What the hell is that supposed to mean?'

She shook her head. 'Stop shouting, can't you?'

'Stop shouting? You saw what he's done to her?'

'Well, he's never snapped before. He's a house-dog.'

'He's a wild beast. He ought to be damn well shot!'

The argument went on, but I was only dimly aware of it, preoccupied as I was in safely manoeuvring the rigid child in my arms through the doorway and then around several corners to the basement stairs. And once I'd begun making my way down them, the raised voices grew faint. I found Betty in the kitchen, heating the water I'd requested. She'd brought the blankets and cushions too, and now, at my direction, and with shaking hands, she cleared the kitchen table and lay sheets of brown paper on it. I set Gillian down with the blankets around her, then opened my bag to sort through my instruments. So absorbed was I in these tasks that, when I took off my jacket to roll up my sleeves and wash my hands, I was astonished to find it a dress-jacket. I'd forgotten where I was, and thought I was in my regular tweeds.

The fact is, I was often obliged to perform this kind of small operation, either in my surgery or in my patients' own homes. Once, while still in my twenties, I had been called to a farmhouse to find a young man with a dreadfully mangled leg, the result of a threshing injury. I had had to cut the leg off at the knee, at the kitchen table, just like this. The family had invited me to take supper with them a few days later, and we had sat at the same table, now cleaned of its stains—the young man sitting there along with us, pale, but cheerfully eating his pie, joking about the money he'd save on boot-leather. But those were country people, used to hardship; to the Baker-Hydes it must have looked dreadful, as I soaked the needle and thread in carbolic and scrubbed my knuckles and nails with a vegetable brush. The kitchen itself, I think, alarmed them, with its blunt Victorian fittings, its flagstones, its monster of a range. And after the over-bright saloon the room seemed horribly dim. I had to have Mr Baker-Hyde bring an oil lamp from the pantry and put it close to his daughter's face, so that I had light enough to stitch by.

Had the girl been older I might have made do with a spray of ethyl chloride to freeze the wound. But I was afraid of her wriggling about, and, after I'd washed her with water and iodine, I put her into a light sort of sleep with a general anaesthetic. Still, I knew the operation would hurt her. I told her mother to rejoin the other guests upstairs in the saloon, and, as I expected, the poor little girl gave off a weak whimpering all the time I worked, the tears flowing ceaselessly from her eyes. There were no severed arteries to deal with, that was a blessing, but the tearing of the flesh made the job a trickier one than I should have liked—my main concern being how to minimise the scarring that would follow, for I knew it would be extensive even with the tidiest of repairs. The child's father sat at the table, holding tightly on to her hand and wincing with every insertion of the needle, but watching me work as though afraid to take his eyes away—as though watching for a slip, so that he might check it. A few minutes after I'd started, his brother-in-law appeared, his face crimson from his argument with Caroline. 'These *bloody* people,' he said. 'That daughter's a lunatic!' Then he saw what I was doing and the crimson sank from his cheeks. He lit himself a cigarette and sat smoking it some distance from the table. Presently—it was the only sensible thing he did all night—he got Betty to brew up a pot of tea and hand round cups.

The others kept upstairs, trying to comfort the girl's mother. Mrs Ayres came down once, to ask how matters were progressing: she stood for a minute and watched me working, anxious for the girl and clearly upset by the sight of the stitching. Peter Baker-Hyde, I noticed, wouldn't turn his head to her.

The job took the best part of an hour, and when I had finished, and while the girl was still woozy, I told her father to take her home. I meant to follow in my car, call in at the surgery for one or two things, and join them at Standish, where I could see her into her bed. I hadn't mentioned the possibility to her parents, because I thought it a very slight one, but there was the risk of blood poisoning or infection to be guarded against.

Betty was sent to alert the girl's mother, and Mr Baker-Hyde and Mr Morley carried Gillian up the stairs and out to their car. She was more sensible now, and as they laid her down on the back seat she began, very pitifully, to cry. I had put strips of gauze across her face—but more for her parents' protection than for hers, for the stitches and the iodine made the wound look monstrous.

When I went back to the bright saloon to say goodbye I found everyone still there, sitting or standing in silence, as if stunned—as if in the aftermath of an air raid. There was still blood on the carpet and the sofa, but someone had taken a cloth and water to it and turned it into creeping pink stains.

'A wretched business,' said Mr Rossiter.

Helen Desmond had been crying. She said, 'That poor, poor child.' She lowered her voice. 'She'll be terribly marked, won't she? What can have prompted it? Gyp isn't a snappy dog, is he?'

'Of course he isn't!' said Caroline, in her new, taut, artificial voice. She was sitting apart from the others, with Gyp beside her; he was visibly trembling, and she was stroking his head. But her own hands were shaking. The rouge was livid on her cheeks and mouth, and the diamanté comb hung crookedly in her hair.

Bill Desmond said, 'Something must have startled him, I suppose. He must have fancied he saw something, or heard something. Did any of us shout, or make some movement? I've been racking my brains.'

'It wasn't *us*,' said Caroline. 'The girl must have been teasing him. I shouldn't be surprised—'

She fell silent, as Peter Baker-Hyde appeared behind me in the passage. He had his coat and hat on, a streak of scarlet just showing on his forehead. He said quietly, 'We're ready, Doctor.' He didn't look at the others. I don't know if he noticed Gyp.

Mrs Ayres moved forward. 'You'll let us know tomorrow, I hope, how the little girl is?'

He was briskly pulling on his driving gloves, still not looking at her. 'Yes, if you wish.'

She took another step, and said gently and earnestly, 'I'm so dreadfully sorry that this has happened, Mr Baker-Hyde—and in my house.'

But he only gave her one quick glance. And what he said was: 'Yes, Mrs Ayres. So am I.'

I followed him out into the darkness and started my car. The ignition turned several times before it caught, for the rain had been falling steadily for hours and the engine was damp: we didn't know it then, but that night was the hinge of the seasons, the start of the gloomy winter to come. I turned the car, then hung back while Peter Baker-Hyde went on ahead of me. He drove with what felt like agonising slowness along the bumpy overgrown route to the wall of the park, but once his brother-in-law had jumped out to open the gate and close it behind us, he put his foot down, and I found myself speeding up in turn—peering through the sweep of the windscreen wipers, fixing my gaze on the piercing red tail-lights of his expensive car until they seemed to float on the darkness of the winding Warwickshire lanes.

FOUR

I left the Baker-Hydes around one, with a promise to return the next day. My morning surgery runs from nine until after ten, so it was almost eleven o'clock when I drew into the courtyard of Standish again; and the first thing I saw there was a muddy maroon Packard I recognised as belonging to Dr Seeley, my local rival. I thought it fair enough that the Baker-Hydes should have brought him in: he was their doctor, after all. But it is always awkward for the practitioners concerned when a patient makes a decision like that without informing them. Some sort of butler or secretary showed me into the house, and I found Seeley just coming down from the girl's bedroom. He was a tall, well-built man, looking larger than ever on the narrow sixteenth-century staircase. He was clearly just as embarrassed to see me there, with my doctor's bag in my hand, as I was to see him with his.

'They called me in first thing this morning,' he said, as he took me aside to discuss the case with me. 'This is my second visit of the day.' He lit a cigarette. 'I gather you were out at Hundreds when it happened? That was a stroke of luck, anyway. Bloody awful for the little girl, isn't it?'

'It is,' I said. 'How does she seem to you? How's the wound?'

'The wound's fine. You made a neater job of it than I could have done. And on the kitchen table! The scarring will be frightful, of course. Such a shame; especially for a girl of her class. The parents are keen to get her up to a London specialist, but I'll be surprised if even in London they'll be able to do much for her. Then again, who knows? The plastics boys have certainly got in enough practice in the past few years. What she needs now is rest. A nurse is coming in, and I've prescribed Luminal, to keep her groggy for a day or two. After that, well, we'll see.'

He spoke a few words to Peter Baker-Hyde, then gave me a nod and went off on his round. I remained in the hallway at the foot of the stairs, still feeling the awkwardness of the situation but, naturally, hoping to see the little girl for myself. Her father made it clear to me, however, that he would rather leave her undisturbed. He seemed genuinely grateful for my assistance—'Thank God you were there last night!' he said, shaking my hand with both of his—but then his arm moved to my shoulder and, lightly but firmly, he guided me to the door. I realised that I had been completely dismissed from the case.

'You'll send me your bill?' he said, as he walked with me out to my car. And when I answered that I wouldn't trouble him with that, he insisted on pressing a couple of guineas on me. Then he thought of the petrol I'd used in coming twice out to Standish, and called for one of his gardeners to fetch a can of fuel. The gesture was extravagant, but at the same time there seemed something hard about it. I had the uneasy feeling he was buying me off. We stood in silence in the spitting rain as the gardener filled up my tank, and I thought what a pity it was that I couldn't just slip upstairs for a final look at the girl. I should have much preferred that to guineas or petrol.

It was only as I was climbing into the car that I thought to ask him whether he'd yet sent word to Hundreds that Gillian was doing well; and at that, his manner grew harder than ever.

'Them,' he said, with a jerk of his chin. 'They'll get word from us, all right. We're taking this matter further, you can be sure.'

I'd been half expecting this, but was dismayed by the bitterness in his voice. Straightening up again, I said, 'What do you mean? You've informed the police?'

'Not yet, but we intend to. At the very least we want to see that dog destroyed.'

'But, well, Gyp's such a foolish old thing.'

'And turning senile, clearly!'

'As far as I know, this incident was quite out of character.'

'That's small comfort to my wife and me. You don't expect us to rest until that dog is got rid of?' He glanced up at the narrow mullioned windows above the porch, one of which was open, and lowered his voice. 'Gillian's life will be fairly ruined by this; you can see that, surely. Dr Seeley tells me it was probably only the merest chance that her blood wasn't poisoned! And all because those people, the Ayreses, think themselves too grand to tie up a dangerous dog! Suppose it attacks another child?'

I didn't believe Gyp would, and though I said nothing, he must have seen the doubt in my expression. He went on, 'Look, I know you're something of a friend to the family. I don't expect you to take my side against them. But I can also see what perhaps you can't: that they believe they can swan it over everyone around here like so many lords of the manor. Probably they've trained the dog up, to see off trespassers! They ought to take a good look at that scrap-heap they're living in. They're out of date, Doctor. To tell you the truth, I've begun to think this whole bloody county's out of date.'

I almost replied that, as I'd understood it, the out-of-datedness of the county was what had attracted him to it in the first place. Instead, I asked him at the very least not to take the matter to the police until he had seen Mrs Ayres again; and he said at last, 'All right. I'll go over there as soon as I know Gillie's out of danger. But if they have any consideration at all, they'll have destroyed the dog before I get there.'

None of the six or seven patients I saw on the rest of my morning round mentioned the affair at Hundreds to me; so swift is local gossip, however, that by the time my evening surgery started I discovered that lurid accounts of Gillian's injury were already doing the rounds of the local shops and pubs. A man I visited after dinner that night described the whole incident to me, correct in every detail except that he had Seeley at the scene, stitching the little girl up, instead of me. He was a labouring man with a long history of pleurisy, and I was doing all I could to prevent the illness turning into something more sinister. But his living conditions were against him—his home was a cramped terraced cottage with a damp brick floor—and, like many labourers, he worked too hard and drank too freely. He spoke to me between bouts of coughing.

'Bit her cheek nearly clean off, they say. Damn near took the nose off, too. There's dogs for you. I've said many times, any dog'll kill you. The breed's not in it. Any dog'll turn.'

Recalling my conversation with Peter Baker-Hyde, I asked him if he thought the dog in this case ought to be destroyed. He answered, without hesitation, that he did not—because, as he'd just said, every dog was a biter, and where was the sense in punishing a creature for what was natural to it?

Was that, I asked, what other people were saying? Well, he'd heard one thing and another. 'Some say it should be whipped, and some say shoot it. Of course, there's the family to think on.'

'You mean, at Hundreds?'

'No, not them. The girl's family, the Baker-Pies.' He laughed, liquidly.

'But won't it be hard on the Ayreses, having to give up their dog?'

'Ah,' he said, coughing again, then leaning to spit into the fireless hearth, 'they've had to give up worse, ha'n't they?'

His words rather unsettled me. I had been wondering all day what the mood was like out at the Hall. And since, when I left his cottage, I found myself close to the gates of the park, I decided to call in there.

It was the first time I had gone to the house without an invitation, and, as on the previous night, the rain was heavy and no one heard my car. I rang, then hurriedly let myself in, and was greeted by poor Gyp himself: he came out into the hall, barking half-heartedly, his claws tapping on the marble. He must have been aware somehow of the shadow of disaster he was under, for he seemed subdued and disconcerted, not at all like himself. He reminded me of a woman I'd once had the care of, an elderly schoolmistress whose mind began to fail her, so that she went wandering out of her house in her slippers and nightdress. For a second I thought to myself, Perhaps he *is* losing his wits. What did I really know about his temperament, after all? But when I squatted at his side and tugged at his ears he seemed very much his ordinary amiable self. He opened his mouth and his tongue showed, pink and healthy against his yellow-white teeth.

'Here's a to-do, Gyp,' I said softly. 'What were you thinking of, boy? Hey?'

'Who's there?' I heard Mrs Ayres call, from further back in the house. Then she appeared, dim in the shadows, in one of her customary dark gowns and with a darker paisley shawl around her shoulders. 'Dr Faraday,' she said in surprise, drawing the shawl closer. Her heart-shaped face was pinched. 'Is everything all right?'

I straightened up. 'I was worried about you,' I said, simply.

'You were?' Her expression softened. 'How very kind of you. But come and get warm. It's chill tonight, isn't it?'

It wasn't really so very cold, but it seemed to me, as I followed her back to the little parlour, that the house, like the season, had undergone some slight but definite shift. The high-ceilinged passage, which had been wonderfully cool and airy throughout the long summer, now had a feel of damp about it, after just two days of rain. In the little parlour itself the curtains were drawn across the windows, a crackling fire of sticks and fir cones was burning in the grate, and the fireside chairs and the sofa had been pulled up to the hearth; but the effect, somehow, was not quite cosy, more as if the seats formed an island of light and warmth with an expanse of worn carpet and pools of shadow just beyond. Mrs Ayres had obviously been sitting in one of the chairs, and in the other, facing me as I went in, sat Roderick. I had seen him only the week before, but his appearance now startled me. He was dressed in one of his bulky old Air Force sweaters, and his hair, like mine, was newly cut; with the wide wing chair behind his head he looked slender as a ghost.

He saw me come in, and seemed to frown; after a fractional delay he gripped the arms of the chair as if to rise and give it up to me. I waved him down, and went over to join Caroline on the sofa. Gyp came and lowered himself onto the rug at my feet, giving, as he did it, one of those expressive doggy groans that sound so startlingly human.

No one had spoken, not even to greet me. Caroline was sitting with her legs drawn up, looking tense and unhappy, picking at the seam of woollen stocking across her toes. Roderick, with jerky, nervous movements, began to roll himself a cigarette. Mrs Ayres rearranged the shawl across her shoulders and said, as she sat, 'We've all been rather at sixes and sevens today, Dr Faraday, as I expect you can imagine. You've been to Standish? Do tell me, how's the child?'

'Doing well enough, as far as I know,' I answered. And then, when she looked at me, not understanding: 'I didn't see her. They've given her over to Jim Seeley. I found him there this morning.'

'Seeley!' she answered, and the scorn in her voice took me by surprise, until I remembered that it was Seeley's father who had had the care of her own little girl—the first little girl, who had died. 'They might as well bring in Crouch the barber! What did he tell you?'

'Not a great deal. Gillian sounds as well as can be expected. The parents mean to take her up to London, apparently, as soon as she can travel.'

'The poor, poor child. She's been on my mind all day. You know I telephoned the house? Three times, and no one would speak to me—only a maid. I thought of sending something over there. Flowers, perhaps? Some sort of gift? The fact is, with people like the Baker-Hydes—well, one could hardly send money. I remember, years ago, a boy being injured—Daniel Hibbit, do you remember, Caroline? He was struck by a horse, on our land, and was left with some sort of a paralysis. We saw to everything, I believe. But with something like this, one hardly knows . . .' Her voice faded.

Beside me, Caroline shifted. 'I feel as badly for that child as anyone,' she said, still plucking at the seam across her toes. 'But I'd feel the same if she'd gone and put her arm through a mangle, or got herself burnt on a hot stove. It was rotten bad luck, wasn't it? Money or flowers won't fix it. What *can* one do?'

Her head was lowered and her chin drawn in, making her tone remote. I said after a second, 'I'm afraid the Baker-Hydes are certainly expecting something.'

But she spoke again, across my words. 'Anyway, there's no reasoning with people like that. Do you know what that brother-in-law told me last night? Not only are they getting rid of practically all the panelling at Standish, they mean to rip open the entire south wing of the house! They're going to make a sort of cinema of it for their friends. They're keeping the gallery, that's all. "The one-and-nines", he called that.'

'Well,' her mother answered vaguely, 'but houses do change. Your father and I made many alterations to this house when we first married. I do think it a pity that the Standish tapestries couldn't have been saved. Did you ever see those tapestries, Dr Faraday? It would break Agnes Randall's heart.'

I didn't reply; and as she and Caroline pursued this subject for another few minutes I couldn't help feeling that, consciously or unconsciously, they were avoiding the more urgent issue.

At last I said, 'You know, with Gillian to worry about, dismantling Standish must be about the last thing on the Baker-Hydes' minds just now.'

Mrs Ayres looked pained. 'Oh, if only, if only,' she said, 'they hadn't brought that child here with them! Why on earth did they? Presumably they have a nurse or a governess for her. They're clearly able to afford one.'

'Probably they think a governess would give her a complex,' said Caroline, moving about. And a second later she added, in a sort of nervous mutter: 'She'll certainly have a complex now.'

I looked at her, shocked. And, 'Caroline!' said her mother, as if aghast.

Caroline herself, to do her credit, seemed as startled by the words as we were. She met my gaze with a horrible expression, her mouth fixed in a nervous smile but her eyes almost anguished; then she turned away. There was no trace of make-up on her now, I noticed: on the contrary, her cheeks looked dry, and her mouth seemed faintly swollen—as if she had taken a flannel to her face and brutally scrubbed it.

I saw Roderick looking over at her as he drew on his cigarette. His own face was flushed unevenly from the heat of the fire, the patches of tight pink skin on his cheeks and jaw standing out like diabolical fingerprints. But, bafflingly, he still said nothing. None of them, I thought, had any idea of just how gravely the Baker-Hydes were treating the affair. Instead they seemed to have turned their backs on it, drawn themselves together, closed ranks . . . I felt the stirrings of a dislike for them, just as I had on my first visit. When the small commotion raised by Caroline's remark had settled I spoke again, telling them, plainly, everything that had passed between Peter Baker-Hyde and me in the courtyard of Standish earlier that day.

Mrs Ayres listened in silence, raising her joined hands together to her face and bowing her head. Caroline looked at me in absolute horror.

'Destroy Gyp?'

'I'm sorry, Caroline. But can you blame them? You must have expected this.'

I think she had. I saw it in her eyes. But, 'Of course I didn't!' she said.

Catching the note of upset in her voice, Gyp himself had risen. He stood with his anxious, bewildered gaze fixed on her face, as if waiting for the word or gesture that would allow him to relax. She leaned forward to put a hand on his neck and draw him closer, but spoke again to me.

'What good do they think it will do? If getting rid of Gyp would mean that that child could somehow be miraculously *un*bitten, then I'd give him up like a shot. I'd rather *I* was bitten than have to go through last night again! They just want to punish him—punish us. They can't be serious.'

I said, 'I'm afraid they are. About bringing in the police, too.'

'Oh, this is dreadful,' said Mrs Ayres, now almost wringing her hands. 'Quite dreadful. What will the police make of the matter, do you think?'

'Well, I suppose they'll have to take it seriously, with a man like Baker-Hyde behind the complaint. And with the injury such an emotive one.' I looked at Roderick, determined now to draw him in. 'Don't you think so, Rod?'

He moved in his chair as if self-conscious, then spoke thickly.

'I really don't know what to think.' He cleared his throat. 'I suppose we've a licence for Gyp, have we? I imagine it'll help if we do.'

'Of course we've a licence!' said Caroline. 'But why on earth should a licence matter? This isn't a case of a dangerous dog running loose in the street. This was a family dog in its own home, being teased out of temper. Everyone who was here last night will say the same. If the Baker-Hydes can't see it— Oh, I can't bear it! I wish those people had never bought Standish! And I wish to God we'd never had that wretched party.'

I said, 'I expect Mr and Mrs Baker-Hyde wish that, too. This business with Gillian has pretty well devastated them.'

'Well, naturally it has,' said Mrs Ayres. 'Anyone could see, last night, that that child will be quite horribly disfigured. It's a frightful thing to happen to any parent.'

There was a silence after her words, and I felt my gaze drawn, unwillingly, from her own face to her son's. He was looking down, as if at his hands. I could make out the movement of some emotion behind his eyes, but his manner still baffled me. He raised his head, and again his voice caught in his throat and he had to clear it. He said, 'I wish I'd been there with you all last night.'

'Oh, so do I, Roddie!' said his sister.

'I can't help but feel,' he went on, as if he hadn't heard her, 'somehow responsible.'

'We all feel that,' I said. 'I feel it myself.'

He looked at me blankly.

Caroline said, 'It wasn't any fault of ours. It was that brother-in-law, messing about on the harpsichord. And if those parents had kept their child where she ought to have been—or better still, not brought her at all—'

And so we were back exactly where we'd started, except that this time it led to Caroline, her mother, and me running over the whole horrible incident from beginning to end, each of us with our own slightly different perspective on events. From time to time as we spoke I looked over at Rod. I saw him light up another cigarette—making a mess of it, dropping tobacco into his lap—and I was aware of him moving restlessly about, as if troubled by our voices. I had no idea how really uncomfortable he was, however, until he got abruptly to his feet.

'God!' he said. 'I can't bear it. I've heard this too many times today. Excuse me, Mother, Doctor: I'm going back to my room. I'm sorry. I—I'm sorry.'

He sounded so strained, and moved so awkwardly, I half rose to help him.

'Are you all right?'

'I'm fine,' he said quickly, putting out his hand as if to push me back. 'No, don't trouble. Honestly, I'm fine.' He gave an unconvincing smile. 'I'm still feeling a bit cheap, that's all, after last night. I'll—I'll have Betty bring me some cocoa. I'll be OK with a decent night's sleep.'

As he spoke, his sister rose. She went across and linked her arm with his.

'You don't need me, Mother?' she said, in a subdued voice. 'Then I'll say good night too.' She looked awkwardly at me. 'Thanks for coming out to us, Dr Faraday. That was thoughtful of you.'

I had got to my feet properly now. 'I'm sorry I didn't bring better news. But do try not to worry.'

'Oh, I'm not worried,' she said, with a smile as brave as her brother's. 'They can say what they like, those people. They won't hurt Gyp. I won't let them.'

She and Roderick moved off, and the dog trotted faithfully after: reassured, for the moment, by the confidence in her voice.

I watched the door close behind them, then turned back to Mrs Ayres. Now that her children had gone she looked terribly tired. I had never spent time with her on her own before, and wondered if I oughtn't to leave her. I had had an early start that day, and was tired myself.

But she beckoned wearily to me. 'Come and take Roderick's place, Dr Faraday, so that I can look at you more easily.'

So I moved to the fire.

I said, as I sat, 'I'm afraid this has all been a dreadful shock for you.'

'It has,' she answered at once. 'I was wakeful, all last night. Thinking of that poor child. That such a ghastly thing should have happened, and here! And then—'

She started to turn the rings indecisively on her fingers, so that I wanted to lean across and place my hand on hers. At last, in a tighter, more anxious voice than before, she said, 'The fact is, I'm rather concerned about Roderick, too.'

I glanced at the door. 'Yes. He certainly seems not quite himself. Has all this upset him as much as that?'

'You didn't notice? Last night?'

'Last night?' I'd forgotten, with all the drama; but remembered now. 'You sent Betty to him—'

'Poor girl, he alarmed her. She came back for me. I found him—oh, in such a strange state!'

'What do you mean? Was he ill?'

She spoke reluctantly. 'I don't know. He said his head was aching. But he looked frightful—half dressed in his evening clothes, sweating, and trembling like a leaf.'

I stared at her. 'He hadn't been . . . drinking?'

It was all I could think of, and I was embarrassed to make the suggestion. But she shook her head, beyond embarrassment.

'It wasn't that, I'm sure it wasn't. I don't know what on earth it was. At first he asked me to stay with him. He caught hold of my hand, like a schoolboy! Then just as suddenly he changed his mind and told me to leave him. He almost bundled me from the room. I had Betty bring him aspirin. There was no question of his coming out, like that. I had to make what excuses I could. What else could I have done?'

'You could have told me.'

'I wanted to! He wouldn't let me. And, naturally, I was thinking of how it might look. I was afraid of his appearing, making some sort of scene. Now I almost wish he had. For then that poor little girl—'

Her voice had grown so tight, it pinched itself out. We sat in an unhappy silence, and once again my mind ran back to the previous evening, to the gristly snap of Gyp's jaws, the shriek and liquid moan that followed. At that very moment, Rod had been sitting in some odd nervous state in his own room; and while I carried Gillian downstairs, while I worked on her cheek, he'd remained in there, presumably hearing the fuss beyond his door but unable to emerge and face it. The thought was horrible.

I seized the arms of my chair. 'Why don't I go and talk to him?'

But Mrs Ayres reached out. 'Don't. I don't think he would want it.'

'What harm could it do?'

'You saw how he was tonight: so unlike himself, so uncertain and subdued. He's been like that all day. I had practically to plead with him to get him to sit in here this evening. His sister doesn't know how I found him last night; she thinks he had a bad headache, that's all, and put himself to bed. I think he's ashamed. I think— Oh, Dr Faraday, I keep thinking about how he was when he came back here from hospital!'

She bowed her head, and started to turn her rings again.

'I've never spoken to you about this,' she said, without quite meeting my eye. 'His doctor at the time called it a depression. But it seemed more than that to me. He seemed never to sleep. He'd fly into rages, or into sulks. His language was filthy. I hardly knew him. My own son! For months and months he was like that. I had to stop asking people to the house. I was ashamed of him!'

I'm not sure if what she told me surprised me. David Graham

had mentioned Rod's 'nervous trouble', after all, back in the summer, and from what I'd seen of Roderick himself since then—his over-preoccupation with his work, his occasional bouts of irritation and impatience—it seemed clear to me that the trouble had not been entirely resolved.

I said, 'I'm sorry. Poor Rod. And poor you, and Caroline! But you know, I've treated many injured men—'

'Of course,' she said quickly, 'I know that what happened to Roderick could have been so much worse.'

'I don't mean that,' I said. 'I'm thinking about healing, about the strangeness of it. It's a different process for every patient. It's no surprise, surely, that Roderick's injury made him angry? A fit young chap like him? I would have been angry, too, at Rod's age, in a situation like his. To have been born with so much, and then to have lost so much: one's health, one's looks—in a sense, one's freedom.'

She shook her head, unconvinced. 'It was more than mere anger. It was as though the war itself had changed him, made an utter stranger of him. He seemed to hate himself, and everyone around him. Oh, when I think of all the boys like him, and all the frightful things we asked them to do in the name of making peace—!'

I said gently, 'Well, it's all done with now. He's young, still. He'll recover.'

'But you didn't see him last night!' she said. 'Doctor, I'm afraid. If he should grow ill again, what on earth will happen? We've already lost so much here. My children try to keep the worst of things from me, but I'm not a fool. I know the estate is living on its capital, and I know what that means . . . But we've lost other things, too. We've lost friends; the trick of society. I look at Caroline: she seems to grow shabbier and more eccentric by the day. It was really for her sake, you know, that I threw the party at all. That was a disaster, like everything else . . . There'll be nothing for her, after I'm gone. If she were to lose her brother, too— And now, to think of those people, talking of bringing in the police! I don't—the fact is, I simply don't know how I shall bear it!'

Her voice had been level but, on these words, darted unsteadily up the scale. She put her hand across her eyes, to cover her face from me.

When I thought about it later, I realised what burdens she'd been living under for so many years: the death of a child, the death of a husband, the stresses of war, her injured son, the lost estate . . . But she had hidden those burdens very successfully behind a veil of breeding and charm, and to see her lose her self-possession now, and openly weep, was shocking. For a second I sat across from her, almost trans-fixed; then I went and squatted beside her chair, and after a slight hesitation I took her hand—just took it, lightly, firmly, as any doctor might. Her fingers tightened around my own, and gradually she grew calmer. I offered her my handkerchief and she dabbed, embarrassed, at her eyes.

'If one of the children should come in!' she said, glancing anxiously over her shoulder. 'Or Betty! I couldn't bear to be found in such a state. I never saw my own mother weep; she always despised a crying woman. Do forgive me, Dr Faraday. The plain fact is, as I told you, I hardly slept last night, and sleeplessness never did agree with me . . . And now, how frightful I shall look. Turn off that lamp for me, would you?'

I switched off the lamp she meant: an ornamental reading-light, hung with lustres, on the table beside her chair. As the ring of the lustres faded I said, 'You've nothing to fear from the light, you know. You never have.'

She was dabbing at her face again, but caught my eye in weary sur-prise. 'I didn't know you were so gallant, Doctor.'

I felt myself blush a little. But before I could answer, she sighed and spoke again.

'Oh, but men acquire gallantry, as women acquire lines in their faces. My husband was a very gallant man. I'm glad he isn't alive to see me as I am now. His gallantry would be sorely tested. I think I grew older by ten years last winter. Probably I'll grow older by another ten, this.'

'Then you will look all of forty,' I said—at which she laughed, properly, so that I was pleased to see the life and colour returning to her face.

We spoke of ordinary things after that. She had me pour her a drink and bring her a cigarette. And only as I rose to leave did I try and remind her why I had come out there in the first place, by mentioning Peter Baker-Hyde.

Her response was to lift her hand as if exhausted by the whole idea.

'That man's name has been heard too often in this house today,' she said. 'If he wants to hurt us, we must let him try. He won't get far. How could he?'

'You really think that?'

'I know it. This horrible business will rage for a day or two, and then blow over. You'll see.'

She seemed as certain as her daughter; so I let the matter rest.

But she and Caroline were wrong. The business did not blow over. The very next day, Mr Baker-Hyde drove out to the Hall to let the family know that he planned to take the case to the police unless they were prepared to destroy Gyp themselves. He sat with Mrs Ayres and Roderick for half an hour—speaking quite reasonably at first, Mrs Ayres told me later, so that for a time she really believed she might persuade him to change his mind.

'No one regrets your daughter's accident more bitterly than I do, Mr Baker-Hyde,' she said to him, with what he must have recognised as genuine feeling. 'But destroying Gyp won't undo it. As to the likelihood of the dog's snapping at another child—well, you can see how we live here, in so quiet a way. There are simply no other children to provoke him.'

That was an unfortunate way to phrase it perhaps, and I can easily picture the hardening effect her words must have had on Peter Baker-

Hyde's expression and manner. Worst of all, at that moment Caroline appeared, with Gyp at her heels. They had been walking in the park and were, I suppose, as I'd often seen them: Caroline flushed, sturdy, untidy, Gyp muddy and contented with a pink open mouth. Mr Baker-Hyde looked at them and must have remembered his daughter, lying wretchedly at home with her savaged face. He later told Dr Seeley, who afterwards reported it back to me, that if he had had a gun in his hand at that moment he would have 'shot the damn dog himself, and the whole bloody family with it'.

The visit swiftly disintegrated into curses and threats, and he drove off in a roar of gravel. Caroline watched him go with her hands on her hips; then, trembling with upset and anger, she strode around to one of the outhouses and dug out a couple of old padlocks and some chains. She went right across the park, first to one gate and then to the other, and locked them shut.

My own housekeeper told me this; she had heard it from one of her neighbours, who was a cousin to Barrett, the Hundreds odd-man. The case was still being very freely talked about in all the local villages, with some people expressing sympathy for the Ayreses, but most apparently feeling that the family's stubbornness over Gyp was simply making a bad situation worse. I saw Bill Desmond on the Friday, and he seemed to think that it was now only a matter of time before the Ayreses 'did the decent thing' and had the poor dog shot. But after that there came a couple of days of silence, and I really began to wonder whether things mightn't be fizzling out. Then, at the start of the following week, a Kenilworth patient of mine asked me how 'that dear little Baker-Hyde girl' was—asked it almost casually, but with an admiring tone to her voice, saying she'd heard I was involved in the case and had practically saved the child's life. When, amazed, I asked her who on earth had told her that, she handed me the latest issue of a Coventry weekly: I opened the paper and found an account of the whole affair. The Baker-Hydes had admitted their daughter for further treatment at a Birmingham hospital, which is where the story had been picked up. The little girl was said to have undergone a 'very savage attack', but to be making good progress. The parents were determined to see the dog in question destroyed, and were taking legal advice as to how best to achieve it. Mrs Colonel Ayres, Mr Roderick Ayres, and Miss Caroline Ayres, the dog's owners, were said to be unavailable for comment.

As far as I knew, the Coventry papers weren't taken at Hundreds, but they had a wide distribution throughout the county as a whole, and I thought the fact of this one's having covered the case rather worrying. I telephoned the Hall, and asked if they had seen the paper; they hadn't, so I took them a copy on my way home. Roderick read it in grim silence before passing it on to his sister. She looked the article over and, for the first time since the thing had started, her confident manner faltered and I saw real fear in her face. Mrs Ayres was frankly appalled. There had been a certain amount of newspaper interest in Roderick's injury during the war, and it had left her, I think, with something of a morbid dread of exposure. For once, when I left them, she walked with me to my car, so that she could speak to me out of earshot of her children.

She said quietly, raising a scarf to cover her hair, 'I've something else to tell you. I haven't told Caroline or Roderick yet. Chief Inspector Allam called me earlier, to let me know that Mr Baker-Hyde is about to go ahead and press charges. He wanted to warn me; he and my husband, you know, were in the same regiment. He made it very plain that, in a case like this, with a child involved, we will have very small chance of winning. I've spoken to Mr Hepton'—this was the family solicitor—'and he agrees. He tells me, too, that there may be more than a fine to pay; there may be damages of some kind . . . I just can't believe it has come this far. Apart from anything else, we don't have the money to take it to trial! I've been trying to prepare Caroline for the worst, but she won't listen. I don't understand her. She's more upset over this than she was over her brother's accident.'

I didn't understand her, either. But I said, 'Well, Gyp means a great deal to her.'

'He means a great deal to all of us! But when all is said and done, he's a dog, and an old one. I simply can't have the family taken to court. I have to think of Roderick, if not of myself. He's still far from well. This is the very last thing he needs.'

She put her hand on my arm and looked squarely into my face. 'You've done so much for us already, Doctor, I hardly like to ask you to do more. But I don't quite want to involve Bill Desmond, or Raymond Rossiter, in our troubles. When it comes to it, with Gyp—I wonder, could *you* help us?'

I said, in bleak surprise, 'You mean, destroy him?'

She nodded. 'I can't expect it of Roderick, and clearly there's no question of Caroline—'

'No, no.'

'I don't know whom else to turn to. If the Colonel were alive—'

'Yes, of course.' I spoke reluctantly, but rather with the feeling that I couldn't very well say anything else. So I said it again, more firmly. 'Yes, of course I'll help you.'

Her hand was still on my arm. I put my own over it, and she bowed her head, in relief and gratitude, the flesh of her face sinking slightly into tired, almost elderly lines.

'But you really think Caroline will allow it?' I asked her, as she drew her hand away.

She said simply, 'She will, for the sake of the family. That's all there is to it.'

And this time, she was right. She called me that evening, to tell me that Chief Inspector Allam had spoken to the Baker-Hydes again, and after a great deal of wrangling they had grudgingly agreed to drop charges, provided that Gyp were destroyed without delay. She sounded desperately relieved about it, and I was pleased that things had been resolved; but I passed a miserable night, thinking of what I'd agreed to do for her the following day. At about three o'clock, too, just as I was sliding at last into something like natural sleep, I was woken by a ringing on the surgery night-bell. A man had run from the neighbouring village to ask me to see to his wife who was having difficulties in labour. I dressed, and drove him home; it was the woman's first confinement and a rather tricky delivery, but the whole business was finished by half past six, the baby bruised at the temples from the grip of my forceps, but noisy and healthy. The man was due in the fields at seven, so we left the mother and child in the care of the midwife, and I gave him a lift as far as his farm. He went off whistling to his work—pleased because the child had been a boy and his brothers' wives, he told me, 'could only make wenches'.

I was glad on his behalf, and I had the slight touch of euphoria that usually follows a successful confinement, particularly when accompanied by a lack of sleep; but when I remembered the task that lay ahead of me at Hundreds, the excitement curdled. I didn't want to go back into Lidcote and have to come out again; I drove the car along a lane I knew, which passed through woods to end in a small clearing beside an overgrown pond. The place, in summer, was picturesque, a haunt of lovers. But it was also, I recalled too late, the scene of a wartime suicide, and the dark water and the wet, bruise-coloured trees looked very melancholy to me as I drew up and switched off my motor. It was too cold to get out: I lit a cigarette and wound down my window, and hugged myself against the chill. I'd occasionally seen herons here in the past, and sometimes courting dabchicks; today the pond seemed lifeless. A single bird called from a branch, called again, but went unanswered. Presently a drizzling rain started, and a breeze seemed to spring from nowhere to cast the stinging little drops against my cheek. I pinched out my cigarette and hurriedly wound the window back up.

A couple of miles down the road was the turning that would take me to the west gate of Hundreds Park. I waited until just before eight, then started the car and made my way over there.

They had taken the chain and padlock from the gate by now, so I got in easily enough. It was lighter in the open park than in the lanes, but the house, which was visible from the west for quite a distance, looked vast and solid in the murky twilight, a great dark cube. But I knew that the family were early risers, and as I drew nearer I could see smoke from some of the chimneys. And when I had rounded the back of the house and my tyres were crunching over the gravel, I saw a light come on at the windows beside the front door.

The door was opened before I reached it, by Mrs Ayres. She looked pale.

I said, 'I'm not too early?'

She shook her head. 'It's all the same to us. Roderick's over at the farm already. I don't think any of us has slept all night. Neither have you, by the look of you. No one's died, I hope?'

'A maternity case.'

'The baby well?'

'The baby, and the mother . . . Where's Caroline?'

'Upstairs, with Gyp. She'll have heard your car, I expect.'

'You warned her I was coming? She knows why?'

'Yes, she knows.'

'How has she taken it?'

She shook her head again, but apart from that made no answer. She took me through to the little parlour and left me there by the spitting logs of a new fire. When she came back she was carrying a tray of tea and bread and cold bacon, and she set it down beside me, and sat with me while I ate, eating nothing herself. Seeing her playing the servant's role only added to my unease. When I had finished the breakfast I didn't linger, but took my bag and let her lead me out into the hall and up the stairs to the first floor.

She left me at Caroline's door. It was slightly ajar, but I tapped, and then, hearing no answer, slowly pushed it open and went in. I found a large, pleasant room, with pale panelled walls and a narrow four-poster bed; but everything, I noticed, was faded, the bed-curtains bleached, the carpets threadbare, the floorboards with a white paint on them, worn to a streaky grey. There were two sash windows and Caroline was sitting at one of them, on a sort of cushioned ottoman, with Gyp at her side. He had his head in her lap, but raised his muzzle when he saw me, and parted his jaws, his tail thumping. Caroline had her face turned to the window and didn't speak until I drew close.

'You came as soon as you could, then.'

I said, 'I was out with a patient. And isn't it better to do it now, Caroline, than to wait and risk the police sending their own man? You wouldn't rather a stranger did it?'

She turned her head to me at last, and I saw she looked ghastly, her hair unbrushed, her face white, her eyes red and swollen with weeping or watching. She said, 'Why must you all talk about it as if it's something ordinary, something reasonable, that has to be done?'

'Come on, Caroline. You know it has to be done.'

'Only because everyone says it does! It's like—like going to war. Why should I do it? It's not my war.'

'Caroline, that little girl—'

'We might have taken this to court, you know, and we might have won it. Mr Hepton said as much. Mother wouldn't let him try.'

'But a court case! Think of the cost of it, if nothing else.'

'I should have found the money somehow.'

'Then think of the attention you'd have received. Think of the look of the thing. Trying to defend yourself, with that child so injured! It wouldn't be decent.'

She made a gesture of impatience. 'What does attention matter? It's only Mother who minds that. And she's only afraid of people seeing how poor we are. As for decency—no one cares about that kind of thing any more.'

'Your family's been through too much. Your brother—'

'Oh yes,' she said, 'my brother! Let's all think of him, shall we? As if we ever do anything else. He could have stood up to Mother over this. Instead he did nothing, nothing at all!'

I had never heard her criticise Roderick before, except in fun, and I was startled by her fierceness. But at the same time, her eyes were growing redder and her voice was weakening, and I think she knew there was no other way. She turned, to gaze back out of the window. I stood watching her in silence, then said gently, 'You must be brave, Caroline. I'm sorry . . . Shall I see to it now?'

'God,' she said, closing her eyes.

'Caroline, he's old.'

'Does that make it better?'

'I give you my word, he won't suffer.'

She sat tensely for a moment; then her shoulders sank, she let out her breath, and all the bitterness seemed to bleed away from her. She said, 'Oh, take him. Everything else has gone, why not take him, too? I'm sick of fighting it.'

Her tone was so bleak, that at last I saw through her stubbornness to other losses and griefs; and I felt I'd been misjudging her. She put her hand on the dog's head as she spoke, and he, understanding that she was talking about him, but also hearing the distress in her voice, looked up at her with trust and concern, then rose on his front legs and moved his muzzle towards her face.

'You idiotic dog!' she said, letting him lick her. Then she pushed him away. 'Dr Faraday wants you, can't you see?'

I said, 'Shall I do it here?'

'No, I don't want that. I don't want to see it. Take him downstairs somewhere. Go on, Gyp.' And she pushed him to me almost roughly, so that he stumbled from the ottoman to the floor. 'Go on,' she said again, when he hesitated, 'you stupid thing! Dr Faraday wants you, I told you. Go on!'

So Gyp came faithfully to me, and after a final glance at Caroline I led him from the room and quietly closed the door behind me. He followed me down through the house to the kitchen, and I took him out to the scullery and had him lie down on an old rug. He knew that was strange, for Caroline was strict about his routines; but then, he must have known there was upset in the house, and perhaps could even guess that he was the cause of it. I wondered what notions were swimming about in his mind—what memories of the party, and whether he thought of what he had done, and was guilty or ashamed. But when I looked into his eyes it seemed to me that I could see only confusion there; and after I had opened my bag and taken out what I needed, I touched his head and said to him, as I'd said to him once before, 'Here's a to-do,

Gyp. But, never mind now. You're a good old dog.' And I went on murmuring nonsense like that, and I held my arm beneath his shoulders, so that after the injection had taken effect he sank on to my hand, and I felt the faltering of his heart against my palm, and then the failing of it.

Mrs Ayres had told me that Barrett would bury him, so I covered him over with the rug, then washed my hands and went back into the kitchen. I found Mrs Bazeley there: she had just arrived and was tying on her apron. When I told her what I'd been doing she shook her head, distressed.

'In't it a shame?' she said. 'The house won't seem right without that old hound in it. Can you make it out, Doctor? I've seen him about the place all his life, and I'd have taken me oath on there being no more harm in him that in the hairs on me own head. I'd have trusted him with me grandchild, I would.'

'So would I, Mrs Bazeley,' I answered miserably; 'if I had one.'

But there was the kitchen table, after all, to remind me of that recent, horrible night. And there, too—I hadn't noticed her before—there was Betty. She was standing half concealed by a door that led to one of the kitchen passages; she had a pile of newly dried dish-cloths and was folding them up. But she moved with an odd jerkiness, her narrow shoulders seeming to twitch, and I realised after a second or two that she was crying. She turned her head and saw me watching, and began to weep harder. She said, with a violence that amazed me: 'That poor old dog, Dr Faraday! Everyone's blaming him, but it wan't his fault! It in't fair!'

Her voice broke down, and Mrs Bazeley went across to her to take her in her arms.

'There, now,' the woman said, awkwardly patting Betty's back. 'You see how this've upset us, Doctor? We dunno what we're about. Betty's got some idea in her head— I dunno.' She looked embarrassed. 'Her thinks that little girl gettin' bit has summat peculiar to it.'

I said, 'Something peculiar? What on earth do you mean?'

Betty drew back her head from Mrs Bazeley's shoulder and said, 'There's a bad thing in this house, that's what! There's a bad thing, and he makes wicked things happen!'

I stared at her for a moment, then lifted my hand, to rub my face. 'Oh, Betty.'

'It's true! I've felt 'm!'

She looked from me to Mrs Bazeley. Her grey eyes were wide, and she was shivering slightly. But I had the sense, as I'd sometimes had before with her, that, at heart, she was enjoying the fuss and attention. I said, less patiently, 'All right. We're all tired, and we're all sorry.'

'It in't tiredness!'

'All right!' Now I spoke sharply. 'This is pure silliness and you know it. This house is big, and lonely, but I thought you were used to that now?'

'I *am* used to it! It in't just *that*.'

'It isn't anything. There's nothing bad here, nothing spooky. What happened with Gyp and that poor child, it was a horrible accident, that's all.'

'It wan't an accident! It were the bad thing, whispering to Gyp, or—or nipping him.'

'Did *you* hear a whisper?'

She spoke reluctantly. 'No.'

'No. And neither did I. And neither did anyone else, in all that crowd of people at the party. Mrs Bazeley, have you seen any sign of this "bad thing" of Betty's?'

Mrs Bazeley shook her head. 'No, I haven't, Doctor. I've never seen nothing queer here at all.'

'And how long have you been coming to this house?'

'Well, very nearly ten years.'

'There you are, then,' I said to Betty. 'Doesn't that reassure you?'

'No, it don't!' she answered. 'Just 'cause she haven't seen it, don't mean it in't true! It might be a—a new thing.'

I said, 'Oh, for goodness' sake! Come on now, be a good girl and wipe your eyes. And I hope,' I added, 'you won't go mentioning any of this to Mrs Ayres, or to Miss Caroline. It's about the last thing they need at the moment. They've been good to you, remember? Remember how they called me in for you, that time you were poorly, in July?'

I looked into her face as I said this. She caught my meaning, and coloured. But her expression, despite the blush, grew mulish. She said in a whisper, 'There *is* a bad thing! There *is*!'

Then she hid her face against Mrs Bazeley's shoulder and wept again, as bitterly as before.

FIVE

~~~

Not surprisingly, in the weeks that followed, life at Hundreds Hall seemed very changed and discouraged and sad. There was, for one thing, simply the physical absence of Gyp to get used to: the days were naturally sombre now, but the house seemed extra dim and lifeless without the dog trotting affably from room to room. Since I was still going out to the Hall once a week to treat Rod's leg, it had become easier for me to let myself in like one of the family, and sometimes, opening up the door, I'd find myself listening out for the click and pad of paws; or else I'd turn my head to a shadow—thinking that the dark shape at the corner of my vision must be Gyp's, and having to suffer, every time, a pang of dismay as all that had happened came rushing back to me.

I mentioned this to Mrs Ayres, and she nodded: she had stood in the hall one rainy afternoon, she said, quite convinced that she could hear the dog pattering about upstairs. The sound was so distinct, she'd gone almost nervously up to look—and realised that what she'd taken as the sound of his claws on the floorboards was really the rapid drip of water from a broken gutter outside. Something similar happened to Mrs

Bazeley. She found herself making up a bowl of bread and gravy and setting it down by the kitchen door, as she'd used to do for Gyp in the old days. She let it sit there for half an hour, all the time wondering where the dog was—and then almost cried, she said, when she remembered he was gone. 'And the queer thing was,' she told me, 'I only done it because I thought I'd heard him coming down the basement steps. You know how he used to huff, like an old chap? I could have sworn I heard it!'

As for poor Caroline—how often she mistook some other sound for the skitter of Gyp's claws, or turned to a shadow supposing it him, I simply don't know. She had Barrett dig a grave for him among the marble headstones that formed a quaint little pet's cemetery in one of the park's plantations. She made a dreary tour of the house, collecting the water-bowls and blankets that had been kept in various rooms for the dog's use, and putting them away. But she seemed, in the process, to seal up her own upset and grief, with a thoroughness that unnerved me. On my first visit to the Hall after that miserable morning when I had put Gyp to sleep, I made a point of seeking her out, not wanting there to be any bad feeling between us. But when I asked her how she was, she said only, in a brisk, expressionless voice, 'I'm fine. It's all done now, isn't it? I'm sorry I spoke so wildly, that time. It wasn't your fault; I know that. It's finished. Let me show you this, that I found yesterday in one of the rooms upstairs—' And she brought out some antique trinket she had unearthed from the back of a drawer; and didn't refer to Gyp again.

I felt I didn't know her well enough to force the issue. But I spoke about her with her mother, who seemed to think that she would 're-cover in her own way'.

'Caroline's never been much of a girl for displaying her feelings,' she told me with a sigh. 'But she's awfully sensible. That's why I brought her back to help with her brother when he was hurt. She was as good as any nurse in those days, you know . . . And have you heard the latest news? Mrs Rossiter came out to tell us, just this morning. Apparently the Baker-Hydes are leaving. They're taking the little girl back to London; the staff are following next week. Poor Standish is to be shut up and sold again. But I do think it's for the best. Imagine Caroline or Roderick or I forever running into that family, in Lidcote or Leamington!'

I was relieved by this news, too. I hadn't relished the prospect of regularly seeing the Baker-Hydes, any more than Mrs Ayres had. I was also pleased that the county newspapers had at last lost interest in the case. And though nothing could be done about local gossip, and though sometimes a patient or colleague of mine would raise the affair with me, knowing I had been slightly involved, whenever the subject arose I always did my best to turn or close it; and talk soon died down.

But still, I wondered about Caroline. Now and then as I drove my car across the park I would catch sight of her, just as I'd used to; and without Gyp trotting beside her she struck me as a terribly forlorn figure. If I stopped the car to speak to her she seemed willing enough to talk, in what was more or less her old manner. She looked as sturdy and as healthy as she always had. Only her face, I thought, betrayed the wretchedness of the past few weeks, for caught at certain angles it seemed heavier and plainer than ever—as if, with the loss of her dog, there had come something like the loss of the last of her optimism and her youth.

D oes Caroline talk to you about how she's feeling?' I asked her brother one day in November, as I was treating his leg.

He shook his head, frowning. 'She doesn't seem to want to.'

'You can't . . . bring her out? Make her open up a little?'

The frown grew deeper. 'I suppose I could try. I never seem to have the time.'

I said lightly, 'No time for your sister?'

He didn't answer, and I remember looking on in concern as his face darkened, and he turned his head from me as if not trusting himself to reply. The fact is, at this point I felt almost more uneasy over him than over Caroline. That the business with Gyp and the Baker-Hydes should have left its mark on her was understandable, but it seemed to have had some sort of devastating impact on him, too, which quite perplexed me. It was not just a question of his being preoccupied and withdrawn, of his spending too much time at work in his room, for that had been true of him for months. It was an extra *something*, that I saw or sensed forever at the back of his expression: some burden of knowledge, or even of fear.

I hadn't forgotten what his mother had told me, about how she had found him on the night of the party. It seemed to me that if this new phase of his behaviour had started anywhere, it was there. I had tried several times to raise the subject with him, and every time he had found some way, through silence or evasion, of putting me off. Perhaps I should have left him to it. I was certainly busy enough on my own account in those days, for the colder weather had brought along its usual rash of winter ailments, and my rounds were heavy. But it was against all my instincts to let the matter rest; and, more than that, I simply felt involved with the family now, in a way I hadn't even three or four weeks before. So, when I had put the electrodes in place and started up the coil, I told him plainly what was bothering me.

His reaction appalled me.

'That's my mother's idea of keeping a confidence, is it?' he said, moving furiously about in his chair. 'I suppose I should have expected it. Just what did she tell you? That she found me in a blue funk?'

'She was worried about you.'

'God! I simply didn't feel like turning out for some idiotic party! My head was killing me. I sat in my room and had a drink. Then I went to bed. Is that a crime?'

'Rod, of course it isn't. It's just, the way she described it—'

'For God's sake. She exaggerates! She imagines things, all the time! As for what's actually under her nose— Oh, forget it. If she thinks I'm about to go off my head, leave her to it. She has no idea. You none of you have. If you only knew—'

He bit the words back. Puzzled by the intensity of his manner, I said, 'If we knew what?'

He sat rigid for a moment, clearly struggling with himself. Then, 'Oh, forget it,' he said again. And he moved sharply forward, catching hold of the wires that ran from his leg to the coil and pulling them free. 'Forget all this, too. I'm tired of it. It's no damn good.'

The electrodes sprang out of their bindings and tumbled to the floor. He tugged the elastics loose, then clumsily rose and, with his trouser leg still rolled high and his foot bare, he went over to stand at his desk, turning his back to me.

I gave the treatment up that day, and abandoned him to his temper. The following week he apologised, and we ran through the process as normal; he seemed to have quite calmed down. By my next visit, however, something new had started happening. I arrived at the house to find him with a cut on the bridge of his nose and a bad black eye.

'Now, don't look like that,' he said, when he saw my face. 'I've had Caroline fussing over me all morning, trying to stick bits of bacon to me and God knows what else.'

I glanced at his sister—she was sitting there with him, in his room; I think she had been waiting for me—then went over to him, to take his head in my hands and turn his face to the light of the window.

'What on earth happened?'

'A very stupid thing indeed,' he said, irritably drawing himself free, 'and I'm almost too embarrassed to mention it. I woke in the night, that's all, and went blundering out to the lavatory, and some fool—i.e., me—had left the door wide open, so that I went smack into the edge of it.'

'He knocked himself out,' said Caroline. 'It's only thanks to Betty that he didn't—I don't know, swallow his own tongue.'

'Don't be silly,' said her brother. 'I didn't knock myself out.'

'You did! He was flat on the floor, Doctor. And he'd given such a cry, he'd woken up Betty, downstairs. Poor girl, I think she thought we had burglars. She crept up and saw him lying there, and very sensibly came and woke me. He was still out cold when I came down to him.'

Rod scowled. 'Don't listen to her, Doctor. She's exaggerating.'

'I'm not, you know,' said Caroline. 'We had to throw water in his face to bring him round, and when he came to he was most ungrateful, told us in very nasty language to leave him alone—'

'All right,' said her brother. 'We seem to have proved that I'm an idiot. But I think I told you that myself. Now, can we leave it?'

He spoke sharply. Caroline looked disconcerted for a moment, then found a way to turn the subject. He wouldn't join in, however, but sat in moody silence while she and I chatted; and for the first time, when I prepared to treat him, he refused outright to let me do it—saying again that he was 'tired of it', that it was 'doing no good'.

His sister stared at him in amazement. 'Oh, Rod, you know that's not true!'

He answered peevishly, 'It's my leg, isn't it?'

'But for Dr Faraday to have gone to so much trouble—'

'Well, if Dr Faraday wants to put himself out for people he hardly knows,' he said, 'that's his look-out. I tell you, I'm tired of being pinched and pulled about! Or are my legs estate property, like everything else around here? Got to patch them up, get a bit more wear out of them; never mind that you're grinding them down to stumps. Is that what you're thinking?'

'Rod! You aren't being fair!'

'It's all right,' I said quietly. 'Rod doesn't have to have the treatment if he doesn't want it. It isn't as though he's paying for it.'

'But,' said Caroline, as if she hadn't heard, 'your paper—'

'My paper's practically written. And, as I think Rod knows, the best effect's already been achieved. All I'm doing now is keeping the muscle ticking over.'

Rod himself had moved away and wouldn't talk to us. In the end we left him to it, and joined Mrs Ayres in the little parlour for a sub-dued tea. But before I left, I went quietly down to the basement to have a word with Betty, and she confirmed what Caroline had told me about the previous night. She had been fast asleep, she said, and had been woken by a cry; muddled with slumber, she'd thought that one of the family wanted her, and had gone dozily upstairs. She found Rod's door open, and Rod himself lying on the floor with blood on his face, so still and white that for a second she'd supposed him dead, and had 'very nearly screamed'. Pulling herself together, she had run to fetch Caroline, and between them they had brought him round. He had woken up 'cursing, and saying funny things'.

I said, 'What sort of things?'

She screwed up her face, trying to remember. 'Just funny things. Queer things. Like when the dentist gives you gas.'

And that was all she could tell me; so I was obliged to let the matter go.

A few days later, however—when the bruise on his eye had turned a lovely shade of what Caroline called 'greenery-yallery', but well before it had faded completely—Rod suffered another small injury. Again he had apparently woken in the night and gone 'blundering' across his room. This time he had walked into a footstool that had mysteriously left its usual place to set itself directly in his path, and he had tripped and fallen, and hurt his wrist. He tried to play the incident down to me, and he let me bind up the injured wrist with a tremendous air of 'humouring the old man'. But I could tell from the look of his arm, and from his reaction when I handled it, that the sprain was quite a bad one, and his attitude baffled me.

I spoke about it later to his mother. She at once looked anxious— putting her hands together, as she often did now, to turn her old-fashioned rings.

'What do you think the matter is, truly?' she asked me. 'He won't tell me anything; I've tried and tried. Clearly, he's not sleeping. Then again, I don't think any of us is sleeping well just now . . . But all this wandering about at night! It can't be healthy, can it?'

'You think he did stumble, then?'

'What else? His leg is at its stiffest when he's been lying down.'

'That's true. But, the footstool?'

'Well, he keeps that room in such a frightful state. He always has.'

'But doesn't Betty tidy it?'

She caught the note of concern in my voice, and her gaze sharpened with alarm. She said, 'You don't think, do you, that there's something seriously wrong with him? He can't have been suffering from more of those headaches?'

But I had already thought of that. I had asked him about his head-aches while bandaging his wrist, and he'd answered that, apart from his two small injuries, he had no physical ailments at all. He seemed to be speaking truthfully; and though he looked tired, I could see no sign of actual illness in him, in his eyes, his manner or complexion. There was only that elusive *something*, faint as a scent or a shadow, that continued to perplex me. His mother looked so concerned I didn't like to burden her further. I remembered her tears on the night I had gone out there after the party. I told her I was probably worrying needlessly—rather playing the whole thing down, just like Rod himself.

But I was bothered enough to want to talk to someone about it. So I made an excuse to call in at the Hall later that week, and I sought out Caroline, to speak to her alone.

I found her in the library. She was sitting cross-legged on the floor with a tray of leather-bound books in front of her; she was rubbing lanolin into their covers. She had just enough weak north light to work by, for in the recent damp weather the window-shutters had begun to warp, and she had only been able to open one of them, and that only partly. White sheets still hung across most of the shelves, like so many shrouds. She hadn't bothered to light a fire, and the room was very chill and cheerless.

She seemed pleasantly surprised to see me there on a weekday afternoon.

'Look at these lovely old editions,' she said, showing me a couple of small tan books, their bindings still glossy and moist from the lanolin, like newly exposed conkers. I hitched up a stool and sat beside her; she opened one of the books and began to turn its pages.

She said, 'I haven't got very far, to tell the truth. It's always more tempting to read than to work. I found something just now, a bit of Herrick, that made me smile. Here it is.' The book creaked as she eased back its covers. 'Just listen to this, and tell me what it reminds you of.' And she began to read aloud, in her low-pitched, pleasant voice:

The tongues of Kids shall be thy meate,
Their Milke thy drinke; and thou shalt eate
The Paste of Filberts for thy bread
With Cream of Cowslips butterèd:
Thy Feasting-Tables shall be Hills
With Daisies spread, and Daffodils;
Where thou shalt sit, and Red-brest by,
For meat, shall give thee melody.

She lifted her head. 'That might have been put out as a broadcast by the Ministry of Food, don't you think? It's all there except the ration book. I wonder what the Paste of Filberts tastes like.'

I said, 'Like peanut butter, I shouldn't wonder.'

'You're right; only even nastier.'

We smiled at each other. She put down the Herrick and picked up the book she had been working on when I arrived, and started rubbing at it with firm, even strokes. But when I told her what was on my mind—that I wanted to talk about Roderick—her hand slowed and her smile faded.

She said, 'I was wondering how much it had all struck you. I've been thinking of talking to you myself. But what with everything else—'

That was as close as she ever came to mentioning the business with Gyp; and as she spoke she dipped her head, so that I saw her lowered eyelids, heavy and moist and curiously nude-looking above her dry cheeks.

She said, 'He keeps saying he's all right, but I know he isn't. Mother knows it, too. That business with the door, for instance. When did Rod ever leave his door open at night? And he *was* almost raving when he came to, despite what he says. I think he's having nightmares. He keeps hearing noises when nothing's there.' She reached for the jar of lanolin and dabbled her fingers inside it. 'He didn't tell you, I suppose, about coming up to my room in the night, last week?'

'To your room?' I'd heard nothing of this.

She nodded, glancing up at me as she worked. 'He woke me up. I don't know what time it was; long before dawn, anyway. I didn't know what on earth was going on. He came barging in, saying would I for God's sake please stop shifting things about, it was driving him mad! Then he saw me in bed, and I swear, he turned *green*—greenery-yallery, just like his eye. His room is almost underneath mine, you know, and he said he'd been lying there for an hour, listening to me dragging things across the floor. He thought I'd been rearranging the furniture! He'd been dreaming, of course. The house was quiet as a church; it always is. But the dream seemed realer to him than I did, that was the horrible thing. It took him forever to calm down. In the end I made him get into bed beside me. I went back to sleep, but I don't know if he did. I think he lay awake all the rest of that night—wide awake, I mean, as if he were watching or waiting or something.'

Her words made me thoughtful. I said, 'He didn't pass out, anything like that?'

'Pass out?'

'He couldn't have been having some sort of . . . seizure?'

'A fit, you mean? Oh, no. It was nothing like that. There was a girl when I was young who threw fits; I remember, they were horrible things. I don't think I could make a mistake about that.'

'Well,' I said, 'not all seizures are the same. It makes a sort of sense, after all. His injuries, his confusion, his queer behaviour . . .'

She shook her head, looking sceptical. 'I don't know. I don't think it was that. And why should he start having seizures now? He's never had them before.'

'Well, perhaps he has. Would he have told you? People have an odd sense of shame about epilepsy.'

She frowned, thinking it over; then she shook her head again. 'I just don't think that's it.'

Wiping the lanolin from her fingers, then screwing on the lid of the jar, she got to her feet. The narrow strip of window showed a swiftly darkening sky, and the room seemed colder and gloomier than ever. She said, 'God, it's like an ice-house in here!' She blew into her hands. 'Help me with this, could you?'

She meant the tray of treated books. I moved forward to lift it with her and we set it on a table. She dusted down her skirt, and said, without looking up, 'Where's Rod now, do you know?'

I said, 'I saw him outside with Barrett when I arrived, heading over to the old gardens. Why? You think we should talk to him?'

'No, it's not that. It's just—have you been to his room lately?'

'His room? Not lately, no. He doesn't seem to want me there.'

'He doesn't seem to want me there, either. But I happened to go in a couple of days ago when he was out, and I noticed something—well, something odd. I don't know if it'll back up your epilepsy theory or not; I rather think not. But will you come and let me show you? If Barrett's got hold of Rod, they'll be ages.'

I didn't care for the idea. 'I'm not sure we ought to, Caroline. Rod wouldn't like it, would he?'

'It won't take long. And it's the sort of thing I'd like you to see for yourself . . . Please will you come? I've no one else to talk to about it.'

That was more or less the feeling that had brought me to her; and since she was clearly so troubled, I said I would. She led me out into the hall, and we went quietly on down the passage towards Rod's room.

It was late in the afternoon, after Mrs Bazeley had gone home, but as we drew near to the curtained arch that led to the service regions we could hear the faint chatter of the wireless that meant that Betty was at work in the kitchen. Caroline glanced over at the curtain as she turned the handle of Roderick's door, and winced at the creaking of the lock.

'You mustn't think I make a habit of this sort of thing,' she murmured, when we were inside. 'If anyone comes, I'll lie, and say we were looking for a book or something. You mustn't be shocked by that, either . . . Here's what I want you to see.'

I'd expected her, I don't know why, to lead me to Rod's desk and papers. Instead she remained at the door she had just closed, and gestured to the back of it.

The door was panelled in oak to match the walls of the room and, like just about everything else at Hundreds, the oak was not at its best. I could imagine the wood, in its heyday, having had a glorious, ruddy lustre; now, though still impressive, it was bleached and slightly streaky, and some of the sections had shrunk and cracked. But the panel at which Caroline pointed had a different sort of mark on it. The mark was at about breast height, and it was small and black, like a scorch-mark—just like a mark I could remember seeing on the floorboards of the little terraced house I grew up in, where my mother had once set down an iron while laundering clothes.

I looked quizzically at Caroline. 'What is it?'

'You tell me.'

I moved in closer. 'Rod's been lighting candles, and let one fall?'

'That's what I thought, at first. There's a table, you see, not too far off. The generator has failed us a couple of times recently; I thought that for some queer reason Rod must have put the table here with a candle on it, and then I supposed he'd fallen asleep or something and the candle had burned itself over. I was pretty annoyed about it, as you can imagine. I told him please not to be such an idiot as ever to do it again.'

'And what did he say?'

'He said he hadn't been lighting candles. If the power goes, he uses that lamp over there.' She indicated an old Tilley lamp, sitting on a bureau on the other side of the room. 'Mrs Bazeley says the same. She keeps a drawer full of candles downstairs for when the generator fails and, according to her, Rod hasn't taken any of them. He says he doesn't know how the mark got here. He hadn't noticed it before I pointed it out. But he didn't seem to like the look of it, either. It seemed to—well, to spook him.'

I moved close to the door again, to run my fingers over the smudge. It left no trace of soot on them, nor any kind of scent, and its surface was quite smooth. The more I studied it, in fact, the more it seemed to me that the mark had the faintest sort of bloom or patina over it—as though it had somehow developed just *below* the surface of the wood.

I said, 'This couldn't have been here for some time, without your having seen it?'

'I don't think so. I think it would have caught my eye whenever I closed or opened the door. And don't you remember—the very first time you treated Rod's leg? I stood just about here and complained about the panels. The mark wasn't there then, I'm certain it wasn't . . . Betty knows nothing about it. Neither does Mrs Bazeley.'

Her casual mention, not of Mrs Bazeley, but of Betty, made me thoughtful. I said, 'You brought Betty here, and showed her the mark?'

'I brought her quietly, like this. She was as surprised by it as I was.'

'Was she really, do you think? You don't think she might have been responsible for it somehow, then been too frightened to own up? She might have been walking past this door with an oil-lamp in her hand. Or maybe she spilled something here. Some sort of cleaning solution.'

'Cleaning solution?' said Caroline. 'There's nothing stronger in the kitchen cupboards than meths and liquid soap! I should know, I've used them often enough. No. Betty has her moods, but I don't think she's a liar.—And anyhow, that's by the bye. I came back in here yesterday when Rod was out, and had another look around. I found nothing strange—until I did this.'

She put back her head and looked upwards, and I did the same. The mark leapt out at me at once. It was on the ceiling this time—that plaster lattice-work ceiling, stained yellow with nicotine. It was a small, dark, formless smudge, exactly like the one on the door; and again, it looked just as though someone had put a flame or an iron there, long enough to scorch the plaster but not to blister it.

Caroline was watching my face. 'I'd like to know,' she said, 'how even a very careless parlourmaid could be careless enough to put a burn mark on the ceiling, twelve feet off the floor.'

I stared at her for a second, then moved across the room until the smudge was right over my head. I said, squinting upwards, 'Is it really the same as the other?'

'Yes. I even brought in the step-ladder and had a look. If anything, it's worse. There's nothing underneath that might account for it—only, as you see, Rod's washing-stand. Even if he'd put the Tilley on that, the distance involved . . . Well.'

'And it's definitely a scorch or a burn? It isn't, I don't know, some sort of chemical reaction?'

'A chemical reaction that can make antique oak panels and plaster ceilings start smouldering all by themselves? Not to mention this. Look over here.'

With a slightly giddy sense, I followed her over to the fireplace and she showed me the heavy Victorian ottoman that sat beside it, on the opposite side to the kindling-box. Sure enough, the leather was marked apparently in exactly the same way as the door and the ceiling, with a small, dark smudge.

I said, 'This is too much, Caroline. The ottoman could have been marked like this for years. Probably a spark from the fire once caught it. The ceiling might have been marked for a long time, too. I don't think I'd have noticed.'

'Perhaps you're right,' she said. 'I hope you are. But you don't think it's odd, about this and the door? The door being the one that Rod walked into, I mean, the night he blacked his eye, and this being the thing he tripped over?'

I said, 'It was *this* he fell over?' I'd been picturing some dainty foot-stool. 'But, this must weigh a ton! How could it have found its way across the room like that?'

'That's what I'd like to know. And why is it marked in this queer way? As if it were, well, *marked out*. It's just so creepy.'

'And you've asked Rod about these?'

'I showed him the mark on the door and the one on the ceiling, but not this. His reaction to the others was too odd.'

'Odd?'

'He seemed . . . furtive. I don't know. Guilty.'

She said the word reluctantly, and I looked at her and began to make out the anxious movement of her ideas. I said quietly, 'You think he's been making these marks himself, don't you?'

She answered unhappily, 'I don't know! But perhaps, in his sleep—? Or in the sort of fit you mentioned? After all, if he can do other things— if he can open doors and move furniture about, and get himself injured; if he can come up to my room at three o'clock in the morning to ask *me* to stop moving furniture!—then couldn't he also do something like this?' She glanced at the door, and lowered her voice. 'And if he can do this, Doctor, well, what else might he do?'

I thought it over for a moment. 'Have you mentioned this to your mother?'

'No. I haven't wanted to worry her. And then, what is there to tell, really? Just a few funny marks. I don't know why they bother me so much . . . No, that's not true. I do know.' She grew awkward. 'It's because we've had trouble with Rod before. Do you know about that?'

'Your mother told me a little,' I said. 'I'm sorry. It must have been tough.'

She nodded. 'It was a bad, bad time. All Rod's injuries were at their worst, his scars ghastly, his leg so bashed about it really seemed as though he might be more or less a cripple for the rest of his life. But he wouldn't do anything to get himself better, that was the maddening thing. He just sat in here, brooding, and smoking—drinking too, I think. You know his navigator died, when their plane came down? I think he blamed himself for that. It was nobody's fault, of course. —No one's but the Germans', I mean. But they say it's always hard on the pilots when their crews are lost. The boy was younger than Roddie; only just nineteen. Rod used to say that it ought to have been the other way around: that the boy had had more to live for than he did. That was fun for Mother and me to hear, as you can imagine.'

I said, 'I can. Has he said anything like that lately?'

'Not to me. Nor to Mother, as far as I know. But I can tell she's afraid of his getting sick again, too. Perhaps it's just because we're afraid, we're imagining too much? I don't know. There's just—something not right here. Something's going on, with Rod. It's as though there's a hoodoo on him. He hardly goes out any more, you know, even to the farm. He just stays in here, saying he's going over his papers. But look at them!'

She gestured to his desk, and to the table beside his chair, both of which were nearly obscured by deep, untidy piles of letters and ledgers and flimsy type-written sheets. She said, 'He's drowning in all this stuff. But he won't let me help him. He says he has a system and I won't understand. Does this look like a system to you? Practically the only person he allows to come in here these days is Betty. At least she keeps the carpet swept, and empties his ashtrays . . . I wish he'd get away for a while, take a holiday or something. But he never would. He won't leave the estate. And it isn't even as though his being here makes any real difference! The estate's doomed, whatever he does.' She lowered herself, heavily, on to the marked ottoman, and rested her chin in her hands. 'Sometimes I think he ought to just let it go.'

She spoke wearily but matter-of-factly, letting her eyes almost close, and again I was conscious of the curious nudeness of her slightly swollen eyelids. I gazed down at her, perturbed.

'You don't mean that, Caroline. You couldn't bear to lose Hundreds, surely?'

Now she spoke almost casually. 'Oh, but I've been brought up to lose it.—To lose it, I mean, once Rod marries. The new Mrs Ayres won't want a spinster sister-in-law about the place; nor a mother-in-law, come to that. That's the stupidest thing of all. So long as Roddie goes on holding the estate together, too tired and distracted to find a wife, and probably killing himself in the process—so long as he goes on like that, Mother and I get to stay here. Meanwhile Hundreds is such a drain on us, it's hardly worth staying for . . .'

Her voice faded, and we stayed without speaking until the silence in that insulated room began to grow oppressive. I looked again at those three queer scorch-marks: they were like the burns, I realised suddenly, on Rod's own face and hands. It was as if the house were developing scars of its own, in response to his unhappiness and frustration—or to Caroline's, or her mother's—perhaps, to the griefs and disappointments of the whole family. The thought was horrible. I could see what Caroline meant about the marked walls and furniture being 'creepy'.

I must have shuddered. Caroline got up. She said, 'Look here, I'm sorry to have told you all this. It really isn't your trouble.'

I said, 'Oh, but it is, in a way.'

'It is?'

'Well, since I've more or less become Rod's doctor.'

She gave her rueful smile. 'Yes, well, but you haven't really, have you? It's just how you said the other day: Rod isn't paying you to come here. You can dress it up how you like, I know you're treating him now more or less as a favour. It's awfully kind of you, but you mustn't let us drag you into any more of our problems. Do you remember what I told you about this house, when I showed you round it? It's greedy. It gobbles up all our time and energy. It'll gobble up yours, if you let it.'

I didn't answer for a second. I'd had a vision, not of Hundreds Hall, but of my own home, with its neat, plain, undemanding, utterly lifeless rooms. I would be returning to them later, to a bachelor's supper of cold meat and boiled potatoes and half a bottle of flat beer.

I said firmly, 'I'm happy to help you, Caroline. Truly I am.'

'You mean it?'

'Yes. I don't know what's going on here, any more than you do. But I'd like to help you figure it out. I'll take my chances with the hungry house, don't worry about that. I'm a pretty indigestible fellow, you know.'

She smiled properly then, and briefly closed her eyes again. 'Thank you,' she said.

After that, we didn't linger. We began to be afraid of Rod's returning and discovering us there. So we made our way quietly back to the library, for Caroline to tidy the room and close the shutter. Then, trying to shake off our anxieties, we went to the little parlour to join her mother.

. . .

B ut I stayed puzzling over Roderick's condition for the next few days; and it must have been on an afternoon early in the following week that the whole thing at last came together—or, depending on how one looks at it, fell apart. I was driving back through Lidcote at about five o'clock, and was surprised to see Rod himself, on the High Street. His presence there would once have been unremarkable, for in the old days he often used to come in on farming business. But, as Caroline had said, he rarely left Hundreds now, and though he still looked very much the young country squire, in an overcoat and tweed cap and with the strap of a leather satchel across his breast, there was something unmistakably burdened and ill at ease about him—about the way he walked, with his collar turned up, and his shoulders hunched, as if against more than the chill November breezes. When I drew up across the street from him to wind down my window and call his name, he turned to me with a startled expression; and just for a second—I could have sworn it—he looked like a frightened, hunted man.

He came slowly over to the car, and I asked him what had brought him into the village. He told me he had been to see Maurice Babb, the big local builder. The county council had recently bought up the last free parcel of Ayres farmland; they planned to build a new housing estate on it, with Babb as the contractor. He and Rod had just been running through the final agreement.

'He makes me come in to his office like a tradesman,' Rod said bitterly. 'Imagine if a man like that had suggested such a thing to my father! He knows I'll do it, of course. He knows I've no choice.'

He drew close the lapels of his overcoat, and again looked burdened and miserable. I couldn't offer him many words of comfort over the sale of the land. In fact, I was pleased to hear about the new houses, which were badly needed in the area. But, thinking of his leg, I said, 'You didn't walk in?'

'No, no,' he answered. 'Barrett managed to whistle me up some fuel, so I drove.'

He gestured with his chin along the High Street, and I caught sight of the Ayres's distinctive car, a shabby old black and ivory Rolls-Royce, parked a little way along it. He said, 'I thought she might give up the ghost on the way here. That would have been just about the last straw. But she made it all right.'

He sounded more like his old self now. I said, 'Well, let's hope she gets you home again! You don't have to hurry back, I take it? Come in with me for a while, and warm yourself up.'

'Oh, I can't,' he said at once.

'Why not?'

His gaze slid away from mine. 'I oughtn't to keep you from your work.'

'Nonsense! I've almost an hour before evening surgery, and this is always a dead time for me. I've hardly seen you lately. Come on.'

He was obviously reluctant, but I kept up a light but determined pressure and he finally agreed to come in with me 'just for five minutes'. I parked the car, and met him at the door to my house. Since none of the upstairs fires were lit, I took him into my dispensary; I brought a chair from behind the counter and set it with another, close to the room's ancient Tortoise stove, which had just enough live embers in it to be kindled into a blaze. I spent a few minutes seeing to that, and by the time I had straightened, Rod had taken off his cap and put down his satchel and was going slowly around the room. He was looking at the shelves, where I kept some of the quaint old jars and instruments that had once belonged to Dr Gill.

His mood, I was glad to see, seemed to have lifted slightly. He said, 'Here's that beastly leech-jar that used to give me such nightmares when I was a kid. Probably old Dr Gill never even kept any leeches in it, did he?'

I said, 'I'm afraid he probably did. He was just the sort of man to have faith in leeches. Leeches, and liquorice, and cod-liver oil. Take your coat off, won't you? I won't be a tick.'

As I spoke I went through to my consulting-room next door, to open a drawer in my desk and bring out a bottle and two glasses.

'Now, I don't want you to think,' I said, showing the bottle as I returned, 'that it's my custom to drink before six. But you look like you need cheering up, and it's only some old brown sherry. I keep it on hand for pregnant women. They either want to celebrate, you see—or they need something to get them over the shock.'

He smiled, but the smile fell quickly from his face.

'I've just been given a drink by Babb. No old brown sherry for him, I assure you! He said we ought to toast the completion of the contract; that if we didn't, it would bring bad luck. I nearly said that as far as I was concerned, I'd had my bad luck; selling the land was part of it. As for the money it's brought in—would you believe me if I told you that's practically spent already?'

But he took the glass I gave him, and touched it to mine. To my surprise, the liquor trembled in his hand and, perhaps to hide the tremor, he took one swift sip, then began to roll the stem of the glass back and forth between his fingers. As we moved to the chairs I looked at him more closely. I saw the tense yet curiously lifeless way in which he lowered himself into his seat. He might have had odd little weights inside him, rolling unpredictably about.

I said lightly, 'You look done in, Rod.'

He lifted his hand to wipe his lip. His wrist was still bandaged, the crepe now soiled and frayed at the palm. 'It must be this business with the land,' he said.

'You shouldn't take it so personally. There are probably a hundred landowners in England in exactly your position, all doing just what you've done today.'

'There are probably a thousand,' he answered, but without much force. 'All the fellows I used to know at school, and all the chaps I used to fly with: every time I hear from one of them, they're telling the same story. Most of them have run through their settlements already. Some are having to take jobs. Their parents are living on their nerves . . . I opened a newspaper this morning: a bishop was sounding off about "the shame of the German". Why doesn't anyone write a piece on "the shame of the Englishman"?—the ordinary hard-working

Englishman, who since the war has had to watch his property and income vanishing like so much smoke? Meanwhile, grubby little businessmen like Babb are doing all right, and men without land, without family, without the eyes of the county on them—men like that bloody Baker-Hyde—'

His voice had tightened, and he didn't finish. He put back his head and swallowed the rest of his sherry, then started to twirl the empty glass between his fingers, even more restlessly than before. His gaze had turned inwards suddenly, he seemed alarmingly out of reach. He made some movement, and again I had that sense that there were unmoored weights inside him, making him jerky and off-balance.

I was dismayed, too, by his reference to Peter Baker-Hyde. It gave me a glimpse, I thought, of what might have been troubling him all this time. It was as though he'd made a sort of fetish of the man, with his handsome wife and his money, and his good war record. I leaned towards him.

'Listen, Rod. You mustn't go on like this. This Baker-Hyde fixation, or whatever it is: let it go, can't you? Concentrate on what you've got, rather than what you think you haven't. Plenty men would envy you, you know.'

He looked at me with a queer expression. 'Envy me?'

'Yes! Look at that house you're living in, for one thing. I know it's tough work keeping it going, but for goodness' sake! Can't you see that by holding on to this sort of resentment you're hardly making life easier for your mother and sister? I don't know what's got into you lately. If there's something on your mind—'

'God!' he said, flaring up. 'If you like the damn house so much, why don't you try running it! I'd like to see you. You've no idea! Don't you know that if I were to stop, even for a moment—' He swallowed, his Adam's apple jerking painfully in his slender throat.

'Stop what?' I said.

'Stop holding everything back. Keeping it at bay. Don't you know that in every second of every day the whole damn thing's in danger of crashing down, and taking me, and Caroline, and Mother down with it? God, you haven't a clue, none of you! It's killing me!'

He put a hand on the back of his chair and made a move as if to push himself up; but then he seemed to change his mind and abruptly sat down again. Now he was definitely trembling—I didn't know if it was with upset or with anger, but I looked away for a minute or two, wanting to give him time to pull himself together. The stove wasn't drawing as it should: I moved forward to fiddle with the draught. But as I did it, I grew aware that Rod was fidgeting; soon he was fidgeting so badly there was something unnatural about it. 'Hell!' I heard him say, in a soft, desperate voice. I looked properly at him and saw that he was pale and sweating and shaking like a man in a fever.

Alarmed, I got up. I thought for a moment that I must have been right about the epilepsy: that he was going into a seizure, right there in front of me.

But he put a hand across his face. 'Don't look at me!' he said.

'What?'

'Don't look at me! Stand over there.'

Then I realised that he was not ill, but in the grip of a dreadful panic, and his embarrassment at my seeing him like this was making him worse. So I turned my back on him and went over to the window, and stood gazing out through the dusty net curtain. I remember the bitter, ticklish scent of it, even now. I said, 'Rod—'

'Don't watch me!'

'I'm not watching. I'm looking out, at the High Street.' I could hear his rapid, laboured breathing, the catch of tears in his throat. I made my voice very level. I said, 'I can see my car. I'm afraid she wants washing and polishing, rather badly. I can see yours, further down, looking even worse . . . There's Mrs Walker and her little boy. There's Enid, from the Desmonds'. She's in a temper by the look of it; she's put her hat on crooked. There's Mr Crouch, come out to his step to shake a cloth . . . May I look at you now?'

'No! Stay like that. Keep talking.'

'Keep talking, all right. Funny how hard it is to keep talking, when someone asks you to start and not stop. And I'm more used, of course, to listening. Have you ever thought of that, Rod? About how much listening one has to do, in this job of mine? I often think that we family doctors are like priests. People tell us their secrets, because they know we won't judge them. They know we're used to looking at human beings as it were without their skins . . . Some doctors don't like it. I've known one or two who've seen so much weakness they've developed a sort of contempt for mankind. I've known doctors—many doctors, more than you'd guess—who've taken to drink. Others of us, though, it humbles. We see what a punishing business it is, simply being alive. Just being alive, not to mention having wars and whatnot thrown at one, and estates and farms to run . . . Most people, you know, seem to muddle through all right in the end . . .'

I slowly turned back to him. He met my gaze with a wretched expression, but didn't protest. He was holding himself impossibly tensely, breathing through his nose with his mouth shut tight. His face was bloodless. Even the taut, smooth skin of his scars had lost its colour. There was only the fading yellow-green bruise at his eye; and his cheeks were wet, with sweat and perhaps with tears. But he was over the worst of it, and growing calmer as I watched. I went across to him, and got out a packet of cigarettes, and he took one gratefully, though he had to hold it to his mouth with both his hands while I put the flame to it.

As he blew out the first uneven plume of smoke, I said quietly: 'What's going on, Rod?'

He wiped his face, and lowered his head. 'Nothing's going on. I'm all right now.'

'All right? Look at you!'

'It's the strain of—of keeping on top of it. It wants me to buckle, that's all. I shan't give in to it. It knows that, you see, and keeps trying harder.'

He spoke breathlessly still, and miserably, but in a measured kind of way, and the combination of anguish and reason in his words and manner was unnerving. I went back to my chair, and when I had sat I said quietly again, 'What's going on? I know something is. Won't you tell me?'

He raised his eyes to me, without lifting his head. 'I want to,' he said, with wretched simplicity. 'But it'll be better for your sake if I don't.'

'Why is that?'

'It might . . . infect you.'

'Infect me! I treat infections every day, don't forget.'

'Not like this.'

'Why, what is this like?'

He dropped his gaze. 'It's a . . . filthy thing.'

He spoke with a look and a gesture of disgust; and at that particular combination of words—'infection', and 'filthy'—an idea began to break upon me about what his trouble might be. I was so surprised and dismayed, and yet so relieved that his predicament should turn out to be such a mundane one, that I almost smiled. I said, 'Is it that, Rod? For God's sake, why didn't you come to me sooner!'

He looked at me, not understanding; and when I spoke more plainly, so that it was clear what I meant, he broke into a ghastly sounding laugh.

'Dear God,' he said, wiping his face. 'If it were as simple a thing as that! As for telling you my *symptoms*—' His expression grew bleak. 'You won't believe me if I do.'

I said urgently, 'Try me, will you?'

'I told you, I want to!'

'Well, when did they first appear, these symptoms of yours?'

'When? When do you think? The night of that wretched party.'

I had sensed this all along. 'You had a headache, your mother said. Was that the start?'

'The headache was nothing. I only said *that* to hide the other thing, the real thing.'

I could see him struggling. I said, '*Tell me*, Rod.'

He put a hand to his mouth, to push his lip between his teeth. 'If it should get out—'

I misunderstood. 'I give you my word, I'll tell no one.'

That alarmed him. 'No, you mustn't do that! You mustn't tell my mother or my sister!'

'Not if you don't want me to.'

'You said you were a sort of priest, remember? A priest keeps se-crets, doesn't he? You must promise me!'

'I promise, Rod.'

'You mean it?'

'Of course.'

He looked away from me, and worked at his lip again, and was silent for so long I thought he'd retreated into himself and I had lost him. But then he drew unsteadily on his cigarette, and gestured with his glass.

'All right. God knows, it'll be a relief to share it with someone at last. But you must give me another drink first. I can't face it sober.'

I poured him out a large measure—his hands were still shaking too hard for him to be able to pour it for himself—and he swallowed it down in one gulp, then asked for another. And when he had drunk that he began, slowly and haltingly, to tell me exactly what had happened to him on the night the little Baker-Hyde girl was hurt.

He had, as I knew, been dubious about the party from the start. He hadn't liked the sound of the Baker-Hydes, he said; he was uncom-fortable with the idea of playing 'master of the house', and he felt a fool about putting on evening clothes, which he hadn't worn in about three years. But he'd gone along with it all for Caroline's sake, and to please his mother. On the evening in question he really had been delayed at the farm, though he knew that everyone would suppose he'd 'simply been dawdling'. He'd been kept there by a piece of failing machinery, for just as Makins had been predicting for weeks, the Hundreds pump had looked like it was finally about to blow, and leaving the farm to deal with the problem without help was out of the question. Rod knew as much about things like that as any mechanic, thanks to his time in the RAF; he and Makins's son patched up the pump and kept it working, but it took until well past eight o'clock. By the time he had crossed the park and was hurriedly letting himself back into the Hall by the garden door, the Baker-Hydes and Mr Morley were already arriving at the front. He was still in his farm clothes, and filthy with dust and grease. He didn't think he had time enough to go upstairs and have a proper wash in the family bathroom; he thought he'd make do with hot water in the bowl of his washing-stand. He rang for Betty, but she was busy with the guests in the saloon. He waited, then rang again; then finally went down to the kitchen to fetch the water himself.

Now, he said, came the first queer thing. His evening clothes were on his bed, laid out and waiting to be put on. Like lots of ex-servicemen he was a neat and orderly dresser, and he had brushed the garments down himself earlier that day, then set them ready. When he had returned from the kitchen and hastily washed, he put on his trousers and his shirt, then looked for his collar—and couldn't find it. He lifted the jacket and looked beneath it. He looked under the bed—looked everywhere, in every likely and unlikely place—the wretched collar was nowhere to be found. This was all the more maddening because the collar in question was, of course, an evening one, meant to go with the shirt he was wearing. It was one of the few unpatched or unturned collars he had left, so he couldn't simply go to the drawer and bring out another.

'How idiotic it sounds, doesn't it?' he said to me, miserably. 'I knew it was idiotic, even at the time. I didn't want to go to the bloody party in the first place, but there I was—the host, supposedly; the master of Hundreds!—keeping everyone waiting, chasing around the room like a twit, because I only owned one decent stand-up collar!'

It was at this point that Betty arrived, sent by Mrs Ayres to find out what was keeping him. He told her what the matter was, and asked if she had moved the collar herself; she said she hadn't seen it since that morning, when she had brought it up to his room with the rest of his laundry. He said, 'Well, for God's sake help me look, will you?' and she spent a minute searching with him—looking in all the places he'd already looked, and finding nothing—until at last he grew so frustrated with the whole business he told her 'rather sharply, I'm afraid' to let things alone and go back to his mother. When she had gone, he gave the search up. He went to his drawer, to do what he could to improvise an evening collar out of one of his daytime ones. Had he known that the Baker-Hydes had arrived so informally dressed, he might have been less anxious. As it was, all he could picture was the disappointed face he thought his mother would turn on him if he stepped into the saloon 'done up like a sloppy bloody schoolboy'.

Then another much odder thing happened. As he was going crossly through the drawers he heard, in the empty room behind his back, a sound. It was a *splash*, soft but quite unmistakable, so he guessed at once that something on his washing-stand must somehow have toppled into the bowl. He turned to look—and couldn't believe his eyes. The thing that had found its way into the water was his missing collar.

Automatically he darted across to fish it out; then he stood with the collar in his hand, trying to figure out how such a thing could possibly have happened. The collar had not been on the washing-stand, he was positive of that. There was no nearby surface it could have slipped from—and no reason for it, anyway, to slip. There was nothing above the stand that might have held it and then let it drop—no dangling light, no sort of hook—even supposing that such a thing as a stiff white collar could have found its way up, unnoticed, to a light or a hook in the first place. All there was, he said, was 'the faintest sort of smudge' on the lattice-work plaster ceiling above his head.

At this point he was baffled, but not unnerved. The collar was dripping soapy water, but a wet collar seemed to him to be better than no collar at all, and he dried it off as best he could, then stood at his dressing-table mirror to fix it to his shirt and to tie his neck-tie. After that he had only to fasten his cuffs, and grease and comb his hair, and he would be ready. He opened up the little ivory tub in which he kept his dress cuff-links; and found it empty.

This, he said, was so absurd and so exasperating that he laughed. He had not seen the links that day with his own eyes, but just that morning he had accidentally knocked against the tub with his fingers,

and he remembered very clearly the rattle of the metal inside. He had
not touched the tub since then. He couldn't believe that Betty or Mrs
Bazeley had removed the links, or that Caroline or his mother could
have come and taken them away. Why would they have? He shook his
head, and glanced around, and addressed himself to the room—to the
'fates', or 'spirits', or whatever it was that seemed to be playing games
with him tonight. 'You don't want me to go to the party?' he said.
'Well, how about this: I don't want to go, either. But want's not in it,
I'm afraid. Just give me back my f—g cuff-links, will you?'

He closed the ivory tub and returned it to its place beside his comb
and brushes; and in the very second of drawing back his hand he saw,
through the dressing-table mirror, and from the corner of his eye, something small and dark dropping down in the room behind him—like a
spider dropping from the ceiling. It was followed almost immediately
by the striking of metal against china: a crash so relatively violent in
that still room that it 'frightened the life out of him'. He turned and,
with a rising feeling of unreality, walked slowly over to the washing-
stand. There at the bottom of the bowl were his cuff-links. The stand
itself was splashed, the cloudy water in the bowl still heaving and slopping about. He put back his head and looked up. Again, the ceiling was
seamless and quite unmarked—except that the 'smudge' he had noticed
before was now considerably darker.

This was the moment, he said, when he realised that something really uncanny was at work in the room. He couldn't doubt his own
senses: he had seen the cuff-links drop, and had heard the tremendous
splash and rattle of them in the bowl. But where on earth could they
have dropped from? He drew over his armchair, and stood precariously
on it to examine the ceiling at closer range. Apart from that queer dark
smudge, there was nothing. It was just as if the links had materialised
into, or out of, thin air. He got heavily down off the chair—his leg
beginning to hurt him now—and peered again into the bowl of his
washing-stand. A whitish scum was already closing over the surface of
the water, but all he had to do was put back his sleeve and dip in his
hand to fish the cuff-links out. But he couldn't bring himself to do it.

He didn't know what the hell to do. He thought again of the brightly lit saloon—his mother and sister waiting, the Desmonds, the Rossiters, the Baker-Hydes—even me, and Betty—all of us waiting, waiting for him, with glasses of sherry in our hands; and he began to sweat. He met his own gaze in his circular shaving-glass and seemed to see the beads of perspiration rising 'like worms' from the pores of his skin.

Now, however, came the most grotesque thing of all. He was still gazing at his own sweating face when, to his disbelief and horror, the shaving-glass gave a sort of shudder. The glass was an old Victorian one, a bevelled circular mirror in a pivoted brass frame, on a porcelain base. It was, as I knew myself, pretty heavy: not a thing that would slip if nudged or shaken by footsteps on the floor around it. Rod stood perfectly still, in that still room, and watched as the shaving-glass shuddered again, then rocked, then began to *inch its way across the washing-stand towards him*. It was just, he said, as if the glass were walking—or, rather, as if it were in that moment discovering its own *ability* to walk. It moved with a jerky, halting gait, the unglazed underside of its porcelain base making a frightful, grating sound on the polished marble surface.

'It was the most sickening thing I ever saw,' said Rod, describing it to me in a shaking voice, and wiping away the sweat which had started out again on his lip and forehead at the memory. 'It was all the more sickening, somehow, for the glass being such an ordinary sort of object. If—I don't know, but if some *beast* had suddenly appeared in the room, some spook or apparition, I think I would have borne the shock of it better. But *this*—it was hateful, it was *wrong*. It made one feel as though everything around one, the ordinary stuff of one's ordinary life, might all at any moment start up like this and—overwhelm one. That was bad enough. But what happened next—'

What happened next was even worse. All this time Rod had been watching the glass make its shuddering way towards him, sick with horror at what, to me, he kept calling the *wrongness* of the thing. Part of this wrongness was his sense that the glass was acting somehow impersonally. It had, God knew how, become animate; but he had the feeling that what was animating it was blind, thoughtless motion. He felt that if he were to put his hand flat in the glass's path the porcelain base would find a creeping, dogged way over his fingers. Naturally, he did not put his hand there. If anything, he shrank back. But he could see that the glass was now approaching the edge of the marble stand, and he felt a horrible fascination in watching it teeter and fall. So he kept his place, a yard or so away from it. The glass crept onwards, until an inch and then a second inch of its base was projecting over the marble edge. He seemed to see the thing groping for another surface; he saw the mirror tilt as, unbalanced, the base rocked forward. He actually started to put out his hand, in an automatic impulse to keep it from tumbling. But as he did it, the glass suddenly seemed to 'gather itself for a spring'—and the next moment it had launched itself at his head. He twisted away, and caught a stinging blow behind his ear. He heard the shattering of the mirror and the porcelain base as the glass struck the floor behind him. He turned, and saw the pieces lying harmlessly on the carpet, as if just knocked there by a clumsy hand.

It was at exactly this moment that Betty returned. She tapped at the door and, tense and startled, Rod cried out. Confused by the sound of his voice, she timidly pushed the door open and saw him gazing, as if transfixed by it, at the broken object on the floor. Not unnaturally, she moved forward, meaning to tidy up the pieces. Then she caught sight of his expression. What he said to her, he couldn't afterwards recall, but he must have spoken pretty wildly, for she left him at once and went hastily back to the saloon—that was when I saw her, going in a flustered way to whisper in Mrs Ayres's ear. Mrs Ayres went straight back with her to Roderick, and realised immediately that something was terribly wrong. He was sweating worse than ever and shaking like a man in a fever. He must have looked, I suppose, pretty much as I'd just seen him when he told me this story. His own first impulse on seeing his mother was, like a child, to clutch at her hand; but he'd also gathered his wits enough, he said, to know that he mustn't in any way involve her in what was going on. He had seen the shaving-glass make that spring at his head: it hadn't been animated by a senseless impulse,

then—he had felt it driven at him by something extraordinarily purposeful and vicious. He didn't want his mother exposed to that. He
gave her a confused, fragmented account of having overtaxed himself
at the farm, and told her his head was aching so badly it felt like it was
splitting in two. He was so obviously ill and upset that she wanted to
send for me, but he wouldn't let her do it; he wanted only to get her
out of that room as quickly as he possibly could. The ten or so minutes
she spent with him were, he said, some of the most dreadful of his life.
The strain of trying to conceal what he had just been through, combined with his fright at the prospect of being left alone, perhaps to go
through it all again, must have made him seem like a madman. Once
he almost broke down in tears—and then, he said, it was only the look
of dismay and anxiety on his mother's face that gave him the strength
to pull himself together. When she and Betty left him, he sat on his bed
in the corner of the room with his back to the wall and his knees drawn
up. His injured leg was throbbing, but he didn't mind it—he was almost
glad of the pain, for keeping him alert. Because what he had to do now,
he said, was *watch*. He had to watch every object, every corner and
shadow in the room, had to keep his gaze moving restlessly from one
surface to another. For he knew that the malevolent thing that had tried
to hurt him before was still in there with him, waiting.

'That was the worst thing about it,' he said. 'I knew it hated me,
really hated me, beyond any sort of logic or reason. I knew it wished
me harm. It wasn't even like being on an op and picking up an enemy
fighter: seeing it coming at you, a machine with a man in it doing his
level best to blast you out of the sky. That was *clean* in comparison.
There was a logic, a fairness to it. This was mean and spiteful and
wrong. I couldn't have held a gun to it. I couldn't have raised a knife
or a poker to it; the knife or the poker might have come to life in my
hand! I felt as though the very blankets I was sitting on might rise up
and throttle me!'

He had kept it up for what might have been thirty minutes—'but
what might as well have been a thousand'—trembling and straining
under the frightful effort of warding the malevolence off; and at last it

had grown too much for him, and his nerve had snapped. He heard himself cry out for the thing to leave him, to leave him alone, for God's sake!—and the sound of his own voice appalled him; perhaps it broke some sort of spell. He felt at once that something had shifted—that the dreadful thing had passed away. He looked at the objects around him, and, 'I can't explain it. I don't know how I knew it. But I knew that they were ordinary and lifeless again.' Utterly shattered, he drank 'a tumblerful' of brandy, got under the covers of his bed, and curled up like a baby. His room, as it always did, had that muted feel to it, as if it were slightly insulated from the rest of the house. If presently there were sounds beyond his door, footsteps and anxious murmurs, he either didn't hear them or was too exhausted to consider what they might mean. He fell into a fretful sleep, and was woken two hours later, by Caroline. She had come to see how he was, and to tell him what had happened with Gyp and Gillian. He listened to her story with mounting horror—realising that the little girl must have been bitten at just about the time he had been calling out at that vicious presence in his room to leave him alone.

He looked at me as he said this, his sore-looking eyes seeming to burn in his scarred face. He said, 'You understand? It was all my fault! I'd willed that thing away from me, through sheer bloody gutlessness; and it had gone there, to hurt someone else. That poor kid! If I had known, I'd have gone through anything—anything at all—' He wiped his mouth, then made an effort and went on more levelly. 'I haven't let my guard slip again like that, I can tell you. Now when it comes, I'm ready. I've been keeping watch for it. Most days are all right. Most days it doesn't come at all. But it likes to surprise me, to catch me out. It's just like a sly, spiteful child. It sets traps for me. It opened the door of my room that time, for me to walk into and bloody my nose. It moves my papers; it puts things in my path, so that I'll stumble over them and break my neck! I don't mind about that. It can do what it wants to me. For so long as I can keep it, you see, in my room, I can contain the infection. That's the vital thing now, don't you agree? To keep the source of the infection away, from my sister and my mother?'

SIX

There have been many times in my medical career when, on examining a patient or on seeing the result of some test or other, it has gradually but ineluctably broken upon me that the case before me is a desperate one. I can think, for example, of a young married woman, just pregnant, who came to see me with a summer cough: I remember very vividly setting the stethoscope to her breast and hearing the first faint but devastating indications of tuberculosis. I can recall a handsome, talented boy brought to me with 'growing pains'—actually, the onset of a muscle-wasting illness which, within five years, was to take his life. The thickening tumour, the spreading cancer, the clouding eye: they are part of a family doctor's case-load alongside the rashes and the sprains, but I have never got used to them, never caught my first certain glimpse of them without the heaviest feeling of impotence and dismay.

Something like that dismay began to creep upon me as I sat listening to Rod tell his extraordinary story. How long it took him, I'm not sure, for he spoke with a certain brokenness, a hesitation and reluctance, a shrinking from the ghastliness of the details of the tale. I kept silent for the most part, and when he had finished we sat together in that quiet room, and I glanced about me at the safe, familiar, fathomable world— the stove, the counter, the instruments and jars, old Gill's hand on their faded labels, *Mist. Scillae, Pot. Iod.*—and seemed to see it all grown slightly strange to me, all knocked slightly askew.

Rod was watching me. He wiped his face, then made a ball of his handkerchief and worked it with his fingers and said, 'You wanted to know. I warned you what a filthy thing it was.'

I cleared my throat. 'I'm very glad you told me.'

'You are?'

'Of course. I only wish you'd done it sooner. It breaks my heart to think of you having gone through this alone, Rod.'

'I had to, you see. For the sake of the family.'

'Yes, I see that.'

'And you don't judge me too badly, over the girl? I swear to God, if I had known—'

'No, no. No one could blame you for that. There's just one thing I'd like to do now. I'd like to examine you, if I may.'

'Examine me? Why?'

'I think you're pretty tired, aren't you?'

'Tired? God, I'm out on my feet! I hardly dare close my eyes at night. I'm frightened this *thing* will return if I do.'

I had risen to fetch my bag, and, as if in obedience to a signal, he began to draw off his sweater and shirt. He stood on the hearth-rug in his vest and trousers, with that dirty bandage on his wrist, rubbing his arms against the chill and looking shockingly thin and vulnerable and young; and I made a brief, basic examination, listening at his chest, reading his blood-pressure, and so on. But I did it, to be honest, mainly to buy myself a little time, for I could see—anyone could have seen— what the real nature of his trouble was. What he had told me, in fact, had pretty well shaken me to the core, and I needed to think about how to proceed with him.

As I'd guessed, there was nothing obviously wrong with him beyond the fact that he was underfed and overtired; and that was true of half my neighbours. I took my time putting my instruments away, still thinking. He stood buttoning up his shirt.

'Well?'

'You said it yourself, Rod: you're exhausted. And exhaustion—well, it does odd things to us, plays odd tricks.'

He frowned. 'Tricks?'

'Listen,' I said. 'I can't pretend to you that what you've told me has made me anything but extremely alarmed. I don't want to mince words with you. I think your problem is a mental one. I think— Listen to me, Rod.' He'd begun to turn away, in disappointment and anger. 'I think that what you've been experiencing can best be described as a sort of nerve-storm. They're more common than you might think, in certain over-stressed people. And let's face it, you've been under an enormous pressure ever since you came out of the Air Force. I think that that pressure, combined with war-shock—'

'War-shock!' he said scornfully.

'Delayed war-shock. That's more common than you would think, too.'

He shook his head, saying firmly, 'I know what I know. I know what I saw.'

'You know what you *think* you saw. What your tired and over-stretched nerves persuaded you to see.'

'It wasn't like that! Don't you understand? God, I wish I'd said nothing. You asked me to tell you. I didn't want to, but you made me. Now you throw it back at me like this, making me out to be some sort of loony!'

'If you could just get a good night's sleep.'

'I told you: the thing will come back if I do.'

'No, Rod. I promise you, it will only return if you *don't*, because it's a delusion—'

'A *delusion*? That's what you think?'

'—a delusion which is feeding on your own tiredness. I think you should get away from the Hall for a while. Right away, on some sort of holiday.'

He was pulling on his sweater, and when his face emerged from the neck of it he looked at me in disbelief. 'Go away? Haven't you been listening to a single thing I've said? If I were to leave, who knows what would happen!' He hastily smoothed down his hair and started putting on his overcoat. He'd caught sight of the clock. 'I've been away too long already. That's your fault, too. I must get back.'

'At least let me give you some Luminal.'

'Dope?' he said. 'You think that'll help me?' And then, with an edge to his voice, seeing me go to a shelf and bring down a tub of tablets: 'No. I mean it. They pumped me full of those after my smash. I don't want them. Don't give them to me, I'll throw the damn things away.'

'You might change your mind.'

'I won't.'

I came back around the counter empty-handed. 'Rod, please. Listen to me. If I can't persuade you to leave the house, well, there's a man I know, a good physician. He has a clinic, in Birmingham, for cases like yours. Let me bring him in to talk to you; to listen to you. That's all he'll want to do: just listen to you while you talk to him as you spoke, just now, to me.'

His face had set. 'A mental doctor, you mean. A psychiatrist, or psychologist, or whatever the hell you call them. That's not my trouble. The trouble isn't mine at all. The trouble's at Hundreds. Can't you see? I don't need a doctor so much as a,' he groped for a word, 'a *vicar* or something. If you'd felt what I had—'

I said on impulse, 'Let me come with you, then! Let me spend some time in your room, and see if this thing appears!'

He hesitated, thinking it over; and the sight of him doing that, treating the idea as if it were possible, sensible, *reasonable*, was almost more disturbing than anything else. But then he shook his head and spoke coldly again.

'No. I can't risk it. I won't tempt it. It wouldn't like that.' He put on his cap. 'I have to go. I'm sorry I told you any of this. I should have known you wouldn't understand.'

'Please listen to me, Rod.' The thought of losing him, now, was dreadful. 'I can't let you go in this state of mind! Have you forgotten how you were just now? That dreadful panic? Suppose that comes over you again?'

He said, 'It won't. You caught me off-guard, that's all. I shouldn't have come here in the first place. I'm needed at home.'

'At least talk to your mother, then. Or let me talk to her for you.'

'No,' he said sharply. He had moved to the door but now turned back to me, and, as once before, I was disconcerted to see real anger in his eyes. 'She mustn't know about any of this. Nor my sister. You're not to tell them. You said you wouldn't. You gave me your word, and I trusted you. You're not to talk to that doctor friend of yours, either. You say I'm going crazy. All right, go ahead and believe that, if it makes you feel better; if you're too much of a coward to face the truth. But at least have the decency to let me go crazy all by myself.'

His tone was hard and level, and absurdly rational-sounding. He put the strap of his satchel over his shoulder and drew together the lapels of his coat, and only the paleness of his face and the slight redness of his eyes hinted at the fantastic delusion that had him in its grip; apart from that he looked, as he'd looked before, like a youthful country squire. I knew there was no keeping him now. He had moved back to the dispensary door, but it was clear, from sounds beyond it, that the first of my evening patients were arriving, so he gestured impatiently to my consulting-room and I took him in there, to let him out into the garden. But I did it with a very heavy heart, and a dreadful sense of frustration; and as soon as the door was closed I went back to the dispensary window and stood at the dusty net curtain to watch him reappear from around the side of the house and make his rapid, limping way along the High Street to his car.

What was I to do? It was clear to me—horribly clear—that over the past few weeks Rod had been the victim of some very powerful hallucinations. That, in a sense, was hardly to be wondered at, given the dreadful mix of burdens he'd recently had to bear. Evidently the sense of threat and strain had overspilled in his mind, to the extent that even 'ordinary things', as he'd repeatedly put it, seemed to be rising up against him. That the delusion had first struck on the night he was meant to host a party for his more successful neighbour was perhaps no surprise; and I thought it sadly significant, too, that the worst of his experience had centred on a *mirror*—which, before it had started on its 'walk', had been reflecting his scarred face, and had ended up shattered. All this, as I say, was shocking enough, but could be explained away as the product of stress and nerve-strain. More upsetting and worrying, to my mind, was the fact that he was still so attached to the delusion he had produced this logical-seeming fear that his mother and sister would be 'infected' by whatever diabolical thing had supposedly invaded his room, unless he was there to ward it off.

I spent the next few hours turning his condition over and over in my mind. Even as I sat with my other patients, a part of me seemed still to be with Rod, listening in horror and dismay as he told his dreadful story. I don't think there has ever been a time in my professional life when I have felt at such a loss as to how to proceed. No doubt my relationship with the family was interfering with my judgement. Probably I should have handed the case over, at once, to another man. But then, it what sense *was* it a case? Rod had not come to me that day for a medical opinion. He had, as he himself had pointed out, been unwilling to confide in me at all. And there was certainly no question of me or any other physician being paid for our assistance or advice. I didn't, at this point, suspect him of being a danger to himself or to others. I thought it much more likely that his delusion would slowly gather strength until it had finally consumed him: that he would wear himself, in other words, into a state of complete mental breakdown.

My biggest dilemma was over what, if anything, to say to Mrs Ayres and Caroline. I had given Rod my word that I would say nothing; and while I had been only half serious in comparing myself to a priest, no doctor takes a promise of secrecy lightly. I passed a terribly fretful evening, deciding now one thing and now another . . . Finally, at almost ten, I ran over to the Grahams' house, to talk the matter through with them. I'd been spending less time with them lately, and Graham was surprised to see me. Anne, he said, was upstairs—one of their children was slightly unwell—but he took me into their sitting-room, and heard the story through.

He was as shocked by it as I had been.

'How on earth did things get so bad? Were there no warnings?'

I said, 'I knew something wasn't right; but not like this.'

'What do you mean to do next?'

'That's what I'm trying to work out. I don't even have a firm diagnosis.'

He thought it over. 'You've considered epilepsy, I suppose?'

'It was my very first idea. I still think it might explain some of it. The aura, producing queer sensations—auditory, visual, and so on. The seizure itself, the weariness after; it all fits, to a degree. But I can't believe it's the whole story.'

He said, 'How about myxœdema?'

'I thought of that, too. But that's pretty hard to miss, isn't it? And there are no indications.'

'Could something be interfering with the brain function? A tumour, for example?'

'Christ, I hope not! It's possible, of course. But again, there are no other signs . . . No, my hunch is it's purely nervous.'

'That's just as bad, in its way.'

I said, 'I know. And his mother and sister have no idea. Do you think I should tell them? That's what's really troubling me.'

He shook his head, blowing out his cheeks. 'You know them better than I do, now. Roderick certainly won't thank you for it. On the other hand, it might push him to some sort of crisis.'

'Or put him completely out of reach.'

'That's certainly a risk. Why not take a day or two to think it over?'

'And meanwhile,' I said gloomily, 'things at Hundreds inch further into chaos.'

'Well that, at least,' he said, 'isn't your problem.'

His tone was rather detached: I could recall it from other conversations of ours about the Ayreses, but it slightly jarred with me now. I finished my drink and went slowly home, grateful to him for having listened, relieved to have shared the details of the case, but no wiser as to how to proceed. And it was only as I stepped into my dark dispensary and saw the two chairs still standing at the stove, and seemed to hear again Rod's halting, desperate voice, that the full force of his story came back to me; and I realised it was my plain duty to the family to give them at least some inkling of his condition, as soon as I could.

But it was a pretty dismal journey I made out to the house the following day. It seemed that all my business with the Ayreses just now lay either in warning them of something or in carrying out some dreary undertaking on their behalf. With the return of daylight, too, there had come a slight failing in my resolve. I thought again of the promise I'd made, and I drove, if such a thing is possible, in a shrinking, reluctant sort of way, hoping more than anything not to encounter Rod himself, either there in the park or in the house. It was only a few days since my last visit, and neither Mrs Ayres nor Caroline was expecting me; I found them both in the little parlour, but could see at once that, by turning up out of the blue like this, I had rather thrown them.

'Why, Doctor, you keep us on our toes!' Mrs Ayres said, raising a ringless hand to her face. 'I shouldn't have dressed so weekdayishly if I had known you were coming. And have we anything in the kitchen, Caroline, to offer the doctor with his tea? I believe we've bread, and margarine. You had better ring for Betty.'

I hadn't wanted to telephone ahead for fear of alerting Roderick, and I was so used now to coming and going to and from Hundreds, it hadn't occurred to me that my visit might put them out. Mrs Ayres spoke politely, but with a faintly querulous tone to her voice. I had never seen her so discomposed before; it was as if I'd surprised her without her charm, as well as without her powder and rings. But the reason for her touch of temper became clear in another moment, for in order to sit down I had to move aside several sagging flat boxes from the sofa: they were boxes of old family photograph albums that Caroline had recently unearthed in one of the morning-room cupboards, and which had proved on inspection to be foxed with damp and spotted with mildew, and practically ruined.

'Such a tragedy!' said Mrs Ayres, showing me the crumbling pages. 'There must be eighty years' worth of pictures here—and not just the Colonel's family, but my side too, the Singletons and Brookes. And you know, I have been asking Caroline and Roderick for months to find these photographs out and make sure they were safe. I had no idea they were in the morning-room at all; I thought they were locked away somewhere up in the attics.'

I glanced at Caroline—who, after having rung for Betty, had returned to her chair, and was turning the pages of a book of her own, with a distant, patient air. Without lifting her eyes from the page before her she said, 'They wouldn't have been any safer in the attics, I'm afraid. The last time I put my head up there it was to take a look at some leak or other. There were baskets of books from when Roddie and I were children, all foxed to death.'

'Then I wish you had told me, Caroline.'

'I'm sure I did, Mother, at the time.'

'I know you have a great deal to think about, you and your brother, but this is awfully disappointing. Just look here, Doctor.' She handed me a stiff old *carte-de-visite*, its already quaint and faded Victorian subject now practically obscured by rust-coloured spots. 'Here's the Colonel's father as a young man. I used to think Roderick very like him.'

'Yes,' I said absently. I was tense now, waiting my chance to speak. 'Where is Roderick, by the way?'

'Oh, in his room, I imagine.' She picked out another. 'Here's another one spoiled . . . This one too . . . This one I remember—oh, how dreadful! It's perfectly ruined! My own family, just before the war. My brothers are all there, look, one can just make them out: Charlie, Lionel, Mortimer, Frank; and my sister, Cissie. I'd been married a year, and was home with Baby, and we didn't know it then, but the family was never to be together like that again, for within six months the fighting had started and two of the boys were lost almost at once.'

Her voice had changed, a note of real distress creeping into it, and this time Caroline looked up, and she and I exchanged a glance. Betty appeared, and was sent off to bring the tea—which I didn't want, and didn't have time for—and Mrs Ayres continued to pick her way, sadly and absently, through the cloudy photographs. I thought of all she had recently been through, and what awful news I had come to break to her; I watched the fretful movement of her hands, which without their rings looked naked, and large at the knuckle. And suddenly the idea of burdening her with yet another anxiety seemed too much. I remembered the conversation I'd had with Caroline about her brother, the week before; it occurred to me that perhaps it was to her I should speak, at least in the first place. I spent a useless few minutes trying to catch her eye again; then, once Betty had returned with the tea things I rose as if to help with the tray, and took Caroline's cup across to her while Betty saw to Mrs Ayres. And as Caroline looked up at me in mild surprise, putting out her hand to receive the saucer, I bent my head to her and whispered: 'Can you find a way of talking to me alone?'

She drew back, startled by the words, or simply by the movement of my breath against her cheek. She looked into my face, glanced at her mother, then gave me a nod. I went back to the sofa. We let five or ten minutes pass while we drank our tea and ate the slim, dry slices of cake that had been served up with it.

Then she moved forward as if just struck by an idea.

'Mother,' she said, 'I meant to tell you. I've put some of our old books together to give to the Red Cross. I thought perhaps Dr Faraday could take them back to Lidcote for us, in his car. I don't like to ask Rod. I'm sorry to trouble you with it, Doctor, but would you mind? They're in the library, boxed up and ready.'

She spoke without a flicker of self-consciousness, and with no trace of colour in her face; but I must confess, my own heart was pounding. Mrs Ayres said discontentedly that no, she supposed she wouldn't miss us for a minute or two, and went back to sorting through the crumbling albums.

'I won't keep you long,' Caroline said to me, still in her ordinary voice, as I opened the door; but she gestured with her eyes along the passage, and we went quickly and softly together to the library, where she made her way to the window and drew back that single functioning shutter. As the wintry light spilled in, the shrouded bookshelves seemed to spring into life around us, like rearing ghosts. I took a few steps forward out of the worst of the gloom, and Caroline came back, away from the window, to stand before me.

'Has something happened?' she asked me gravely. 'Is it Rod?'

'Yes,' I said. And I proceeded to tell her, as briefly as I could, everything her brother had confessed to me in my dispensary the night before. She listened in growing horror—but also, I thought, with a sort of dawning comprehension, as if my words made a ghastly sense to her, put into her hands the clue to a dark puzzle that up till now had been lying just out of her reach. The only time she interrupted me was when I repeated what Rod had said about the smudge appearing on his ceiling, and then she seized my arm and said, 'That mark, and the others! We saw them! I *knew* there was something odd about them. You don't think—? It couldn't be—?'

I realised with surprise that she was almost ready to take her brother's claims seriously. I said, 'Anything could have made those marks, Caroline. Rod might have made them himself, simply to back up his own delusion. Or maybe it was the marks appearing in the first place that set the whole thing off in his head.'

She drew her hand away. 'Yes, of course . . . And, you really think that's how it is? It couldn't be what you said before? Seizures, and so on?'

I shook my head. 'I'd rather there *were* some physical problem here;

it would be easier to treat. But I'm afraid that what we're dealing with is some kind of, well, mental illness.'

The words shocked her. She looked frightened for a second, then said, 'Poor, poor Rod. This is dreadful, isn't it? What on earth can we do? Do you mean to tell my mother?'

'I did. That's why I came out here. But seeing her with those photographs—'

'It isn't just the photographs, you know,' she said. 'Mother's changing. Most days she's quite her old self. But other days she's like this, vague and maudlin, thinking too much of the past. She and Rod have started almost quarrelling, about the farm. Apparently there are new debts. He takes it all so personally! Then he shuts himself away. Now I understand why. It's too horrible . . . He really said those frightful things, and meant them? You couldn't have misunderstood?'

'I wish for all our sakes that I had. But no, I'm afraid there was no mistaking him. If he won't let me treat him, we can only hope that his mind will somehow clear itself. It might do, now that the Baker-Hydes have left the county and all that dreadful business is settled at last; though that's bad news about the farm. Certainly there's nothing I can do for him while he remains so fixated on this idea of his that he's protecting you and your mother.'

'You don't think, if I were to talk to him—?'

'You might try; though I shouldn't like you to have to hear what I heard, from his own lips. Perhaps the best thing now is for you simply to keep an eye on him—for us both to watch him, and hope to God he doesn't grow any worse.'

'And if he does?' she asked.

'If he does,' I replied, 'well, if this were another house, with a more ordinary family in it, I know what I'd do. I'd bring in David Graham, and have Rod forcibly committed to a psychiatric ward.'

She put a hand across her mouth. 'It couldn't come to that, surely?'

'I'm thinking of those injuries of his. It looks to me like he's punishing himself. He clearly feels guilty, perhaps because of what's happening now with Hundreds; perhaps even because of what happened to his navigator, back in the war. He might be trying to harm himself, almost unconsciously. On the other hand, he might be seeking our help. He knows what powers I have, as a doctor. He might be hurting himself precisely in the hope that I'll step in and do something drastic—'

I stopped. We were standing in the faint light of the unshuttered window, and we had been talking tensely, in murmurs, all this time. Now, from somewhere over my shoulder, as if from the deepest shadows of the room, there came the small sharp creak of metal; we both turned our heads to it, startled. The creak came again: it came, I realised, from the handle of the library door, which was slowly twisting in its socket. Seen through the gloom like that, in our already keyed-up condition, the thing looked almost uncanny. I heard Caroline draw in her breath, and felt her move a little closer to me, as if afraid. As the door was pushed slowly open and the light of the hall revealed Roderick standing there, I think we were both, for a second, relieved. Then we saw the expression on his face, and moved hastily apart.

We looked, I suppose, about as guilty as we felt. Rod said coldly, 'I heard your car, Doctor. I'd half expected it.' And then, to his sister: 'What's he been telling you? That I'm touched or cracked or something? I suppose he's told Mother the same thing.'

'I haven't said anything to your mother yet,' I said, before Caroline could answer.

'Well, isn't that big of you.' He looked again at his sister. 'He gave me his word, you know, that he wouldn't say anything at all. That's how much a doctor's word is worth, clearly. A doctor like him, anyway.'

Caroline ignored that. 'Roddie,' she said, 'we're worried about you. You aren't yourself, you know you aren't. Come into the room, can't you? We don't want Mother or Betty to hear us.'

He kept still for a moment, then moved forward, closed the door, and stood with his back to it. He said flatly, 'So *you* think I'm cracked, too.'

'I think you need a rest,' said Caroline, 'a break—anything, to get you away from here for a while.'

'Away from here? You're as bad as him! Why is everyone trying to get me away?'

'We just want to help you. We think you must be ill, and need treatment. Is it true you've been . . . seeing things?'

He lowered his gaze, impatiently. 'God, it's just like after my smash! If I'm to be watched, endlessly watched and fussed and nannied—'

'Just tell me, Rod! Is it true you believe there's something—something in the house? Something that wants to hurt you?'

He didn't answer for a moment. But then he lifted his eyes to hers and said quietly, 'What do you think?'

And to my surprise, I saw her flinch as if from something in his gaze.

'I—I don't know what to think. But Rod, I'm frightened for you.'

'Frightened! You ought to be frightened, both of you. But not for me. Not *of* me, either, if that's what's worrying you. Don't you understand? I'm all that's holding this place together!'

I said, 'I know it seems that way to you, Rod. If you'd just let us help you—'

'This is your idea of helping me, is it? Running straight to my sister, when you *promised*—'

'This *is* my idea of helping you, yes. Because I've been turning it over in my mind and I don't think you're in a position to help yourself.'

'But don't you see? How can you not see, after all I told you yesterday! It isn't *myself* I'm thinking of. God! I've never been given any credit for the work I've done for this family—not even now, when I'm thrashing myself to death! Perhaps I should pack the whole thing in, close my eyes for once, look the other way. Then we'll see what happens.'

He sounded almost sulky now—like a boy trying to argue down a bad school report. He folded his arms, and hunched his shoulders, and the darkness and the horror of what we were actually talking about, which a moment before had felt so palpable, began somehow to slip away from us. I saw Caroline looking at me, for the first time with doubt in her eyes, and I took a step forward, saying urgently, 'Rod, you must understand, we're desperately worried. This can't go on.'

'I don't want to talk about it,' he said firmly. 'There's no point.'

'I think you're really ill, Rod. We need to work out exactly what the illness is, so that we can cure it.'

'All that's making me ill is you and your prying! If you'd let me alone, if you'd just let all of us alone— But you two have always been in league against me. All that guff about my leg, saying I was doing the hospital a favour.'

'How can you say that,' said Caroline, 'when Dr Faraday was so kind!'

'Is he being kind now?'

'Rod, please.'

'I told you, didn't I? I don't want to talk about it!'

He turned, to wrench open the heavy old library door and go out. And as he went he gave the door such a slam, a line of dust came down, like a veil, from a crack in the ceiling, and two of the sheets slid from the bookshelves to land in a musty heap on the floor.

Caroline and I looked helplessly at each other, then went slowly across to lift the sheets back up.

'What can we do?' she asked me as we fastened them. 'If he's really as bad as you say he is, but won't let us help him—'

'I don't know,' I answered. 'I truly don't know. We can only, as I said before, watch him, and hope to try and regain his trust. Most of that will fall to you, I'm afraid.'

She nodded, then gazed into my face. And after a little hesitation she said, 'You are sure? About what he told you? He sounds so— so sane.'

'I know he does. If you'd seen him yesterday you wouldn't think that. And yet, even then, he spoke so reasonably— I swear, it's the strangest mix of sanity and delusion I've ever seen.'

'And you don't think— There couldn't be anything, really—any truth in what he's saying?'

Again, I was surprised that she would even consider it. I said, 'I'm sorry, Caroline. It's terribly hard, when this sort of thing happens to a person one loves.'

'Yes, I suppose so.'

She spoke doubtfully, then put her hands together, working the thumb of one over the knuckles of the other, and I saw her shiver.

I said, 'You're cold.'

But she shook her head. 'Not cold—frightened.'

With an uncertain movement, I put my own hands over hers. At once, her fingers moved gratefully against mine.

I said, 'I didn't mean to frighten you. I'm so sorry to burden you with this.' I glanced around. 'This house is gloomy, on a day like today! That's probably part of Rod's trouble. If only he hadn't let things slip so far! And now— Damn.' Frustrated, I'd caught sight of the time. 'I have to go. You'll be all right? And you'll let me know at once, if anything changes?'

She promised she would. 'Good girl,' I said, squeezing her fingers.

Her hands stayed in mine for another second, then slid away. We headed back to the little parlour.

'What an age you've been!' said Mrs Ayres as we went in. 'And what on earth was that great crash? Betty and I supposed the roof was falling in!'

She had the girl at her side: she must have kept her back when she came to take away the tea-tray, or perhaps had rung for her deliberately; she was showing her the spoiled photographs—had laid out half a dozen of them, apparently pictures of Caroline and Roderick as infants—and now began to pick them impatiently back up.

Caroline said, 'I'm sorry, Mother. I let a door slam. Now there's dust, I'm afraid, on the library floor. Betty, you'll have to see to that.'

Betty put down her head and gave a curtsey. 'Yes, miss,' she said, moving off.

Not having any time to linger, I said a polite but hasty goodbye—meeting Caroline's gaze, and trying to will into my expression all the sympathy and support I could—and more or less followed the girl out.

I reached the hall, and glanced in through the open library door, and saw her down on her knees with a dustpan and brush, dabbing without enthusiasm at the threadbare carpet. And it was only as I saw the dipping and rising of her slender shoulders that I remembered that queer outburst of hers, on the morning I had destroyed Gyp. It seemed a strange coincidence that her claim that Hundreds had a 'bad thing' in it should have found an echo, now, in Roderick's delusion . . . I went in and spoke quietly to her, wanting to know if she had said anything that might have put the germ of an idea into his head.

She swore she had said nothing.

'You told me not to, didn't you?' she said. 'Well, I haven't said a word!'

'Not even in fun?'

'No!'

She spoke with great earnestness—but also, I thought, with the faintest touch of relish. I recalled suddenly what a good little actress she was: I looked into her shallow grey eyes, and for the first time I was uncertain whether her gaze was guileless or sly. I said, 'You're quite sure, now? You haven't been saying anything, or doing anything? Just to liven things up? Moving things around? Putting things where they oughtn't to be?'

'I haven't done nothing,' she said, 'and I haven't said nothing! I don't like to think of it, anyhow. It makes me frit if I think about it when I'm downstairs on me own. It in't *my* bad thing; that's what Mrs Bazeley says. If I don't go bothering him, she says, he won't come bothering me.'

And I had to be satisfied with that. She went back to dabbing at the carpet. I stood and watched her for a few moments longer, then left the house.

I spoke to Caroline several times over the following week or two. She told me that nothing much had changed, that Rod was as secretive as ever but, apart from that, quite rational; and he himself, on my next visit, came to the door of his room when I knocked on it, only to tell me in sober tones that he 'had nothing to say to me, and simply wanted to be left alone'—then closed the door, with horrible finality, in my face. My interference, in other words, had had exactly the effect I'd feared most. There was no question now of my continuing with the treatment of his leg: I finished my writing up of the case and submitted my paper, and without that reason to call at the house, my visits rather fell away. I found myself missing them, surprisingly badly. I missed the family; I missed Hundreds itself. I worried about poor, burdened Mrs Ayres, and I thought often of Caroline, wondering how on earth she could be coping out there, with things so bad; thinking back to that time in the library and remembering the tired, reluctant way her hand had moved away from mine.

December arrived, and the weather grew more wintry. There was an outbreak of influenza in the district: the first of the season. Two of my elderly patients died, and several others were badly affected. Graham came down with the illness himself; our locum, Wise, took on some of his workload, but the rest of his rounds were added to mine and I was soon working every spare hour. For the first few days of the month I got no nearer to the Hall than the Hundreds farm, where Makins's wife and daughter were both lying ill, the milking suffering as a result of it. Makins himself was sour and grumbling, talking of throwing in the whole business. He hadn't seen hide nor hair of Roderick Ayres, he told me, for three or four weeks—not since the most recent rent day, when he had come to collect his money. 'That's the so-called gentleman farmer for you,' he said bitterly. 'When the sun is shining, all's well and good. The first trace of bad weather and he's at home with his feet up.'

He would have gone grumbling on; I didn't have time to stay and listen. I didn't have time, either, to call in at the Hall as I would once have done. But what Makins had told me had worried me, and that night I telephoned the house. Mrs Ayres answered, sounding weary. 'Oh, Dr Faraday,' she said, 'how nice it is to hear your voice! We've had no visitors in ages. This weather makes everything so hard. The house is so comfortless, just now.'

'But you're all right?' I asked. 'All of you? Caroline? Rod?'

'We're—fine.'

'I spoke to Makins—'

The line crackled. 'You must come and see us!' she called, through the interference. 'Will you? Come and dine! We'll give you a proper old-fashioned dinner. Should you like that?'

I called back that I should, very much. The line was too bad for us to continue. We fixed on a date, between crackles, for two or three days off.

The weather, in that short time, seemed only to decline. It was a wet, blowy night, moonless and starless, when I went up to Hundreds again. I don't know if the damp and the darkness were to blame, or whether, in keeping away for a while, I had forgotten how really shabby and neglected the house had become: but when I stepped into the hall the cheerlessness of it struck me at once. Some of the bulbs in the wall-lights had blown, and the staircase climbed into shadows, just as it had on the evening of the party; the effect, now, was a strangely lowering one, as if the inclement night itself had found a way in through seams in the brickwork, and had gathered to hang like smoke or must in the very core of the house. It was also piercingly cold. A few ancient radiators were bubbling and ticking away, but their heat was lost as soon as it rose. I went along the marble-floored passage and found the family gathered in the little parlour, their chairs drawn right up to the hearth in their efforts to keep warm, and their outfits eccentric— Caroline with a short cape of balding sealskin over her dress, Mrs Ayres in a stiff silk gown and an emerald necklace and rings, with clashing Spanish and Indian shawls around her shoulders and, on her head, her black mantilla; and Roderick with an ointment-coloured woollen waistcoat underneath his evening jacket, and a pair of fingerless gloves on his hands.

'Forgive us, Doctor,' said Mrs Ayres, coming forward as I went in. 'I'm ashamed to think how we must look!' But she said it lightly, and I could tell from her manner that, in fact, she had no idea how truly outlandish she and her children appeared. That made me uneasy, some-how. I suppose I was seeing them all, as I'd seen the house, as a stranger might.

I looked closest at Rod; and was pretty dismayed by what I saw. When his mother and sister greeted me he hung back, pointedly. And though he did shake my hand at last, he did it limply, without speaking, and barely raising his eyes to mine, so that I could see he only meant to go through the motions of making me welcome, perhaps for his mother's sake. But all this I'd expected. There was something else, which troubled me more. His whole manner had changed. Where be-fore he'd carried himself in the tense, hunted way of someone braced against disaster, now he seemed to *slouch*, as if barely caring whether disaster struck or not. While Mrs Ayres and Caroline and I chatted together, with an attempt at normality, of county matters and local gossip, he sat the whole time in his chair, watching us from under his brows but saying nothing. He rose only once, and that was to go to the drinks table to top up his glass of gin and French. And from the way he handled the bottles, and from the stiffness of the cocktail he mixed, I realised that he must have been drinking steadily for some time.

It was horrible to see. Presently Betty came, to call us to dinner, and in the movement that followed I drew close to Caroline and murmured, 'Everything all right?'

She glanced at her mother and brother, then gave a tight shake of her head. We stepped out into the passage and she drew close the collar of her cape, against the chill which seemed to rise up from the marble floor.

We were to eat in the dining-room, and Mrs Ayres, in order I sup-pose to make good her promise to give me a 'proper, old-fashioned dinner', had had Betty lay the table rather elaborately, with Chinese porcelain to match the oriental paper on the walls, and with ancient silverware. The ormolu candelabra were lit, and the flames of their candles dipped alarmingly in the draught from the windows. Caroline and I sat face to face across the width of the table between them, while

Mrs Ayres took her place at the table's foot; Roderick made his way to the master's chair—his father's old chair, I suppose it was—at the head of it. Almost as soon as he had sat down he poured himself a glass of wine, and when Betty had taken the bottle to the other end of the table and approached him with the tureen of soup, he put his hand across his bowl.

' "Oh, take the nasty soup away! I won't have any soup today!"' he said, in a foolish, jarring voice. Then: 'Do you know what happened to the naughty boy in that poem, Betty?'

'No, sir,' she said uncertainly.

'*No, zir,*' he repeated, mimicking her accent. 'Well, he was burnt in a fire.'

'No, he wasn't,' said Caroline, with an attempt at a smile. 'He wasted away. Which is what you'll do, Rod, if you're not careful. Though goodness knows, I don't think any of us would care. Have some soup.'

'I told you,' he answered, putting on his silly voice again, ' "I *won't* have any soup today!" But you may bring back the wine please, Betty. Thank you.'

He topped up his glass. He did it heavily, the neck of the bottle striking the glass and making it ring. The glass was a lovely Regency one, brought out of storage, I imagine, along with the porcelain and the silver; and at the little concussion Caroline's smile faded and she looked at her brother, suddenly, with real annoyance—so that I was almost startled by the flash of distaste in her eyes. Her gaze stayed hard, then, for the rest of the meal, and I thought it a pity, for in the light of the candles she looked her best, with her heavy features softened, and the angular lines of her collarbones and shoulders concealed by the folds of her cape.

Mrs Ayres, too, was flattered by the candle-light. She said nothing to her son, but kept up a light, smooth flow of conversation with me, just as she had in the little parlour. I thought this simply a sign of good breeding, at first; I supposed she was embarrassed by Rod's behaviour and was doing her best to cover it up. Gradually, though, I became aware of a certain brittleness to her tone, and I remembered then what Caroline had told me, that time in the library, about her mother and brother having 'started quarrelling'. And I found myself wishing—what I couldn't remember ever having done before, at Hundreds—I found myself wishing that I hadn't come out there, and I began to long for the meal to end. The house, I thought, didn't deserve their bad feeling; and neither did I.

Presently Mrs Ayres and I fell to talking about a patient I'd recently been treating for the influenza, an old Hundreds tenant who lived a quarter of a mile from the west gates. I said how lucky it was that I was able to use that road across the park in order to reach him; that it made a great difference to my round. Mrs Ayres agreed—then added, cryptically, 'I do so hope that's allowed to continue.'

'You do?' I asked, surprised. 'Well, why shouldn't it?'

She looked pointedly at her son, as if expecting him to speak. He said nothing, only gazed into his wine glass, so she dabbed at her mouth with her linen napkin, then went on: 'I'm afraid, Doctor, that Roderick's had to give me some unhappy news today. The fact is, it looks as though we'll soon be obliged to sell off more of our land.'

'You will?' I said, turning to Rod. 'I thought there wasn't any more to sell. Who's the buyer this time?'

'The county council again,' said Mrs Ayres, when Rod didn't answer, 'with Maurice Babb to build, as before. Their plans are for twenty-four extra houses. Can you imagine? I thought the regulations would forbid it; they seem to forbid everything else. But it seems this government is quite happy to hand out permits to men who intend to break up parklands and estates so that they might cram twenty-four families into three acres of ground. It will mean putting a breach in the wall, laying pipes, and so on—'

'The wall?' I said, not understanding.

Caroline spoke. 'Rod offered them farmland,' she said quietly, 'and they didn't want it. They'll only take the grass-snake field, over to the west. They finally made up their minds, you see, about the water and electricity: they say they won't extend the mains to Hundreds simply for our use, but they'll bring them out if it's for the sake of new houses. It seems we might just be able to raise the money to lay the pipes and wires the extra distance to the farm.'

For a moment I was too dismayed to answer. The grass-snake field— as I knew Caroline and Roderick had named it, as children—was just within the park wall, about three-quarters of a mile from the house itself. It had been hidden from view in high summer, but with the thinning of the trees in autumn it became visible from all the south- and west-facing windows of the Hall, a distant swathe of green and white and silver, rippling and lovely as fingered velvet. The thought that Rod was seriously prepared to give it up bothered me horribly.

'You can't mean it,' I said to him. 'You simply can't break up the park. There must be some alternative, surely?'

And again his mother answered. 'Nothing at all, apparently, aside from selling the house and park completely; and even Roderick feels that that's not to be thought of, not after we've given up so much already in order to hang on to it. We'll make it a condition of the sale that Babb puts up a fence around the building-work—and then at least we won't have to look at it.'

Now Roderick did speak. He said thickly, 'Yes, we must have a fence to keep out the mob. Not that that will stop them, mind. They'll soon be scaling the walls of the house at night, with cutlasses between their teeth. You'd better sleep with a pistol under your pillow, Caroline!'

'They're not pirates, you oaf,' she murmured, without looking up from her plate.

'Aren't they? I'm not so sure. I think they'd like nothing better than to hang us all from the mainbrace; they're just waiting for Attlee to give them the word. He probably will, too. Ordinary people hate our sort now, don't you see?'

'Please, Roderick,' said Mrs Ayres uncomfortably. 'Nobody hates our sort. Not in Warwickshire.'

'Oh, especially in Warwickshire! Over the border, in *Gloz*tershire, they're still feudal at heart. But Warwickshire people have always been good business people—right back to the days of the Civil War. They were all for Cromwell then, don't forget. Now they can see which way the wind is blowing. I wouldn't blame them if they decided to chop off our heads! We've certainly put up a pretty poor show of saving ourselves.' He made a clumsy gesture. 'Just look at Caroline and me, prize heifer and prize bull. We're hardly doing our bit to further the herd! Anyone would think we were going out of our way to make ourselves extinct.'

'Rod,' I said, seeing the look on his sister's face.

He turned to me. 'What? You ought to be glad. You're from pirate stock, aren't you? You don't think you'd have been invited along tonight, otherwise! Mother's too embarrassed to let any of our real friends see us as we are now. Hadn't you figured that out yet?'

I felt myself blush, but more in anger than anything else; and I wouldn't give him the satisfaction of showing any other discomfort, but kept my eyes on his as I ate—wanting to stare him out, one man to another. The tactic worked, I think, for he met my gaze with a flutter of his lashes, and just for a moment he looked ashamed and somehow desperate, like a boasting boy secretly daunted by his own bravado.

Caroline had lowered her head, and went on with her dinner. Mrs Ayres said nothing for a minute or two, then set her knife and fork together. And when she spoke again, it was to ask after another patient of mine, as if our earlier conversation had had no interruption. Her manner was smooth, her voice quite soft; she didn't look at her son after that. Instead she seemed to cut him from the table—to plunge him into darkness, just as if she were reaching and snuffing out the candles in front of him, one by one.

The dinner, by then, was beyond recovery. The dessert was a bottled-raspberry pie, slightly sour, served with artificial cream; the room, after all, was damp and chill, the wind was moaning in the chimney, the table not the sort of pre-war one it was possible to linger over, even if the mood had been better. Mrs Ayres told Betty that we would take our coffee in the little parlour, and she, Caroline, and I rose and put down our napkins.

Only Rod hung back. At the door he said moodily, 'I shan't come with you, I'm sure you won't mind. I've some papers I need to look over.'

'Cigarette papers, I suppose,' said Caroline, going down the passage to open the door to the little parlour for her mother.

Roderick blinked at her, and again I had the feeling that he was trapped in his own bad humour and secretly abashed by it. I watched him turn away from us to begin the short, gloomy journey to his room, and I felt a rush of angry pity for him; it seemed brutal of us to let him go. But I joined his mother and sister, and found them adding wood to the fire.

'I must apologise for my son, Doctor,' said Mrs Ayres as she sat. She put the back of her wrist to her temple as if her head ached. 'His behaviour tonight was unforgivable. Can't he see how unhappy he makes us all? If he means to start drinking now, on top of everything, I shall have to ask Betty to keep back the wine. I never saw his father drunk at the table . . . I hope you know how very welcome you are in this house. Will you sit here, across from me?'

I did sit, for a time. Betty brought us our coffee, and we talked more about the sale of the land. I asked them again if there were no alternative, pointing out the disruption that the building-work would lead to, and the impact such a thing would inevitably have on life at the Hall. But they had thought it through already, and had evidently surrendered themselves to the idea. Even Caroline seemed curiously passive about it all. So I thought I would try Roderick again. It was bothering me, too, to picture him alone and unhappy on the other side of the house. Once my coffee was finished I put down my cup and said I would just look in on him to see if I could be any help with his work.

As I'd suspected, the work was all bluff: when I went in he was sitting more or less in darkness, with only the fire to light the room. I hadn't knocked this time, so as not to give him the opportunity of refusing me, and he turned his head and said sulkily, 'I thought you'd come.'

'May I join you for a while?'

'What do you think? You can see how frightfully busy I am.—No, don't put on the light! I've rather a headache.' I heard him setting down a glass and moving forward. 'I'll stoke this up a bit instead. God knows it's cold enough for it.'

He caught up a couple of pieces of log from the box beside the fire-place and flung them clumsily into the hearth. They sent sparks flying up the chimney and cinders leaping out of the grate, and had the effect, for a moment or two, of damping the fire and making the room even darker. But by the time I had picked my way over to him and drawn up the other armchair the flames were beginning to lap and crackle around the damp raw wood and I could see him clearly. He had slouched back in his chair and stuck out his legs. He was still in his evening clothes, his woollen waistcoat and fingerless gloves, but he had loos-ened his tie and taken out a collar-stud, so that one side of the collar sprang up like a comedy drunk's.

This was the first time I had been in his room since he had told me that fantastic story in my dispensary, and as I sat I found myself glanc-ing uneasily around. Away from the light of the fire the shadows were so thick and so shifting as to be almost impenetrable, but I could just make out the rumpled blankets of his bed, with beside it his dressing-table and, close to that, his marble-topped washing-stand. Of the shaving-glass—which I'd last seen sitting on the stand along with his razor and soap and brush—there was no sign.

By the time I looked back at Roderick he'd begun fiddling in his lap with papers and tobacco, rolling himself a cigarette. Even in the shifting glow of the firelight I could see that his face was flushed and thick with drink. I began to talk, as I'd intended, about the sale of the land—leaning forward, speaking earnestly, trying to get some sense into him. But he turned his head and wouldn't listen. At last I gave the subject up.

Sitting back, I said instead, 'You look terrible, Rod.'

That made him laugh. 'Ha! I hope that's not a professional opinion. I'm afraid we can't afford it.'

'Why are you doing this to yourself? The estate's falling to pieces around you, and look at you! You've had gin, vermouth, wine, and'— I nodded to his glass, which was sitting on a mess of papers on the table at his elbow—'what's in there? Gin again?'

He cursed quietly. 'Jesus! What of it? Can't a bloke get lit up now and then?'

I said, 'Not a bloke in your position, no.'

'What position's that? Lord of the manor?'

'Yes, if you want to put it like that.'

He licked the gum of his cigarette paper, looking sour. 'You're thinking of my mother.'

'Your mother would be miserable,' I said, 'if she saw you like this.'

'Do me a favour then, old chap, will you? Don't tell her.' He put the cigarette into his mouth, and lit it with a newspaper spill from the fire. 'Anyway,' he said, as he sat back, 'it's a bit late for her to begin acting the devoted matron. Twenty-four years too late, to be exact. Twenty-six, in Caroline's case.'

I said, 'Your mother loves you dearly. Don't be stupid.'

'You know all about it, of course.'

'I know what she's told me.'

'Yes, you're great chums, you and she, aren't you? What *has* she told you? How frightfully *disappointed* I've made her? She's never forgiven me, you know, for letting myself get shot down and lamed. We've been disappointing her all our lives, my sister and I. I think we disappointed her simply by being born.'

I didn't answer, and for a time he was silent, gazing into the fire. And when he spoke again, it was in a light, almost casual tone. He said, 'Did you know I ran away from school when I was a boy?'

I blinked at the change of subject. 'No,' I said reluctantly, 'I didn't know that.'

'Oh, yes. They kept it quiet, but I bolted twice. The first time I was only eight or nine; I didn't get far. The second time, though, I was older, maybe thirteen. I just walked out, no one stopped me. I got as far as the public bar of an hotel. I telephoned Morris, my father's chauffeur, and he came and got me. He was always a pal of mine. He bought me a ham sandwich and a glass of lemonade, and we sat at a table and talked it through . . . I had thought it all out. I knew he had a brother who ran a garage, and I had fifty pounds of my own, and I thought I might go shares in the garage—live with the brother and be a mechanic. I really knew, you see, about engines.'

He drew on his cigarette. 'Morris was awfully good about it. He said, "Well, Master Roderick"—he had the most terrible Birmingham accent, just like that—"Well, Master Roderick, I think you'd make a fine mechanic, and my brother would be honoured to have you, but don't you think it would break your parents' heart, you being heir to the estate and all?" He wanted to take me back to school, but I wouldn't let him. He didn't know what else to do with me, so he brought me back here, and gave me to Cook, and Cook got me quietly up to my mother. They were imagining that Mother would look after me, make things easy with the old man—like mothers do in the pictures and on the stage. But, no: she just told me what a great *disappointment* I was, and she sent me down to Father, to explain to him for myself what I was doing here. The old man ramped like the devil, of course, and thrashed me—thrashed me right by the open window, where any out-doors servant could have seen.' He laughed. 'And I had only run away because a boy was thrashing me at school! A beastly boy, he was: Hugh Nash. He used to call me "Ayres-and-Graces". But even he had the decency to whip me in private . . .'

His cigarette was burning itself out in his fingers, but he sat still, and his voice dipped. 'Nash went into the Navy in the end. He was killed off Malaya. And do you know, when I heard he'd been killed, I felt relieved. I was already in the Air Force by then, and I felt relieved—just as if I were still at school, and another boy had told me that Nash had been taken out of class by his parents . . . Poor Morris died, too, I think.

I wonder if his brother did all right.' His voice grew harsh. 'I wish I *had* gone shares in that garage. I'd be a happier man than I am now, pouring everything I've got into this bloody estate. Why the hell am I doing it? *For the sake of the family*, you're going to say, with that wonderful insight of yours. Do you really think this family's worth saving? Look at my sister! This house has sucked the life out of her—just as it's sucking it out of me. That's what it's doing. It wants to destroy us, all of us. It's all very well my standing up to it now, but how long d'you think I can go on like that? And when it's finished with me—'

'Rod, stop it,' I said, for his voice had risen suddenly and he was becoming agitated: realising his cigarette had gone out, he'd leaned forward to put another paper spill to the fire, and he had thrown the spill violently down so that it bounced back over the marble fender and lay burning at the edge of the rug. I picked it up and tossed it into the grate; then, seeing the state of him, I reached for the edge of the fire-curtain—for his was one of those fireplaces that had a piece of fine old mesh hung across it, like a nursery guard—and drew it closed.

He sat back in his chair, his arms folded defensively. He took one or two furtive puffs on his cigarette, then tilted his head and began to glance around the room, his eyes seeming very large and dark in his lean, pale face. I knew what he was watching for, and felt almost sick with frustration and dismay. There had been no mention of the old delusion before this; his behaviour had been troubling, unpleasant, but rational enough. But I could see now that nothing had changed. His mind was still clouded. The drinking, perhaps, was simply to give him courage, and the truculence was a desperate form of bluster.

He said, with his gaze still moving, 'There'll be tricks, tonight. I can sense it. I've a feeling for it now. I'm like a weather-vane, I start twitching when the wind's on the turn.'

He spoke almost lugubriously, so that I couldn't tell how much of this was theatrics, how much was in deadly earnest. But—it was impossible to resist—I found my gaze following his. Again my eye was drawn to the washing-stand; this time, too, I tilted back my head to look at

the ceiling above it. I could just make out, through the darkness, that
peculiar stain or smudge—and then my heart sank as I spotted, a yard
or so from it, a similar mark. Further off I thought I saw another. I
looked at the wall behind Rod's bed, and saw one there. Or, thought I
did. I couldn't be sure; the shadows played such tricks. But my gaze
went darting about from one surface to another until it seemed to me
that the room might be teeming with those mysterious smudges; and
suddenly the thought of leaving Rod among them for another night—
another hour!—was too much. I drew my eyes away from the darkness
and leaned forward out of my chair to say urgently, 'Rod, come back
to Lidcote with me, will you?'

'To Lidcote?'

'I think you'll be safer there.'

'I can't leave now. I told you, didn't I? The wind's on the turn—'

'Stop talking like that!'

He blinked, as if in sudden understanding. He tilted his head again
and said, almost coyly, 'You're afraid.'

'Rod, listen to me.'

'You can feel it, can't you? You can feel it, and you're afraid. You
didn't believe me before. All that talk of *nerve-storms*, of *war-shock*.
Now you're more frightened than I am!'

I *was* afraid, I realised—not of the things he'd been babbling about,
but of something vaguer and more dreadful. I reached to try and catch
hold of his wrist.

'Rod, for God's sake! I think you're in danger!'

The action startled him; he moved back. And then—it was the drink,
I suppose—he flew into a rage.

'God damn you!' he cried, pushing me away. 'Get your hands off
me! Don't you f—g well tell me how to behave! That's all you ever do.
And when you're not doling out your doctor's advice you're making a
grab at me, with your filthy doctor's fingers. And when you're not grab-
bing you're watching, watching, with your filthy doctor's eyes. Who
the f—g hell are you, anyway? Why the hell are you here? How did you

manage to get such a footing in this house? You're not a part of this family! You're no one!'

He thumped his glass down on the table, so that the gin slopped over the papers. 'I'm calling for Betty,' he said absurdly, 'to see you out.'

He moved clumsily to the chimney-breast and caught hold of the lever that worked the call-bell, jerking and jerking it, so that we could hear the faint hectic clanging of it down in the basement. It sounded bizarrely like the bell that the village air-raid wardens had used to ring, and it added an extra atavistic flutter of agitation to the shock and upset that had already begun to swirl inside me at his words.

I rose and went across to the door, and opened it just as, breathless and startled, Betty appeared. I tried to keep her from coming in.

I said, 'It's all right, nothing's wrong. There's been a mistake. Go back downstairs.'

But, 'Dr Faraday's leaving, Betty!' called Roderick, over my words. 'He has other patients to see. Isn't that a pity? Take him out to the hall, will you, and pick up his coat and his hat on the way?'

The girl and I looked at each other; but what on earth could I do? I myself had reminded Rod, a few minutes before, that he was 'the head of the household', a grown man, master of the estate and its servants. I said stiffly at last, 'Very well.' She stepped aside so that I could pass her, and then I heard her hurrying off to fetch my things.

I felt so agitated now, I actually had to stand for a minute at the little parlour door, to collect myself; and when finally I went in I was still so shaken, I imagined my face or manner would betray me at once. But my entrance impressed no one. Caroline had an open novel in her lap, and Mrs Ayres, in her chair beside the fire, was frankly snoozing. That gave me another jolt: I had never seen her sleeping before, and when I went over to her and she woke, she looked at me, briefly, with what might have been the frightened, unmoored gaze of a bewildered old woman. She had placed a shawl across her lap and it was slipping to the floor. I bent to retrieve it, and by the time I had straightened up, she could take it from me and tuck it back around her knees, herself again.

She asked me how Roderick was. I hesitated, then said, 'Not wonderful, to be honest. I—I wish I knew what to say. Caroline, you might look in on him, in a minute or two?'

'Not if he's drunk,' she answered. 'He's too boring.'

And, 'Drunk!' said Mrs Ayres, with a touch of scorn. 'Thank goodness his grandmother isn't alive to see him—the Colonel's mother, I mean. She always said there was nothing more depressing than the sight of a man in liquor; I must say I agree with her. As for my own mother's side—I think my great-grandparents were Temperance people. Yes, I'm almost sure they were.'

'Still,' I said, looking hard at Caroline, 'you might just pay your brother a visit, before you go to bed, to be sure all's well?'

She at last caught the meaning behind my words, and looked up to meet my gaze. She closed her eyes in a weary gesture, but gave me a nod.

That reassured me a little, but I was quite unable to sit calmly beside the fire and talk of ordinary things. I thanked them for my supper and said good night. Betty was waiting out in the hall with my hat and overcoat, and the sight of her brought Rod's words back to me: *Who the hell are you? You're no one!*

Outside, the weather was still filthy, and seemed to whip up my mood. The upset and anger grew on me as I drove home—so that I drove badly, clashing the gears, once taking a curve too sharply and very nearly running the car off the road. In an effort to calm myself down I worked on various bills and papers until well past midnight; but when I finally went to bed I lay fretful—almost hoping for a call to a patient, to take my mind away from the snag of my own thoughts.

No call came, and at last I switched on the lamp and got up to pour myself a drink. On my way back to bed I caught sight of that old photograph of the Hall, in its handsome tortoiseshell frame: I had kept it out all this time, together with that Empire Day medal, on my bedside table. I picked it up, and looked at my mother's face. Then I shifted my gaze to the house behind her, and, as I'd sometimes done before, I thought of the people inside it now, wondering if they were lying more restfully than I was, in their chill, dark, separate rooms. Mrs Ayres had given me the picture in July, and it was now early December. How on earth, I asked myself, had my life, in those few months, become so tangled with that family's as to trouble and unsettle me like this?

With the alcohol inside me my anger blunted, and eventually I slept. But I slept badly; and while I lay tussling with dark, violent dreams, something dreadful happened out at Hundreds Hall.

SEVEN

The story, as I pieced it together afterwards, was this.

Once I left the house, Mrs Ayres and Caroline stayed in the little parlour for just over an hour; and during that hour, feeling slightly uneasy after what I'd hinted to her, Caroline went in to check on Rod. She found him sprawled open-mouthed, nursing an empty gin bottle, too drunk to speak, and her first reaction, she said, was one of annoyance: she was very tempted simply to leave him there, to 'stew in his chair'. But then he gazed blearily up at her, and there was something in his eyes that moved her—some spark of his former self. For a moment she was almost overcome with the hopelessness of their situation. She knelt beside him and took his hand, lifting it to her face and resting her brow against his knuckles. 'What's happened to you, Roddie?' she asked him quietly. 'I don't know you. I miss you. What's happened?'

He moved his fingers against her cheek, but didn't or couldn't answer. She stayed at his side for another few moments, then, pulling herself together, decided to put him into his bed. She guessed he needed the lavatory, so she got him to his feet and sent him off to the 'gentlemen's hoo-hah' along the passage, and when he'd come lurching back she took off his shoes and his collar and got him out of his trousers. She was used to helping him in and out of his clothes, from having nursed him after his accident, so this sort of thing was nothing to her. She said he more or less passed out the moment his head touched his pillow, and then he lay snoring, and reeking horribly of drink. He was lying on his back, and that made her remember some wartime training and try to heave him over on to his side, in case he should be sick. But he resisted all her efforts, and finally, tired and frustrated, she gave them up.

She made sure he was well covered with blankets before she left him, and she went to the fire, drew back the mesh guard, and added more wood. She closed the guard again when she had finished, she was later quite certain of that; and she was equally certain that no cigarettes were burning in any of the ashtrays, and that no lamps or candles were lit. She returned to the little parlour, where she spent another half-hour with her mother. They went to bed well before midnight; Caroline read for ten or fifteen minutes before putting out her light; and she fell asleep almost at once.

She was woken a few hours later—around half past three, as it turned out—by the faint but distinctive sound of breaking glass. The sound came from just below her own windows—that is, from one of the windows of her brother's room. Startled, she sat up in bed. She assumed that Rod had woken and was blundering about, and her one thought was to prevent him from coming upstairs and disturbing their mother. She got wearily to her feet and put on her dressing-gown; she was just nerving herself up to go downstairs and deal with him when it occurred to her that the sound might not have been made by her brother at all, but might have come from a burglar trying to force a way into the house. Perhaps she was remembering Rod's words about pirates and cutlasses. Anyway, she went softly across to her window, put back the curtain, and looked out. She saw the garden bathed in a leaping yellow light, and smelt smoke—and realised that the house was on fire.

Fire is a thing that is always dreaded in a great house like Hundreds

Hall. Once or twice in the old days there had been small kitchen fires, which had fairly easily been put out. During the war Mrs Ayres had had a constant fear of air raids, and buckets of sand and water, and hoses and stirrup-pumps, had been left out on every floor—and, as it turned out, were never needed. Now those pumps had been put away; there were no mechanical extinguishers; there was only, hanging up in one of the basement passages, a line of ancient leather pails, bloomy with age and probably leaky—kept there more for picturesque value than anything else. It is a wonder that Caroline, knowing all this, and seeing the dancing yellow light, did not panic. Instead, she confessed to me later that, for a single, wild moment, what she felt was a sort of *excitement*. She thought of all the problems that would be solved if the Hall were simply to burn to the ground. She had a vision of the work she had done on the house in the past few years, all the wooden floors and panels she had polished, all the glass, all the plate; and instead of resenting the fire for threatening to snatch these things from her, she wanted to give them all up in a sort of orgy of surrender.

Then she remembered her brother. She caught up the rug from before her hearth, and the blankets from her bed, and went racing out to the staircase—calling wildly to her mother as she went. Downstairs in the hall the smell of smoke grew stronger; in the passage the air was already soupy, and began to prickle at her eyes. She ran through the boot room to the gentlemen's lavatory, to douse the rug and blankets with water at the basin. She found the call-bell, and rang and rang on it—much, I suppose, as I'd seen Roderick ringing, a few hours before. By the time she had gathered together the sodden blankets and gone staggering out with them, a frightened-looking Betty had appeared at the curtained arch, barefoot and in her nightdress.

'Bring water!' Caroline called to her. 'There's a fire! Can't you smell it? Bring your bedclothes, bring anything! Quickly!'

And, hoisting the wet blankets higher against her breast, she ran panting and sweating to Roderick's room.

She began to cough and catch at her breath, she said, even before opening the door. When she went in, the smoke was so thick and so stinging, she was reminded of a gas-practice chamber she had once been sent into during her time in the Wrens. Then, of course, she had had a respirator with her; the point of the exercise was to put it on. Now she could do nothing but bury her nose and mouth in the wet bundle in her arms and fight her way forward. The heat was already terrific. She could see flames on every side of the room: there seemed to be fire everywhere, so that for one desperate moment she thought she was beaten and would have to turn back. But then she *did* turn—and lost her bearings, and grew sick with absolute panic. She saw flames close beside her, and wildly flung her blankets at them. She began to beat at another patch of fire with the rug, and soon she became aware of Betty and her mother, beating with blankets of their own. The smoke billowed and briefly thinned, and she caught a glimpse of Roderick, on the bed where she had left him, dazed and coughing, as if just coming to. Two of the brocade curtains at the windows were alight; two others had burned almost completely and were in the process of falling away. She was able to force a path to them and reach between them to fling open the glass doors.

I shuddered when she told me this, for had the fire's grip on the room been much stronger, the sudden rush of cold air would surely have been fatal. But the flames, at that point, must have already been under control, and the night, thankfully, was still a damp one. Caroline helped a staggering Roderick out on to the stone steps, and then went back to see to her mother. The smoke was clearing, she said, but the room as she plunged back into it was like some small scene from hell: unimaginably hot, lit up at a thousand diabolical points, and thick with whirling embers and tongues of fire that seemed to dart viciously at her face and hands. Mrs Ayres was coughing and gasping for breath, her hair wild, her nightdress filthy. Betty had begun to bring pans of water, and the ash and smoke and smouldering fragments of carpet, blanket, and paper were turning to pools of thick black sludge beneath the three women's feet.

They worked on the room for far longer, probably, than they really needed to, for at first they would beat out a patch of flame, only to turn their backs on it and find that, a few minutes later, it had begun to glow again; so after that they took no chances, and made their grim, methodical way from one ruined surface to another, pouring water, and using pokers and fire-tongs to riddle up and beat out embers and sparks. They were all three of them sick and wheezing from the smoke, with running eyes that left pale tear-marks on their soot-stained cheeks, and soon they found themselves shivering, partly in response to the drama of it all, partly simply with the cold, which seemed to rise up in the hot room with appalling swiftness the moment the last flame was doused.

Roderick, apparently, kept at the open window, clinging to the frame. He was still very drunk, but added to that—and not surprisingly, I suppose, bearing in mind everything he'd been through during the war—the sight of the flames and the choking smoke seemed to paralyse him. He looked on wildly but uselessly as his mother and sister made the room safe; he let himself be helped indoors, but by the time they had got him down to the kitchen and put him to sit at the table with a blanket around him he had begun to understand just how near they had all come to disaster, and he clutched at his sister's hand.

'You see what's happened, Caro?' he said to her. 'You see what it wanted? My God, it's cleverer than I thought! If you hadn't woken—! If you hadn't come—!'

'What is he saying?' asked Mrs Ayres, distressed by his manner and not understanding. 'Caroline, what does he mean?'

'He doesn't mean anything,' answered Caroline—knowing full well what he meant, but wanting to protect her mother from it. 'He's still drunk. Roddie, please.'

But now, she said, he started acting 'like a madman', putting the heels of his hands to his eyes, then catching at his hair, then looking in horror at his fingers—for his hair had oil on it, and the oil had turned, in the smoke, to a gritty sort of tar. He wiped his hands on his blackened shirt-front, compulsively. He began to cough, and then to struggle for his breath, and the struggling sent him into one of his panics. He reached for Caroline again. 'I'm sorry!' he kept saying, over and over.

His breath was ragged and boozy, his eyes were crimson in his sooty face, his shirt was soaked through with rainwater. He grabbed, with shaking hands, at his mother. 'Mother, I'm sorry!'

After their ordeal in the burning room, his behaviour was too much. Mrs Ayres looked at him for a second in absolute horror, then, 'Be quiet!' she cried, her voice breaking. 'Oh, for God's sake, be quiet!' And when he still babbled and wept, Caroline went to him, and swung back her hand, and struck him.

She said she felt the sting of it in her palm almost before she knew that she had done it; and then she put her hands to her mouth, as startled and as frightened as if it were she herself who'd been hit. Rod abruptly fell silent, and covered his face. Mrs Ayres stood watching him, her shoulders twitching as she caught after her breath. Caroline said unsteadily, 'We're all a little mad, I think. We're all a little crazy . . . Betty? Are you there?'

The girl came forward, her eyes wide, her face pale, and striped like a tiger's with streaks of soot. Caroline said, 'You're all right?'

Betty nodded.

'Not burnt, or anything like that?'

'No, miss.'

She spoke in a whisper; but the sound of her voice was reassuring, and Caroline grew calmer.

'Good girl. You've been very good, and very brave. Don't mind my brother. He—he isn't himself. We're none of us ourselves. Is there any hot water? Light the boiler, will you, and put some pans on the stove, enough for tea and three or four wash-bowls. We can take off the worst of the muck before we go up to the bathroom. Mother, you should sit down.'

Mrs Ayres looked vague. Caroline went around the table to help her into a chair and to tuck a kitchen blanket around her. But her own limbs trembled as she did it, she felt as nerveless suddenly as if she'd been lifting impossible weights, and when her mother was settled, she drew out a chair for herself and sank heavily into it.

For five or ten minutes after that, the only sounds in the kitchen were the roars of flame at the stove, the rising stir of warming water, and the clink of metal and china as Betty went about setting down bowls and gathering towels. Presently the girl called softly to Mrs Ayres; she helped her over to the sink, where she washed her hands, her face, and her feet. She did the same for Caroline; then looked doubtfully at Rod. He, however, had calmed himself down sufficiently to see what was wanted of him and to stumble over to the sink. But he moved like a sleepwalker, putting his hands into the water and letting Betty soap and rinse them, then standing limp and staring while she wiped the smudges from his face. His tarry hair resisted all her attempts to wash it: she took a comb to it instead, catching the crumbs of cindery oil in a sheet of newspaper, then screwing the paper up and setting it down on the draining board. When she had finished, he moved dumbly to one side, to let her pour the filthy water down the sink. He looked across the kitchen and caught his sister's eye, and his expression was such a mixture, Caroline said, of fear and confusion, she couldn't bear it. She turned away from him, meaning to rejoin her mother.

Then a very strange thing happened. Caroline had just taken a step towards the table when, from the corner of her eye, she saw her brother make some movement—something as simple, she thought at the time, as putting up his hand to his face to bite at a fingernail or to rub at his cheek. At the same moment, Betty also moved—turning briefly away from the sink to drop a towel into a bucket on the floor. But as she turned back, the girl gave a gasp: Caroline looked properly and, to her absolute amazement, saw, beyond her brother's shoulder, more flames. 'Roddie!' she called, afraid. He turned, saw what she had seen, and darted away. On the wooden draining-board, a few inches from where he had been standing, there was a small bundle of fire and smoke. It was the newspaper Betty had used to catch the cinders from his hair. She had screwed it into a loose sort of parcel—and now, somehow, unbelievably, it had managed to set itself alight.

The fire was nothing, of course, compared to the terrifying small inferno they had tackled in Roderick's room. Caroline went quickly across the kitchen and knocked the bundle into the sink. The flames rose higher, then rapidly dwindled; the blackened paper, gossamer-like, held its shape for a moment before collapsing into fragments. But the dumbfounding thing was how such a fire could have started at all. Mrs Ayres and Caroline looked at each other, thoroughly unnerved. 'What did you see?' they asked Betty, and she answered, with frightened eyes, 'I dunno, miss! Nothing at all! Only the smoke and the yellow flames, coming up behind Mr Roderick's back.'

She seemed as bewildered as everyone else. After thinking the matter over, they could only conclude, doubtfully, that one of the cinders she had combed from Roderick's hair still had the germ of a fire in it, and the dryness of the newspaper had encouraged it back into life. Naturally, this was a very disturbing thought. They began to glance nervously about, half expecting other flames. Roderick, in particular, was distressed and panicky. When his mother said that perhaps she, Caroline, and Betty ought to go back up to his room for another rake at the ashes, he cried out that they mustn't leave him alone! He was afraid to be on his own! He 'couldn't stop it!' So, mainly in fear of his breaking down altogether, they took him with them. They found him an undamaged chair, and he sat in that with his legs drawn up, his hands at his mouth, his eyes darting, while they went wearily from one blackened surface to another. But all was cold and dead and filthy. They gave up searching just before dawn.

I woke an hour or two later, rather wearied by my bad dreams, but blissfully ignorant of the catastrophe that had very nearly swallowed up Hundreds Hall in the night; in fact, I knew nothing of the fire until I heard of it from one of my evening patients, who in turn had had the damage reported to him by a tradesman who'd been out at the house that morning. I didn't believe him at first. It seemed impossible to me that the family could have gone through such an ordeal and not sent me word of it. Then another man mentioned the incident to me as if it were already common knowledge. Still dubious, I telephoned

Mrs Ayres, and to my amazement she confirmed the whole story. She sounded so hoarse and so tired, I cursed myself for not having called her sooner, when I might have gone out there—for I had recently started spending an evening a week on the wards of the district hospital, tonight was one of those evenings, and I simply could not get away. She promised me that she, Caroline, and Roderick were all quite well, only weary. She said the fire had given them all 'a little fright': that was how she phrased it, and perhaps because of those words I pictured the incident as something relatively minor. I remembered all too vividly the state that Rod had been in when I had left him; I recalled the bullishness with which he'd been slopping his drinks around, the way he had dropped a lighted spill so that it burned unheeded on the carpet. I supposed he'd started a small blaze with a cigarette . . . But I knew that even a small fire can produce a great deal of smoke. I knew, too, that the effects of smoke inhalation are often at their worst a day or two after the fire itself. So I went to bed worried about the family, and passed another uneasy night on their behalf.

I drove out to the house at the end of my round next morning and, just as I'd feared, they were all suffering. In purely physical terms, Betty and Roderick were the least affected. She had kept close to the door while the fire was raging, and had been darting back and forth to the lavatory for water. Roderick had been lying flat in his bed, breathing shallowly while the worst of the smoke collected high above his head. But Mrs Ayres was by now quite wretched—breathless and weak, and more or less confined to her room—and Caroline looked and sounded ghastly, with a swollen throat, and singed hair, and her face and hands marked crimson from embers and sparks. She met me at the front door as I arrived, and the sight of her was so awful, and so much worse than I'd been expecting, I found myself putting down my bag so that I could take her by the shoulders and gaze properly into her face.

'Oh, Caroline,' I said.

She blinked self-consciously, and smiled, but her eyes began to glisten with tears. 'I look like a poor Guy Fawkes,' she said, 'that got snatched off the bonfire at the very last minute—'

She turned away, and started coughing. I said hastily, 'Go in, for heaven's sake, out of the cold.'

By the time I had picked up my bag and joined her, her cough had subsided, she had wiped her face, and the tears were gone. I closed the door—but did it blindly, shocked now by the frightful scent of burning that met me in the hall; shocked by the appearance of the hall itself, which might have been hung with mourning-veils, so thickly spotted and smeared was every surface with smuts and blacks and soot.

'Rotten, isn't it?' said Caroline hoarsely, following my gaze. 'And it only gets worse, I'm afraid. Come and see.' She led me along the north passage. 'The smell's right through the house, even up in the attics, I don't know how. Don't mind your muddy shoes, we've given up on this floor for now. But be careful of your jacket against the walls. The soot sticks like anything.'

The door of Rod's room was ajar, and as we drew closer to it I could see enough to prepare me for the devastation that lay beyond. Even so, when Caroline went in, for a second I stayed at the threshold, too appalled to follow. Mrs Bazeley—who was in there with Betty, washing down the walls—met my gaze and nodded, grimly.

'You look like I done, Doctor,' she said, 'when I come in yesterday morning. And this is nothing to how it were then. We was wading in filth up to our ankles, wan't we, Betty?'

The room had been cleared of most of its furniture, which was standing higgledy-piggledy down on the terrace on the other side of the open French window. The carpet had also been rolled up and moved out, and sheets of newspaper had been laid on the wide wooden floorboards, but the boards were still so wet and ashy that the paper was turning to a thick grey pulp, like sooty porridge. The walls were running with more ashy water where Mrs Bazeley and Betty were scrubbing at them. The wooden panelling was scorched and charred, and the ceiling—that notorious lattice-work ceiling—was perfectly black, its mysterious smudges lost for ever.

'This is unbelievable,' I said to Caroline. 'I had no idea! If I had known—'

I didn't finish, for my knowing or not knowing was beside the point, there was nothing I could have done. But I felt extremely unsettled to think that such a serious thing could have happened to the family in my absence. I said, 'The whole house might have been lost. It doesn't bear thinking about! And Rod was *here*, in the middle of it? Is he really all right?'

She gave me, I thought, an odd sort of look, then glanced over at Mrs Bazeley.

'Yes, he's all right. Only wheezy like the rest of us. Most of his things have been lost, though. His chair—you can see it out there—seemed to get the worst of the fire; that, and his desk and his table.'

I looked through the open window and saw the desk, its legs and drawers intact but its surface as blackened and crisped as if someone had lit a bonfire on it. Suddenly I understood why there was so much ash in the room. I said, 'His papers!'

Caroline nodded tiredly. 'Probably the driest things in the house.'

'Were any spared?'

'A few. I don't know what's been lost. I don't really know what was in here. There were plans of the house and estate, weren't there? I think there were all sorts of maps, copies of the deeds to the farms and cottages, and letters, and bills, notes of my father's . . .' Her voice grew thicker. She began to cough again.

'What a dreadful, dreadful shame,' I said, looking around, and seeing new damage with every glance: a painting on the wall with its canvas charred, lamps with blackened globes and lustres. 'This lovely room. What will you do with it? Can it be saved? The worst of the panels might be replaced, I suppose. The ceiling you could whitewash.'

She gave a gloomy shrug. 'Mother thinks that once the room has been cleaned, we might as well just close it up like the others. We certainly don't have the money to restore it.'

'What about insurance money?'

She glanced again at Mrs Bazeley and Betty. They were still scrubbing at the walls, and under cover of the rasp of their brushes she said quietly, 'Rod let the insurance payments go. We just found out.'

'He let them go!'

'Months ago, apparently. As a way of saving money.' She closed her eyes, and slowly shook her head, then moved to the French window. 'Come outside for a minute, would you?'

We went down the stone steps and I surveyed the damaged furniture, the ruined desk and table, the armchair with its leather covering gone, its springs and horsehair stuffing laid bare like the diseased bones and intestines of some fantastic anatomical model. It made very bleak viewing, and the day, though rainless, was cold; I saw Caroline shiver. I wanted to examine her and Betty, along with her mother and brother, so I said she ought to take me back into the house, to the little parlour or somewhere warm. But after a slight hesitation she looked in through the open window, then drew me further away from it. She coughed again, grimacing against her swollen throat as she swallowed.

She said very quietly, 'You spoke to Mother yesterday. Did she say anything to you about how the fire might have started?'

She kept her eyes on mine. I said, 'She told me only that it had broken out in Rod's room after all of you had gone to bed, and that you found it and put it out. I guessed that Rod, being so drunk, had done something silly with a cigarette.'

'We thought the same,' she said, 'at first.'

I was struck by that 'at first'. I said warily, 'What does Rod himself remember?'

'Nothing at all.'

'I suppose he passed out, and then—what? Could he have woken later, gone to the fire, lit a spill?'

She swallowed uncomfortably again, and spoke with something of an effort. 'I don't know. I just don't know what to think.' She nodded back in through the window. 'Did you notice the fireplace?'

I looked, and saw the grate covered over with the grey mesh guard. Caroline said, 'That's exactly how it was when I left Rod, a few hours before the fire started. When I went back in, the grate was dark as if it hadn't been disturbed. But the other fires, well, I keep picturing them.

There wasn't just one, you see. There were, I don't know, maybe five or six.'

'As many as that?' I said, shocked. 'It's a miracle, Caroline, that none of you is more seriously hurt!'

'That isn't what I mean . . . They taught us about fire in the Wrens. They talked about how fire spreads. It creeps, you know. It doesn't leap. These fires, they were more like the separate small fires that might have been started by—by incendiaries or something. Look at Rod's chair: it's as though flames broke out right in the middle of it; the legs are un-touched. The desk and table are the same. And, these curtains.' She caught up the pair of brocade curtains that had burned themselves free from their rings, and which had been slung over the back of the ruined armchair. 'The fire starts here, look, half-way up. How can that be? The walls to either side of them are only scorched. It's as if—' She glanced back into the room, more afraid than ever of being overheard. 'Well, Rod's having been careless with a cigarette or a candle is one thing. But it's as if these fires were set. Deliberately set, I mean.'

I said, appalled, 'You think that Rod—?'

She answered quickly, 'I don't know. I simply don't know. But I've been thinking about what he told you, that time at your surgery. And those marks we found on his walls—they were burns, weren't they? Well, weren't they? They make a horrible sort of sense now. Besides, there's another thing.'

And then she told me about that odd little incident down in the kitchen, when the parcel of newspaper had apparently burst into flame behind Rod's back. At the time, as I've reported, they'd all supposed it the work of a cinder. But since then Caroline had gone to have another look at the scene, and had found a box of kit-chen matches on one of the shelves close by. She didn't think it very likely, but it seemed to her just possible that, with no one's eyes upon him, Roderick could have got hold of one of the matches and started the blaze himself.

This seemed to me to be simply too much. I said, 'I don't want to doubt you, Caroline. But you'd all been through such an ordeal. I'm not surprised you saw more flames.'

'You think we imagined the burning paper? All four of us?'

'Well—'

'We didn't imagine it, I promise you that. The flames were real. And if Roddie didn't start them, then . . . what did? That's what scares me, almost more than anything. That's why I think it *has* to have been Rod.'

I didn't quite know what she was getting at; but she was plainly very frightened. I said, 'Look, let's be calm about this. There's no proof, is there, that the fire was anything other than an accident?'

She said, 'I'm not so sure. I wonder, for instance, what a policeman would make of it. You heard that Paget's man was out here yesterday, bringing the meat? He smelt the smoke, and wandered round to look through the windows before I could stop him. He was a fireman in Coventry during the war, you know. I told him some slush about an oil-heater, but I saw him having a good look round, taking everything in. I could see in his face that he didn't believe me.'

'But what you're suggesting,' I said softly, 'is monstrous! To think of Rod, cold-heartedly going about the room—'

'I know! I know, it's horrible! And I don't say he did it deliberately, Doctor. I don't believe he wanted to hurt anyone. I'll believe anything but that. But, well—' Her expression grew pinched, and desperately unhappy. 'Can't people do hurtful things, sometimes, and not even know they're doing them?'

I didn't answer. I looked around me again, at the ruined furniture: the chair, the table, the desk with its charred and ashy surface, over which I had so often seen Rod poring in a state very like despair. I remembered how, a few hours before the fire, he had been raging against his father, against his mother, against the whole estate. *There'll be tricks tonight*, he had said to me, with dreadful coyness; and I'd looked from him—hadn't I?—into the shadows of his room, and seen the walls and ceiling of it marked—almost swarming!—with those unnerving black smudges.

I passed a hand across my face. 'Oh, Caroline,' I said. 'What a ghastly business. I can't help but feel responsible.'

She said, 'What do you mean?'

'I should never have left your brother alone! I let him down. I've let you all down . . . Where is he now? What does he say?'

Her look grew odd again. 'We've put him upstairs in his old room. But listen, we can't get anything sensible out of him. He—he's in pretty dreadful shape. We think we can rely on Betty, but we don't want Mrs Bazeley to see him. We don't want anyone to see him, if we can help it. The Rossiters called yesterday, and I had to send them away, in case he made some sort of fuss. It isn't shock, it—it's something else. Mother's taken his cigarettes and everything like that. She's—' Her eyelids fluttered, and a little blood crept into her cheeks. 'She's locked him in.'

'Locked him in?' I couldn't believe it.

'She's been thinking about the fire, you see, like I have. She supposed it an accident at first; we all did. Then, from the way he was behaving and the things he said, it was clear that something else was going on. I had to tell her about the other things. Now she's afraid of what he'll do next.'

She turned away and started coughing, and this time the cough would not subside. She had spoken too long and too feelingly, and the day was too cold. She looked terribly weary and ill.

I took her through to the little parlour, and it was there that I examined her. Then I went upstairs, to look at her mother and her brother.

I went to Mrs Ayres first. She was propped up against her pillows, swathed in bedjackets and shawls, her long hair loose about her shoulders, making her face seem pale and pinched. But she was clearly very glad to see me.

'Oh, Dr Faraday,' she said hoarsely. 'Can you believe this new calamity? I'm beginning to think my family must have some sort of curse upon it. I don't understand it. What have we done? Whom have we angered? Do you know?'

She asked this almost seriously. I said, as I hitched up a chair and began to examine her, 'You've certainly had more than your share of bad luck. I'm so sorry.'

She coughed, leaning forward to do it, then sinking back into her pillows. But she held my gaze. 'You've seen Roderick's room?'

I was moving the stethoscope. 'Just a second, please . . . Yes.'

'You saw the desk, the chair?'

'Do try not to speak for a moment.'

I drew her forward again, in order to listen at her back. Then, putting my stethoscope away, and feeling her eyes still on me, I nodded. 'Yes.'

'And what do you make of them?'

'I don't know.'

'I think you do. And oh, Doctor, I never imagined I would live to be afraid of my own son! I keep picturing what might have happened. Every time I close my eyes, I see flames.'

Her voice caught. Another fit of coughing overtook her, more serious than the first, and she couldn't finish. I held her shoulders as she shook, then gave her water to sip, and a clean handkerchief with which to wipe her mouth and eyes. She fell back into her pillows again, flushed and exhausted.

I said, 'You're talking too much.'

She shook her head. 'I have to speak! I've no one to discuss this with save you and Caroline, and she and I have been talking each other in circles. She told me things, yesterday—extraordinary things! I couldn't believe it! She said that Roderick's been behaving almost like a madman. That his room was burned, before this. That she showed you the marks?'

I moved uncomfortably. 'She showed me something, yes.'

'You wouldn't come to me, either of you?'

'We didn't want to unsettle you. We wanted to spare you if we could. Naturally, if I had had any idea that Roderick's condition would lead to something like this—'

Her expression grew unhappier. 'His "condition", you call it. So you knew he was ill.'

I said, 'I knew he wasn't well. To be frank, I suspected he was far from well. But I made him a promise.'

'He came to you, I think, and told you some tale about this house. About there being something in it, wishing him harm? Is that true?'

I hesitated. She saw, and said, with humble earnestness, 'Please be honest with me, Doctor.'

So I said, 'Yes, it's true. I'm sorry.' And I recounted everything that had happened: Rod's fit of panic in my dispensary, his bizarre and frightening story, his sulkiness and temper since then, the threats implicit in some of his words . . .

She listened in silence—putting out her hand, after a moment, and blindly catching hold of mine. Her fingernails, I saw, were ridged and elderly, and still dirty with soot. Her knuckles were marked from flying embers, the scars a little echo of her son's. Her grip grew tighter the more she learned, and when I had finished speaking she looked at me as if bewildered.

'My poor dear boy! I had no idea. He was never strong like his father, I knew that. But to think of his mind giving way like this! Did he really—' She put her other hand to her breast. 'Did he really speak like that against Hundreds? Against me?'

I said, 'You see? This is precisely why I hesitated to tell you. He wasn't himself when he said those things. He hardly knew what he was saying.'

She seemed not to have heard me. 'Can it be true that he hates us all so much? Is that why this has happened?'

'No, no. It's clearly the strain—'

She looked more bewildered than ever. 'The strain?'

'The house, the farm. The after-shock of his accident. His time in the service.—Who knows? Does it matter what's caused it?'

Again, she didn't seem to be listening. She clutched my fingers and said, as if really anguished, 'Tell me, Doctor: am I to blame?'

The question, and the obvious force of emotion behind it, surprised me. I said, 'Of course you aren't.'

'But I'm his mother! This is his home! For this thing to have happened—it isn't natural. It isn't right. I must have failed him in some way. Have I? Suppose there were something, Dr Faraday—'

She drew away her hand, and lowered her eyes as if ashamed. 'Suppose there were something,' she went on, 'that had got in the way of my feelings for him, when he was a boy. Some shadow, of upset, or grief.' Her voice flattened. 'I expect you know that I once had another child, before Caroline and Roderick were born. My little girl, Susan.'

I nodded. 'I remember it. I'm sorry.'

She made a gesture, turned her head, acknowledging my sympathy, but also shrugging it off, as if it could have no bearing on her grief. She said, in the same almost matter-of-fact way as before, 'She was my one true love. Does that sound odd to you? I never expected, when I was young, that I should fall in love with my own child, but she and I were like sweethearts. When she died, I felt for a long time that I might as well have died with her. Perhaps I did . . . People told me that the best and soonest way to get over the loss of a child was to start another, as quickly as one could. My mother told me that, my mother-in-law, my aunts, my sister . . . And then, when Caroline was born, they said something else. They said, "Well, naturally, a little girl will put you in mind of the lost one, you must try again, you must try for a boy; a mother always loves her sons . . ." And, after Roderick: "Why, what's the matter with you? Don't you know that people of our sort don't make a fuss? Here you are, in your fine home, with your husband who came through the war, and two healthy children. If you can't find a way to be happy with that, you must simply stop complaining—"'

Again she coughed, and wiped her eyes. I said, when the cough had subsided, 'It was hard for you.'

'Harder for my children.'

'Don't say that. Love isn't a thing that can be weighed and measured, surely?'

'Perhaps you're right. And yet— I *do* love my children, Doctor; truly I do. But what a very dull and half-alive thing that love has seemed to me, sometimes! Because *I* have been half alive, you see . . . Caroline, I think, it hasn't harmed. Roderick was always the sensitive one. Could it be that he grew up feeling a sort of falseness in me, and hating me for it?'

I thought of how Rod himself had spoken on the night of the fire. I remembered him saying that he and his sister had disappointed his mother 'simply by being born'. But her expression, now, was so anguished; and I had already told her so much. What good would it have done, to share that with her, too? So I took her hand again and said, very firmly, 'You're being fanciful. You're ill, and tired. One upset summons up a crowd of others, that's all it is.'

She looked into my face, wanting to believe me. 'You really think so?'

'I know so. You mustn't brood on things from the past. The issue we've to deal with now is not what's made Rod ill, but how we're to get him well again.'

'But suppose this is too deep a thing for that? Suppose he can't be cured?'

'Of course he can. You're talking as though he's beyond help! With proper care—'

She shook her head, beginning to cough again. 'We can't care for him here. We simply haven't the strength for it, Caroline and I. Remember, we've been through this before.'

'Then, perhaps a nurse?'

'I don't believe a nurse could cope with him!'

'Oh, but surely—'

Her gaze moved from mine. She said as if guiltily, 'Caroline told me you spoke of a hospital.'

I said, after a slight pause, 'Yes. I hoped at one point to be able to persuade Rod to admit himself. The place I had in mind was a specialist private nursing home. For mental disorders, like this.'

'Mental disorders,' she repeated.

I said quickly, 'Don't let that phrase alarm you too much. It covers all sorts of conditions. The clinic is up in Birmingham, and quite discreet. But, well, it's not cheap. Even with Rod's disability pension I'm afraid the fees would be hefty. Perhaps, after all, a reliable nurse, here at Hundreds, would be the better option . . .'

She said, 'I'm frightened, Dr Faraday. A nurse could only do so much. Suppose Roderick were to start another fire? Next time, perhaps, he'd succeed in burning the Hall to the ground, or in killing himself—or in killing his sister, or me, or one of the servants! Have you thought of that? Imagine what would follow! Inquiries, and policemen, and newspaper-men—all in earnest this time; not like that wretched business with Gyp. And what would become of him then? As far as anyone knows, this fire was an accident and Roderick had the worst of it. If we send him away now, we can say we're simply sending him out of the Warwickshire winter in order for him to recover. Don't you agree? I'm asking you now as our friend, as well as our doctor. Please help us. You were so good to us, before.'

I saw the sense in her words. I was very conscious that I had already dragged my heels over Roderick, with near-disastrous results. It could certainly do him no harm to get away from the estate for a while; I had wanted that for him from the start. And yet, there was a great deal of difference between encouraging him to admit himself to a clinic, and packing him off there by force.

I said, 'It's certainly an option. Naturally, I would have to bring in another man, get a second opinion. But we mustn't act too hastily. As frightful as this incident has been, it may well have the effect of jolting him out of his delusion. I still can't believe—'

'You haven't seen him yet,' she whispered, across my words.

She had that odd look of Caroline's. I said, after a moment, 'No, not yet.'

'Go and speak to him now, will you? Then come back and tell me your thoughts.—Just a second.'

I had risen, but she beckoned me back. And while I watched, she reached into the drawer of her bedside cabinet and took something from it. It was a key.

Reluctantly, I held out my hand.

．　．　．

The room they had put him in was the bedroom he'd had as an older child: the room, I suppose, in which he'd slept during his school holidays and, later, in his brief leaves from the Air Force, before his smash. It was just around the landing from his mother's, separated from it only by her old dressing-room, and it was horrible to think of his having been in there all this time—horrible, too, to have to tap at his door and brightly call his name, and then, receiving no answer, put the key to the lock like a gaoler. I don't know what I expected to find when I went in to him. I wouldn't have been surprised if he had come charging after his freedom. As I opened the door I remember I flinched, prepared for anger and abuse.

But what I found was, in a way, far worse. The curtains at the windows were half drawn, and the room was gloomy. It took me a moment to see that Rod was sitting in bed, in a pair of boyish striped pyjamas and an old blue dressing-gown, and instead of making a rush at the open door, he watched me approach, keeping very still. He had one hand at his mouth, the fingers made loosely into a fist; he was rapidly. flicking at his lip with his thumb-nail. Even in the poor light and from a distance I could see how unwell he looked. Drawing closer, I made out the greasy yellowish-white of his face, and his swollen, sore-looking eyes. There seemed to be traces of soot, still, in the pores of his skin and in the oil of his unwashed hair. His cheeks were unshaven, the stubble growing patchily because of his scars; his mouth was pale, the lips drawn in. I was struck, too, by the *odour* of him: the odour of smoke and perspiration and sour breath. Under his bed was a chamber-pot, which had evidently recently been used.

He kept his eyes on my face as I approached, but didn't answer when I spoke to him. Only when I sat beside him and opened my bag, and gently parted the lapels of his dressing-gown and pyjama top to put the stethoscope to his chest, did he break his silence. And what he said was, 'Can you hear it?'

His voice had only a hint of hoarseness. I drew him forward to put the stethoscope to his back. 'Hear what?'

His mouth was close to my ear. He said, 'You know what.'

'All I know is that, like your mother and sister, you breathed in a good deal of smoke the other night. I want to be sure it didn't hurt you.'

'Hurt me? Oh, it wouldn't do that. It doesn't want that. Not any more.'

'Be quiet for a moment, will you?'

I moved the bulb. His heart was thumping and his chest was tight, but I could find no trace of stickiness or deadness in his lungs, so I settled him back against his pillow and refastened his clothes. He let me do it, but his gaze moved away, and soon he returned his hand to his mouth and started flicking again at his lip.

I said, 'Rod, this fire has frightened everybody terribly. No one seems to know how it started. What do you remember? Can you tell me?' He seemed not to be listening. 'Rod?'

He gaze came back to mine and he frowned, growing almost peevish. 'I've told everyone, already: I don't remember anything. Just you being there, and then Betty coming, and then Caroline, putting me to bed. I had a dream, I think.'

'What sort of dream?'

He was still flicking at his mouth. 'Just a dream. I don't know. What does it matter?'

'You might have dreamed, say, that you got up. That you tried to light a cigarette or a candle.'

His hand grew still. He looked at me in disbelief. 'You're not trying to make out it was all an accident!'

'I don't know what to think, yet.'

He moved around in the bed, growing excited. 'After all I've told you! Even Caroline can see it wasn't an accident! There were lots of fires, she says. She says those other marks, in my room, they were little fires, too. Little fires that didn't take.'

I said, 'We don't know that for sure. We may never know.'

'*I* know. I knew, that night. I told you, didn't I, that a trick was coming? Why did you leave me on my own? Couldn't you see I wasn't strong enough?'

'Rod, please.'

But he was shifting around now as if he could hardly control his own movements. He was like a man with DT; it was terrible to see.

At last he reached for my arm and held on to it. 'What if Caroline hadn't come in time?' he said. His eyes were blazing in his face. 'The whole house might have burnt down! My sister, my mother, Betty—'

'Come on, Rod. Calm down.'

'Calm down? I'm practically a murderer!'

'Don't be foolish.'

'That's what they're saying, aren't they?'

'No one's saying anything.'

He twisted the sleeve of my jacket. 'But they're right, don't you see? I thought I could keep this thing at bay, stop the infection. But I'm too weak. The infection's been too long inside me. It's *changing* me. It's making me *like* it. I thought I was keeping it away from Mother and Caroline. But all this time it's been working *through* me, as a way of getting at them. It's been— What are you doing?'

I had drawn away from him to reach for my bag. He saw me bringing out a tub of tablets.

'No!' he cried, hitting out with his hand so that the tub went flying. 'Nothing like that! Don't you understand? Are you trying to help it? Is that what you're doing? I mustn't go to sleep!'

The blow of his hand against mine, and the obvious madness of his words and expression, frightened me. But I looked in anxiety at his swollen eyes and said, 'You haven't been sleeping? Not since the night before last?' I took hold of his wrist. His pulse was still racing.

He pulled himself free. 'How can I? It was bad enough before.'

'But Rod,' I said, 'you must sleep.'

'I daren't! And you wouldn't, either, if you knew what it was like. Last night—' He lowered his voice, and glanced craftily about. 'Last night I heard noises. I thought there was something at the door, something scratching, wanting to get in. Then I realised that the noise was *inside me*, that the thing that was scratching was inside me, trying to get *out*. It's waiting, you see. It's all very well them locking me in, but if I go to sleep—'

He didn't finish, but looked at me with what he evidently thought was tremendous meaning. Then he drew up his knees, put his hands before his mouth, and went back to flicking at his lip. I left the bed, to gather up the pills that he had knocked from the tub to the floor; I found my hand was trembling as I did it, for I'd realised at last how deeply, deeply lost he was to his delusion. I stood up and looked help-lessly at him, and then I gazed around the room, seeing tragic little tokens of the charming, lively boy he must once have been: the shelf of adventure books still on the wall, the trophies and models, the Air Force charts, with annotations added in an untidy teenage hand . . . Who ever could have predicted this decline? How had it happened? It seemed to me, suddenly, that his mother must be right: no amount of strain or burden could explain it. There had to be something else at the root of it, some clue or sign I could not read.

I returned to the bed, and looked into his face; but finally looked away, defeated. I said, 'I have to leave you, Rod. I wish to God I hadn't. Can I send Caroline to sit with you?'

He shook his head. 'No, you mustn't do that.'

'Well, is there anything else I can do?'

He looked me over, considering. And when he spoke again his voice had changed, he was as polite and apologetic, suddenly, as the boy I had been picturing a few moments before. He said, 'Let me have a cigarette, would you? I'm not allowed to, when I'm on my own. But if you stay with me while I smoke it, that'll be all right, won't it?'

I gave him a cigarette, and lit it for him—he wouldn't do it with his own hands, and he screwed up his eyes and covered his face while I struck the flame—then I sat with him as, wheezing slightly, he smoked it through. When he had finished he gave me the stub, so that I could take it away with me. 'You haven't left your matches, by mistake?' he asked anxiously as I rose again. I had to show him the box, and make a sort of pantomime of putting it back into my pocket, before he'd let me go.

And then, most poignantly of all, he insisted on coming to the door with me, to make sure that, after I left him, I locked it. I went twice, the first time to take his chamber-pot to the bathroom, where I emptied and rinsed it; but even for that short trip he insisted I turn the key on him, and when I returned I found him hovering on the other side of the door as if disturbed by the coming and going. Before I left the second time I took his hand—but again, the delay seemed only to agitate him, his fingers were lifeless in mine and his gaze slid nervously from my face. When I finally closed the door I did it very firmly, and turned the key with great deliberateness, so that there should be no mistake about it; but as I was walking quietly away I heard the creaking of the lock, and looked back to see the handle moving and the door shifting in its frame. He was making sure he couldn't get out. The handle twisted two or three times in its socket before it was still. The sight of that, I think, upset me almost more than anything else.

I took the key back to his mother. She could see how shocked and distressed I was. We sat in silence for a moment, and then, in low, dismal voices, began to talk over the arrangements that must be made for taking him away.

It was a simple enough business, after all. I brought in David Graham first, to confirm that Rod was beyond ordinary medical help, and then the director of the clinic—a Dr Warren—came down from Birmingham to make his own examination, and to bring the necessary papers. This was on the Sunday of that week, four days after the night of the fire: Rod had gone sleepless all that time, violently refusing my attempts to sedate him, and had passed into a near-hysterical state which I think shocked even Warren. I didn't know how he would take the news that we planned to commit him to what was effectively a psychiatric hospital; to my very great relief—but also, in a sense, to my dismay—he was almost pathetically grateful. Clutching desperately at Warren's hand, he said, 'You'll watch me there, won't you? Nothing will get out of me, if you're watching. And even if it does, well, it won't be my fault, will it, if something happens, if someone gets hurt?'

His mother was there in the room while he babbled on like this. She was still weak and very wheezy, but had risen and dressed in order to receive Dr Warren. Seeing how upset the sight of Roderick made her, I took her downstairs. We joined Caroline in the little parlour, and Warren came down to us a few minutes later.

'This is terribly sad,' he said, shaking his head. 'Terribly sad. I see from his records that Roderick was treated for nervous depression in the months after his injury; but there was no hint, in those days, of serious mental imbalance? And nothing's happened to bring this on? A loss of some kind? Another shock?'

I'd already given him, by letter, a pretty thorough account of the case. It was clear he felt—as I did, at heart—that there was something missing, that no young man as essentially healthy as Roderick could have deteriorated so badly and so rapidly without some cause. We told him again about Rod's delusions, his panics, those disturbing marks on his walls. I described the various burdens he'd had placed on him lately, as a landowner and master of the estate.

'Well, we may never get to the real root of the problem,' he said at last. 'But, as his GP, you're definitely prepared to put him into my care?'

I said I was.

'And as his mother, Mrs Ayres, you're also willing for me to take him?'

She nodded.

'In that case, I think I can do no better than take him with me at once. I hadn't planned to. I'd intended only to come and examine him, and return with proper assistance in a few days. But my driver's a capable man, and I'm sure you won't mind me saying that it's doing no good at all, you keeping Roderick here. He certainly seems very ready to go.'

He and I attended to the paperwork while Mrs Ayres and Caroline went gloomily upstairs to prepare Rod's things, and to fetch Rod himself. When they brought him to us, he came haltingly down the stairs like an old man. They had dressed him in his ordinary clothes and his tweed overcoat, but he was so painfully thin and shrunken, the garments seemed three sizes too big. His limp was very pronounced—quite as bad as it had been six months before, so that I thought with dismay of all those wasted hours of treatment. Caroline had made an effort to shave him, and done it badly: there were cuts on his chin. His dark eyes darted, and his hands kept fluttering up to his mouth to pluck at his lips.

'Am I really going with Dr Warren?' he asked me. 'Mother says I am.'

I told him he was, and I took him to a window to show him Warren's handsome black Humber Snipe parked outside, with its driver beside it smoking a cigarette. He looked at the car with such interest, in such an ordinary, boyish kind of way—even turning to ask Dr Warren a question about the engine—that for a second he was himself again as he hadn't been for weeks, and I had a dizzying moment of doubt about the whole grim affair.

But it was too late. The papers were signed, and Dr Warren was ready to go. And Roderick grew edgy once we'd stepped forward to say our goodbyes. He returned his sister's embrace very warmly, and allowed me to shake his hand. But as his mother was kissing his cheek his eyes were darting again. He said, 'Where's Betty? I ought to say goodbye to Betty too, oughtn't I?'

He threatened to grow so agitated about it, Caroline went hastily off to the kitchen to bring Betty back. The girl stood shyly in front of Roderick, and he gave her a quick jerky nod.

'I'm going away for a while, Betty,' he said. 'So there'll be one less of us for you to look after. But you'll keep my room neat and tidy for me, while I'm gone?'

She blinked, looked quickly at Mrs Ayres, and then said, 'Yes, Mr Roderick.'

'Good girl.' His eyelid quivered, in the ghost of a wink. He patted his pockets for a moment, and I realised that, grotesquely, he was feeling for a coin. But, 'That will do, Betty,' his mother said quietly; and, obviously grateful, the girl slipped away. Rod watched her go, still fumbling with his pockets, his brow creasing into a frown. Afraid that he might grow agitated again, Warren and I moved forward and led him out to the car.

But he went into the back of it quite without fuss. Dr Warren shook my hand. I returned to the steps and stood with Mrs Ayres and Caroline until the Snipe had creaked its way across the gravel and driven from sight.

This was all done, as I've said, on a Sunday, in Mrs Bazeley's absence. How much she knew about Roderick's condition—how much she'd guessed, or been told by Betty—I don't know. Mrs Ayres informed her that Roderick had gone away out of the county 'to stay with friends': that was the story she put about, and if anyone locally asked me about it I said only that, having seen him after the fire, I'd advised him to take himself off on a holiday for the good of his lungs. At the very same time I was taking the contradictory line of trying to play the fire down. I didn't want the Ayreses to come under any sort of special scrutiny, and even to people like the Desmonds and the Rossiters, who knew the family well, I told a mixture of lies and half-truths, hoping to steer them away from the facts. I am not naturally a duplicitous man, and the strain of warding off gossip was at times a tiring one. But these were busy days for me in other ways, for—ironically enough, partly as a result of the success of that paper of mine, on Rod's treatment—I'd recently been asked to become a member of a hospital committee, and had a host of new duties. The extra work, in fact, was a welcome distraction.

Once a week for the rest of that month I took Mrs Ayres and Caroline to visit Roderick in the Birmingham clinic. It was a very mournful journey, not least because the clinic lay in a suburb of the city that had been badly bombed in the war: we weren't used to ruins and broken roads around Lidcote, and the sight of the hollowed-out houses with their jagged, gaping windows, rising eerily through what seemed to be a perpetual city fog, never ceased to depress us. But the visits were not a great success, for other reasons. Roderick was nervy and uncommunicative, and the supposed treat of showing us around, of taking us for walks in the bare wintry garden, of sitting at a tea-table with us in a room full of other listless or wild-eyed men, seemed to fill him with shame. Once or twice in the early days he asked after the estate, wanting to know how the farm was doing; as time went on, however, he seemed to lose interest in Hundreds affairs. We kept the conversation, as much as we could, to neutral village matters, but from certain things he said it was obvious to me—and it must have been clear to his mother and sister, too—that his sense of what we were talking about was shockingly dim. Once he asked after Gyp. Caroline said, in frightened tones, 'But Gyp died. You know that, Rod'—at which he screwed up his eyes as if making an effort at remembering, and said vaguely, 'Oh, yes. There was some trouble, wasn't there? And Gyp got hurt? Poor old boy.'

He might have been in hospital for years rather than weeks, so sluggish and cloudy were his thoughts; and after our third visit to him, just before Christmas, when we'd arrived to find the clinic decked out in muddy-coloured paper chains and garlands, and the men with absurd little cardboard crowns on their heads, and Roderick more vague and lifeless than ever, I was glad to be taken aside by Dr Warren's assistant and given a report on his progress.

'He's not doing too badly, all in all,' said the man. He was a younger man than Warren, with a slightly breezier approach. 'He seems to have shaken off most of his delusions, anyway. We've managed to get some lithium bromide into him, and that's helped. He's certainly sleeping better. I wish I could say his case was an isolated one, but, as I expect you've noticed, we've lots of fellows of about his age: dipsomaniacs, nervous cases, men still claiming "shell-shock" . . . It's all part of a general post-war malaise, in my opinion; all essentially the same problem, though it affects individuals differently depending on type. If Rod wasn't the boy he was, with the background he's had, he might have turned to gambling, or womanising—or suicide. He still likes to be locked into his room at night; we hope to break him of that. You haven't seen much change in him, but, well'—he looked embarrassed—'the reason I called you in is because I think it's these visits of yours that are holding him back. He's still convinced he's some sort of danger to his family; he feels he has to keep that danger in check, and the effort exhausts him. With no one here to remind him of home he's a different man, much brighter. The nurses and I have watched him, and we all feel the same.'

We were standing in his office, which had a window overlooking the clinic's courtyard, and I could see Mrs Ayres and Caroline making their way back to my car, hunched and wrapped against the cold. I said, 'Well, these visits put a strain on his mother and sister, too. I could certainly dissuade them from coming, if you like, and come on my own.'

He offered me a cigarette from a box on his desk.

'To be honest, I think Rod would like it if you *all* kept away for a while. You bring back the past to him, too vividly. We must think of his future.'

'But, surely—' I said, with my hand poised above the box. 'I'm his doctor. And quite apart from that, he and I are good friends.'

'The fact is, Rod has specifically requested that he be left alone for a time, by all of you. I'm sorry.'

I didn't take a cigarette after all. I said goodbye to him, then made my own way across the courtyard to rejoin Mrs Ayres and Caroline and drive them home; and in the weeks that followed, though we wrote regularly to Roderick and received occasional spiritless replies, none of his letters encouraged us to make another visit. His room at Hundreds, with its charred walls and blackened ceiling, was simply shut up. And since Mrs Ayres now often woke breathless and coughing in the night, needing medicine or a steam inhaler, his old schoolboy bedroom just around the landing from hers was given over to Betty.

'It makes much more sense to have her sleep up here with us,' Mrs

Ayres told me, wheezily. 'And heaven knows, the girl deserves it! She's been very good and loyal to us in all our troubles. That basement's too lonely for her.'

Betty, not surprisingly, was delighted with the change. But I found myself faintly unsettled by it, and when I looked into the room shortly after she had moved in, I felt more unnerved than ever. The Air Force charts, the trophies, and the boyish books had all been put away, and her few poor possessions—the petticoats and darned stockings, the Woolworth hairbrush and scattering of grips, the sentimental postcards tacked to the wall—were somehow enough to transform it. Meanwhile, the whole north side of the Hall, which Caroline had once described to me as 'the men's side', went practically unvisited. Occasionally I wandered over there, and the rooms seemed dead as paralysed limbs. Soon it was eerily as though Rod had never been master of the house at all— as if, more thoroughly even than poor Gyp before him, he had vanished and left no trace.

EIGHT

With Roderick's removal, it was clear to all of us that Hundreds had entered a distinct new phase. In purely practical terms, changes occurred almost at once, for the estate's already overstretched finances were hit hard by the fees of his clinic, and drastic extra economies had to be put in place in order to accommodate them. The generator, for example, was now routinely turned off for days at a stretch, and going up to the Hall on those wintry evenings I'd often find the place plunged into nearly total darkness. There would be an old brass lantern left out for me on a table just inside the front door, and I'd pick my way through the house with it—the smoke-scented walls of the passages, I remember, seeming to dance forward into the soft yellow light, and then to recede again into shadow as I moved on. Mrs Ayres and Caroline would be together in the little parlour, reading or sewing or listening to the wireless by the light of candles and oil-lamps. The flames would be weak enough to make them squint, but the room would seem a sort of radiant capsule in comparison with the inkiness all about it. If they rang for Betty she'd come with an old-fashioned candlestick, wide-eyed, like a character in a nursery rhyme.

They all put up with the new conditions with what struck me as amazing fortitude. Betty was used to lamps and candles; that was all she had grown up with. She seemed used to the Hall now, too, as if all the recent dramas had served to fix her in her place in the household, even as they'd shaken Roderick from his. Caroline claimed to like the darkness, pointing out that the house hadn't been designed for electricity anyway; saying that they were finally living in it as they were meant to. But I thought I could see through the bravado of comments like that, and it bothered me terribly that she and her mother were so reduced. My visits had fallen off during the last, worst part of Rod's illness, but now I began to go out to the Hall once or even twice a week, often taking up small presents of groceries and coal; sometimes pretending that the gifts came from patients. Christmas Day drew near—always a slightly awkward day for me, as a single man. This year there was talk of my spending it, as I'd sometimes done in the past, with a former colleague and his family over in Banbury. But then Mrs Ayres said something that made me realise that, quite as a matter of course, she was expecting me to dine with them at Hundreds; so, touched, I made my apologies to my Banbury friends, and she, Caroline, and I enjoyed a subdued dinner at the long mahogany table in the draughty dining-room—dishing up the meat on to our own plates, while Betty, for once, spent a day and a night with her parents.

But here was another effect of Roderick's absence. Gathered there together like that, I don't think any of us could have failed to remember the last time we had sat at that table, a few hours before the fire, when Rod himself had cast such a brooding, unpleasant shadow over the meal. I don't think any of us, in other words, could have failed to feel a guilty sense of relief at that shadow's removal. There was no question that Rod was missed, and missed very keenly, by his mother and sister. The Hall at times seemed terribly muted and lifeless, with only the three hushed women in it. But life there was unmistakably less tense, too. And on the business side of things, for all Rod's obsessing over the estate, the fact that he was no longer there to manage it seemed—as Caroline, I remembered, had once predicted—to make astonishingly little difference. Things continued to stagger along. If anything, they staggered rather less. Caroline herself sent for bankers' and brokers' reports to replace the ones that had been lost in the blaze, and discovered what a really parlous state the family finances had reached. She had a long, frank talk with her mother, and between them they started up those grim new economies over fuel and light. She went ruthlessly through the house looking for anything that might be sold, and soon pictures, books, and pieces of furniture which in the past had sentimentally been retained while lesser pieces were let go went off to Birmingham dealers. Perhaps most drastically, she continued negotiations with the county council over the sale of Hundreds parkland. The deal was struck at the New Year, and only two or three days later, driving into the park at the west gates, I was dismayed to see the developer, Babb, going over the site with a couple of surveyors, already pegging off the ground. Digging began soon after, and the first of the pipes and foundations were speedily laid. Overnight, it seemed, a section of the Hundreds boundary wall was demolished, and from the road that ran beside the breach one could stare right across the parkland to the Hall itself. The house looked somehow more remote, I thought, and yet oddly more vulnerable, than it had ever looked with its wall intact.

Caroline clearly thought the same. 'Mother and I feel horribly exposed,' I remember her telling me when I called in there one day in the middle of January. 'It's as if we're permanently out in our petticoats, like in some awful dream. But we've made up our minds to it, and that's that. We heard from Dr Warren again this morning, you know, and Rod's no better; it sounds to me as though he's worse. The plain fact is, no one knows when he'll be fit enough to come home again. The money from this sale will see us through the rest of the winter, and by spring the water pipe will be laid to the farm. That will change everything, Makins says.'

She rubbed her eyes with the heel of her hand, her eyelids creasing. 'I don't know. It's all so uncertain. As for all this—!' We were in the little parlour, waiting for her mother to come down, and she made a hopeless, helpless gesture towards Mrs Ayres's writing table, which she was using for her estate correspondence, and which was smothered with letters and plans. 'I swear,' she said, 'this stuff is like ivy. It positively creeps! For every letter I send to the county council they want two more copies. I've started *dreaming* in triplicate.'

'You sound like your brother,' I said warningly.

She looked startled. 'Don't say that! Poor Roddie, though. I understand better now why the business so consumed him. It's like gambling: always the very next wager that promises to turn one's luck. But look here.' Drawing back the cuff of her sweater, she offered me her bare forearm. 'Pinch me, will you, if you ever catch me sounding like him again?'

I reached for her wrist and, instead of pinching it, gently shook it, for there wasn't flesh enough to pinch; her freckled brown arm was as lean as a boy's, her well-shaped hand looking larger but oddly more feminine as a result. Feeling the bone of her wrist move smoothly against my palm as she drew away, I had a queer little surge of feeling for her. She met my gaze, smiling, but I caught hold of the tips of her fingers for a second and said seriously, 'Be careful, won't you, Caroline? Don't take on too much. Or, let me help you.'

She pulled the fingers free, self-conscious, folding her arms.

'You help us quite enough as it is. To be honest, I don't know how we'd have managed without you in the past few months. You know all our secrets. You, and Betty. What a funny thought that is! But then, it's your job to know secrets, I suppose; and hers too, in a way.'

I said, 'I hope I'm your friend, not just your doctor.'

'Oh, you are,' she answered automatically. Then she thought it over, and said it again, with more warmth and conviction: 'You are. Though heaven knows *why* you are, since we're nothing but a nuisance to you, and you've your patients to be that. Aren't you tired of nuisances?'

'I like all my nuisances,' I said, beginning to smile.

'They keep you in business.'

'Some are definitely good for business. Others I like for their own sake. But they're the ones I tend to worry about. I worry about you.'

I put a slight emphasis on the 'you', and she laughed, but looked startled again.

'Good heavens, why? I'm all right. I'm always all right. That's my "thing"—didn't you know?'

'Hmm,' I said. 'I'd be more convinced by those words if you weren't looking so tired as you said them. Why not, at least—'

She tilted her head. 'Why not what?'

I'd been meaning to broach this with her for weeks, but the moment had never felt right. I said now, in a rush, 'Well, why not get yourself a dog again?'

At once, her expression changed, seemed to shut. She turned away. 'I don't want to do that.'

'I was out at Pease Hill Farm on Monday,' I went on. 'Their retriever's in pup, a lovely bitch.' Then, seeing her resistance, I said gently, 'No one would think you were replacing Gyp.'

But she shook her head. 'It isn't that. It . . . wouldn't feel safe.'

I stared at her. 'Not safe? For you? Your mother? You mustn't let what happened with Gillian—'

'I don't mean that,' she said. And she added, reluctantly, 'I mean, for the dog.'

'The dog!'

'I'm just being silly, I expect.' She half turned away from me. 'It's just, sometimes, I can't help thinking about Roddie, and all the things he said about this house. We packed him off to that clinic, didn't we? We sent him away, because it was easier to do that than to listen to him properly. I came almost to hate him, you know, in those last few weeks. But suppose it was our hating him, our not listening to him, that made him so ill? Suppose—'

She had drawn down the cuffs of her jersey, and they drooped almost to her knuckles. Fidgeting, she tugged them further, working at them with her fingers until her thumbs found a weakness in the wool and went right through. She said quietly, 'Sometimes this house *does* seem changed to me, you know. I can't tell if it's just the way I've come to feel about it, or if it's the way it feels about me, or—' She caught my eye, and her voice changed. 'You must think me crazy.'

I said, after a second, 'I could never think you crazy. But I can see how the house, and the farm, in the state they're in now, could make you feel gloomy.'

'Gloomy,' she repeated, still working at her cuffs. 'You think that's all it is?'

'I know it. Once spring is here, and Roderick's better, and the estate gets back on its feet, you'll feel very different. I'm sure you will.'

'And you really think it's worth us . . . persevering, with Hundreds?'

The question shocked me. 'Of course! Don't you?'

She didn't answer; and in another moment the little parlour door had opened, and her mother had joined us, and the chance for further discussion was lost. Mrs Ayres came in coughing, and Caroline and I moved forward to help her to her chair. She took my arm, saying, 'Thank you, I'm fine. Truly I am. But I've been lying down for an hour, and that's a foolish thing to do at the moment, for now my lungs feel just as though they've the bottom of a duck-pond inside them.'

She coughed again, into her handkerchief, then wiped her watering eyes. There were several shawls across her shoulders, and around her head she had her lace mantilla. She looked pale and delicate, like some slender sheathed flower: the stresses of the past few weeks had aged her, the fire had slightly weakened her lungs, and the weakness had turned into a touch of winter bronchitis. Even the short journey she had just made down through the chilly house had wearied her. Her cough subsided, but left her wheezy.

She said, 'How are you, Doctor? Did Caroline tell you we've heard again from Dr Warren?' She shook her head, tight-lipped. 'Not good news, I'm afraid.'

'Yes, I'm sorry.'

The three of us talked this over for a while, and then we were led back to that other cheerless topic of the moment, the building-work. But soon Mrs Ayres's voice began to fail her, and her daughter and I took up the conversation and continued it more or less on our own: she sat listening to us for a minute or two as if frustrated by her own silence, her ringed hands restless in her lap. At last, while we spoke on, she gathered her shawls and went across to her writing-table, and started going through the papers.

Caroline followed her with her gaze.

'What are you searching for, Mother?'

Mrs Ayres was peering into an envelope as if she hadn't heard. 'So much nonsense from the council!' Her voice was like cobwebs now. 'Doesn't the government talk of paper shortages?'

'Yes, I know. It's tiresome. What are you after?'

'I'm looking for your Aunt Cissie's last letter. I'd like to show it to Dr Faraday.'

'Well, I'm afraid the letter isn't there any more.' Caroline rose as she spoke. 'I had to move it. Come and sit back down, and I'll fetch it for you.'

She went across the room to a cabinet, took the letter from one of its compartments, and handed it to her mother. Mrs Ayres returned with it to her chair, one of her Spanish shawls slipping, its long, knotted fringe beginning to trail. She spent a moment settling herself before she opened up the paper. Then she found that she had mislaid her reading-glasses.

'Oh, good Lord,' she whispered, closing her eyes. 'What next?'

She began to look about her. After a moment, Caroline and I joined in the search.

'Well, where did you have them last?' Caroline asked as she lifted a cushion.

'I had them in here,' answered Mrs Ayres. 'I'm certain I did. I had them in my hand when Betty brought in Dr Warren's letter this morning. You haven't moved them?'

Caroline frowned. 'I haven't seen them.'

'Well, someone must have moved them. Oh, I do apologise, Doctor. This is awfully boring for you.'

We spent a good five minutes making a search of the room, disturbing papers and opening drawers, peering under chairs and so on; all without success. Finally Caroline rang for Betty and—her mother protesting all the time that the journey would be fruitless, since she could remember very well where she last had the glasses, and it was right there, in the little parlour—she sent the girl off to look upstairs.

Betty returned almost at once, having found the spectacles on one of the pillows of her mistress's bed.

She held them out with an air of apology. Mrs Ayres gazed at them for a second, then took them from the girl's hand, turning her head in a gesture of disgust.

'This is what it means to be old, Betty,' she said.

Caroline laughed. The laughter, I thought, was faintly forced. 'Don't be silly, Mother!'

'No, really. I shouldn't be surprised, you know, if I were to finish up like my father's Aunt Dodo. She used to mislay her things so often, one of her sons gave her a little Indian monkey. He strapped a basket to its back and she kept her scissors and thimbles and so on in it, and led it around on a ribbon.'

'Well, I'm sure we could find you a monkey, if you'd like one of your own.'

'Oh, one could never do such a thing today,' said Mrs Ayres, as she put the glasses on. 'Some society or other would prevent it, or Mr Gandhi would object. Probably monkeys have the vote in India now.—Thank you, Betty.'

The spell of breathlessness had passed and her voice was almost her own again. She shook open the paper, found the passage she wanted, and read it aloud. It turned out to be some piece of advice sent on by her sister from a Conservative MP very concerned about the breaking up of the old estates; and in fact it only confirmed for us what we already knew, that there would be nothing but penalties and restrictions for rural landowners so long as the present government was in power, and the best the gentry could do was to 'sit tight and draw in its belt' until the next election.

'Yes, well,' said Caroline, when her mother had finished. 'That's all right for those with belts, but suppose one hasn't so much as a buckle? If one could make a sort of *bois dormant* of one's estate in the hope of a gallant Conservative government's turning up in a few years' time, that would be fair enough. But if we were to sit and do nothing to Hundreds for even one more year, we'd be sunk. I could almost wish the council wanted more of our land. Fifty or so more houses would probably just about pay off our debts . . .'

We discussed this in a dispirited way until Betty brought up the tea-tray, and then we lapsed into silence, each of us lost to our own thoughts. Mrs Ayres still struggled slightly after her breath, now and then sighing, now and then coughing into her handkerchief. Caroline kept glancing at the writing-table, her mind presumably on the failing estate. I sat with the china cup in my hands, light and warm against my fingers, and found myself, I don't know why, looking from one thing to another in that room and thinking back to my first visit there. I remembered poor Gyp, lying on the floor like a bowed old man while Caroline carelessly worked her toes through the fur of his belly. I recalled Rod, idly reaching to pick up his mother's fallen scarf. *My mother's like a paper-chase, Doctor. She leaves a trail of things behind her wherever she goes* . . . Now both he and Gyp were gone. The French window, which had been open then, was closed against the bitter weather; a low screen had been bolted across it to keep out the worst of the draughts, and it cut out some of the daylight, too. There was still the sour scent of burning in the air; the moulded plaster walls were full of greasy-looking shadows where soot had drifted during the fire. The room also smelt faintly of damp wool, for a few rain-soaked outdoor garments of Caroline's had been put to dry before the hearth on an ancient clothes-horse. I couldn't imagine Mrs Ayres, six months ago, allowing the room to be used as a laundry. But then I thought back to the tanned, handsome woman who had come stepping in from the garden in those distracting shoes of hers, that day in July; and I looked at her now, coughing and sighing in her mismatched shawls, and realised how much she had changed, too.

I glanced at Caroline; and found her looking at her mother with an anxious expression, as if thinking the same thing. Her gaze met mine, and she blinked.

'How dreary we all are today!' she said, finishing her tea and getting up. She went to a window and stood looking out, her arms folded against the chill, her face lifted to the low grey sky. 'The rain's easing off at last, anyway. That's something. I think I'll go down to the building-work before it gets dark.—Oh, I go down nearly every day,' she added, turning, and catching my look of surprise. 'Babb's given me a copy of the building-schedule, and I'm working my way through it. He and I are great friends now.'

I said, 'I thought you wanted him to fence the whole thing off?'

'We did, at first. But there's something horribly fascinating about it. It's like some grisly sort of wound: one can't help lifting up the bandage.' She came back from the window, took her coat and hat and scarf from the clothes-horse, and began to put them on. And as she did it she said to me, casually, 'Come with me, if you like. If you have time.'

I did, in fact, have time, for my list that day was a light one. But I had been to bed late the night before, and had been woken very early, and was feeling my age; I didn't really relish the thought of a walk across the cold, wet ground of the park. Nor did I think it quite polite of Caroline to suggest that we leave her mother. Mrs Ayres, however, when I looked doubtfully in her direction, said, 'Oh yes, do go down there, Doctor. I should so like a man's opinion of the work.' And after that I could hardly say no. Caroline rang for Betty again, and the girl brought in my outdoor things. We built up the fire in the grate, and made sure that Mrs Ayres had everything she needed. When we left the house, to save time we went directly from the little parlour, hopping over the screen at the French window and going down the flying stone steps, then striking off across the south lawn. The grass clung damply to our shoes, instantly soaking the cuffs of my trousers and darkening Caroline's stockings. Where the lawn grew even wetter we went on tiptoe, awkwardly joining hands, then separating once we'd reached the dryer surface of a gravel path that cut across the rough open ground beyond the garden fence.

The wind there was as solid as a velvet curtain; we had almost to fight our way through it. But we walked briskly, Caroline setting the pace, clearly glad to be out of the house, moving easily on those long, thickish legs of hers, her stride more than matching my own. She had her hands thrust deep into her pockets, and her coat, pulled tight by her arms, showed up the flare of her hips and bosom. Her cheeks had pinked with the sting of the wind; her hair, which she had inexpertly tucked up inside a rather frightful wool hat, had here and there escaped and was being lashed by the breezes into dry, demented locks. She seemed not at all breathless, though. Unlike her mother, she'd quickly shaken off the after-effects of the fire, and her face had lost the signs of tiredness I'd seen in it just a few minutes before. Altogether, there was an air of health and easy power to her—as if she could no more help being robust, I thought with a trace of admiration, than a beautiful woman could help good looks.

Her pleasure in the walk was infectious. I began to warm up, and finally to enjoy the buffets of crisp, cold air. It was novel, too, being out in the park on foot, as opposed to driving across it, for the ground that I saw from my car window as a uniform tangle of green looked very different at close range: we found patches of snowdrops, bending gamely in the agitated grass, and here and there, where the grass thinned, tight little coloured buds of crocuses were thrusting their way out of the earth as if ravenous for air and sunlight. All the time we walked, however, we could see ahead of us, at the farthest point of parkland, the breach in the wall and the stretch of muddy ground before it, with six or seven men moving over the area with barrows and spades. And as we drew closer and I caught more detail, I began to understand the true scale of the work. The lovely old grass-snake field was gone completely, gone for ever. Instead, a patch of land a hundred yards or more in length had been stripped of its turf and levelled, and the hard raw earth was already parcelled off into sections by poles and channels and rising walls.

Caroline and I approached one of the trenches. It was still in the process of being filled in, and as we stood at the edge of it I saw with dismay that the rubble being used for the foundations of the new houses consisted mainly of pieces of broken brown stone from the demolished park wall.

'What a pity!' I said, and Caroline answered quietly: 'I know. It's somehow horrible, isn't it? Of course people must have homes, and all that. But it's as if they're chewing Hundreds up—just so they can spit it all out again in nasty little lumps.'

Her voice dipped lower as she spoke. Maurice Babb himself was there at the edge of the site, talking with his foreman at the open door of his car. He saw us come and, in a leisurely fashion, began picking his way towards us. He was a man in his early fifties, short and rather barrel-chested: prone to boasting, but clever; a good businessman. Like me, he came from labouring stock and had pulled himself up in the world—and he'd done it all, as he'd reminded me once or twice over the years, without the help of a patron. To Caroline he raised his hat. To me, he offered his hand. Despite the coldness of the day his hand was warm, the fingers plump and bunchy and tight in their skin, like half-cooked sausages.

'I knew you'd be down, Miss Ayres,' he said affably. 'My men said the rain would keep you away, but I told them, Miss Ayres isn't the sort of lady to be kept off by a bit of bad weather. And here you are. Come to keep your eye on us, as usual? Miss Ayres puts my foreman to shame, Doctor.'

'I can believe it,' I said, smiling.

Very slightly, Caroline blushed. A few strands of hair were being blown across her lips, and she drew them free to say, not quite truthfully, 'Dr Faraday was wondering how you're getting on, Mr Babb. I've brought him down to see the work.'

'Well,' he answered, 'I'm very glad to show it! Especially to a medical man. I had Mr Wilson, the sanitary inspector, out here last week. He said there'll be nothing to beat these places in the way of air and drainage, and I think you'll find you'll agree. You see how the ground's laid out?' He gestured with one of his thick, short arms. 'We shall have six houses here, then a break at the curving of the road; and over there, six more. Two homes per house, done semi-detached. Red brick, you'll notice—' he indicated the livid, brutal-looking machine-made bricks at our feet—'to match the Hall. A nice little estate! Step along over here, if you'd care to, and I'll show you about. Watch your step, Miss Ayres, on these ropes.'

He offered her his bunchy hand. Caroline didn't need it—she was several inches taller than he was—but obligingly let him guide her over the trench, and we moved further along the site, to a spot where the work was more advanced. He explained again exactly how each house would sit in relation to its neighbours, and then, warming to his theme, he took us into one of the squared-off spaces and sketched the rooms it would soon contain: the 'lounge', the fitted kitchen with its gas stove and electric points, the indoor bathroom with a built-in bath . . . The whole patch looked scarcely bigger than a boxing-ring to me, but apparently they had already had people coming out there, wanting to know how to get their names down for a house. He himself, he told us, had been offered money and 'any amount of cigarettes and meat', to 'pull a few strings'.

'I told them, it in't up to me! I said, Go and talk to the Town Hall!' He lowered his voice. 'Just between us three, mind, they could talk to the Town Hall till they're blue in the face. That list's been filled six months already. My own brother's boy, Dougie, and his wife, they've got their names down for a place, and I hope they gets it, for you know where they're living just now, Miss Ayres, in two rooms in Southam with the girl's mother? Well, they can't go on like that. One of these'd be just the thing for them. Patch of garden they shall have out at the back there, you see, with a path and a chain-link fence. And the Lidcote bus is to be brought this way—had you heard that, Doctor? It's to come along the Barn Bridge Road. June, I think they're starting that.'

He ran on like this for a while, until called to by his foreman, at which he made his apologies, offered me his sausage-like hand again, and left us. Caroline moved away to watch another man at work, but I stayed in the squared-off concrete space, standing more or less where I guessed the kitchen window would be placed, and looking back across the park to the Hall. It was clearly visible in the distance, especially with the trees before it so bare; it would be very visible indeed, I realised, from this house's upper floor. I could see very well, too, how the flimsy wire fences that were to be strung at the back of the houses would do nothing to keep the children of the twenty-four families out of the park . . .

I joined Caroline at the edge of concrete, and we chatted for a minute with the man she had been watching at work. He was a man I knew quite well; in fact, he was a sort of cousin of mine, on my mother's side. He and I had shared a desk in the two-roomed council school I'd attended as a young boy; we had been good pals then. Later, once I'd started at Leamington College, the friendship had soured, and for a time he and his elder brother Coddy had rather persecuted me—lying in wait for me, with handfuls of gravel, as I came cycling back home in the late afternoons. But that was a long time ago. Since then he had married, twice. His first wife and child had died, but he had two grown-up sons who had recently moved to Coventry. Caroline asked how they were getting on, and he told us, in the ripe Warwickshire accent I could never quite believe had once also been mine, that they had gone straight into factory jobs, and between them were bringing home a weekly wage of over twenty pounds. I should have been glad to earn that myself; and it was probably more, I thought, than the Ayreses had to live on over a month. But still, the man removed his cap in order to talk to Caroline—though he looked more shyly at me, giving me an awkward sort of nod as we moved off. I knew that even after all this time it was queer for him to call me 'Doctor', but out of the question, too, for him either to use my Christian name or to address me as 'sir'.

I said, as easily as I could, 'Goodbye, Tom.' And Caroline said, with real warmth, 'See you again, Pritchett. It was nice to talk to you. I'm glad your boys are doing so well.'

I wished suddenly, and without quite knowing why, that she wasn't wearing that ridiculous hat. We turned and began to make our way back to the Hall, and I felt Pritchett pause in his work to watch us, and perhaps to glance at one of his mates.

We went in silence across the grass, following the line of our own dark footprints, both made thoughtful by the visit. When she spoke at last, it was quite brightly, though without meeting my eye.

'Babb's a character, isn't he? And don't the houses sound marvellous? Very good for your poorer patients, I suppose.'

'Very good,' I answered. 'No more damp floors and low ceilings. Fine sanitation. Separate rooms for the boys and the girls.'

'A proper start for the children, and so on. And awfully nice for Dougie Babb, if it means he can get away from his horrible mother-in-law . . . And, oh, Doctor—' She looked at me at last, then glanced unhappily over her shoulder. 'I would as soon want to move into a little brick box like that, with a lounge and a fitted kitchen, as live in our old cowshed.' She leaned to pick up a piece of branch that had been blown across the park, and began to swipe at the ground with it. 'What *is* a fitted kitchen, anyhow?'

'There are no nasty gaps,' I said, 'and no odd corners.'

'And no character, I bet. What's wrong with gaps and odd corners? Who'd want a life without any of those?'

'Well,' I said, picturing some of the squalider homes on my round, 'it's possible, after all, to have too many.' And I added almost as an afterthought, 'My mother would have been glad of a house like that. If I'd been born a different sort of boy, she might well be living in one now, along with my father.'

Caroline looked at me. 'What do you mean?'

And I told her, briefly, about the struggle my parents had had, simply to keep up with the scholarships and grants that had got me through Leamington College and medical school: the debts they had taken on, the grim economies they had made, my father working extra hours, my mother taking in sewing and laundry when she was barely strong enough to lift the wet clothes from the copper to the pail.

I heard my voice grow bitter, and could not stop it. I said, 'They put everything they owned into making a doctor of me, and I never even realised my mother was ill. They paid a small fortune for my education, and all I learned was that my accent was wrong, my clothes were wrong, my table manners—all of it, wrong. I learned, in fact, to be ashamed of them. I never took friends home to meet them. They came once to a school speech day; I was receiving a science prize. The look on some of the other boys' faces was enough. I didn't invite them again. Once, at seventeen, in front of one of his own customers, I called my father a fool—'

I didn't finish. She waited a moment, then said, as gently as the blustery day would allow, 'But they must have been very proud of you.'

I shrugged. 'Perhaps. But pride doesn't make for happiness, does it? They'd have been better off, really, if I'd been like my cousins—like Tom Pritchett back there. Maybe I'd have been better off, too.'

I saw her frown. She swiped at the ground again. 'All this time,' she said, without looking at me, 'I thought you must hate us slightly, my mother, my brother, and I.'

I said, astonished, 'Hate you?'

'Yes, on your parents' behalf. But now it sounds almost as though— well, as though you hate yourself.'

I didn't answer, and we walked in silence again, both of us grown rather awkward. Conscious that the day was sliding into evening, we made an effort to quicken our pace. Soon we left our own dark trail, looking for drier ground, and approached the house by a different route, arriving at a spot where the garden fence gave way to an ancient ha-ha, its sides so collapsed and overgrown it was more truthfully, I suggested, a boo-hoo. The comment made Caroline smile, and lifted us out of our low spirits. We struggled through the tangled ditch, then found ourselves in a patch of waterlogged lawn and, as before, had to tiptoe messily across it. My smooth-soled shoes weren't made for that sort of treatment, and once I slithered very nearly into a splits. She laughed properly at that, the blood creeping up through her throat and into her already pink cheeks, making them glow.

Mindful of our filthy footprints, we went around the house to the garden door. The Hall, as usual now, was unlit, and, though the day was sunless, to move towards it was like stepping into shadow, as if its sheer, rearing walls and blank windows were drawing to themselves the last of the light from the afternoon. When Caroline had wiped her shoes on the bristle mat she paused, looking up, and I was sorry to see lines of tiredness reappearing in her face, the flesh about her eyes puckering faintly like the surface of warming milk.

She said, as she studied the house, 'The days are still so short. I hate them, don't you? They make every hard thing harder. I do wish Roddie were here. Now that it's just Mother and me—' She lowered her gaze. 'Well, Mother's a darling, of course. And it isn't her fault that she's unwell. But, I don't know, sometimes she seems to be growing sillier by the day, and I'm afraid I don't always keep patience. Rod and I, we used to have fun. Just nonsense things. Before he got ill, I mean.'

I said quietly, 'It really won't be too long, before he's back.'

'You truly think so? I wish we could see him. It's so unnatural, to think of him there, ill and alone! We don't know what's happening to him. You don't think we should visit him?'

'We can go, if you like,' I said. 'I'll happily take you. But Rod himself, he's given no sign, has he, that he'd like us to visit?'

She shook her head, unhappy. 'Dr Warren says he likes the isolation.'

'Well, Dr Warren should know.'

'Yes, I suppose so . . .'

'Give it more time,' I told her. 'As I said before: soon it'll be spring, and everything will look different then, you'll see.'

She nodded, briskly, wanting to believe it. Then she kicked her shoes across the mat again and, with a sigh of reluctance, headed back into the chill and gloomy house to rejoin her mother.

I found myself recalling that sigh a day or two later, as I was making my arrangements for the district hospital dance. The dance was an annual event, meant as a fund-raiser; no one except the younger people treated it very seriously, but the local doctors liked to attend, along with their wives and grown-up children. We Lidcote physicians took it in turns to go along, and this year it was the turn of Graham and me, while our locum, Frank Wise, and Dr Seeley's partner, Morrison, remained on call. As a bachelor I was at liberty to take along a guest or two, and a few months earlier, thinking ahead to the night, I'd actually considered asking Mrs Ayres. Now that she was still so relatively unwell, her attendance was out of the question; but it occurred to me that Caroline might be willing to partner me, if it was for the sake of an evening away from Hundreds. Of course, I thought it just as possible she'd be appalled to be asked along, at the last minute, to what was essentially a 'works do', and I dithered over whether or not to suggest it. But I'd forgotten that ironic streak of hers.

'A doctors' dance!' she said, delighted, when I finally called her up to invite her. 'Oh, I should love to.'

'Are you sure? It's a funny old event. And it's more of a nurses' dance than a doctors'. The women usually far outnumber the men.'

'I bet they do! All pink and hysterical at being let off the wards, just like the junior Wrens used to be, at naval parties. And does Matron drink too much, and disgrace herself with the surgeons? Oh, say she does.'

'Now, steady on,' I said, 'or there'll be no surprises.'

She laughed, and even over the imperfect telephone line I could hear the note of real pleasure in her voice, and I was glad I'd asked her. I don't know if, in agreeing to be my guest, she had any other motive in mind. It would be odd, I suppose, for an unmarried woman of her age to look forward to a dance without giving a thought to the single men who might be there. But if her ideas were running that way, she hid them well. Perhaps her little humiliation with Mr Morley had taught her to be cautious. She spoke about the dance as if she and I would be a pair of elderly lookers-on at the fun. And when I picked her up on the night in question I found her dressed very unshowily, in an olive-coloured sleeveless gown, with her hair hanging loose and uncurled, her throat and hands, as usual, bare, and her heavy face almost free of make-up.

We left Mrs Ayres in the little parlour, apparently not at all unhappy to have an evening to herself. She had a tray across her lap and was going through some old letters of her husband's, putting them in neat, ordered bundles.

Still, I felt awkward about leaving her alone. 'Will your mother really be all right?' I asked Caroline, as she and I set off.

She said, 'Oh, she has Betty, don't forget. Betty will sit with her for hours. They've started playing games together, did you know that? Mother came across some old boards when we were going through the house. They play draughts, and halma.'

'Betty, and your mother?'

'I know, it's queer, isn't it? I don't remember Mother ever wanting to play board-games with Roddie and me. She seems to like it now, though. Betty likes it, too. They play for ha'pennies, and Mother lets her win . . . I don't think Betty had much fun at home over Christmas, poor thing. Her own mother sounds frightful, so I suppose it isn't surprising she prefers mine. And people *do* like Mother, it's just one of those things . . .'

She yawned as she said this, and drew in her coat against the cold. And after a while, lulled by the sound and motion of the car—for it was almost a thirty-minute drive to Leamington on the wintry country roads—we lapsed into companionable silence.

But once we reached the hospital grounds and joined the stir of vehicles and people, we both perked up. The dance was held in one of the lecture halls, a large room with a parquet floor; tonight it had been cleared of its desks and benches, its harsh central lights were turned off, and pretty coloured lamps and bunting had been draped from beam to beam. A band, not terribly good, was playing an instrumental number when we went in. The slippery floor had been liberally powdered with chalk, and several obliging couples were already up and dancing. Other people sat at tables around the edge, getting up their nerve to join them.

A long trestle arrangement did service as a bar. We started across towards it, but after only a few yards I was hailed by a couple of colleagues: Bland and Rickett, one a surgeon, the other a Leamington GP. I introduced them to Caroline, and there followed the usual sort of chat. They had paper cups in their hands and, seeing me glancing at the bar, Rickett said, 'Headed for the chloroform punch? Don't be taken in by the name; it's like flat cherryade. Hang on a sec. Here's the fellow we need.'

He reached around Caroline's back to catch hold of somebody by the arm: the man was a porter, 'our resident spiv', Bland explained to Caroline, while Rickett murmured in the man's ear. The porter went off, and returned a minute later with four more cups, each brim-full of the watery pink liquid I could see being ladled out from the punch-bowls at the bar, but each, too, as soon became apparent, rather stiffly laced with brandy.

'Vastly improved,' said Rickett, having tasted and smacked his lips. 'Don't you think so, Miss—?' He had forgotten Caroline's name.

The brandy was rough, and the punch itself had been sweetened with saccharine. When Bland and Rickett had moved on I said to Caroline, 'Can you drink this stuff?'

She was laughing. 'I'm not going to waste it, after all that. Is it really black?'

'Probably.'

'How shocking.'

'Well, I dare say a bit of black brandy won't do us any harm.' I put my hand to the small of her back, to steer her out of the traffic of people going to and from the bar. The hall was filling up.

We began the search for a vacant table. But soon another man greeted me—one of the consultants this time, and, as it happened, the man to whom I'd submitted my paper on the successful treatment of Rod's leg. There was no question of my not stopping for him, and he ran on for ten or fifteen minutes, wanting my opinion on some therapeutic process of his own. He made little effort to include Caroline, and I kept glancing at her as he spoke: she was gazing around the hall, taking rapid sips from her paper cup, self-conscious. But from time to time, too, she looked at me as the man addressed me, as if seeing me in a slightly new way.

'You're quite the somebody here,' she said to me, when the consultant had finally moved on.

'Ha!' I took a mouthful of punch. 'Quite the nobody, I assure you.'

'Well, then we can be nobodies together. It makes a nice change from home. I can't go into any of the villages these days without feeling everyone's watching me, thinking, *There goes poor Miss Ayres, from up at the Hall* . . . And now, look.' She had turned her head. 'All the nurses have arrived, in a great big flock, just as I'd pictured them! Like blushing goslings. I thought of nursing, you know, during the war. So many people told me I was just cut out for it, it put me off. I couldn't make that out as a compliment, somehow. That's why I joined the Wrens. Then I ended up nursing Roddie.'

Catching the touch of wistfulness in her voice, I said, 'Did you miss it, service life?'

She nodded. 'Badly, at first. I was good at it, you see. That's a shameful thing to admit, isn't it? But I liked all the mucking about with boats. I liked the routines of it. I liked there being only one way to do things, only one sort of stocking, one sort of shoe, one sort of way to wear one's hair. I was going to stay on at the end of the war, go out to Italy or Singapore. But once I was back at Hundreds—'

Her arm jolted, as a man and a girl pushed hastily past her; her drink slopped, she raised the cup to her mouth to catch the drips with her tongue, and after that she was silent. The band had been joined by a singer, and the music was louder and livelier. People were moving in some excitement to the dance-floor, making it harder for us to stand and talk.

Raising my voice above the music, I said, 'Let's not stay here. Why don't I find you someone to dance with? There's Mr Andrews, the house surgeon—'

She touched my arm. 'Oh, don't introduce me to any more men just yet. Especially not to a surgeon. Every time he looks at me I shall be thinking he's sizing me up for the knife. Besides, men hate dancing with tall women. You and I can dance, can't we?'

I said, 'Of course. If you like.'

We finished our drinks, set down our cups, and made our way on to the floor. There was an awkward moment as we put up our arms and moved together, trying to overcome the essential artificiality of the pose and join the jostling, unwelcoming crowd.

Caroline said, 'I hate this bit. It's like having to hurl oneself on to a paternoster lift.'

'Close your eyes, then,' I answered, and guided her out in a quick-step. After a moment of being clipped and scuffed by the heels and el-bows of other dancers, we found the rhythm of the crowd, and a route through it.

She opened her eyes, impressed. 'But how on earth will we get off again?'

'Don't worry about that just yet.'

'We'll have to wait for the slow numbers . . . You dance rather well, in fact.'

'So do you.'

'You sound surprised. I love to dance. I always have. I danced like mad in the war. It was very best thing about it: all that dancing. When I was young I danced with my father. He was so tall, it didn't matter that I was tall, too. He taught me all my steps. Rod was hopeless. He said I heaved him about, he might as well have been dancing with a boy. I'm not heaving you about, am I?'

'Not at all.'

'And I'm not talking too much? I know some men don't like that. I gather it puts them off their stroke.'

I said she could talk as much as she liked. The fact is, I was delighted to see her in such good spirits, and to feel her so relaxed, so yielding and mobile in my arms. We kept a slight formal distance between us, but every now and then the pressure of the crowd would send her more firmly into my grip and I'd feel the spring of her full bosom against my chest, the solid push of her hips. As we made a turn, the muscular flesh of her lower back would tense and shift beneath my palm and out-spread fingers. Her hand in mine was sticky, from the spilled punch; once she turned her head to look across the dance-floor and I caught the scent of brandy on her mouth. I realised that she was slightly drunk. Perhaps I was slightly drunk, too. But I felt a rush of fondness for her, so sudden and so simple it made me smile.

She put back her head to look into my face. 'Why are you grinning like that? You look like a dancer in a contest. Have they pinned a num-ber on your back?' She peered over my shoulder, pretending to check; again her bosom came springily against me. Then she spoke into my ear. 'There's Dr Seeley! Whizz me round, so you can see his bow-tie and his buttonhole!'

I made a turn, and caught sight of the man, large and bearish, danc-ing with his wife. The tie was a polka-dotted one, the flower some sort of fleshy orchid; goodness knows where he'd got hold of it. A blade of hair, over-greased, had fallen forward over his brow.

I said, 'He thinks he's Oscar Wilde.'

'Oscar Wilde!' Caroline laughed. I felt the laughter in my arms. 'If only he were! When I was young the girls called him "The Octopus". He was always terribly keen to give one a lift. And no matter how many hands he had on the steering-wheel, there always seemed to be at least one more . . . Guide me away where he can't see us. You still have to dish out all the gossip, don't forget. Keep to the edge of the floor—'

'Look here, who's leading? I'm beginning to think I know what Roderick meant, when he said you heaved him about.'

'Keep to the edge,' she said, laughing again, 'and as we go round you can tell me who everybody is, and who has killed the most patients, and which doctors are going to bed with which nurses; and all the scandals.'

So we stayed on the floor through two or three more songs, and I did my best to point out the major hospital personalities, and to offer up a few mild pieces of gossip; after that the music reverted to a waltz and the dancing thinned. We moved back to the bar for more punch. The hall was growing warmer. Looking up, I saw David Graham, just arrived with Anne and making his way through the crowd in our direction. Thinking of the last time he and Caroline had met—when he had come up to Hundreds to second my opinion of Roderick, the day before Rod was taken from the house—I leaned close to her and said, as quietly as I could over the music, 'Here's Graham headed our way. Will you mind seeing him?'

She didn't look, but gave a small, tight shake of her head.

'No, I don't mind. I guessed he'd be here.'

The slight awkwardness of the Grahams' arrival, anyway, was soon dispelled. They had brought guests, a middle-aged Stratford man and his wife and their married daughter; and the daughter and Caroline turned out to be old friends. Laughing and exclaiming, they moved together to exchange kisses.

'We knew each other,' Caroline told me, 'oh, years ago! Way back in the war.'

The daughter, Brenda, was blonde, good-looking—rather worldly looking too, I thought. I was pleased for Caroline's sake that she had turned up, but also vaguely sorry, for with her and her parents' arrival it was as if a line were drawn between the older people and the younger. She and Caroline stood slightly apart from the rest of us, and lit cigarettes; and soon they linked arms and headed off in the direction of the Ladies'.

By the time they returned, I'd been thoroughly claimed by the Graham party, who had found a table away from the blare of the band and produced a couple of bottles of Algerian wine. Cups of this were given to Caroline and Brenda, and chairs offered; but they wouldn't sit, they stood looking over the dance-floor, Brenda swinging her hips impatiently to the rhythm of the music as she drank. The tunes were picking up again and they both wanted to dance.

'You don't mind?' Caroline asked apologetically as she moved away. 'Brenda knows some people here, she wants to introduce me.'

'You go and dance,' I said.

'I shan't be long, I promise.'

'It's good to see Caroline out and about enjoying herself,' Graham said to me, when she had gone.

I nodded. 'Yes.'

'You and she see a lot of each other?'

I said, 'Well, I call in, whenever I can, at the house.'

'Of course,' he answered, as if having waited for me to say more. And then, more confidentially: 'No progress with the brother, I suppose?'

I gave him the latest report I'd had from Dr Warren. We passed from that to exchanging news about one or two of our other patients, and from that to a discussion, with the Stratford man, of the forthcoming Health Service. The Stratford man, like most GPs, was violently opposed to it; David Graham was passionately for it, while I was still gloomily convinced it would mean the end of my career, so the debate was pretty lively and went on for some time. Every so often I'd lift my head and look for Caroline on the dance-floor. Now and then she and Brenda returned to the table for more wine.

'OK?' I'd call to her, or mouth to her, over Graham's shoulder. 'I'm not neglecting you?'

She'd shake her head, smiling. 'Don't be silly!'

'Do you really think Caroline's all right?' I asked Anne, as the evening wore on. 'I feel I've rather abandoned her.'

She glanced at her husband, and said something that didn't quite carry over the music, something like, 'Oh, we're used to that!' or even, 'She'll have to get used to that!'—something, anyway, that gave me the impression she had misheard me. But seeing the puzzlement on my face she added, laughing, 'Brenda's looking after her, don't worry. She's fine.'

Then, at half past eleven or so, someone got hold of the microphone to announce a Paul Jones, and there was a general migration to the dance-floor which Graham and I were persuaded to join. Automatically I looked for Caroline again, and saw her being pulled into the women's circle on the other side of the hall; after that I kept my eye on her, hoping to coincide with her at the breaks of music. But with every reshuffle we'd go galloping towards each other, only to be helplessly tugged away in opposite directions. The ring of women, swollen with nurses, was fuller than the ring of men: I saw her smile and almost stumble as her feet tangled with the other girls' and, once as she flew past me, she caught my eye and grimaced. 'This is murder!' I think she called. The next time she came she was laughing. Her loose hair had fallen forwards and was clinging in darkening strands to the sheen of perspiration on her face and lips. At last she finished a place or two to my left, and in the polite but determined jostling that followed I moved to claim her—only to be beaten to her side by a large, damp, hot-looking man I recognised, after a second, as Jim Seeley. He was, I think, her rightful partner in the ring, but she gave me an alarmed, comical look as he drew her into a close embrace, then led her off in a slow foxtrot with his chin against her ear.

I danced that number with one of the younger nurses, and when it ended and the circles formed more rowdily than before, I left the floor. I went to the bar for another cup of watery punch, then moved out of the thickest part of the crowd, to watch the dancing. Caroline, I saw, had extricated herself from Seeley and found a less overbearing partner, a young man in horn glasses. Seeley himself, like me, had given up on the floor altogether in favour of the bar. He had knocked back his punch and was taking out cigarettes and a lighter— and, happening to look up and catch my eye as he did it, he came over to offer me his case.

'On nights like this I feel my age, Faraday,' he said, when our cigarettes were lit. 'Don't these damn nurses seem young to you? I swear, there's a little thing I danced with earlier on, she looked barely older than my twelve-year-old daughter. That's all right for a filthy old pervert like—' and here he named one of the senior surgeons, who'd been at the centre of a minor scandal a year or two before. 'But when I'm dancing with a girl and I ask her how she likes the district, and she tells me it reminds her of the place she was evacuated to in 1940—well, it's hardly conducive to romance. As for all this thundering about in circles, I'd sooner an old-fashioned waltz. I suppose they'll break out the rumbas in a minute. God help us then.'

He took out a handkerchief and mopped his face, then passed the handkerchief under his collar and wiped all round his neck. His throat was scarlet, his bow-tie limp. His orchid was lost, I noticed now, only the fleshy green stalk of it remaining at his lapel, slightly milky at the tip. Fuelled by drink and exercise, he gave off heat like a brazier, so that it was impossible to stand beside him in that over-warm hall and not want to move away. But having accepted one of his cigarettes, I thought it only fair to keep him company while I smoked it. So he mopped and puffed and grumbled on for another minute or two; then our gazes moved naturally back to the dance-floor and we both fell silent, watching the couples jog by.

I didn't see Caroline at first, and thought she might have left the floor. But she was dancing, still, with the young man in glasses, and once my eyes had found her out they tended to return to her. The Paul Jones had finished and this dance was more sedate, but there was a general air of subsiding hilarity and Caroline, like everybody else, was damp in the face, her hair untidy, her shoes and stockings streaked with chalk, her throat and the flesh of her arms still flushed and glowing. The heightened colour suited her, I thought. For all that her dress was so unshowy and her pose so plain, she looked very young—as if her youth had been whipped to the surface, by motion and laughter, along with her blood.

I watched her through all of that dance, and into the start of another; and only when Seeley spoke did I realise that he had been watching her, too.

He said, 'Caroline Ayres looks well.'

I took a step away from him, to stub out my cigarette at the nearest table. Moving back, I said, 'Yes, doesn't she.'

'She's a good dancer, that girl. Knows she's got hips, and what to do with them. Most Englishwomen dance from the feet.' His tone and expression grew more speculative. 'You've seen her on horseback, I suppose? There's something there, definitely. A pity she doesn't have the looks to match. Still,' he took a last draw on his cigarette, 'I shouldn't let that put you off.'

For a second I thought I had misheard him. Then I saw by his face that I had not.

He saw my expression, too. He had pursed his lips, to direct away a plume of smoke, but he laughed, and the plume grew ragged. 'Oh, come on! It's no secret, is it, how much time you've been spending with that family? I don't mind telling you, there's quite a little debate locally as to which of the women you've set your sights on—the daughter or the mother.'

He spoke as if the whole thing were a tremendous joke—as if amusedly egging me on in some ambitious piece of mischief, like a prefect applauding a junior boy for having the pluck to peep through Matron's window.

I said coldly, 'What terrific fun for you all.'

But he laughed again. 'Don't take it like that! You know what village life is like. Almost as bad as hospital life. We're all so many bloody prisoners; we have to take our entertainment where we can get it. Personally, I don't know why you've been dragging your heels. Mrs Ayres has been a handsome woman in her day, I'll give you that. But if I were you I'd plump for Caroline—purely on the basis, you know, of her having so many good years left in her.'

His words, as I recall them now, strike me as so offensive I'm astonished to think that I stood there, letting him say them, gazing into his boozy hot red face, without wanting to punch him. But what impressed me most at the time, still, was that hint of condescension. I felt I was being made an ass of, and it seemed to me that to strike him would only serve to give him the satisfaction that I was, at root, what he supposed me to be—a sort of rustic booby. So I stood tensely, saying nothing, wanting to shut him up but not quite knowing how. He saw my confusion, and actually nudged me.

'Set you thinking, have I? Well, make your move tonight, old man!' He gestured to the dance-floor. 'Before that twerp in the horn-rims gets a chance to make his. After all, it's a long dark drive back to Hundreds.'

At last I woke up. 'I think I see your wife,' I said, nodding over his shoulder into the crowd.

He blinked, and turned; and I moved away from him, finding an awkward, interrupted route around the tables and chairs. I was heading for the door, meaning to stand for a minute or two in the chill night air. But as I went, I passed close to the table I had been sharing with the Grahams, and the Stratford couple, seeing me going by with such a fixed expression, naturally assumed I'd lost my way back to my seat, and called out to me. They looked so pleased by my return—the wife walked with a cane, and was kept from the dancing—that I hadn't the heart to press on, but rejoined their table, and stayed talking to them, then, for the rest of the night. What we talked about, I have no idea. I was so thrown by what Seeley had said, and in such a mixture of ways, I could hardly sort out my own feelings.

The fact that I had brought Caroline there, with no thought for how the thing would look, seemed suddenly incredible. I suppose I'd grown used to the idea of spending time with her, out in the isolation of Hundreds; and if I'd once or twice had a surge of feeling for her—well, that was one of those things brought on, between men and women, by simple closeness: like matches sparking as they jostled in the box. To think that all this time people had been watching us, speculating— rubbing their hands—! It made me feel fooled, somehow; it made me feel exposed. A part of my upset, I'm sorry to say, was simple embar- rassment, a basic masculine reluctance to have my name romantically linked with that of a notoriously plain girl. Part of it was shame, at discovering I felt this. A contradictory part, too, was pride: for why the hell shouldn't I—I asked myself—bring Caroline Ayres along to a party, if I chose to? Why the hell shouldn't I dance with the squire's daughter, if the squire's daughter wanted to dance with me?

And mixed up with it all was a kind of nervous possessiveness of

Caroline herself, which seemed to have leapt upon me from nowhere. I recalled the smirk on Seeley's face as he watched her moving about the floor. *Knows she's got hips, and what to do with them . . . You've seen her on horseback, I suppose?* I should have hit him when I had the chance, I thought furiously. I would certainly have hit him now, if he'd come and said the same thing again. I even peered around the hall, with the crazy idea of going after him . . . I couldn't see him. He wasn't dancing, he wasn't standing looking on. But I couldn't see Caroline, either; nor the boy with the horn-rims. That began to bother me. I was still politely chatting with the Stratford couple, still sharing cigarettes and wine. But as we talked, my eyes must have been darting. The dancing looked nonsensical to me now, the dancers themselves like gesturing lunatics. All I wanted was for Caroline to emerge from the jolting, red-faced crowd so that I could put her into her coat and take her home.

Finally, at just after one, when the music had finished and the lights had come up, she reappeared at the table. She came with Brenda, both of them fresh from the dance-floor, with blurred eyes and mouths. She stood a couple of feet away from me, yawning, and plucking at the bodice of her dress to free it from the tug of moist skin beneath, exposing an edge of brassière strap at her armpit—exposing the armpit itself, a muscular hollow shadowed with fine stubble and faintly streaked with talcum. And though I had longed for her return, when she met my gaze and smiled, I felt, unaccountably, the sting of something that was almost anger, and had to turn away from her. I told her, rather stiffly, that I would fetch our things from the cloakroom, and she and Brenda went off again to the Ladies'. When they came back, still yawning, I was relieved to see that she had tidied her hair and made a neat, conventional mask of her face and throat with lipstick and powder.

'God, what a fright I looked!' she said, as I helped her into her coat. She gazed around the hall, up into the rafters at the bunting, which had revealed itself in all its faded VE colours. 'A bit like this place. Isn't it awful how the glamour goes, once the lights come on? Still, I wish we didn't have to leave . . . A girl was crying in the lavatory. I suppose one of you beastly doctors has broken her heart.'

Without meeting her gaze, I nodded to her coat, which she'd left unfastened.

'You ought to do that up. It'll be freezing outside. Didn't you bring a scarf?'

'I forgot.'

'Well, close your lapels, will you?'

She drew the coat together with one hand, and slipped the other through my arm. She did it lightly, but I wished she hadn't done it at all. We stood saying our goodbyes to the Grahams, to the Stratford couple and to blonde, worldly Brenda, and I felt horribly self-conscious, imagining I could see mirth in all their gazes, and guessing what they were thinking as they watched us heading off together for—as Seeley had put it—'the long dark drive back to Hundreds'. Then I remembered the queer thing Anne Graham had laughingly said when I'd asked after Caroline: that Caroline would 'have to get used to being abandoned', as if she were soon to be a doctor's wife . . . That made me more self-conscious still. When we had said good night and were crossing the emptying hall, I found a way of handing Caroline before me so that our arms became disengaged.

Out in the car park the ground was so frosty, and the cold so instantly penetrating, she caught hold of me again.

'I warned you you'd freeze,' I said.

'Either that or break a leg,' she answered. 'I'm in heels, don't forget. Oh, help!' She stumbled, and laughed, and seized my arm with both her hands, to draw herself even closer.

The gesture jarred with me. She had had that brandy early in the evening, and, after that, a glass or two of wine, and I'd been glad to see her—as I'd thought of it then—letting off steam. But where, for those first few dances, she'd been genuinely loose and tipsy in my arms, it seemed to me now that her giddiness had something just slightly forced about it. She said again, 'Oh, isn't it a shame we have to leave!'—but she said it too brightly. It was as if she wanted more from the night than the night had so far given her, and was broadening and hardening her strokes against it in an effort to make it pay up. Once more before we reached my car she stumbled, or pretended to; and when I got her inside and put a blanket around her shoulders she sat and shivered unrestrainedly, her teeth chattering like dice in a cup. Since my car had no heater I had brought along a hot-water bottle for her, and a thermos of water with which to fill it. I saw to that, and handed it over, and she tucked it gratefully inside her coat. But as I started the engine she wound down her window and, still shivering, stuck out her head.

I said, 'What on earth are you doing?'

'I'm looking at the stars. They're rather brilliant.'

'Well, for God's sake look with the window up. You'll catch a chill.'

She laughed. 'You sound almost like a doctor.'

'And you,' I said, catching hold of her sleeve and pulling her back in, 'sound almost like the silly young girl I know for a fact you're not. Now sit up straight and close your window.'

She did as she was told, suddenly meek, perhaps chastened by the note of irritation in my voice, perhaps puzzled by it. I was puzzled by it myself, for the fact is, she had done nothing to deserve it. It was all filthy-minded Seeley's fault; and I had let him walk away.

We drove without speaking out of the hospital grounds, part of a lively gush of traffic at first, but soon breaking free of the tooting horns, the cheers and calls and bicycle bells, and entering quieter roads. Caroline sat huddled in the blanket and, little by little, as she grew warmer, I felt her long limbs begin to loosen. My mood softened slightly in response.

'Better?' I asked.

'Yes, thank you,' she replied.

By now we had left the outskirts of Leamington and passed into unlit country lanes. The ground was frostier here, the road and hedges white and sparkling: they seemed to part around our headlamps, to froth and rush back into darkness, like water churned by the prow of a boat. Caroline gazed for a time through the windscreen, then rubbed her eyes.

'The road's hypnotising me! Don't you mind it?'

I said, 'I'm used to it.'

She seemed struck by that. 'Yes,' she said, looking at me, 'of course you are. Driving through the night. How people must listen out for your car, and watch for the headlamps. And how glad they must be when you arrive. If we were dashing to a bedside now, how badly those people would be longing for us. I never thought of that before. Doesn't it almost frighten you?'

I reached to change gear. 'Why should it frighten me?'

'The responsibility of it, I suppose.'

I said, 'I told you before, I'm a nobody. People don't even see me half the time. They see "Doctor". They see the bag. The bag's the thing. Old Dr Gill told me that. My father bought me a fine new leather bag when I first qualified. Gill took one look at it and said I wouldn't get anywhere with a thing like that, no one would trust me. He gave me a battered old bag of his own. I used it for years.'

'Still,' she said after a moment, as if she hadn't been listening. 'How those people must watch, and wait, and want you. Perhaps you like it. Is that it?'

I glanced at her, through the darkness. 'Is what what?'

'Do you like it, that there's always someone longing for you, in the night?'

I didn't make her any answer. She didn't seem to want any. More than ever I had the feeling of there being something false about her, as if she were playing on the dark, dislocated intimacy of the car to try out another personality—Brenda's personality, perhaps. She was silent for a moment, then started humming. It was one of the songs she had danced to with the young man in glasses, and, realising that, I felt my mood harden again. She reached for her evening bag and fumbled for something inside. 'Has your car one of those lighter things?' she asked, bringing out a packet of cigarettes. Her hand moved palely over the dashboard, then drew back. 'Never mind, I've matches here some- where . . . Shall I light one for you?'

I said, 'I can light my own, if you'll pass it to me.'

'Oh, let me do it. It'll be just like in the pictures.'

There came the rasp and flare of a match, and from the corner of my eye I saw her face and hands spring into luminous life. She had two cigarettes at her mouth: she lit them both, then took one from between her lips and reached across to put it between mine. Faintly disturbed by the sudden brush of her cold fingers—and by the dry nudge of the cigarette, which had a suggestion of lipstick about it—I at once took it out again and held it at the steering-wheel.

We smoked in silence for a while. She put her face close to her window, and started drawing lines and circles where her breath clouded the glass. Then, abruptly, she said, 'That girl Brenda I met tonight: I don't much like her, you know.'

I said, 'You don't? I'd never have guessed. You greeted each other like long-lost sisters.'

'Oh, women always go on like that.'

'Yes, I've often thought it must be exhausting to be a woman.'

'It is, if you do it properly. Which is why I so seldom do. Do you know how I know her?'

'Brenda? I imagined, from the Wrens.'

'No, from just before that. We firewatched together, for about six weeks, that's all. We were not at all alike, but I suppose the boredom made us talk. She'd been seeing a boy—sleeping with him, I mean—and she'd just found out that she was pregnant. She wanted to get rid of it, and she was after a girl to go with her to a chemist's and help her buy some stuff; and I said I'd go. We went into Birmingham, where no one knew us. The man was horrible: prim and withering and excited, just as you'd expect. I can never decide if it's reassuring when people turn out to be just what one's expected, or depressing . . . The stuff worked, though.'

Reaching to change gear again, I said, 'I doubt that it did, actually. That sort of stuff hardly ever does.'

'No?' said Caroline, surprised. 'Just a coincidence, then?'

'Just a coincidence.'

'Just a bit of good luck, for good old Brenda. And after all that. But Brenda's the sort of person that luck happens to—good luck and bad.

Some people are like that, don't you think?' She drew on her cigarette. 'She asked who you were.'

'What? Who did?'

'Brenda did. She thought you might be my stepfather! And when I told her you weren't, she looked at you again with a horrid narrowing of her eyes and said, "Your sugar-father, then." That's the way her mind works.'

Christ! I thought. That seemed to be the way that everyone's minds worked; and I supposed it was a marvellous joke to all of them. I said, 'Well, I hope you swiftly put her right.' She didn't answer. She was still drawing lines on the window. 'Well, did you?'

'Oh, I let her think it for a minute—just for a minute, just for the fun of trying it out. She must have remembered that time in Birmingham, too. She said the best of its being a medical man was, one was never so afraid of "tripping up". I said, "My dear, you needn't tell me! I've sprained my ankle four times! Doctor's been a lamb!"'

She took another puff on her cigarette, then spoke flatly. 'I didn't really. I told her the truth: that you were a friend of the family, being kind, taking me dancing as a treat. I think she thought rather the worse of me for it.'

'She sounds like a thoroughly unpleasant young woman.'

She laughed. 'How prim you are! Most young women talk like that—to other young women, I mean. I told you, I've never much liked her. God, my feet are perished!'

She fidgeted about for a second, trying to warm herself up. I realised she was kicking her shoes off; soon she hitched up her legs and tucked the skirts of her dress and coat behind her knees, and turned sideways towards me, setting her stockinged feet down over the slight gap between her seat and mine. Reaching forward with her hands, one of them with the half-smoked cigarette in it, she caught hold of her toes and began to chafe them.

She kept this up for a minute or two, finally getting rid of the cigarette in the dashboard ashtray, then breathing into her palms and laying them flat and still on the back of her feet. And after that, she was silent; she tucked in her head and seemed to doze. Or perhaps she only pretended to sleep. At a turn in the road I felt the car meet a patch of ice and glide a foot or two across it: I had to pump the brake and slow almost to a standstill, which surely would have roused her if she'd been slumbering naturally, but she didn't stir. A little later I stopped for a crossroads, and turned to look at her. Her eyes were still closed, and in the darkness, in her dark dress and coat, she seemed an assemblage of angular fragments: the squarish face with its heavy brows, the full red diamond of her mouth, her uncovered throat, her muscular calves, those long pale hands.

The fragments shifted as she opened her eyes. She held my gaze, her own gaze gleaming very slightly in the reflected sparkle of the frosty road. When she spoke, the touch of brashness had gone from her voice; she sounded flat, almost unhappy. She said, 'The first time you gave me a lift in this car, we ate blackberries. Do you remember?'

I put the car into gear, and moved on. 'Of course I remember.'

I felt her eyes still on my face. She turned to her window and peered out.

'Where are we now?'

'On the Hundreds road.'

'As close as that?'

'You must be tired.'

'I'm not. Not really.'

'Not after all that dancing, all those young men?'

'The dancing woke me up,' she said, in the same subdued tone as before, 'though it's true that one or two of the young men nearly put me to sleep again.'

I opened my mouth to speak; then closed it. Then spoke anyway.

'What about the fellow with the specs?'

She turned back to me, curious. 'You saw him, did you? He was the worst. Alan—or Alec, I suppose it might have been. He said he works in one of the hospital laboratories, tried to make it sound frightfully technical and important; but I don't think it can be. He lives "in town", with his "mum and dad". That's as much as I know. He couldn't really talk while he was dancing. He couldn't really dance, either.'

She lowered her head again, so that her cheek touched the back of her seat, and again I found myself struggling with a curious mix of emotions. I said with a touch of bitterness, 'Poor little Alan or Alec.' But she didn't catch the change in my voice. She had drawn in her chin, so that when she spoke again her words were muted. She said, 'I don't think I enjoyed any of the dances, actually, so much as the ones that you and I had at the start.'

I didn't answer. She went on, after a pause, 'I wish we had some more of that black brandy. Don't you keep a flask of something in the car?' And she reached and opened up a pocket in the dashboard and started feeling about inside, among the papers and spanners and empty cigarette packets.

I said, 'Please don't do that.'

'Why not? Have you a secret? There's nothing there, anyway.' She closed the pocket with a snap, then turned to look over at the back seat. The hot-water bottle fell out of her coat and went slithering to the floor. She had grown lively again. 'Isn't there anything in your bag?'

'Don't be silly.'

'There must be something.'

'You can have some ethyl chloride if you like.'

'That would put me to sleep, wouldn't it? I don't want to go to sleep. I might as well be back at Hundreds then. God, I don't want to go back to Hundreds! Take me somewhere else, can't you?'

She moved about like a child; and either with that, or simply with the jolting of the car, her feet crept further over the gap between our seats, until I could just make out the small blunt movement of her toes against my thigh.

I said uneasily, 'Your mother will be waiting for you, Caroline.'

'Oh, Mother doesn't care. She'll have gone to bed, and put Betty to wait. Besides, they know I'm with you. The noble chaperon, and all that. It won't matter how late we are.'

I glanced at her. 'You're not serious? It's past two o'clock. I have my surgery at nine.'

'We might stop the car, go for a walk.'

'You're in dancing shoes!'

'I don't want to go home yet, that's all. Couldn't we drive somewhere, sit, smoke more cigarettes?'

'Drive where?'

'Drive anywhere. You must know a place.'

'Don't be silly,' I said again.

But I said it rather weakly. For, despite myself—as if the image had been waiting just under the surface of my mind, and now, at her words, sprang upwards—despite myself, I thought of that spot I sometimes drove to: the dark pond, with its border of rushes. I imagined the smooth, starred water, the grass silvered and crisp underfoot; the hush and stillness of the place. The turning was a mile or two ahead, that was all.

Perhaps she sensed some change in me. She stopped moving about, and we fell into a tight sort of silence. The road rose, then curved and dipped; another minute, and we were approaching the entrance to the lane. I really didn't know, I think, until the very last moment, whether I would make the turn or not. Then abruptly I slowed, and put in the clutch, and changed hastily down the gears. Beside me, Caroline reached out a hand to the dashboard, to brace herself against the turn. She'd expected it even less than I had. Her feet slid further forward with the motion of the car, so that for a second I felt them right under my thigh, solid and purposeful as burrowing creatures. Then we ran more smoothly and she drew them back, and her seat creaked and tilted as she pressed in her heels to keep them from sliding further.

Had she meant it, when she'd talked of sitting, smoking cigarettes? Had I, in picturing this place, somehow forgotten that it was two o'clock in the morning? With the fading of the headlamps that came when I turned off the engine, there was nothing to be seen of the pond, the grass, the circling rushes. We might have been anywhere, or nowhere at all. Only the hush was as I'd imagined it: a hush so deep it seemed to magnify every sound that broke it, so that I was unnaturally aware of the movement of Caroline's breath, of the tightening and unclenching of her throat as she swallowed, of the unsticking of her tongue and palate as she slightly opened her mouth. For a minute, perhaps longer, we sat with no more motion between us than that, I with my hands on the steering-wheel, she with her arm out to the dashboard as if still bracing herself against jars.

Then I turned and tried to look at her. It was too dark to make her out properly, but I could picture vividly enough her face, with its unhandsome combination of strong family lines. I heard again Seeley's words: *There's something there, definitely* . . . Oh, I had felt it, hadn't I? I think I had felt it the very first time I'd met her, watching her work her bare brown toes through the fur of Gyp's belly; and I had felt it a hundred times since then, catching sight of the flare of her hips, the swell of her bosom, the easy, solid movement of her limbs. But—again, I was ashamed to acknowledge it, am ashamed to remember it now— the feeling stirred something else in me, some dark current of unease, almost of distaste. It wasn't the difference in our ages. I don't think I even considered that. It was as if what pulled me to her also repelled me. As if I desired her despite myself . . . I thought again of Seeley. None of this, I knew, would have made any sense to him. Seeley would have kissed her and to hell with it. I've imagined that kiss, many times. The chill of her lip, and the surprise of the heat beyond it. The teasing open, in the darkness, of a seam of moisture, movement, taste. Seeley would have done it.

But I am not Seeley. It was a long time since I had kissed a woman; years, in fact, since I had held a woman in my arms with anything other than a rather perfunctory passion. I had a brief flare of panic. Suppose I had lost the trick of it? And here was Caroline beside me, possibly as uncertain as myself, but youthful, alive, tense, expectant . . . At last I took my hand from the steering-wheel and placed it tentatively upon one of her feet. The toes shifted as if tickled, but apart from that she made no response. I kept the hand there for perhaps six or seven heart-beats, and then, slowly, I moved it—just moved my fingers across the

fine, unresisting surface of her stocking, up over the arch of her foot
and the jut of her ankle bone and into the dip of heel behind it. When
again she kept quite still, I inched the hand steadily higher, until it was
held in the cleft, slightly warm, slightly moist, between her calf and the
back of her thigh. And then I turned and leaned towards her, putting
out my other hand, meaning to catch at her shoulder and draw her face
to mine. But the hand, in the darkness, found the lapel of her coat; my
thumb slid just beyond the inner edge of it, and met the start of the
swell of her breast. I thought she flinched, or shivered, as the thumb
moved lightly over her gown. Again I heard the movement of her tongue
inside her mouth, the parting of her lips, an indrawn breath.

The gown had three pearl buttons to it, and I awkwardly opened
them up. Beneath was a slip, some overlaundered thing with a limp lace
trim. Beneath that was her brassière, solid, unfussy, severely elasticated,
the kind of thing I'd seen many times on female patients since the war,
so that, for a moment, recalling those unerotic consulting-room scenes,
my faltering desire almost dwindled completely. But then she moved,
or took a breath; her breast lifted into my hand and I became aware,
not of the stiffly tailored cup of the brassière, but of the warm, full flesh
inside it, hard at the tip—hard, it seemed to me, as the point of one of
her own shapely fingers. That somehow gave the missing charge to my
desire, and I leaned further into her, my hat slipping from my head. The
leg that gripped my left hand I eased open and drew behind me. Her
other leg came across my lap, heavy and warm. I put my face to her
breast, and then must have reached for her mouth. I moved awkwardly
over and upon her—wanting to kiss her, that was all. But she gave a
sort of buck, and her chin clipped my head. She shifted her legs—
shifted them further—it took me a moment to realise she was trying to
draw them back.

'I'm sorry,' she said, her movements growing stronger. 'I'm sorry,
I—I can't.'

Again, I think I understood her just a beat too late; or perhaps it was
simply that, having got so far with her, I found myself suddenly desperate to see the thing through. I put down my hands and caught hold of

her hips. With a violence that astonished me, she twisted free. For a moment we actually tussled. Then she drew in her knees, and kicked out at me, blindly. Her heel caught my jaw, and I fell back.

I think the blow must have stunned me for a second. I became aware of the jolting of the seats: I couldn't see her, but realised that she had put down her legs and was straightening her skirt, refastening her gown—doing it all with hasty, jerky movements, as if almost panicked. But then she tightened the blanket around herself and turned and moved away from me, shuffling over as far as the narrowness of the car would allow, and putting her face against the window, pressing her forehead to the glass; and after that she was horribly still. I didn't know what to do for her. I reached, uncertainly, and just touched her arm. She flinched at first, then let me stroke her—but it might as well have been the blanket letting me do it, or the leather seat; she felt dead to my hand.

I said miserably, 'For God's sake! I thought you wanted it.'

She answered, after a moment, 'So did I.'

That was all she would say. So presently, embarrassed, uncomfortable, I drew my hand away, and retrieved my hat. The windows of the car, with appalling comedy, had grown cloudy. I wound mine down, hoping to do something to relieve the atmosphere of intimacy and blunder. The night air came in like a flood of frigid water, and after a minute I felt her shiver. I said, 'Shall I take you home, Caroline?' She didn't reply, but I started the engine—the sound was brutal in the silence—and slowly turned the car around.

She began to stir only once we had rejoined the Hundreds road and were running alongside the wall of the park. She roused herself properly as we drew up at the gates, tidying her hair, working her feet back into her shoes, but not looking at me. By the time I had got out to push the gates open and had climbed back in, she had removed the blanket from her shoulders and was sitting up straight and ready. I took us carefully along the frosty drive and around to the sweep of gravel. A couple of windows caught the light of the headlamps, sending it back with the soft, irregular sheen of oil on water. But the windows themselves were dark, and when I switched the engine off the great house seemed somehow to edge closer, until it was impossibly looming and forbidding against the densely starred sky.

I reached for the catch of my door, meaning to get out and open hers. But she beat me to it, saying hastily, 'No, please don't. I can manage. I don't want to keep you.'

There was no trace of drunkenness in her voice; no girlishness; but no upset, either. She sounded slightly subdued, that was all. I said, 'Well, I'll sit here and watch until you're safely inside.'

But she shook her head. 'I'm not going in that way. Now Roddie's gone, Mother has Betty bolt the front door at night. I'm going in the garden way. I've brought a key.'

I said that in that case I would certainly go with her, so we both got out, and started silently and awkwardly together past the shuttered library windows, then turned on to the terrace to go along the north side. It was so dark we had to make our way almost by trust. Now and then our arms touched and we moved elaborately apart, only to step blindly onwards and find ourselves veering back together. At one point our hands met and snagged; she drew away her fingers as if scalded, and I winced, remembering that terrible little tussle in the car. The darkness began to feel almost stifling. It was like a blanket over one's head. When we rounded the next corner and even the starlight was blotted out by the elms on that side of the house, I brought out my cigarette lighter and made a lantern of my palms. She let me guide her to the door, her key ready.

Once the door was open, however, she stood on the threshold as if suddenly uncertain. The stairs beyond were faintly lit, but for a second, after I had blown out my flame, we were blinder than we had been in the total darkness. When my eyes had readjusted, I could see that her face was turned to mine, but her gaze lowered. She said, quietly and slowly, 'That was stupid of me, before. The night had been such a nice one, too. I enjoyed our dances.'

She raised her eyes, and might have said more, I don't know. At that moment the stairs were lit up properly and she said quickly, 'There's Betty coming down for me. I must go.' She leaned to me and kissed my cheek, quite primly at first; then, as the corner of her mouth overlapped with the corner of mine, she put up a hand to the side of my head and clumsily drew my face around. Just for a second, as our lips met, I felt a sort of tremor pass over her features, her mouth twitching and her eyes shutting tight. Then she moved away from me.

She went into the house as if stepping through a rip in the night and instantly sealing it up behind her. I heard her key turn in the lock, and caught the diminishing tap of her heels on the bare stone stairway. And somehow the loss of her made me want her, plainly and physically, more than the nearness of her had done: I stepped to the door and stood against it, frustrated, willing her to return. But she did not return. The silent house was closed to me, the tangled garden still. I waited another minute, and another; then slowly picked my way back, through the almost impenetrable darkness, to my car.

NINE

After that I didn't see her for more than a week; I was too busy.
And to be honest, I was grateful for the delay. It gave me a
chance, I thought, to sort through my feelings: to recover from
my embarrassment at the blunders of the night; to tell myself that, after
all, nothing much had passed between us; to put the whole thing down
to the drink, and the darkness, and the giddy after-effects of the dance.
I saw Graham on the Monday, and made a point of mentioning Caroline's name, telling him she'd fallen asleep in the car on the way out of
Leamington and had slept 'like a child' until we reached the Hundreds
gate; and then changing the subject. As I think I have said before, I'm
not a naturally mendacious man. I've seen too many of the complica-
tions, in the lives of my patients, to which lies lead. But in this instance
I thought it best to try and put a definite end to any speculation regard-
ing Caroline and me; I thought this for Caroline's sake as much as my
own. I rather hoped to run into Seeley. I planned to ask him, baldly, to
do all he could to quash those rumours he'd mentioned, which suggested that I was romantically interested in one or both of the Ayres
women. Then I even began to wonder whether there really *had* been

rumours. Couldn't the whole thing have been simply a tipsy piece of mischief on Seeley's part? I decided that it could, and when my path did at last cross his, I made no mention of the dance, and neither did he.

But still, as that week ran busily on I thought of Caroline often. The frosty weather grew wet again, but I knew that rain rarely kept her from walking: taking my short-cut across the park, I found myself looking out for her. I looked out for her, too, in the lanes around Lidcote, and was aware of a sense of disappointment at not seeing her. And yet, when an opportunity arose for dropping in at the Hall itself, I didn't take it . . . I realised, almost to my own surprise, that I was nervous. Several times I picked up the telephone, meaning to call her; always I put the receiver down with the call unmade. Soon the delay began to feel unnatural. It occurred to me that her mother might start to think it odd that I was keeping away. And it was the prospect of inadvertently arousing Mrs Ayres's suspicions, as much as anything, that sent me over there at last, for I found I almost dreaded them.

I went out there on a Wednesday afternoon, in a spare hour between cases. The house was empty, save for Betty, happily cleaning brass at the kitchen table with the wireless on; she told me that Caroline and her mother were somewhere in the gardens, and after a brief search I discovered them making a gentle tour of the lawns. They were surveying the effects, on the already untidy flower-beds, of some recent driving rains. Mrs Ayres was well wrapped up against the damp and the cold, but seemed very much better than when I'd last seen her. She caught sight of me before her daughter did, and came across the grass to greet me, smiling. Caroline, as if self-conscious, bent to the ground to pick up a sprig of slick brown leaves. But when she had straightened, she followed her mother, meeting my gaze without a blush, and one of the first things she said to me was, 'You've recovered, then, from all that dancing? My feet were killing me last week. You should have seen how we punished the parquet, Mother! We were rather splendid, weren't we, Doctor?'

She was the squire's daughter again, her tone light, deliberate, seamless. I said, 'We were'—and had to turn away, unable to look at her, for it was only in that moment, feeling the sudden violent dropping or dashing of something inside me, that I knew what she meant to me. All my careful reasoning of the past ten days, I understood, was a sort of sham, a sort of blind, thrown up by my own unsettled heart. She herself had done the unsettling, had raised a cloudy stir of emotions between us; and the thought that she might be able now to seal those emotions up—seal them up, for example, as she had sealed up her grief over Gyp—was very hard to bear.

Mrs Ayres had moved away from me, to examine another flower-bed. I went to her and offered my arm, Caroline joined her on her other side, and the three of us moved slowly on from one lawn to another, Caroline every so often stooping to pull up the worst of the battered plants, or to press the less damaged of them back into the soil. I don't know if she looked at me at all. When I glanced at her she was looking ahead, or looking down, so that I saw mainly her flattish profile, and because we walked with Mrs Ayres between us, her face was often partially or wholly hidden from me by her mother's. They talked a great deal about the gardens, I recall. The rains had brought a fence down, and they were debating whether or not it ought to be replaced. An ornamental urn had also become broken, and the large rosemary bush it held needed to be moved elsewhere. The urn was an old one, brought over from Italy as part of a pair by the Colonel's great-grandparents. Did I think it might be repaired? We stood and stared at the forlorn-looking thing, its bowl jagged and gaping, exposing a mass of tangled roots. Caroline squatted down beside it and gave the roots a prod. 'One half expects it to twitch,' she said, her eyes on the rosemary plant above. Mrs Ayres also went closer, passing her gloved hands over the green and silver branches as if combing tresses of hair, then holding her fingers to her face to inhale the fragrance.

'So lovely,' she said, extending her hand for me to inhale it too, and automatically I bent my face to her fingers, and smiled—though all I could smell, I remember, was the bitter scent of her damp wash-leather gloves. My mind was all on Caroline. I saw her prod at the roots again, then straighten up and wipe her hands. I saw her adjust the belt of her coat, I saw her lightly kick one foot against the other to remove a clump of earth from her heel. I saw her do all these things without once actually looking at her—as if with a new, secret eye that she herself had called into being and now, in her carelessness, meant to trouble like a stray lash.

Mrs Ayres led us over to the west lawn. She wanted to examine the house on that side, for Barrett had told her that one of the drainpipes might be blocked and leaking water. Sure enough, when we turned and looked back we could see a large dark irregular stain where water had spread from a joint in the pipe. The stain ran right over the roof of the saloon, disappearing into the lead-and-brickwork seam where the exterior half of the room jutted out from the house's flat rear face.

'I bet that saloon's been a blasted nuisance since the moment they added it,' Caroline said, putting a hand on her mother's shoulder and raising herself on tiptoe, trying to see. 'I wonder how far the rainwater has seeped. I hope the bricks won't need repointing. We might manage a repair to the pipe itself, but we haven't the budget for anything more serious.'

The subject seemed to preoccupy her. She discussed it with her mother, both of them weaving about on the lawn for a better perspective on the damage. Then we all moved up to the terrace for a closer look. I went quite silently, unable to summon up much enthusiasm for the task; I found myself glancing over to the other side of the angular bay of the saloon, to the garden door, where I had stood with Caroline in the darkness, and where she had lifted her head and clumsily moved her mouth to mine. And for a moment I was seized so vividly by the memory of it all, I felt almost giddy. Mrs Ayres called me over to the house; I made what can only have been a few rather idiotic observations about the bricks. But then I drew away, passing on around the terrace until that troubling door was well out of my sight.

I had turned to face the parkland, and was gazing sightlessly across it, when I became aware that Caroline had also drawn away from her mother. Perhaps, after all, she had been bothered by the sight of the door, too. She came slowly over to my side, putting her ungloved hands into her pockets. She said, without looking at me, 'Can you hear Babb's men?'

'Babb's men?' I repeated stupidly.

'Yes, it's clear today.'

She nodded to where, in the distance, giant webs of scaffolding were now being erected, with houses rising inside them, square and brash. Tuning my ears to the sound, I caught, on the still, damp air, the faint concussive clamour of the work, the calling of the men, a sudden tumbling of planks or poles.

'Like the sounds of a battle,' Caroline said. 'Don't you think? Perhaps like that phantom battle people are said to be able to hear in the middle of the night when they go camping on Edge Hill.'

I looked into her face but didn't answer, not quite trusting my voice; and I suppose my saying nothing was as good as murmuring her name or putting out a hand to her. She saw my expression, then glanced over at her mother, and—I don't know how it happened, but some charge or current at last passed between us, and in it everything was acknowledged, the spring of her hips against mine on the dance-floor, the chill dark intimacy of the car, the expectation, the frustration, the tussle, the kiss . . . Again I felt almost giddy. She lowered her head, and for a second we stood in silence, uncertain what to do. Then I said, very quietly, 'I've been thinking of you, Caroline. I—'

'Doctor!' Her mother was calling to me again. She wanted me to take a look at another patch of brickwork. An old lead clamp had worked its way loose, and she was concerned that the wall it supported might be beginning to weaken . . . The charge of the moment was lost. Caroline had already turned and was making her way over. I joined her at her mother's side; we gazed gloomily at the bulging bricks and the cracks in the mortar, and I offered up a few more inanities about possible repairs.

Soon, beginning to feel the cold, Mrs Ayres put her arm through mine again, and let me lead her back indoors, to the little parlour.

She had spent the past week, she told me, hardly venturing from her room, in an attempt to drive away the last of her bronchitis. Now, as we sat, she held her hands to the fire, rubbing the warmth back into them with obvious relish. She had lost weight recently; the rings moved on her fingers, and she straightened the stones. But, 'How marvellous it is,' she said, in a clear voice, 'to be up and about again! I'd begun to think myself like the poet. Which poet do I mean, Caroline?'

Caroline was lowering herself on to the sofa. 'I don't know, Mother.'

'Yes, you do. You know all the poets. The lady poet, frightfully bashful.'

'Elizabeth Barrett?'

'No, not her.'

'Charlotte Mew?'

'Good heavens, how many there were! But I meant the American one, who kept to her room for years and years, sending out little notes and so on.'

'Oh, Emily Dickinson, I expect.'

'Yes, Emily Dickinson. A rather exhausting poet, now I come to think of it. All that breathlessness and skipping about. What's wrong with nice long lines and a jaunty rhythm? When I was a girl, Dr Faraday, I had a German governess, a Miss Elsner. She was terribly keen on Tennyson . . .'

She went on to tell us some tale of her childhood. I'm sorry to say I barely heard it. I had taken the chair across from hers, which meant that Caroline, on the sofa, was to my left, just far enough out of the range of my vision for me to have to make a deliberate movement of my head to catch her eye. The movement grew more strained and unnatural every time I made it; it felt unnatural, too, not to turn to her at all. And though sometimes our gazes would meet and snag, more often her eyes would seem guarded to me, her expression almost dead. 'Have you been down to the new houses this week?' I asked her, when Betty had brought our tea, and 'Have you any plans to visit the farm today?'—thinking I could offer her a lift, and get some time with her on her own. But she answered in a level voice that, No, she had various chores to see to and meant to stay at home now for the rest of the afternoon . . .

What more could I do, with her mother there? Once, when Mrs Ayres turned aside, I looked over more frankly, with a sort of shrug, and a frown, and she looked quickly away, as if flustered. The next moment I watched her casually drawing down a tartan rug from the back of the sofa, and I had a sudden brutal memory of her tightening the blanket around herself in my car, pulling away from me. I heard her voice: *I'm sorry. I'm sorry. I can't!* And the whole thing seemed hopeless to me.

At last Mrs Ayres noticed my distraction.

'You're quiet today, Doctor. Nothing on your mind, I hope?'

I said apologetically, 'My day started early, that's all. And I still have patients to call on, alas. I'm very glad to see you looking so much better. But now'—I made a show of looking at my watch—'I'm afraid I must go.'

'Oh, what a pity!'

I got to my feet. Mrs Ayres rang for Betty again and sent her off to fetch my things. As I put on my overcoat, Caroline rose, and I thought with a surge of apprehension and excitement that she planned to walk with me to the front door. But she went only as far as the table, to load the teacups on to the tray. While I stood exchanging a final word with her mother, however, she drew close to me again. Her head was bent, but I saw her glance in a noticing way at the front of my coat. She said quietly, 'You're coming apart at the seams, Doctor,' reaching out and taking hold of my top button, which was dangling by a couple of threads of fraying brown cotton. Caught off guard by the gesture, I jerked back slightly, and the threads unravelled; the button came free in her hand, and we laughed. She ran her thumb over its plaited leather surface, and then, with a touch of self-consciousness, dropped it into my outstretched palm.

I put the button into my pocket. 'One of the perils of being a bachelor, I'm afraid,' I said as I did it.

And the truth is, I meant absolutely nothing by the comment, it was the sort of thing I had said at Hundreds a thousand times before. But when the implications of the words struck me I felt the blood rush into my face. Caroline and I stood as if frozen; I didn't trust myself to look at her. It was Mrs Ayres my gaze was drawn to. She was looking at her daughter and me with an expression of mild inquiry—as if we were 'in' on some joke that excluded her, but that she naturally assumed we would now make clear. When we said nothing—simply stood there, blushing and awkward—her expression changed. It was like light moving rapidly over a landscape, the inquiry giving way to a sudden blaze of astonished understanding, the astonishment swiftly transforming itself into a tight, self-deprecating smile.

She turned to the table at her side, putting out her hand as if absently searching for something, then got to her feet.

'I'm afraid I've been rather tiresome today,' she said, drawing in her shawls.

I said nervously, 'Good heavens, you could never be that!'

She wouldn't look at me. She glanced at Caroline instead. 'Why don't you walk Dr Faraday to his car?'

Caroline laughed. 'I think, after all this time, Dr Faraday is capable of finding his own car.'

'Of course I am!' I said. 'You mustn't trouble.'

'No,' said Mrs Ayres, 'it's I who've been the trouble. I see that now. Chattering on . . . Doctor, do take off your coat and stay longer. You mustn't think of hurrying away on my account. I have chores to finish upstairs.'

'Oh, Mother,' said Caroline. 'Really. What on earth's got into you? Dr Faraday has patients to visit.'

Mrs Ayres was still gathering her things together. She said, as if Caroline hadn't spoken, 'I dare say you have lots to discuss, the two of you.'

'No,' said Caroline, 'I assure you! Nothing at all.'

I said, 'I really must go, you know.'

'Well, Caroline will walk with you.'

Again Caroline laughed, her voice hardening. 'No, Caroline won't! Doctor, I'm sorry. What nonsense this all is! All because of a button. I wish you were handier with your needle. Mother will give me no peace, now . . . Mother, sit down again. Whatever you're thinking, it's quite wrong. You needn't leave the room. I'm going upstairs myself.'

'Please, don't do that,' I said quickly, putting out my hand to her; and the touch of feeling that crept into my voice and pose must have done more than anything to give us away. She had already begun moving purposefully across the room; now she made an almost impatient gesture—shaking her head at me. And in another moment she was gone.

I watched the closing of the door behind her, then turned back to Mrs Ayres.

'*Is* it nonsense?' she asked me.

I said helplessly, 'I don't know.'

She drew in her breath, and her shoulders sank as she released it. She returned to her chair, sitting down heavily, and gesturing for me to return to mine. I perched at the front of it, still in my overcoat, my hat and scarf in my hand. We said nothing for a moment. I could see her thinking it all through. When she did at last speak, her voice had a false brightness to it—like a dull metal, overpolished.

'Naturally,' she said, 'I've thought of you and Caroline making a match, many times! I think I thought of it the very first time you came here. There's the difference in ages; but that means nothing to a man, and Caroline's too sensible a girl to be troubled by those sort of considerations . . . But you and she seemed good friends merely.'

'We're still good friends, I hope,' I said.

'And something more than friends, clearly.' She glanced at the door, and frowned, perplexed. 'How secretive she is! She'd have told me nothing of this, you know. And I, her mother!'

'There's scarcely anything to tell, that's why.'

'Oh, but this isn't the sort of thing one does by degrees. One crosses the floor, as it were. I shan't ask exactly when the floor was crossed, in this case.'

I shifted about uncomfortably. 'Very recently, as it happens.'

'Caroline's of age, of course. And she always did know her own mind. But, with her father dead, and her poor brother so unwell, I suppose I should ask you something. Your intentions, and so on. How Edwardian that sounds! You'll have no illusions about our finances; that's a blessing.'

I shifted again. 'Look, you know, this is all a little awkward. You'd do better talking to Caroline herself. I can't speak for her.'

She laughed, unsmiling. 'No, I shouldn't recommend you try.'

'I'd be happier, to be honest, if we could let the subject drop. I really do have to go.'

She bowed her head. 'Of course, if you wish.'

But I sat struggling with my feelings for a few more moments, perturbed at the turn my visit had taken, unhappy that this thing—which still struck me as having come more or less from nowhere—had put such an obvious distance between us. At last, abruptly, I got up. I drew close to her chair, and she tilted back her head to look at me, and I was amazed and alarmed to see that her eyes were wet with tears. The flesh around them seemed to have darkened and slackened, and her hair—for once, without its silk square or mantilla—was, I realised, streaked with grey.

The artificial brightness of manner had gone, too. She said, with a touch of playful self-pity, 'Oh, what's to become of me, Doctor? My world is dwindling to the point of a pin. You won't abandon me completely, you and Caroline?'

'Abandon you?' I stepped back, shaking my head, trying to laugh the whole thing off. But my tone sounded as false to my ears as hers had, a few minutes before. I said, 'This is all absurdly precipitate, you know. Nothing has changed. Nothing has changed, and no one's to be abandoned. I can promise you that.'

And I left her, going rather dazedly along the passage, more unsettled than ever by the turn of events and by the speed with which, in such a short space of time, things seemed to have jolted forward. I don't think I even thought of going after Caroline. I simply made my way to the front door, putting on my hat and scarf as I went.

But as I crossed the hall, some sound or movement alerted me: I glanced up the staircase and saw her there, on the first landing, just beyond the turn of the banister. She was lit from above by the dome of glass, her brown hair looking almost fair in the soft, kind light, but her face in shadow.

I took off my hat again, and went over to the lowest stair. She didn't come down, so I called softly up to her.

'Caroline! I'm so sorry. I really can't stay. Talk to your mother, will you? She—she has an idea that we're about to elope or something.'

She didn't answer. I waited, and then added more quietly: 'We aren't about to elope, are we?'

She hooked a hand around one of the balusters and slightly shook her head.

'Two sensible people like us,' she murmured. 'It seems unlikely, doesn't it?'

Her face being in shadow, her expression was unclear. Her voice was low, but level; I don't think she meant it playfully. But she must, after all, have been waiting there for me to appear; and it struck me suddenly that she was still waiting—waiting for me to climb the stairs, go up to her, nudge the thing forward, put it well beyond question or doubt. But when I did take a step upwards, it was as though she couldn't help herself: a look of alarm came into her face—I caught it, even through the shadow—and she took a swift step back.

So, defeated, I moved down again, to the pink and liver-coloured marble floor. And I said, not warmly, 'Yes, it seems awfully unlikely, at the moment'—putting on my hat and turning away from her, and letting myself out through the buckled front door.

I began to miss her almost at once, but the feeling irritated me now, and a sort of stubbornness or tiredness kept me from pursuing her. I spent a few days avoiding the Hall altogether—taking the longer route around the park; wasting fuel in the process. Then, quite unexpectedly,

I ran into her and her mother on one of the streets of Leamington. They had driven in to do some shopping. I came upon them too late to pretend I hadn't seen them, and we stood and chatted, awkwardly, for five or ten minutes. Caroline was wearing that unflattering wool hat of hers, together with a jaundice-coloured scarf I hadn't seen on her before. She looked plain and sallow and remote, and once the first shock of bumping into her had worn away, I realised unhappily that there was no leaping charge between us, no special sympathy at all. She had clearly spoken to her mother, who made no reference to my last visit; indeed, we behaved, all three of us, as if that visit had never occurred. When they left me I raised my hat to them, as if to any acquaintance on the street. Then I went moodily on to the hospital—and started a dreadful row, I remember, with the most ferocious of the ward sisters.

Over the next few days I threw myself back into my rounds, not wanting to give myself any time to be idle and brooding. And then a piece of luck came my way. The committee on which I'd been sitting was due to present its findings at a London conference; the man who was meant to give the paper fell ill, and I was invited to take his place. With things with Caroline so muddled, I leapt at the chance; and as the conference was a long one, involving a few days' stay as an observer on one of the wards of a London hospital, for the first time in several years I took a complete break from my practice. My cases were handed over to Graham and to our locum, Wise. I left Warwickshire for London on the fifth of February, and altogether was away for almost two weeks.

My absence couldn't, in practical terms, have had much impact on life at Hundreds, for I was often unable to call in at the Hall for longish spells of time. But I learned later that they missed me there. I suppose they had come to rely on me, and liked feeling that I was on hand, ready to drop in, if I had to, in response to a telephone call. My visits had eased their sense of isolation; now it seemed to rush back upon them, more dismal than before. Looking for distractions, they spent an afternoon in Lidcote with Bill and Helen Desmond, followed by an evening with elderly Miss Dabney. Another day they went into Worcestershire, to visit some old family friends. But that journey took most of their petrol-ration; and then the weather grew wet again, and it became more difficult to get about on the bad country roads. Fearful for her health, Mrs Ayres kept safely indoors. Caroline, however, was made restless by the constant rain: she put on her oilskins and wellingtons and worked hard on the estate. She spent some days with Makins at the farm, helping with the first of the spring sowing. Then she turned her attention to the garden, fixing up the broken fence with Barrett, and doing what she could with the blocked drainpipe. This last task was a dispiriting one: going closer to the problem she could see how very badly the water had seeped. When she had cleared it, she went back into the house, to check for damage in all the rooms on the west side. Her mother went with her; they found minor leaks in two of the rooms, the dining-room and 'boot-room'. Then they opened up the saloon.

They did this rather reluctantly. On the morning following the disastrous party back in October, Mrs Bazeley and Betty had gone in there to try and remove the traces of blood from the carpet and the sofa—working at them for two or three hours apparently, taking away pail after grisly pail of cloudy pink water. After that, with the house so depressed, and with all the anxiety over Rod, no one had had the heart to go back in there, and the saloon had been more or less shut up. Even when Caroline had gone through the Hall in search of items to auction, she had left this room untouched—almost as if, I remember thinking at the time, she'd developed a sort of superstition about disturbing it.

But now, putting back its creaking shutters, she and her mother cursed themselves for not having looked it over sooner. The room was more damaged than they could have guessed, its decorative ceiling so bloated with water it actually sagged. In other spots rain had simply worked its way through seams in the plaster to fall unchecked on the carpet and furniture below. The harpsichord, fortunately, had escaped the worst of the damage, but the tapestried seat of one of the gilt Regency chairs was quite ruined. Most startling of all, the yellow Chinese wallpaper had tugged its corners from the rusting drawing-pins with which Caroline had fixed them up, and was drooping in ragged strips from the damp plaster behind.

'Well,' said Caroline, sighing, gazing at the mess, 'we had our trial by fire. I suppose we should have expected to be tried by water, too . . .'

They called for Betty and Mrs Bazeley, and had them build up a blaze in the grate; they started up the generator, brought electric heaters and oil-stoves, and for the rest of that day, and through the whole of the day that followed, they devoted themselves to airing the room. The ceiling they knew they could do nothing for. The crystal cups of the chandelier held pools of cloudy water, and fizzed and crackled alarmingly when they tried its switch, so after that they dared not touch it. The wallpaper was beyond salvage. But the carpet they thought they could rescue, and the pieces of furniture too large to be taken for storage elsewhere they planned to clean, then bag or drape. Caroline herself joined in the work, putting on some ancient drill trousers and tying up her hair with string. Mrs Ayres's health, however, had taken another slight dip, and she was not quite well enough to do much more than watch unhappily while the room was stripped and diminished.

'Your grandmother would have broken her heart,' she said on the second day, fingering a pair of silk curtains fantastically stained by creeping water.

'Well, it can't be helped,' said Caroline wearily. Her long spell of work was catching up with her. She was struggling with a roll of felt, brought down from upstairs and meant for the sofa. 'The room has had its life, and that's that.'

Her mother looked almost stricken. 'You talk as though we were making a tomb of it!'

'I wish we were! We might get a grant from the county council for that. No doubt Babb could do the conversion.—What a beast this thing is!' She flung the roll down. 'I'm sorry, Mother. I don't mean to be flippant. Why not go back to the little parlour if the sight of all this is upsetting you?'

'When I think of the parties your father and I hosted here, when you were small!'

'Yes, I know. But Daddy never did much like this room, remember? He said the wallpaper made him seasick.'

She glanced around, searching for some gentle chore with which to occupy her mother; and finally, taking her hand, she led her to a chair beside the cabinet of the gramophone.

'Look here,' she said, opening the cabinet up and bringing out a heap of old records. 'We might as well do things properly. I've been meaning to go through these for ages. Let's you and I sort through them now, and see what we can throw away. I'm sure most of them are rubbish.'

She meant only, really, to distract her mother from the depressing business going on around her. But the records were all mixed up with other things, pieces of sheet music, concert and theatre programmes, dinner-menus and invitations, many of them dating from the early years of her mother's marriage or from her own childhood; and the task became an absorbing and rather sentimental one for them both. They sat there for almost an hour, exclaiming over the things they turned up. They found music bought by the Colonel, and old dance-tunes of Rod's. They found recordings of a Mozart opera that Mrs Ayres had first seen sung on her honeymoon in 1912.

'Why, I remember the gown I was wearing!' she said, letting the record sink in her lap and gazing softly into her own memory. 'A blue chiffon, with handkerchief sleeves. Cissie and I had argued about which of us should have it. One felt one was floating in a gown like that. Well, at eighteen one does float, or we girls did then, we were mere children . . . And your father, in his dress-suit—and walking with a cane! He'd twisted his ankle. Only twisted his ankle, jumping down off a horse, but he carried that cane about for a fortnight. I think he thought it distinguished. He was a child, too: only twenty-two, younger than Roderick is now . . .'

The thought of Roderick was obviously a hard one, coming as it did upon her other memories, and she looked so wistful that, after watching her for a moment, Caroline gently took the record from her hands, opened up the gramophone, and set it to play. The disc was old, and the gramophone needle badly wanted replacing: at first all they heard was the hiss and crackle of the shellac. Then, slightly chaotically, there came the boom of the orchestra. The singer's voice seemed to struggle against it, until finally the soprano rose purely, 'like some lovely, fragile creature,' Caroline told me later, 'breaking free of thorns.'

It must have been an oddly poignant moment. The day was dark with rain again, and the saloon was quite dim. The fire and the purring heaters cast an almost romantic light, so that for a minute or two the room—for all that the paper was hanging from its walls and its ceiling bulging—seemed alive with glamour. Mrs Ayres smiled, her gaze loose again, her hand stirring, the fingers sinking and falling in response to the swells of the music. Even Mrs Bazeley and Betty were awed. They kept up their progress around the room, but did so stealthily, like dumb-show artists, softly unrolling lengths of drugget across the last uncovered strips of carpet, and gently easing mirrors from the walls.

The aria drew to its close. The gramophone needle caught in its groove and gave a harsh repetitive crackle. Caroline rose and lifted it free, and across the ensuing silence there broke the steady drip, drip of water tumbling from the ruined ceiling into buckets and bowls. She saw her mother look up, blinking, as if waking from a dream; and so, to dispel the melancholy, she started up a second record, a brisk old music-hall song that she and Roderick had used to march about to as children.

'*Jolly good luck to the girl who loves a sol-dier!*' she sang lightly. '*Girls, have you been there?*'

Mrs Bazeley and Betty, relieved, began to move about more freely, picking up the pace of their work to match the clip of the music.

'Now, there's a fine old song,' said Mrs Bazeley approvingly.

'You like this one?' called Caroline. 'So do I! Don't tell me you saw Vesta Tilley singing it on *your* honeymoon?'

'Honeymoon, miss?' Mrs Bazeley pulled in her chin. 'I never had one! Only a night at me sister's, at Evesham. Her and her husband went in with the kids, for Mr Bazeley and me to have the room. After that we went straight to me mother-in-law's place, where we never even had so much as a bed to ourselves—no, not for nine years, until the poor old lady died.'

'Good gracious!' said Caroline. 'Poor Mr Bazeley.'

'Oh, he never minded. He kept a bottle of rum by the bed, and a jar of black treacle; he gave his mother a spoonful of them o'nights, and her slept like a dead un.—Pass us that old tin box there, Betty, there's a good girl.'

Caroline laughed, then looked on, still smiling, as Betty handed Mrs Bazeley the box. It held a number of narrow sandbags, used in the house for stopping up draughts, and known in the family as 'snakes': they were very familiar from Caroline's childhood, and she watched with a touch of nostalgic pleasure as Mrs Bazeley crossed to the windows of the saloon and began to lay them down on the sills and over the gaps between the sashes. She even, finally, went over and drew a spare sandbag from the box, taking it back to the heap of records so that she could turn it in her hands as she went through the last of the papers and discs.

She was vaguely aware, in time, of Mrs Bazeley making a soft exclamation of annoyance, then calling to Betty for water and a cloth. But it was another minute or two before she thought to look over to the window again. When she did look, she saw the two servants kneeling side by side, alternately frowning and rubbing gingerly at some spot on the wainscot. She called out, more or less idly, 'What is it, Mrs Bazeley?'

'Well, miss,' Mrs Bazeley answered, 'I don't quite know. I can only think as it's some mark left here by that poor little girl that was bit.'

Caroline's heart sank. She realised that the window alcove they were looking at was the one in which Gillian Baker-Hyde had been sitting when Gyp had snapped at her. The wainscot and floorboards there had been badly splashed with blood, but that whole area had been thoroughly washed down along with the sofa and the carpet. She supposed now that some stain had managed to escape notice.

Something in Mrs Bazeley's voice or manner, however, made her curious. She let the sandbag fall from her fingers and went to join her at the window.

Her mother looked up as she moved away. 'What is it, Caroline?'

'I don't know. Nothing, I expect.'

Mrs Bazeley and Betty drew back to let her see. The mark they'd been rubbing at wasn't a stain, but a number of childish scrawls on the woodwork: a jumble of Ss, done apparently in pencil, randomly placed, and roughly or hastily drawn. The effect was like this:

    S Ss   SSSS

             SS S

  SS   SsS

'God!' said Caroline under her breath. 'As if tormenting Gyp wasn't enough for her!' Then, catching Mrs Bazeley's eye: 'I'm sorry. What happened to that little girl was frightful, and I'd give anything to undo it. She must have brought a pencil with her that night. Unless she took one of ours. I suppose it *was* the Baker-Hyde girl? Do the marks look fresh to you?'

She moved slightly as she spoke: her mother had been drawn across the room by her words, and was standing at her side. She was gazing at the scribbles, Caroline thought, with an odd expression, half in great dismay, half as though she wanted to go closer, perhaps run her fingers over the wood.

Mrs Bazeley wrung out her wet cloth and started to rub at the scribbles again.

'I can't say how they look, miss,' she said, puffing as she worked. 'I know they're harder to get off than they should be! They weren't here though—were they, Betty?—when we did out the room in the days before that party.'

Betty looked nervously at Caroline. 'I don't think so, miss.'

'I know they weren't,' said Mrs Bazeley. 'For I went over this paint-work myself, every inch of it, while Betty done the carpets.'

'Well, then it must have been that child,' said Caroline. 'It was naughty of her; very naughty indeed. Do the best you can to remove them, will you?'

'I'm doing it!' said Mrs Bazeley, indignant. 'But I'll tell you something. If this is pencil, I'm King George. This is stuck fast, this is.'

'Stuck? It isn't ink, or crayon, is it?'

'I don't know what it is. I could almost fancy it's come up from *under* the paint.'

'*Under* the paint,' repeated Caroline, startled.

Mrs Bazeley looked up at her for a second, struck by her tone; then she saw the clock, and tutted. 'Ten more minutes, now, and there's me time done. Betty, you shall have to try soda on this after I've gone. Not too much, mind, or you'll blister it . . .'

Mrs Ayres turned away. She had said nothing about the marks, but it seemed to Caroline that her pose was a burdened one, as if this unexpected reminder of the party and all it had led to had put the final gloomy seal on her day. With slow and fumbling gestures she gathered together her things, saying she was tired and meant to rest for a while upstairs. And since the saloon had now well and truly lost its glamour, Caroline also decided to leave it. She picked up the box of rejected records and followed her mother to the door—looking back only once to the patch of scrubbed wainscot, with its indelible swarm of *S*s like so many wriggling little eels.

This was on the Saturday—probably at just about the time I was delivering my report to the London conference, with the whole affair with Caroline still niggling darkly at the back of my mind. By the end of that afternoon the work on the saloon was finished, and the room was effectively sealed up again, its shutters fastened and its door closed; and the scribbles on the wainscot—which, after all, were very small annoyances in the wider scheme of the family's misfortunes—were more or less forgotten. Sunday and Monday passed off without incident. Both those days were cold, but dry. So Caroline was surprised, on passing the door of the saloon on Tuesday afternoon, to hear from the room beyond it a regular soft tapping sound, which she took to be the drip of rainwater. Dismayed to think that the ceiling must have sprung some mysterious new leak, she opened the door and looked inside. The tapping ceased as she did it. She stood still with her breathing softened, peering into the lightless room, just about making out the strips of torn paper on the walls, and the odd, lumpy-looking pieces of wrapped-up furniture, but hearing nothing more. So she closed the door and went on her way.

Next day, re-passing the saloon, she again heard the noise. A rapid drumming or pattering it was this time, so unmistakable that she went right into the room and drew back a shutter. As before, the noise had stopped by the time she had quite opened up the door: she checked the bowls and pails that had been left out to catch drips from the ceiling, and made a quick inspection of the drugget-covered carpet, but all was dry. She was just deciding to give the thing up, baffled, when the noise started again. This time it seemed to her to be coming not from inside the saloon at all, but from one of its neighbouring rooms. A soft but smart *rat-tat-tat* she said it was now, like a schoolboy idly drumming with a stick. More baffled and intrigued than ever, she went back out into the passage and stood listening again. She pursued the sound to the dining-room, but there it again abruptly fell silent—only to restart a few seconds later, this time apparently on the other side of the wall, in the little parlour.

She found her mother in there, reading a week-old newspaper. Mrs Ayres had heard nothing. 'Nothing?' asked Caroline. 'Are you sure?' Then: 'There! Do you hear that?' She held up her hand. Her mother listened, and after a moment agreed that, yes, there was certainly some sort of sound. A 'knocking', she called it, as opposed to Caroline's 'tapping'; she suggested it might be the result of air or water being trapped in the central-heating pipes. Doubtfully, Caroline crossed to the room's ancient radiator. It was tepid to her touch and quite lifeless, and even as she drew her hand away from it, the knocking grew louder and clearer: it seemed now to be over her head. So distinct a sound was it, she and her mother were able to 'watch' its progress in the ceiling and the walls: it travelled from one side of the room to the other like 'a small hard bouncing ball'.

This was sometime in the afternoon, after Mrs Bazeley had gone home; but now, naturally, they thought of Betty, wondering if she mightn't simply be at work in one of the rooms upstairs. When they rang for her, however, she came straight up from the basement: she had been down there for half an hour, she said, preparing their tea. They kept her with them in the little parlour for almost ten minutes, during which time the house was perfectly silent and still; but no sooner had she left them than the knocking started again. This time it was back out in the passage. Caroline went quickly to the door, and looked out to find Betty standing bewildered in the middle of the marble floor while a soft, crisp drumming sounded from the panels of the wall high up above her head.

They were none of them afraid, Caroline said, not even Betty herself. The sound was queer, but not menacing; it seemed to lead them almost playfully, in fact, from one spot to another, until the pursuing of it along the passage began to feel like 'a bit of a lark'. They followed it right out into the hall. This was always the chilliest place in the house, and today it seemed almost like an ice-box. Caroline rubbed her arms, glancing up the draughty staircase.

'If it means to go upstairs,' she said, 'then it can go on its own. I don't care about the idiotic thing that much.'

Rat-tat-tat! went the drumming loudly, as if in indignant response to her words, and after that the sound seemed grudgingly to 'settle' in one spot, giving the bizarre impression that it was coming from a shallow laburnum-wood cabinet that stood against the panelled wall beside the staircase. The effect was so vivid, Caroline felt wary about opening the cabinet up. She caught hold of its handles, but stood well back as she turned them—half expecting the thing to spring open, she said, like a jack-in-the-box. But the doors swung harmlessly towards her, revealing nothing but a few odd bits of ornament and clutter, and when the tapping sounded again, it became clear that it was coming not from inside the cabinet, but from somewhere behind it. Caroline closed the doors, and moved to peer into the slender dark space between the cabinet and the wall. Then, with an understandable touch of reluctance, she lifted her hand and slowly slid her fingers into the gap. She stood still, her breath held, her palm flat on the dry wood panel.

The knocking came again, louder than before. She started back, alarmed but laughing.

'It's there!' she said, shaking her arm as if to drive pins and needles from it. 'I felt it in the wall! It's like a little hand, rapping. It must be beetles or mice or something. Betty, come here and help me with this.' She took hold of one side of the cabinet.

Betty looked fearful now. 'I don't want to, miss.'

'Come on, it won't bite you!'

So the girl moved forward. The cabinet was light but unwieldy, and it took the two of them a minute to shift it. The tapping faded again as they set it down, so that when Mrs Ayres, struck by the sight of something on the newly exposed wall, drew in her breath, Caroline heard her very clearly; and she saw her make a movement—stretch out her hand, then draw it back to her bosom as if in fright.

'What is it, Mother?' she said, still struggling with the placing of the cabinet's feet. Mrs Ayres didn't answer. Caroline made the cabinet steady, then went to her mother's side and saw what had startled her.

The wall was marked with more of that childish scribbling: *SSS SSSS S SU S*.

Caroline stared. 'I don't believe it. This is simply too much! She couldn't have— That child couldn't possibly have— Could she?' She looked at her mother; her mother didn't answer. She turned to Betty.

'When was this cabinet last moved?'

Betty looked really frightened now. 'I don't know, miss.'

'Well, think! Was it after the fire?'

'I—I think it must have been.'

'I think it must have been, too. Didn't you wash this wall, along with all the others? And you saw no writing then?'

'I don't remember, miss. I don't think so.'

'You would have seen it, wouldn't you?'

Caroline moved right up to the wall as she spoke, to examine the marks more closely. She gave them a rub with the cuff of her cardigan. She licked her thumb, and rubbed with that. The marks remained. She shook her head, utterly perplexed.

'*Could* the little girl have done it? Would she have? I think she went to the lavatory at some point, that night. She might just, perhaps, have slipped out here. She might have thought it funny, making a mark where we wouldn't find it for months and months—'

'Cover it up,' said Mrs Ayres abruptly.

Caroline turned to her. 'Oughtn't we to wash it?'

'There isn't any point. Can't you see? The marks are just like those others. We oughtn't to have found them. I don't want to look at them. Cover them up.'

'Yes, of course,' said Caroline, with a glance at Betty. They manoeuvred the cabinet back into place.

And it was only when that was done, she told me, that the queerness of the whole thing began to strike her. She had been unafraid before, but now the taps, the discovery of the marks, her mother's response, the current silence: she thought it all through, and felt her courage begin to waver. With an attempt at bravado, she said, 'This house is playing parlour games with us, I think. We shan't pay it any mind if it starts up again.' She lifted her voice, and spoke into the stairwell. 'Do you hear me, house? It's no good your teasing us! We simply shan't play!'

There were no answering knocks this time. Her words were swallowed up by the silence. She caught Betty's apprehensive gaze, then turned away and spoke more quietly.

'All right, Betty, you go on back to the kitchen now.'

But Betty hesitated. 'Is madam all right?'

'Madam's fine.' Caroline put a hand on her mother's arm. 'Mother, come through to the warm, will you?'

As on that other day, however, Mrs Ayres said she preferred to go alone to her room. She tightened her shawl, and Caroline and Betty watched her softly climb the stairs. She stayed up there until almost dinner-time; by which point, apparently, she was more herself again. Caroline, too, had recovered her nerve by then. Neither of the women mentioned the scribbles. That evening, and the day or two that followed, passed uneventfully.

But some time later that week, Mrs Ayres had her first broken night. Like many women who had lived through the war, she was easily woken by unfamiliar sounds, and one night she started up out of sleep with the distinct impression that someone had called for her. She kept still in the deep winter darkness, listening hard; when she heard nothing more for several minutes, she began to relax back into slumber. Then, settling her head against her pillow, she thought she caught, beyond the rustling of the linen against her ear, another sound, and again sat up. After a moment the sound came again. It was not a voice, after all. It was not a rapping or a drumming, either. It was a fluttering, faint but distinct; and it was coming, unmistakably, from the other side of a narrow jib door beside her bed—that is, from her old dressing-room, which she now treated as a box-room for the storing of trunks and hampers. The sound was such an odd one, it conjured up a particular and peculiar image, and for a moment she was really frightened. She supposed that someone had got into the dressing-room and was plucking clothes from one of the hampers and letting them flutter to the floor.

Then, as the sound continued, she realised that what she could hear was in fact the beating of wings. A bird must have found its way down the chimney and become trapped.

This was a relief, after her rather wild imaginings; but it was also a nuisance, for now she lay wide awake, listening to the poor thing making its panicked attempts at escape. She didn't relish the idea of going into the dressing-room and trying to catch it. As it happened, she had never much cared for birds or other fluttering things; she had a childish fear of them flying into her face, becoming tangled in her hair. But at last she could stand it no longer. She lit a candle and got out of bed. She put on her dressing-gown, taking care to button it right up to her throat; she tied a scarf very securely over her head, and drew on shoes and her wash-leather gloves. She did all this—making 'a complete guy of myself', as she later told her daughter—then gingerly drew back the dressing-room door. As with Caroline's experience in the saloon, the fluttering ceased the moment the door began its swing, and the room beyond it seemed undisturbed. There were no bird droppings on the floor, no fallen feathers; and the flap of the chimney, she found when she went to examine it, was rusted shut.

She lay awake for the rest of that night, unsettled and wary, but the house stayed silent. The next night she went to bed early, and slept without much difficulty. On the night after that, however, she was again woken, and in exactly the same way as before. This time she went around the landing and woke Betty, and had her return with her and stand listening at the dressing-room door. It was about a quarter to three. Betty said she heard 'something, she wasn't sure what'; but again, when they nerved themselves up to look inside the little room, they found it lifeless . . . It then occurred to Mrs Ayres that her first instinct must have been right. She could not have imagined the sounds, they were too distinct for that; the bird must be inside the chimney itself, just behind the breast of it, unable to find its way back up the flue. The thought took hold of her, horribly. It was made all the worse, I suppose, by the lateness of the hour, by the stillness and the dark. She sent Betty back to her bed but again lay awake, upset and frustrated, and by the time Caroline went in to see her next morning she was already up, and back in the dressing-room; she was down on her knees in front of the hearth, prising with a poker at the rusted chimney-flap.

For a moment, it seemed to Caroline that her mother might have lost her mind. Once she understood what the matter was, she helped Mrs Ayres to her feet and took over the prising of the flap herself, and when she had opened it up she fetched a broomstick and poked about in the flue until her arm ached. By then she was black as a minstrel, having brought down a shower of soot. The soot had not so much as a feather in it, but so certain was Mrs Ayres about the trapped bird— and so 'peculiarly upset about it' was she, apparently—that Caroline cleaned herself up and went out into the garden with a pair of opera glasses to examine the chimney-stack. She found the pots of all the chimneys on that side of the Hall covered with wire guards, the wire here and there broken, but so pasted with wet, dead leaves it seemed unlikely to her that a bird could have made its way into one of those cages and gone from there into a flue. But after thinking the matter over on her way back into the house, she told her mother that the pot in question looked to her as though it might recently have held a nest. She said she had seen a bird 'go into it and then fly out again, quite freely'. That seemed to reassure Mrs Ayres a little, and she dressed and took her breakfast.

But only an hour or so later, while Caroline was finishing off her own breakfast in her room, she was startled to hear her mother cry out. The cry was a piercing one, and sent her running across the landing. She found Mrs Ayres at the open door of her dressing-room, apparently backing feebly away, her arms held out, from something inside it. Only much later would it occur to Caroline that her mother's pose at this moment might not, in fact, have been one of retreat; at the time she simply dashed to her mother's side, imagining she'd been struck seriously ill. But Mrs Ayres was not ill—at least, not in the ordinary way. She let Caroline walk her to her chair, pour a glass of water, kneel at her side with her hand in hers. 'I'm all right,' she said, wiping her glistening eyes; startling Caroline all the more by her tears. 'You mustn't trouble. So foolish of me, after so much time.'

As she spoke, she kept looking over at the dressing-room. Her expression was so odd—so apprehensive and yet somehow so *avid*— Caroline grew afraid.

'What *is* it, Mother? Why are you looking? What can you see?'

Mrs Ayres shook her head and wouldn't answer. So Caroline rose

and went warily across to the dressing-room door. She told me later
that she didn't know what frightened her more, the prospect of discovering something dreadful in the room beyond it, or the possibility—
which at that moment, given her mother's behaviour, seemed quite
strong—of there being nothing untoward in there at all. All she saw at
first, in fact, was a jumble of boxes, which her mother had obviously
pulled out of their usual place in an attempt to dust them free of the
soot that had settled on them from the unsealed chimney. Then her gaze
was caught by what in the dimness she took to be a thicker smear of
soot low down on one of the walls, which the drawing back of the
boxes had exposed. She moved closer and, as her eyes grew used to the
light, the patch resolved itself into a block of smudged dark childish
writing, exactly like the scribbles she had recently seen downstairs:

SSu SS Su

            SSu

     SSuCKY

          SuCKeY

At first all she was struck by was the *age* of the marks. They were
clearly much older than everyone had been guessing so far, and must
have been made not by poor Gillian Baker-Hyde, but by another child
entirely, years before. Could she herself, she wondered, have made
them? Or Roderick? She thought of cousins, family friends . . . And
then, with a queer little dropping of her heart, she looked again at what
had been written, and suddenly understood her mother's tears. To her
own amazement, she felt herself blush. She had to stay in the small dim
room for a minute or two in order to let the blush subside.

'Well,' she said, when she finally rejoined her mother, 'at least now
we can be sure it wasn't the Baker-Hyde girl.'

Mrs Ayres answered simply, 'I never thought it was.'

Caroline stood at her side. 'I'm sorry, Mother.'

'What have you to be sorry for, darling?'

'I don't know.'

'Don't say it, then.' Mrs Ayres sighed. 'How this house likes to catch us out, doesn't it? As if it knows all our weaknesses and is testing them, one by one . . . God, how dreadfully tired I am!' She made a pad of her handkerchief and pressed it to her forehead, tightly closing her eyes.

'Is there something I can do for you, or fetch for you?' asked Caroline. 'Why don't you go back to bed for a while?'

'I'm tired even of my bed.'

'Stay in your chair and doze, then. I'll make up the fire.'

'Like an old woman again,' grumbled Mrs Ayres.

But she wearily settled herself in the chair, while Caroline saw to the grate; and by the time the flames were lapping at the wood she had put back her head and appeared to be dozing. Caroline looked at her for a moment, struck by the lines of age and sadness in her face, and suddenly seeing her—as, when we are young, we are now and then shocked to see our parents—as an individual, a person of impulses and experiences of which she herself knew nothing, and with a past, with a sorrow in it, which she could not penetrate. All she could do for her mother just then, she thought, was to make her more comfortable, so she moved softly around the room, drawing the curtains part-way across, closing the dressing-room door, adding a blanket to the shawl that lay across her mother's knees. Then she went downstairs. She didn't mention the incident to Betty or Mrs Bazeley, but she found she wanted company, so she made up some chore to see to in the kitchen. When she looked in on the bedroom again later she saw her mother sleeping soundly, her pose apparently unchanged.

Mrs Ayres must have woken at some point, though, for now the blanket lay in a heap on the floor, as if brushed or tugged aside; and the dressing-room door, Caroline noticed, which she had gently but firmly closed, stood open again.

I was still in London while all this was going on. I came home, in the third week of February, in a rather perturbed state of mind. My trip, in many ways, had been a great success. The conference had gone well for me. I'd made the most of my time at the hospital, and become good friends with its staff; in fact, on my final morning one of the doctors had taken me aside to suggest that at some point in the future I might like to consider joining them down there on the wards. He was a man, like me, who had made the move into medicine from humble beginnings. He was determined, he said, to 'shake things up', and preferred to work with doctors who had 'come in from outside the system'. He was the sort of man, in other words, I had once naively imagined I might myself become; but the fact was, he was thirty-three and already head of his department, while I, several years older, had achieved nothing much at all. I spent the train journey back to Warwickshire thinking over his words, wondering if I could live up to his estimation of me, debating with myself whether I could seriously consider abandoning David Graham; wondering, too, rather cynically, what really bound me to my Lidcote life, and whether anyone would miss me if I left it.

The village looked desperately narrow and quaint as I made my way home from the station, and the list of calls awaiting me was the usual round of country ailments—arthritis, bronchitis, rheumatism, chills—it seemed to me suddenly that I had been battling uselessly against conditions like that for the whole of my career. Then there were one or two other cases, discouraging in a different way. A thirteen-year-old girl had got herself pregnant, and had been badly beaten by her labourer father. A cottager's son had contracted pneumonia: I went to see him at the family home and found him appallingly ill and wasted. He was one of eight children, all of them sick in one way or another; the father was injured and out of work. The mother and grandmother had been treating the boy with old-fashioned remedies, binding fresh rabbit-skins to his chest to 'draw out the cough'. I prescribed penicillin, more or less paying for the mixture myself. But I doubted they would even use it. They gazed warily at the bottle, 'not liking the look of the yellow'. Dr Morrison was their regular doctor, they told me, and his mixture was red.

I left their cottage with my spirits thoroughly depressed, and on my way home I took my short-cut across Hundreds Park. Letting myself in through the gate, I planned to call in at the Hall; I'd already been back three days by then, and had had no contact with the Ayreses. But as I drew closer to the house, and saw its marred and wasted faces, I felt a surge of angry frustration, and put my foot down and carried on. I told myself that I was too busy, that there was no point calling in there only to have to give my apologies and rush straight off again . . .

I told myself something similar the next time I crossed the park, and again the time after that. So I had no clue as to the latest shift in mood in the house until, a few days later, I received a telephone call from Caroline, asking me if I wouldn't mind dropping in and, as she put it, 'seeing if I thought everything was all right'.

She rarely called me by telephone, and I wasn't expecting her to call now. The sound of her low, clear, handsome voice sent a thrill of surprise and pleasure through me, that almost at once became a flutter of concern. Was something wrong? I asked her, and she answered vaguely that, no, nothing was wrong. They had had 'some trouble with leaking water', but that was 'all fixed now'. And, she was well? And her mother? Yes, they were both quite well. There were just 'one or two things' she'd like my opinion on, if I could 'spare the time for it'.

That was all she would say. A sense of guilt flared up in me and I drove more or less straight out there, putting off a patient in order to do it; worrying about what was awaiting me; imagining that she had graver things to tell me but wouldn't share them on the open line. But when I arrived at the house I found her in the unlit little parlour, in a pose that couldn't have been more mundane. She was kneeling at the hearth with a pail of water and some crumpled sheets of newsprint, making balls of papier-mâché and rolling them in coal-dust, to be burned on the fire.

Her sleeves were turned up to her elbows and her arms were filthy. Her hair was straggling over her face. She looked like a servant, a plain Cinderella; and the sight of her, for some reason, absolutely enraged me.

She got awkwardly to her feet, trying to wipe off the worst of the muck. She said, 'You needn't have come so quickly. I wasn't expecting you to.'

'I thought something was the matter,' I said. '*Is* something wrong? Where's your mother?'

'She's up in her room.'

'Not ill again?'

'No, not ill. At least— I don't know.'

She was looking about for something with which to clean her arms, and finally caught up a piece of newspaper and rubbed ineffectually with that. I said, 'For goodness' sake!'—moving forward, offering her my handkerchief.

She saw the crisp white square of linen and began to protest. 'Oh, I mustn't.'

'Just take the wretched thing,' I said, holding it out. 'You aren't a skivvy, are you?' And when she still hesitated, I dipped the handkerchief into the pail of ink-stained water and, possibly not very kindly, rubbed at her arms and hands myself.

In the end we were both slightly filthy, but she, at least, was cleaner than before. She drew down her sleeves and moved back. 'Sit down, will you?' she said. 'Can I get you some tea?'

I stayed standing. 'You can tell me what the trouble is, that's all.'

'There's nothing to tell, really.'

'You've brought me all this way for nothing?'

'All this way,' she repeated, quietly.

I folded my arms, and spoke more gently. 'I'm sorry, Caroline. Go on.'

'It's just,' she began hesitantly; then, bit by bit she told me what had happened since my last visit: the appearance of the scribbles, first in the saloon and then in the hall; the 'bouncing ball' and the 'trapped bird'; her mother's discovery of that final patch of writing. To be honest, at this point it didn't sound like much. I hadn't then seen the scribbles for myself, but even when I did eventually go to the saloon and examine those phantom irregular *S*'s, I didn't find them particularly troubling.

Now, in response to Caroline's story, I said, 'But isn't it clear what's happened? Those marks must have been there,' I thought it over, 'well, nearly thirty years. The paint must be thinning and letting them through. Probably the damp has caused that. No wonder they won't rub away; there must be still just enough of a varnish to seal them in.'

'Yes,' she said doubtfully, 'I suppose so. But those creaks, or raps, or whatever you want to call them?'

'This house creaks like a galleon! I've heard it, many times.'

'It's never creaked quite like that before.'

'Perhaps it's never been quite so damp before; and the place has certainly never been so neglected. Probably the timbers are shifting about.'

She still looked doubtful. 'But isn't it strange, the way the tapping seemed to lead us to the scribbles?'

I said, 'There have been three young children living here. There could be scribbles on every wall . . . It's possible too,' I added, as I thought it over, 'that your mother knew—I mean, as a sort of forgotten memory—where that second and third patch of handwriting were. The uncovering of the first one might have put the idea in her head. And then, once the creaking started, she might unconsciously have guided the search.'

'She couldn't have made those knocks! I felt them!'

'That, I must admit, I can't explain—except to suppose that your first idea was right: that it was mice or beetles or some other creature, the sound of it getting magnified somehow by the hollowness of the walls. As for the trapped bird—' I lowered my voice. 'Well, I expect it's already crossed your mind that your mother might have imagined that whole incident?'

'Yes, it has,' she answered, speaking quietly too. 'She hadn't been sleeping. But then again, according to her it was the bird that was keeping her awake. And Betty also heard the sound, don't forget.'

I said, 'I think Betty, in the middle of the night, would hear just about any sound suggested to her. These things have a circularity to them. Something woke your mother, I don't doubt that, but then her

very sleeplessness may have kept her awake—or kept her dreaming she
was awake—and after that, her mind was vulnerable in some way—'

'I think it's vulnerable now,' she said.

'What do you mean?'

She hesitated. 'I'm not sure. She seems . . . changed.'

I said, 'Changed, how?'

But I think a note of weariness was creeping into my tone, for it
seemed to me that she and I had had this conversation, or others very
like it, several times before. She turned away from me, clearly disappointed, and said, 'Oh, I don't know. I'm imagining things, I expect.'

She wouldn't say any more. I watched her, with a disappointment
of my own. I said I would go up and see her mother, and I took my bag
and climbed the stairs.

I did it with a slight sense of foreboding, expecting from Caroline's
manner to find Mrs Ayres looking really ill, perhaps back in her bed.
But when I knocked on her door I heard her call out brightly for me to
enter; I went in and found the room with its curtains almost closed,
but, in stark contrast with the little parlour, with two or three lamps lit
and a good fire in the grate. The smell was of camphor, maiden-auntish:
the dressing-room door was wide open and the bed was heaped with
gowns and furs, and with the loose silk bags, like deflated bladders, in
which the furs had been stored. Mrs Ayres looked up from them as I
went in, seeming perfectly happy to see me. She and Betty, she told me,
were looking through some of her old clothes.

She didn't ask after my trip, nor did she show any consciousness of
the fact that I had just been downstairs, alone with her daughter. She
moved forward to take my hand, then led me back towards the bed,
nodding to the tangle of gowns upon it.

'I felt so guilty,' she said, 'with the war on, hanging on to all this. I
gave away what I could, but some of these, oh, I just *couldn't* see them
go, to be hacked about and so on, made into blankets for refugees and
goodness knows what. Now I'm awfully glad I kept them. Do you think
it very wicked of me?'

I smiled, pleased to see her looking so well, so like her old self.

Her hair still startled me by its greyness, but she had dressed it with extra care, though in a curiously pre-war style, rather looped about the ears. Her lips had a genteel touch of lipstick, her fingernails were a polished pink, and the skin of her heart-shaped face seemed almost unlined.

I turned to the heap of old-fashioned silks. 'It's certainly difficult to imagine these being handed round in a refugee camp.'

'Isn't it? Far better to keep them here, where they'll be appreciated.' She picked up a flimsy satin gown with a flapperish droop to its shoulders and skirt. She held it up to show Betty, who was just emerging from the dressing-room with a shoe-box in her hand. 'What do you say to this one, Betty?'

The girl caught my eye, and I gave her a nod. 'Hello, Betty. All right?'

'Hello, sir.' Her face was pink; she seemed excited. She was clearly trying to hold the excitement in, but as she looked at the dress her plump little mouth broke into a smile. 'It's lovely, madam!'

'Things were made to last, in those days. And such colours! One simply doesn't see them now. And what have you there?'

'Slippers, madam! Gold uns!'

'Let me look.' Mrs Ayres took the box, and put back the lid and then the paper inside it. 'Ah, now these cost the devil. And they pinched like the devil, too, as I remember. I only wore them once.' She held them up. Then she said, as if on impulse: 'You try them, Betty.'

'Oh, madam.' Betty blushed, glancing self-consciously at me. 'Shall I?'

'Yes, go on. Show the doctor and me.'

So the girl unlaced her stout black shoes and shyly slipped on the gold leather slippers; then, encouraged by Mrs Ayres, she walked from the dressing-room door to the fireplace, and back again, like a mannequin. She burst out laughing as she did it, raising a hand to cover up her crooked teeth. Mrs Ayres laughed too, and when Betty stumbled because the slippers were too big, she stuffed the toes of them with stockings to make them fit. She spent several minutes doing that, and then she dressed the girl with gloves and a stole, and had her stand, and walk, and turn, lightly applauding as she did it.

I thought again of the patient I had put off in order to come out here. But after another minute or two Mrs Ayres seemed suddenly to tire. 'There,' she said to Betty, sighing, looking over the cluttered bed. 'You had better tidy these things away, or I shall have nowhere to sleep tonight.'

'You're sleeping well, though?' I asked, as she and I moved over to the fire. And then, seeing Betty disappearing into the dressing-room with an armful of furs, I said quietly, 'I hope you don't mind, but Caroline told me about your . . . discovery, last week. I gather it quite unsettled you.'

She was bending forward to pick up a cushion. She said, 'It did, rather. Wasn't that foolish of me?'

'Not foolish at all.'

'After so much time,' she murmured, sitting back, lifting her face, and surprising me with her expression, which showed no trace of worry or anguish but, on the contrary, was almost serene. 'I didn't suppose there was any trace of her left, you see.' She placed her hand above her heart. 'Except in here. She has always been real to me, in here. More real, sometimes, than anything else . . .'

She kept her hand upon her breast, lightly smoothing the fabric of her gown. Her look had grown vague—but then, a certain amount of vagueness was habitual with her, and part of her charm. Nothing about her behaviour struck me as odd, or made me anxious; I thought she seemed pretty healthy and content. I spent about fifteen minutes with her, then headed back downstairs.

Caroline was where I had left her, standing limply at the hearth. The fire was low in the grate, the light was dimmer than ever, and again I was conscious of the great contrast between the cheerlessness of this room and the cosiness of her mother's. And again the sight of her, with her housemaid's hands, unreasonably annoyed me.

'Well?' she asked me, looking up.

I said, 'I think you're worrying about nothing.'

'What's my mother doing?'

'She's been going through some old clothes, with Betty.'

'Yes. That's all she wants to do now, things like that. Yesterday she brought out those photographs again, the ones that were spoiled—you remember?'

I spread my hands. 'She's entitled to look at photographs, isn't she? Can you blame her for wanting to think about the past, when her present is so joyless?'

'It isn't just that.'

'What is it, then?'

'It's something in her manner. She isn't just *thinking* about the past. It's as though, when she looks at you, she isn't really seeing you at all. She's seeing something else . . . And she tires so easily. She isn't at all old, you know, but she takes a rest now, like an old lady, nearly every afternoon. She never mentions Roderick. She's not interested in Dr Warren's reports. She doesn't want to see anybody . . . Oh, I can't explain it.'

I said, 'She's had a jolt. Coming across those scribbles, being reminded again of your sister. It's bound to have shaken her up.'

I realised, as I said the words, that she and I had never spoken about Susan, the lost little girl. The same thing must have occurred to her: she stood in silence, raising her dirty fingers to her mouth and starting to pick and pull at her lip. And when she spoke again, her voice had changed.

She said, 'It's queer to hear you say "your sister" like that. It doesn't sound right. Mother never mentioned her, you see, when Rod and I were children. I knew nothing about her for years and years. Then one day I came across a book with "Sukey Ayres" written in it, and asked Mother who she was. She reacted so oddly, I was frightened. That's when Daddy told me all about it. He called it "awfully bad luck". But I don't remember being sorry for him or for Mother. I just remember being cross, because everyone had always told me I was the eldest child, and I thought it wasn't fair if I hadn't been really.' She gazed down at the fire, her forehead creasing. 'I seem to have been cross all the time, somehow, when I was a girl. I was horrid to Roddie; I was horrid to the maids. You're supposed to grow out of horridness, aren't you? I don't think I ever grew out of mine. Sometimes I think it's still inside me, like something nasty I swallowed, that got stuck . . .'

She did, at that moment, look rather like a moody child, with her dirty hands, and a couple of locks of unbrushed brown hair beginning to droop across her face. Like other bad-tempered children, however, she also looked desperately sad. I made a half-movement towards her. She lifted her head as I did it, and must have caught my hesitation.

And at once, the air of childishness fell away. She said, in a hard, society tone, 'I haven't asked after your trip to London, have I? How did it go?'

I said, 'Thank you. It went well.'

'You spoke at the conference?'

'Yes, I did.'

'Did people like what you said?'

'Very much. In fact—' I hesitated again. 'Well, there's been some talk of my going back down there. Going down there to work, I mean.'

Her gaze changed, seemed to quicken. 'There has? Do you mean to do it?'

'I don't know. I should have to think about it. About what I was . . . giving up.'

'And that's why you've been keeping away from us? You haven't wanted the distraction? I saw your car in the park on Saturday. I thought you might be going to call in. Then, when you didn't, I guessed that something must have happened; that something must have changed. That's why I called you up today, because I couldn't count on your coming out here in the ordinary way. The way you used to, I mean.' She tucked back the drooping hair. 'Did you ever mean to visit us again?'

'Of course I did.'

'But you *have* been keeping away. Haven't you?'

She tilted up her chin as she asked this. That was all she did. But, like stubborn milk finally yielding to the motion of the churn, the anger shifted inside me and became something else, something quite different. My heart began to beat faster. I said, after a moment, 'I've been a little afraid, I think.'

'Afraid of what? Of me?'

'Hardly.'

'Of my mother?'

I took a breath. 'Listen, Caroline. That time in the car—'

'Oh, *then*.' She turned her head. 'I behaved like a fool.'

'I was the fool. I'm sorry.'

'And now everything's changed and wrong.—No, please don't.'

For she looked so unhappy I had gone across and started to embrace her; and though she stood rigid and resisting for a moment or two, when she realised I meant to do nothing more than put my arms around her, she slightly relaxed. The last time I had held her like this had been to dance with her; she had been in heels, her eyes and mouth on a level with mine. Now her shoes were flat ones and she was an inch or two shorter: I moved my chin, and the stubble of it caught at her hair. She bent her head, her cool dry brow sliding into the hollow beneath my ear . . . And then somehow she was standing full against me, I felt the push and yield of her breasts, the pressure of her hips and heavy thighs. I moved my hands across her back and drew her to me more tightly still. 'Don't,' she said again; she said it pretty weakly, though.

And the surge of my feelings astonished me. A few moments before, I had looked at her and felt nothing but exasperation and annoyance. Now I said her name, speaking breathily into her hair, moving my cheek roughly against her head.

'I've missed you, Caroline!' I said. 'God, I've missed you like hell!' I wiped my mouth, unsteadily. 'Look at me! Look what a bloody idiot you've made of me!'

She began to pull away. 'I'm sorry.'

I gripped her harder. 'Don't be sorry. For God's sake!'

She said miserably, 'I've missed you, too. Whenever you go away, something happens here. Why is that? This house, and my mother—' She closed her eyes, put her hand to her forehead as if against a bad headache. 'This house makes one think things.'

'This house is too much for you.'

'I've been almost afraid.'

'There's nothing to be afraid of. I shouldn't have left you, to be cooped up here on your own.'

'I wish—I wish I could get away. I can't, with Mother.'

'Don't think about your mother. Don't think about going away. You don't need to go away.'

And neither did I, I thought. For everything seemed clear to me suddenly, there, with Caroline in my arms. My plans—the consultant—the London hospital—all of it, all of it melted away. 'I've been a fool,' I said. 'Everything we need is right here. Think about that, Caroline. Think about me. About us.'

'No. Someone might come—'

I had started to nudge at her mouth with mine. But now we swayed, and, in swaying, moved our feet to find our balance; and somehow separated. She took a step out of my reach, putting up one of her filthy hands. Her hair was untidier than ever from the rub of my cheek; her lips were parted, faintly damp. She looked like a woman who'd just been kissed and who, to be honest, wanted to be kissed again. But when I moved towards her she took a second step back, and I saw then that her desire had another quality mixed up with it—innocence, or something stronger; reluctance, a touch even of fear. So I didn't try to embrace her again. I didn't trust myself to do it without frightening her away. Instead I caught hold of one of her hands, and lifted it, and touched the dirty knuckles to my lips. And as I gazed at her fingers, rubbing my thumb over the blackened nails, I said, with a tremor of desire and daring, 'Look what you've done to yourself. You perfect child! There'll be no more of this sort of thing, you know, once we are married.'

She said nothing. I was briefly aware of the house, as still and as silent around us as if it were holding its breath. Then she slightly bowed her head again—and at that, with a rush of triumph, I did pull her to me, to kiss not her mouth, but her throat, her cheeks and hair. She gave a burst of nervous laughter.

'Wait,' she said, half playful, half serious; almost struggling. 'Wait. Oh, wait!'

TEN

I think now of the three or four weeks that followed as Caroline's and my courtship; though the truth is, what passed between us was never so settled, nor so uncomplicated, as really to deserve that name. For one thing I was still very busy, and could rarely get to see her for more than hurried snatches of time. For another, she turned out to be surprisingly squeamish about exposing this definite shift in our relationship to her mother. I was impatient to get things moving, have some sort of announcement made. She felt her mother 'wasn't well enough yet'; that the news would simply 'make her worry'. She would tell her, she assured me, 'when the moment was right'. That moment seemed terribly slow in arriving, however, and as often as not when I called in at the Hall in those weeks, I'd end up sitting with the two women in the little parlour, taking tea and drily chatting—just as if nothing had really changed.

But, of course, everything had changed, and from my point of view those visits were sometimes rather hard to bear. I thought of Caroline constantly now. Looking into her strong, angular face, I couldn't believe that I had ever found it plain. Meeting her eye across the teacups

I felt like a man made of tinder, flaring up at the simple friction of her gaze against mine. Sometimes when I had said my goodbye she would walk with me to my car; we'd go in silence through the house, passing room after shadowy room, and I'd think of leading her into one of those wasted chambers and pulling her into my arms. Now and then I chanced it; but she was never at ease. She'd stand against me with her head averted, her arms hanging loosely at her sides. I'd feel the softening and warming of her limbs against mine—but slowly, slowly, as if they begrudged even their own slight yielding. And if ever, frustrated, I pressed further, the result was disaster. Her soft limbs would harden, her hands come up across her face. 'I'm sorry,' she'd say—just as she had on that chilling occasion in my car. 'I'm sorry. It isn't fair of me, I know. I just need a little time.'

So I learned not to ask too much of her. My great fear now was of pushing her away. I had the sense that, overburdened as she was with Hundreds business, our engagement was simply one complication too many: I supposed she was waiting until things at the Hall improved before allowing herself to plan for the time beyond.

And at that point, real improvement seemed close at hand. Work on the council houses was progressing; the extending of water and electricity out to the park was underway; things at the farm, apparently, were looking up, and Makins was pleased with all the changes. Mrs Ayres, too, despite Caroline's doubts about her, still seemed healthier and happier than she had in months. Every time I called at the house I found her carefully dressed, with touches of rouge and powder on her face; as usual, in fact, she was far better turned out than her daughter, who, despite the change in our relationship, continued to wear her shapeless old sweaters and skirts, her rough wool hats and stout shoes. But since the weather remained wintry, I felt I could forgive her that. Once the season turned, I planned to take her into Leamington and quietly kit her out with some decent dresses. I thought often, and longingly, of the summer days to come: the Hall with its doors and windows thrown open, Caroline in short sleeves and loose-necked blouses, her long limbs brown, her dusty feet bare . . . My own cheerless house felt as dim as a stage-set to me now. At night I would lie in my bed, weary but wakeful, thinking of Caroline lying in hers. My mind would go softly across the darkened miles between us, to slip like a poacher through the Hundreds gate and along the overgrown drive, to nudge open the swollen front door, to inch across the chequered marble; and then to go creeping, creeping towards her, up the still and silent stairs.

Then, one day in early March, I dropped in at the house as usual to find that something had happened. Those mysterious tricks, or 'parlour games'—as Caroline had once dubbed them—had started up again, in a new form.

She didn't want to tell me about them at first. She said they were 'too boring to mention'. But she and her mother both looked tired, and I happened to comment on it; and then she confessed to me that, for the past few nights, they had been woken in the early hours of the morning by the ringing of the telephone bell. It had happened three or four times, she said, always between two and three o'clock; and every time, when they had gone down to unhook the receiver, the line had been dead.

They had wondered, at one point, if the caller could be me. 'You were the only person we could think of,' Caroline said, 'who might be up at that sort of time.' She glanced at her mother, colouring slightly. 'It wasn't you, I suppose?'

'No, it wasn't!' I replied. 'I wouldn't dream of calling so late! And at two o'clock this morning, as it happens, I was tucked up in bed. So unless I put through the call in my sleep—'

'Yes, of course,' she said, smiling. 'There must have been some sort of muddle at the exchange. I just wanted to be sure.'

She spoke as if that put an end to the matter, so I let the subject drop. The next time I visited, however, I learned that another call had come, again around half past two, a night or two before. Caroline had left the telephone to ring this time, lying in bed, unwilling to get up in the cold and the darkness. But at last its hard, hectic clamour had been too much to ignore and, hearing her mother stirring in her room, she had gone down and picked up the receiver—only to find that, as usual, the line was dead.

'At least, no,' she corrected herself, 'it wasn't dead. That's the funny thing. There was no voice, but I thought—oh, it sounds silly, but I could have sworn there was someone there. Someone who'd rung particularly for Hundreds, particularly for us. Again, you see, I thought of you.'

'And once again,' I said, 'I was fast asleep and dreaming.' And since we were on our own this time, I added, 'Dreaming of you, very probably.'

I put up my hand to her hair; she caught my fingers and stilled them. 'Yes. But *someone* called. And what I've been thinking—I can't get the idea out of my mind. But you don't think it could have been Roddie, do you?'

'Rod!' I said, startled. 'Oh, surely not.'

'It's possible, isn't it? Suppose he's in some sort of trouble—at that clinic, I mean. We haven't seen him for so long. Dr Warren just says the same thing every time he writes. They could be doing anything to him, trying any sort of medicine or treatment. We don't know what they're doing, really. We just pay the bills.'

I took both her hands in mine. She saw my face and said, 'It's only this feeling I had, that someone had rung up, well, with something to tell us.'

'It was half past two in the morning, Caroline! Anybody would feel like that. It must be just what you thought last time; there must have been a mix-up in the lines. In fact, why don't you ring the exchange right now, and talk to the girl, explain what's happened?'

'Do you think I should?'

'If it will set your mind at rest, why not?'

So, frowning, she went over to the old-fashioned little parlour extension, and dialled for the operator. She stood with her back to me as she did it, but I listened to her running through the story of the calls. 'Yes, if you wouldn't mind,' I heard her say, her voice artificially bright; and then, a moment later, with some of the brightness gone, 'I see. Yes, I expect you're right. Yes, thank you. I'm sorry to have troubled you.'

She set down the telephone and its ear-piece and turned back to me, her frown deeper than ever. Raising her fingers to her mouth to bite at the tips of them, she said, 'The woman who works the night shift isn't there now, of course. But the girl I spoke to looked at the tickets—their log, or whatever, where they keep a record of the calls. She said no one telephoned Hundreds this week, no one at all. She said no one called last week, either.'

'Then,' I said, after a moment, 'that puts the whole thing beyond doubt. There's clearly a fault with the line—or more probably with the wiring in this house. It wasn't Rod at all. You see? It wasn't anyone.'

'Yes,' she said slowly, still nibbling at her fingers. 'That's what the girl said. Yes, it must be that, mustn't it?'

She spoke as if wanting to be convinced. But the telephone rang again that night. And because when I next saw her she was still irrationally troubled by the idea that her brother might be trying to contact her, to put her mind completely at rest I called up the Birmingham clinic, to ask if there was any possibility of Rod's having made the calls. I was assured that there was not. It was Dr Warren's assistant I spoke to, and his tone, I noticed, was less breezy than when I had seen him just before Christmas. He told me that Rod, after seeming to have made some slight but definite progress at the start of the year, had recently disappointed them all by having 'a bad couple of weeks'. He didn't go into details, but, like a fool, I made this call with Caroline at my side. She caught enough of the conversation to realise that the news was not good; and after that she was more subdued and preoccupied than ever.

And as if in response to this shift in her anxieties, the telephone calls ceased, and a fresh set of nuisances took over. This time I was there the day they began, having dropped in between cases: Caroline and I

were again alone together in the little parlour—in fact I had been kissing her goodbye and she had just stepped out of my arms—when the
door opened, surprising us both. Betty came in, made a curtsey, and
asked 'what was wanted of her'.

'What do you mean?' asked Caroline, flustered, speaking sharply,
brushing back her hair.

'The bell rung, miss.'

'Well, I didn't ring it. It must be my mother who wants you.'

Betty looked confused. 'Madam's upstairs, miss.'

'Yes, I know she's upstairs.'

'But please, miss, it were the little parlour bell that rung.'

'Well, it couldn't have been, could it, if I didn't ring it, and neither
did Dr Faraday! Do you think it rang itself? Go on upstairs, if my
mother wants you.'

Blinking, Betty backed away. When the door was closed I caught
Caroline's eye, wiping my mouth and almost laughing. But she wouldn't
return my smile. She turned away as if impatient. And she said, with
surprising force, 'Oh, this is hateful. I can't bear it! All this slinking
around, like cats.'

'Like cats!' I said, amused by the image. I reached for her hand to
pull her back. 'Come here, puss. Nice puss.'

'Stop it, for heaven's sake. Betty might come.'

'Well, Betty's a country girl. She knows about the birds and the
bees, and the cats . . . Besides, you know the solution, don't you? Marry
me. Next week—tomorrow—whenever you like. Then I can kiss you,
and to hell with who sees. And little Betty will be busier than ever,
bringing us our eggs and bacon in bed in the morning, and nice things
like that.'

I was still smiling, but she turned back to me with an odd expression. She said, 'But, what do you mean? We wouldn't—we wouldn't be
here, would we?'

We had never discussed the practical side of the life we would have
together, married. I had taken it for granted that I would live with her

there at the Hall. I said, less certainly than before, 'Well, why not? We couldn't leave your mother, could we?'

She was frowning. 'But how would it work, with your patients? I'd assumed—'

I smiled. 'You wouldn't rather live with me in Lidcote, in that dreadful old house of Gill's?'

'No, of course not.'

'Well, we can sort something out. I'll keep the surgery going in the village, perhaps start up some night-system with Graham . . . I don't know. Everything will change, anyway, in July, when the Health Service comes in.'

'But when you came back from London,' she said, 'you told me there might be a post for you there.'

She took me by surprise; I'd forgotten all about it. My trip to London felt an age away now; the affair with her had put the whole thing out of my head. I said carelessly, 'Oh, there's no point thinking about it now. July will change everything. There might be posts galore after that; or posts for no one.'

'For no one? But, then how would we ever leave?'

I blinked. 'Would we want to leave?'

'I thought,' she began, and she looked so anxious, I reached for her hand again, saying, 'Look, don't worry. There'll be plenty of time for all this sort of thing once we are married. That's the main thing, isn't it? The thing we want most of all?'

She said that yes, of course it was . . . I raised her hand to my mouth to kiss it, then, putting on my hat, I made my way to the front door.

And there I saw Betty again. She was coming down the staircase, looking more confused than ever, and slightly sulky, too. Mrs Ayres, it seemed, was fast asleep in her bedroom, so it couldn't possibly have been she who had rung for a maid. But then, Betty told me, she had never supposed that it had been: it was the little parlour bell that had rung—she would swear to it on her own mother's life—and if Miss Caroline and I didn't believe it, well, it wasn't fair, to have her word doubted like that. Her voice rose as she spoke, and soon Caroline appeared, wondering what the commotion was. Glad to escape, I left them arguing together, and thought nothing more of it.

By the time I returned at the end of that week, however, the Hall was, in Caroline's words, 'a madhouse'. The call-bells had developed a mysterious life of their own, ringing out at all sorts of hours, so that Betty and poor Mrs Bazeley were continually traipsing from room to room asking what was wanted of them, sending Caroline and her mother to distraction. Caroline had examined the junction-box of bells and wires down in the basement and could find nothing wrong with it.

'It's as though an imp gets in there,' she told me, taking me down to the vaulted passage, 'and plays on the wires to torment us! It isn't mice or rats, either. We've put down trap after trap and caught nothing.'

I looked at the box in question: that imperious device, as I had once thought of it, to which wires ran, like the nerves of the house, through tubes and channels from the rooms above. I knew from experience that the wires were not especially sensitive things, and that sometimes one had to tug at a lever quite vigorously in order to set a bell ringing, so Caroline's story rather bemused me. She brought me a lamp and a screwdriver, and I poked around at the workings for a while, but the mechanism was very simple, none of the wires was overtaut, and, like Caroline herself, I could find no fault. I could only, with some unease, recall those creaks or raps that the women had heard, a few weeks before; I thought, too, of the sagging saloon ceiling, the spreading damp, the bulging brickwork . . . I said nothing about it to Caroline, but it seemed pretty clear to me that the Hall had reached a point of dilapidation where one defect was almost setting off another; and I felt more dismayed and frustrated by the house's decline than ever.

Meanwhile, the call-bells continued their restless, maddening activity, until finally, sick and tired of the whole thing, Caroline took a pair of wire-snippers and put the junction-box out of use. After that, whenever she or her mother wanted Betty they had to go to the head of the service staircase and shout for her. Often they'd simply carry on down to the kitchen and see to the chore themselves—just as if they had no servants at all.

But the house, it seemed, would not be so easily subdued, and before another week had passed, a new trouble had emerged. The problem this time lay with a relic of the Hall's Victorian years—an old speaking-tube, which had been installed in the 1880s to allow the nursery staff to communicate with the cook, and which ran right down through the house from the day-nursery on the second floor, to finish at a small ivory mouthpiece in the kitchen. The mouthpiece was stoppered by a whistle, fastened to it by a slim brass chain, and designed to sound when the tube was blown into at the other end. Naturally, with Caroline and Roderick both grown up, it was a very long time since the speaking-tube had last been put to serious use. The nurseries themselves had been stripped of their fittings at the start of the war, so that the rooms could be occupied by the officers of the army unit that had been billeted with Mrs Ayres. Altogether, in fact, the tube must have lain there, mute and dusty and undisturbed, for fifteen years.

Now, however, Mrs Bazeley and Betty went to Caroline to complain that the disused mouthpiece had started giving off eerie little whistles.

I had the whole story from Mrs Bazeley herself, when I went down to the kitchen a day or two later to see what the trouble was. She said that, at first, they'd heard the whistling and couldn't imagine what was making it. It had been faint, then—'Faint,' she said, 'and gusty; all blow. Well, just like the sound of a kettle working himself up to a boil'—and they'd concluded doubtfully that it must be the hiss of air escaping from the central-heating pipes. But one morning the whistle had sounded so clearly there could be no mistaking the source of it. Mrs Bazeley had been on her own in the kitchen at the time, putting loaves into the oven, and the sudden piercing blast had so startled her, she'd burned her wrist. She didn't, she told me as she showed me the blister, even know what the speaking-tube was. She hadn't been at Hundreds long enough ever to have seen the contraption in use.

She'd always thought the tarnished mouthpiece and whistle 'part of the electrics'.

It had taken Betty to work the thing out and explain it to her; and so when, a day later, the whistle sounded shrilly again, Mrs Bazeley naturally supposed that Caroline or Mrs Ayres wanted to talk to her from one of the rooms upstairs. She went doubtfully to the mouthpiece, drew out the whistle, and set her ear to the ivory cup.

'And what did you hear?' I asked her, following her apprehensive gaze across the kitchen to the now-silent tube.

She made a face. 'A queer sort of noise.'

'Queer, how?'

'I can't say. Like a breath.'

'A breath?' I said. 'You mean a person, breathing? Was there a voice?'

No, there wasn't a voice. It was more of a rustling. Then again, not quite a rustling . . . 'Well, like hearing the operator,' she said, 'over the telephone. You don't hear her speak, but you know her's listening. You know her's there. Oh, it were queer!'

I stared at her, struck for a moment by the similarity between her words and Caroline's description of the mysteriously ringing phone. She met my gaze, and shuddered; she said she had stuck the whistle hastily back in its socket, and run from the room to fetch Betty, and Betty, after nerving herself up to it, had put her own ear to the mouthpiece, and had also had the feeling of 'something queer' being in the tube. That's when they had gone upstairs to complain about the business to the Ayreses.

They had found Caroline, alone, and told her everything that had happened. She must have been struck by Mrs Bazeley's words, too: she listened carefully to their story, then accompanied them back to the kitchen and gingerly listened at the tube herself. But she heard nothing, nothing at all. She said they must have been imagining things; or that the whistles were caused by 'the wind playing tricks'. She hung a tea-cloth over the mouthpiece and told them that, if the noise were to start again, they must simply ignore it. And she added, as an afterthought, that she hoped they would say nothing of this new nuisance to Mrs Ayres.

Her visit didn't do much to reassure them. In fact, the tea-cloth seemed only to make things worse. For now the speaking-tube became 'like a parrot in a cage': every time they found themselves starting to forget about it, and to sink back into their old routines, it would let out one of its awful whistles and frighten them to death.

In any other setting, such a story would have struck me as farcical. But the Hall, by now, had a disconcertingly palpable air of stress and tension: the women in it were tired and nervous, and I could see that Mrs Bazeley's fear, at least, was very real. When she'd finished speaking, I left her side, and went across the kitchen to look at the speaking-tube myself. Lifting the tea-cloth I found a bland ivory cup and whistle, fixed to the wall at head height on a shallow wooden mount. A less sinister-looking thing it would have been hard to imagine—and yet, when I thought of the disquiet it had managed to inspire, the very quaintness of the object before me began to seem slightly grotesque. I was reminded uneasily of Roderick. I remembered those 'ordinary things'—the collar, the cufflinks, the shaving-mirror—which had seemed, in his delusion, to come to crafty, malevolent life.

Then, as I drew the whistle free, another thought struck me. This was a nursery-servants' speaking-tube; my mother had been nursery-maid here. She must have spoken many times into this device, forty years before . . . The thought caught me off guard. I had the sudden irrational idea that, in putting my ear to the cup, I would hear my mother's voice. I had the idea that I'd hear her calling my name, exactly as I'd used to hear her, calling me home at the end of the day, when I was a boy playing out in the fields at the back of our house.

I became aware of Mrs Bazeley and Betty, watching, perhaps beginning to wonder at my delay. I dipped my head to the mouthpiece . . . And, like Caroline, I heard nothing, only the faint surge and echo of the blood in my ear—sounds which, I suppose, might easily have been translated, by an overwrought imagination, into something more sinister. Straightening up, I laughed at myself.

'I think Miss Caroline had the right idea,' I said. 'This tube must be sixty years old, at least! The rubber must be perished; the wind gets in, and makes those whistles. I dare say it's the wind that's been setting the bells off, too.'

Mrs Bazeley looked unconvinced. She said, with a glance at Betty, 'I dunno, Doctor. This child's been saying for months that the house has something queer about it. Suppose—'

'This house is falling apart,' I said firmly. 'That's the sad truth, and all there is to it.'

And to put a stop to the whole business I did what Mrs Bazeley or Caroline, if they had been less distracted, might easily have done for themselves: I tugged the ivory whistle from its chain and put it in my waistcoat pocket, and I replaced it with a cork.

I assumed that that would be the end of the matter; and for several days, I believe, there was calm in the house. But then, on the following Saturday morning, Mrs Bazeley came into the kitchen as usual and noticed that the tea-cloth, which she had hung back over the speaking-tube after my visit, and which had remained there undisturbed since then, had somehow fallen to the floor. She supposed that Betty must have knocked it, or a breeze from the passage dislodged it, so, with shrinking fingers, she picked it up and put it back in place. An hour later she noticed that the cloth had fallen again. By now Betty was with her, having come down from her duties upstairs: *she* picked up the cloth and returned it to the mouthpiece—taking care, she told me earnestly, to tuck it tightly into the crack between the wooden mount and the wall. Again the cloth came free, and this time Mrs Bazeley actually caught a glimpse of it falling. She saw it from the corner of her eye as she stood at the kitchen table: she said it didn't flutter, as if caught by a breeze; instead it slid straight down to the floor as if someone had tugged it.

By now she was tired of her own fear, and the sight exasperated her. She caught the cloth up and flung it aside, then stood squarely before the stopped-up tube and shook her fist at it.

'Go on,' she cried, 'you hateful old thing! No one's minding you!

Do you hear me?' She put a hand on Betty's shoulder. 'Don't look at him, Betty. Come away. If he wants to go on pranking, let him try. I'm sick to death of him.' And she turned on her heel and headed back to the table.

She had taken only two or three steps when she heard the sound of something softly striking the kitchen floor. She turned back to see that the cork, which a week before she had watched me screw snugly into the ivory mouthpiece, had been plucked or pushed from its socket and was rolling around at her feet.

At that, all her bravado left her. She gave a scream, and darted to Betty—who had also heard the cork fall, though she hadn't seen it rolling—and the two of them ran from the room, banging the door closed behind them. They stood for a moment in the vaulted basement passage, almost frightened out of their wits; then, hearing movement on the floor above, they stumbled together up the stairs. They were hoping for Caroline, and I wish now that they had found her; I think she would have been able to calm them down and keep the matter in check. But Caroline, unfortunately, was down at the building-work with Babb. It was Mrs Ayres they met, just coming out of the little parlour. She had been sitting quietly reading, and, taken by surprise by them now, she imagined from the wildness of their manner that some new catastrophe had taken place—another fire broken out, perhaps. She knew nothing of the whistling speaking-tube, and when she finally pieced together their confused account of the falling tea-towel and the tumbling cork, she was nonplussed.

'But, what has frightened you so much?' she asked them.

They couldn't properly say. All she could understand, finally, was how shaken they both were. The thing didn't strike her as very serious, but she agreed to go and take a look. It was rather a nuisance, she said; but then, the house was full of nuisances these days.

They followed her down to the threshold of the kitchen, but further than that they would not go. When she went in they stayed at the door, clutching at the frame and watching in dismay as, bemused, she examined the lifeless cloth, the cork, and the tube; and when she delicately tucked back her loops of greying hair and lowered her head to the mouthpiece, they stretched out their arms and said, 'Oh, madam, be careful! Oh, madam, do please take care!'

Mrs Ayres hesitated just for a moment—struck, perhaps, as I had been a few days before, by the sincerity of fear in their voices. Then she carefully put her ear to the cup and listened. When she straightened up, her expression was almost apologetic.

'I'm afraid I don't quite know what I ought to have heard. There seems to be nothing.'

'There's nothing there, now!' said Mrs Bazeley. 'But it'll be back, madam. It's in there, waiting!'

'Waiting? But, what do you mean? You talk as though there's a sort of genie! How could there be anything there? The tube runs right up to the nurseries—'

And here, Mrs Bazeley told me later, Mrs Ayres stumbled, and her look changed. She said, more slowly, 'Those rooms are shut up. They've been shut up since the soldiers left us.'

Now Betty spoke, in a voice of horror. 'Oh, madam, you don't suppose—you don't suppose summat's got up there, and is up there now?'

'Oh, my Lord!' cried Mrs Bazeley. 'The girl's right. With them rooms all shut and dark like that, how do we know what's been going on in them? Anything could've been going on! Oh, why don't you call for Dr Faraday and make him go up and have a look? Or let Betty run and fetch Makins, or Mr Babb.'

'Makins or Babb?' said Mrs Ayres, coming back to herself. 'No, I certainly shan't. Miss Caroline will be home soon, and what she'll make of this I can't imagine. If you'll just get on with your tasks—'

'We can't put our minds to house-work, madam, with that nasty thing a-watching us!'

'Watching you? A minute ago it only had ears!'

'Well, whatever he've got, he in't normal. He in't nice. Oh, at least let Miss Caroline go up and take a look, when she comes back. Miss Caroline won't stand for no nonsense.'

But just as Caroline herself, a week before, had tried to keep her mother from being drawn into this matter, so, now, it occurred to Mrs Ayres that she might very easily sort this out before her daughter's return. Whether she had any other motive in mind, I don't know. I think it likely that she did—that, having just glimpsed the first, faint thread of a particular idea, she felt almost compelled to pursue it. Anyway, much to Mrs Bazeley's and Betty's horror, she declared that she would put an end to the whole business by going upstairs and examining the empty rooms herself.

So once again they followed her, this time up through the north passage to the hall; and just as they had stuck at the threshold of the kitchen so now, at the foot of the staircase, they hung fearfully back, clutching at the serpent-headed banister and watching her climb. She went briskly and almost silently in her indoor shoes, and once she had rounded the first landing all they could do was put back their heads and lean into the stairwell, to watch her go higher. They saw the flash of her stockinged legs between the graceful rising balusters, and the grip and slide of her ringed fingers on the mahogany rail. They saw her, high up on the second floor, pause and give a single glance back down at them; and then she moved off, over creaking boards. The creaks continued to sound after her footsteps faded, but at length even they died away. Mrs Bazeley overcame her fear enough to advance a little higher; further than the first landing, however, nothing would induce her to go. She kept hard at the banister, straining her ears: trying to pick out sounds in the Hundreds silence, 'like trying to spy figures in a mist'.

Mrs Ayres, too, as she left the stairwell behind, was aware of the thickening silence. She was not afraid of it, she told me later, but something of Mrs Bazeley's and Betty's suspense must have infected her, even if ever so slightly, for though she had started up the staircase boldly enough, she now found herself moving more cautiously. This floor was laid out differently from the two floors below, with narrower corridors and noticeably lower ceilings. The dome of glass in the roof lit up the stairwell with a chill, milky light, but, as in the hall downstairs, this had the effect of filling the spaces to every side of it with shadows. The rooms Mrs Ayres had to pass on her journey to the nurseries were mostly box-rooms, or servants' bedrooms, and had long lain empty. Their doors were shut to prevent draughts, and some had been made fast in their frames with rolls of paper or chips of wood. This meant that the corridor was gloomier than ever; and with the generator off, the electric light-switches were useless.

So she moved on through the shadows until she reached the nursery passage, where she found the door to the day-nursery closed like all the others, with the key turned in its lock. It was as she put her hand to the key that she experienced the first touch of real apprehension, conscious again of the heavy Hundreds silence, and suddenly irrationally fearful of what she might find when the door was opened. She felt, almost too vividly, the stir of old emotions; she remembered coming here, quietly like this, to visit her children when they were small. She recalled odd scenes: Roderick running into her arms, clinging to her like a monkey, putting his wet mouth to her gown; Caroline polite, stand-offish, busy with paints, her hair falling forward into the colours . . . And then, as if from a different, distant era, she saw Susan, in a creaseless dress. She remembered her nurse, Nurse Palmer. Rather sharp, rather stern, always giving the impression that one's visits were a trouble, as if one wanted to see one's child more than was really proper or nice . . . Unlocking the door, Mrs Ayres half expected to hear her voice, half expected to find everything unchanged. *Here's mummy come up for you again, look, Susan. Why, mummy can't keep away!*

But the room in which she found herself could not, after all, have been more anonymous, nor more dismal. It had, as I've said, been stripped of its nursery furniture and fittings years before, and it now had the plangent echoing quality of all bare, neglected rooms. Its floorboards were dusty, and the faded paper on its walls was stained with damp. A set of black-out curtains, streaked indigo by the sun, still hung from a wire at the barred sash windows. The old-fashioned hob hearth was swept, but the brass fender was spotted with smuts where rainwater had found its way down the chimney; a corner of the mantelpiece was broken, and showed pale as the exposed enamel on a freshly

chipped tooth. But there on the chimney-breast, just as Mrs Ayres remembered, was the speaking-tube: it finished on this floor in a short
length of braided pipe, with another tarnished mouthpiece at its end.
She went across to it, lifted it, and took out its whistle, and it at once
gave off a musty, unpleasant odour—something like bad breath, she
said, so that, as she put the cup to her ear, she was uncomfortably
aware of all the lips which, over the years, must have pressed and slid
against it . . . As before, she heard nothing save the muffled roar of her
own blood. She listened for almost a minute, trying the mouthpiece at
different angles against her ear. Then she fitted the whistle back in its
socket, let the tube fall, and wiped her hands.

She was disappointed, she realised—quite horribly disappointed.
Nothing about the room seemed to want or welcome her: she gazed
around, trying to find a trace of the nursery life that had gone on in it,
but there was no sign of the sentimental pictures that had used to hang
on the walls, or anything like that. There were only grubby echoes of
the soldiers' occupation, rings and scratches and cigarette-burns, scuffs
on the skirting-boards; and the window-sills, as she found when she
crossed to one of them, were ugly with little grey circles of gum. It was
bitterly cold there, before the ill-fitting window sashes, but she stood
for a moment, gazing at the view across the park, mildly intrigued by
the high, oblique perspective it gave her on the far-off building-work,
and able, presently, to pick out the figure of Caroline, who was just
beginning her journey back to the house. The sight of her tall, eccentric-
looking daughter making her solitary way across the fields made Mrs
Ayres feel bleaker than ever, and after a moment of watching she stepped
back from the glass. To her left was another door, communicating with
the neighbouring room, the old night-nursery. That was the room in
which her first daughter had lain sick with diphtheria; the place, in fact,
where she had died. The door was ajar. Mrs Ayres found she couldn't
resist the dark temptation to open it properly and go inside.

But again, there was little here that she remembered, nothing but
wear and waste and neglect. A couple of panes in the windows were
cracked, the sash frame crumbling around them. A corner hand-basin

gave off a sour, uriney smell, and the boards beneath were almost rotting where a leaking tap had dripped. She went across to examine the damage; leaning, she put a hand to the wall. The wallpaper had a raised pattern of loops and arabesques that had once, she recalled suddenly, been very colourful. It had been painted over with a drab distemper, which the damp was turning to a sort of curd. She looked at the stains on her fingers with a feeling of distaste, then stood and worked her hands together, trying to brush the distemper from her skin. She was sorry, now, that she'd come in here—sorry that she'd come up to these rooms at all. She went to the basin and ran some frigid, spluttering water over her hands. She wiped her fingers against her skirt, and turned to leave.

And as she did that, she felt the starting up of a breeze—or, anyway, something like a breeze, a cold movement of air, which came suddenly against her, striking her cheek, disarranging her hair, making her shiver; and a second later she was shocked and jolted almost out of her skin by a violent slamming in the neighbouring room. She guessed pretty much at once what had happened—that the door she'd unlocked and left open had been swung to by a draught from the badly fitting windows. But still, the sound was so unexpected, and so sickeningly loud in the stripped, silent room, it took her a moment to recover herself and steady her lurching heart. Trembling slightly, she went back through to the day-nursery and, as she'd expected, its door was closed. She crossed to it, and caught hold of its handle; and couldn't open it.

She stood still for a second, perplexed. She turned the handle to left and to right, supposing in dismay that the spindle must have broken, thinking that the violence with which the door had blown shut must have jolted the mechanism. But the lock was the old rim kind, fitted to the door and painted over: there was a slight gap between it and its keep, as there usually is, and when she stooped and put her eye to this she could see very clearly that the spindle was working as it should— and that the bolt of the lock had been shot home, just as if the key on the other side had been deliberately turned. Could a breeze have done that? Could a slamming door have locked itself? Surely not. She grew a little uneasy. She went back through to the night-nursery, to try the door there. That was locked, too—but then, there was no reason to expect to find it otherwise. It was locked fast, like all the others on this floor, against the cold.

So she returned to the first door, to try it again—struggling, now, to hold on to her patience and her nerve; reasoning with herself that the wretched thing could *not* be locked, that it must simply be warped, as lots of Hundreds doors were warped, and sticking in its frame. But the door had moved easily enough when she had first opened it, and when she peered again into the gap between the lock and the keep, she again saw the shot bolt, unmistakable even in the gloom. Putting her eye to the keyhole, she could even make out the rounded end of the shaft of the turned key. She tried to see if there were some way she might get at that—perhaps with a hairpin?—and work it back. She still supposed that the door had managed, in some extraordinary way, to lock itself.

Then she heard something. Quite distinct through the silence it rose: the swift, soft patter of footsteps. And in the inch of murky, milky light that showed at the keyhole, she saw a movement. It came, she said, like a flash of darkness, as of someone or something passing very rapidly along the corridor, from left to right—in other words, as if heading along the nursery passage from the back stairs at the north-west corner of the house. Since she supposed, reasonably enough, that the person could only be Mrs Bazeley or Betty, her first response was one of relief. She got to her feet, and tapped on the door. 'Who's there?' she called. 'Mrs Bazeley? Betty? Betty, is it you? Whoever you are, you've locked me in, or someone has!' She rattled the handle. 'Hi! Do you hear me?'

Bafflingly, no one answered, no one came; and the footsteps faded. Mrs Ayres lowered herself back down before the keyhole and again looked out, until at last—and again, to her considerable relief—the pattering returned and drew nearer. 'Betty!' she called—for she realised now that the footsteps, so rapid and soft, could hardly belong to Mrs Bazeley. 'Betty! Let me out, child! Can't you hear me? Can't you see the key? Come and turn it, can't you?' But, much to her bewilderment, there came only another flash of darkness—moving from right to left, this time—and, instead of pausing at the door, the footsteps went on. 'Betty!' she called again, more shrilly. A moment of silence; then the footsteps returned. And after that the quick dark figure passed and re-passed the door, again and again: she could see the blur of it as it ran; it moved like a shadow, without face or feature. All she could think, with growing horror, was that the figure must be Betty's after all, but that the girl had somehow lost her wits and was racing up and down the nursery passage like a lunatic.

But then, the next time it came, the pattering figure seemed to draw closer to the door, seemed to brush against it with an elbow or a hand; and the times after that, the pattering footsteps were accompanied by a light sort of grating sound . . . Mrs Ayres understood suddenly that, as it ran, the figure was catching at the panels of wood with its finger-nails. She had a distinct impression of a small, sharp-fingered hand—a child's hand, she realised it was; and the thought was such a startling one, she scrambled back from the door in sudden panic, tearing her stockings at the knee. She got to her feet in the centre of the room, chilled and shaking.

At that, at their loudest point, the footsteps abruptly ceased. She knew now that the figure must be standing on the other side of the door; she even saw the door move a little in its frame, as if just nudged or pressed or tested. She looked at the lock, expecting to hear the turn-ing of the key and see the twisting of the handle, and nerving herself for what would be revealed when the door was opened. But after a long moment of suspense the door relaxed back on its hinges. She held her breath, until all she could hear, as if on the surface of the silence, was the rapid thumping of her own heartbeats.

Then, from over her shoulder, there came a sudden piercing blast from the whistle of the speaking-tube.

So completely had she been bracing herself for some quite different shock that she started away from the ivory mouthpiece, crying out and almost stumbling. The tube fell silent, then whistled again; the whistle, after that, came regularly, a series of shrill, prolonged blasts. It was impossible, she said, to suppose that the sound might be the product of a breeze or a freak of acoustics: the whistle was purposeful, demanding—something like the wail of a siren, or the cry of a hungry baby. It was so deliberate a signal, in fact, that the thought at last broke through her panic that there might, after all, be a simple enough explanation; for wasn't it possible that Mrs Bazeley, anxious for her safety but still unwilling to follow her upstairs, had returned to the kitchen and was trying to communicate with her? The tube, anyway, was at least a part of the ordinary human Hundreds world—nothing like that inexplicable pattering figure out in the passage. So, again screwing up her courage, Mrs Ayres went to the chimney-breast and picked the shrieking thing up. With clumsy, shaking fingers she drew the ivory whistle from it— and was plunged back, of course, into silence.

But the thing in her hand was not quite silent, after all. As she raised the cup to her ear she could hear, coming from it, a faint, moist susurration—as if wet silk, or something fine like that, were being slowly and haltingly drawn through the tube. The sound, she realised with a shock, was that of a laboured breath, which kept catching and bubbling as if in a narrow, constricted throat. In an instant she was transported back, twenty-eight years, to her first child's sickbed. She whispered her daughter's name—'Susan?'—and the breathing quickened and grew more liquid. A voice began to emerge from the bubbling mess of sound: a child's voice, she took it to be, high and pitiful, attempting, as if with tremendous effort, to form words.

And Mrs Ayres let the speaking-tube drop, in absolute horror. She ran to the door. She didn't care what might be on the other side of it now: she hammered on the panels, calling wildly for Mrs Bazeley, and when no answer came she darted unsteadily back across the room to one of the barred nursery windows, and plucked at its catch. She had, by this time, begun to weep tears of fright, which almost blinded her. They, and her panic, must have stripped her of sense and strength, for the catch was a simple one, and quite loose, but somehow it cut into her fingers and would not give.

But there, below her, was Caroline, just making her brisk way up from the lawn to the south-west corner of the terrace; and at the sight of her, Mrs Ayres abandoned the catch and starting banging on the window. She saw her daughter pause and raise her head, looking about, hearing the sound but unable to place it; a second later, to Mrs Ayres's unutterable relief, she saw her lift up her hand in a gesture of recognition. But then she made out more clearly the direction of Caroline's gaze. She realised that she was looking, not up at the nursery window, but straight ahead, across the terrace. Pressing closer to the glass, she caught sight of a stoutish female figure running across the gravel, and recognised Mrs Bazeley. She saw her meet Caroline at the top of the terrace steps, and begin making quick, frightened gestures back to the Hall. They were joined, after a moment, by Betty, who also ran across the terrace, beckoning them agitatedly on . . . All this time, the unstoppered mouthpiece had been sending out its pitiful whisper. Now, seeing the three women below, Mrs Ayres realised that she and the feeble, clamourous presence at the other end of the tube were alone together in that vast house.

This was the moment when her panic tipped over into hysteria. She raised her fists and pummelled on the window—and two of the fine old panes gave way beneath her hands. Caroline, Mrs Bazeley, and Betty, hearing the sound of the breaking glass, looked up in amazement. They saw Mrs Ayres shrieking from between the nursery bars—shrieking like a child, Mrs Bazeley said—and beating her hands against the edges of broken window.

What happened to her in the time it took the women to make their stumbling, frightened way up to the nursery, no one could afterwards say. They found the door to the room ajar and the speaking-tube silent, the ivory whistle fixed neatly in its socket. Mrs Ayres had worked herself rigidly into a corner and, effectively, 'blacked out'. She was bleeding badly from the cuts on her hands and arms, so the three of them did what they could to bind up her wounds, tearing up one of her own silk scarves for bandages. They got her to her feet and half walked, half carried her downstairs to her bedroom, where they gave her brandy and tried to warm her, building up the fire in the grate and loading her with blanket after blanket—for now, in her shock, she'd begun to shake.

She was still shaking when I saw her, just over an hour later.

I had been visiting a patient—luckily, a private patient with a telephone, so when Caroline put through a call to my surgery, the girl at the exchange was able to pass on her urgent request that I stop off at Hundreds on my way home. I drove to the Hall as soon as I could, with no idea of what was awaiting me. I was utterly flabbergasted to find the house in such a state. A white-faced Betty took me up to Mrs Ayres: she was sitting with Caroline at her side, hunched and shivering, starting like a hare at every slight unexpected movement or sound; and at the first sight of her, I faltered. Her expression was so wild, she looked just like her son, just like Roderick in the last, worst phase of his delusions. Her hair was straggling around her shoulders, and her arms and hands were ghastly. The blood had caught in her bulky rings, turning all the stones to rubies.

But her wounds, by a miracle, turned out to be fairly superficial. I cleaned them up, and dressed and bound them, and then, taking Caroline's place, I simply sat and gently held her hands. Bit by bit, the worst of the wildness faded from her gaze and she told me what had happened to her—shuddering and weeping with every fresh twist of it, and covering her face.

But at last she looked squarely and urgently into my eyes.

'You understand what's happened?' she said. 'You see what this means? I failed her, Doctor! She came, and I failed her!'

She clutched my fingers—clutched them so hard, I saw the blood rising to the surface of her dressings as her wounds reopened.

'Mrs Ayres,' I said, trying to steady her.

She wouldn't listen. 'My darling girl. I've wanted her to come, you see, so desperately. I've *felt* her, here in this house. I've lain in my bed, and felt her near. So near, she was! But I was greedy. I wanted her nearer. I drew her, by wishing for her to come. And then she came—and I was afraid. I was afraid of her, and failed her! And now I don't know what frightens me more, the thought that she'll never come to me again, or the thought that, in failing her, I've made her hate me. Will she hate me, Doctor? Say she won't!'

I said, 'Nobody hates you. You must be calm.'

'But I've failed her! I've failed her!'

'You've failed no one. Your daughter loves you.'

She looked into my face. 'You think she does?'

'Of course she does.'

'You promise me?'

'I promise you,' I said.

I would have said anything, at that moment, simply to calm her down; and soon I forbade her to speak any more, and I gave her a sedative and put her to bed. She lay fretful for a time, with her bandaged hands still clasped in mine, but the sedative was a strong one, and once she was sleeping I gently disengaged my fingers from hers and went downstairs, to go over the incident with Caroline, Mrs Bazeley, and Betty. They were gathered together in the little parlour, looking as pale and as shaken almost as Mrs Ayres herself. Caroline had handed out glasses of brandy, and the alcohol, on top of the shock, had made Mrs Bazeley tearful. I questioned her and Betty as closely as I could, but all they could confirm of Mrs Ayres's story was that she had gone up to the second floor alone; that she had stayed there so long—they thought, about fifteen or twenty minutes—they had grown anxious about her, and had gone out to alert Caroline; and then, that all three of them had seen her crying out in that dreadful way at the broken window.

When I had pieced together their side of things I went up to the day-nursery to examine the scene for myself. I had never been up to the second floor before, and I made the ascent warily, pretty shaken by the mood of the house. I found the bare room looking hideous, with its broken window and its streaks and splashes of darkening blood. But its door moved smoothly on its hinges, and the key moved glibly, too, in the lock. I tried turning the key with the door both closed and open; I even gave the door a slam, to see if that might jar the mechanism—it had no effect at all. I listened again at that wretched speaking-tube and, as before, heard nothing. So then I went through to the old night-nursery, just as Mrs Ayres had, and I stood very still and expectant—thinking of the dead child, Susan; thinking of my mother; thinking a thousand gloomy things—holding my breath, almost daring something to happen, someone or something to come. But nothing did happen. The house seemed deathly silent and chill, the room felt bleak, un-happy—but quite lifeless.

I did consider one explanation: that somebody had staged the whole affair with the intention of tormenting Mrs Ayres, either as a sort of ghastly joke, or out of simple malice. I could hardly suspect Caroline; and since I wouldn't believe it of Mrs Bazeley, who'd been a servant at the house since before the war, my suspicions had to fall on Betty. It was possible that she, after all, had somehow been behind the business with the speaking-tube in the first place; and Mrs Ayres herself had said that the footsteps she had heard, going back and forth beyond the door, were light ones—light as a child's. According to Mrs Bazeley, Betty had been down in the hall with her throughout the entire incident, though she also admitted that, in her anxiety for Mrs Ayres, she had gone fur-ther up the staircase while Betty had hung back. Could the girl have run to the servants' stairs, made her rapid way up them, locked the nursery door, and then gone pattering back and forth in the passage—all without the other woman's having missed her? It seemed very un-likely. I had come up by the back stairs myself, and had examined them pretty closely by the flame of my lighter. They were covered with a fine layer of dust, which my own shoes instantly disturbed, but there were no other footmarks, heavy or soft, I was quite certain. And then, Betty's distress over the incident seemed very genuine; I knew she was fond of her mistress; and finally, of course, there was Mrs Ayres's own word against her involvement, for she had seen the girl with Mrs Bazeley outside the house while the sounds in the speaking-tube went on . . .

I ran through all this in my mind, looking over that bleak room; but soon the oppressions of the place proved too much for me. I wet my handkerchief at the basin and cleared up the worst of the blood. I found a few loose pieces of linoleum and did what I could to block up the broken panes of window. Then I went heavily back downstairs. I went down by the main staircase, and met Caroline on the first landing, just coming out of her mother's room. She touched her finger to her lips, and we carried on silently together to the little parlour.

When we were inside with the door closed, I said, 'How is she?'

She shivered. 'She's sleeping. I thought I heard her call out, that's all. I don't want her to wake up and be frightened.'

'Well,' I said, 'she should sleep for hours with the Veronal inside her. Come and sit by the fire. You're cold. And God knows, so am I.'

I led her to the hearth, drew the chairs close together before it, and we sat. I put my elbows on my knees, and my face in my hands. Beaten and weary, I rubbed my eyes.

She said, 'You've been upstairs.'

I nodded, gazing blearily at her. 'Oh, Caroline, that horrible room! It looks like a lunatic's cell up there. I've locked the door of it. I think you should leave it locked, now. Don't go up there.'

She looked away from me, towards the fire. 'Another room shut up,' she said.

I was still rubbing at my sore eyes. 'Well, that's the least of our worries right now. It's your mother we need to think about. I just can't believe this has happened, can you? And she was quite herself, this morning?'

She said, without drawing her gaze from the flames, 'She was no different from how she was yesterday, if that's what you mean.'

'She'd slept well?'

'As far as I know . . . I oughtn't to have gone down to the houses, I suppose. I oughtn't to have left her.'

I lowered my hands. 'Don't be silly. If anyone's at fault here, it's me! You've been telling me for weeks that she hasn't been herself. I wish to God I'd paid more attention. I'm so sorry, Caroline. I had no idea her mind was as unsettled as this. If those cuts had been deeper, if she'd caught an artery—'

She looked frightened. I reached for her hand. 'Forgive me. This is dreadful for you. To see your mother in such a state . . . These—these fantasies of hers.' I spoke reluctantly. 'These ideas about your sister, that your sister's been . . . visiting her. Did you know about that?'

She gazed back at the fire again. 'No. But it makes sense now. She's been spending so much time alone. I thought it was tiredness. Instead, up in her room, she must have been thinking that, that Susan— Oh, it's grotesque! It's—it's filthy.' Her pale cheeks had coloured. 'And it *is* my fault, no matter what you say. I knew that something like this would happen. That it was only a matter of time.'

'Well,' I said miserably, 'then I should have known it, too. And I could have kept a closer eye on her.'

'It doesn't matter how closely you watch,' she said. 'We watched Roderick, remember? I should have taken her away—right away, from Hundreds.'

There was something odd about the way she said this; and as she spoke she looked at me, then almost furtively dropped her gaze. I said, 'What do you mean? Caroline?'

'Well, isn't it obvious?' she said. 'It's something in this house! Something that's been here all along, and has just . . . woken up. Or something that's come here, to punish and spite us. You saw how my mother was, when you arrived. You heard what happened to her. You heard Mrs Bazeley, and Betty.'

I was gazing at her in disbelief. I said, 'You can't seriously mean— You can't believe— Caroline, listen.' I reached across her for her other hand, and held her fingers tightly in mine. I said, 'You, your mother, Mrs Bazeley, Betty: you're all of you at the end of your tethers! This house, yes, has put thoughts in your heads. But is that so surprising? One grim thing has led so clearly to another: first Gyp, then Roderick, and now this. Surely you can see that? You aren't your mother, Caroline. You're stronger than she is. Why, I remember her sitting, weeping, where you're sitting now, months ago! She must have been fretting over the memory of your sister ever since those wretched scribbles appeared. She's been unwell, not sleeping; her age is against her, too. And then that foolish business with the speaking-tube—'

'And the locked door? The footsteps?'

'The door was probably never even shut! It was open, wasn't it, when you and Mrs Bazeley went up there? And the whistle was back in its place? As for the footsteps—I dare say she heard some sound. She thought she heard Gyp's footsteps once, you remember? That must have been all it took, for her mind to begin to give way.'

She shook her head, frustrated. 'You have an answer for everything.'

'A rational answer, yes! You aren't seriously suggesting that your sister—'

'No,' she said firmly. 'No, I'm not suggesting that.'

'What, then? That some other ghost entirely is haunting your mother? The same ghost, presumably, that made those marks in Roderick's room—'

'Well *something* made them, didn't it?' she cried, pulling her hands out of my grip. 'Something's here, I know it is. I think I've known it ever since Rod got ill, but I was too afraid to face it . . . I keep thinking, too, of what my mother said, when that last set of scribbles was found. She said the house knows all our weaknesses and is testing them, one by one. Roddie's weakness was the house itself, you see. Mine—well, perhaps mine was Gyp. But Mother's weakness is Susan. It's as if, with the scribbles, the footsteps, the voice—it's as if she's being *teased*. As if something's *playing* with her.'

I said, 'Caroline, you can't possibly believe that.'

'Oh,' she answered angrily, 'it's all right for you! You can talk about delusions and fantasies, and things like that. But you don't know this family; not really. You've only seen us like this. We were different, a year ago. I'm sure we were. Things have changed—gone wrong—so badly, so quickly. There has to be *something*, don't you see?'

Her face was white now, and stricken. I put my hand on her arm.

'Look, you're tired. You're all of you tired.'

'You keep on saying that!'

'Well, unfortunately it keeps on being true!'

'But this is more than mere tiredness, surely? Why won't you see that?'

'I see what's in front of me,' I said. 'Then I make sensible deductions. That's what doctors do.'

She gave a cry that was part frustration, part a sort of disgust; but the cry seemed to use up the last of her strength. She covered her eyes, sat still and stiff for a second, and then her shoulders sank.

'I just don't know,' she said. 'Sometimes it seems clear. Other times, it's just—too much. It's all too much.'

I drew her towards me, to kiss and smooth her head. Then I spoke to her, quietly and calmly.

'My darling, I'm so sorry. This is hard, I know. But it won't help anyone, your mother least of all, if we avoid the obvious . . . Things have clearly become too difficult for her. There's nothing odd or super-natural about that. I think she's been trying to retreat to an era, that's all, when her life was easier. How many times has she spoken wistfully about the past? She must have made your sister into a sort of figure for everything she's lost. I think her mind, with rest, will clear. Truly I do. I think it would help her, too, if the estate could get back on its feet.' I paused. 'If we were to marry—'

She moved away. 'I can't think of marrying, with my mother like this!'

'Surely it would reassure her, to see things settled? To see *you* settled?'

'No. No, it wouldn't be right.'

I struggled for a second with a frustration of my own; then spoke measuredly again.

'Very well. But your mother's going to need careful nursing now. She's going to need all our help. She doesn't need to be frightened or alarmed with any sort of fancy. You understand me? Caroline?'

After a slight hesitation, she closed her eyes and gave me a nod. But after that we sat in silence. She folded her arms and moved forward in her chair, gazing into the fire again as if brooding over the flames.

I stayed with her as long as I could, but at last had to leave for the hospital. I told her to rest. I promised to return first thing in the morning, and meanwhile she was to call me if her mother showed any signs of upset or agitation. Then I went softly back down to the kitchen to say the same thing to Betty and Mrs Bazeley—adding that I wanted them to keep an eye on Caroline herself, who I thought was 'feeling the strain a little'.

And before I left, I looked in on Mrs Ayres. She was sleeping heavily, with her poor bandaged arms flung out, her long hair tangled on her pillow. She began to stir and murmur as I stood beside her bed, but I laid my hand across her forehead, and stroked her pale, anxious face; and soon she was still.

ELEVEN

I didn't know what to expect when I returned to Hundreds next morning. Life at the house had reached a point where it seemed to me that, in my absence, absolutely anything might happen. But when I stepped into the hall at around eight o'clock I found Caroline coming downstairs to greet me, looking tired, but with reassuring touches of life and colour in her cheeks. She told me that they had all passed an uneventful night. Her mother had slept deeply, and since waking had been quite calm.

'Thank God!' I said. 'And how does she seem? There's no confusion?'

'Apparently not.'

'Has she spoken about what happened?'

She hesitated, then turned and began to head back upstairs.

'Come and talk to her yourself.'

So I followed her up.

The room, I was pleased to see, was light, with its curtains drawn wide, and Mrs Ayres, though still in her night-clothes, was out of her bed, sitting by the fire, her hair tied back in a loose plait. She looked apprehensively at the opening door as we went in, but the alarm passed from her face when she saw Caroline and me. Her gaze met mine, and she blinked, and coloured, as if in simple embarrassment.

I said, 'Well, Mrs Ayres! I came early, thinking you might need me. I see I'm hardly needed at all.' I crossed to her, pulling over the padded stool from beneath her dressing table so that I could sit at her side and examine her. I said quietly, 'How are you feeling?'

Close to, I could see that her eyes were dark and still glassy from the sedative I'd given her the day before, and her pose was a rather weak one. But her voice, though low, was clear and steady. She put down her head and said, 'I feel like a perfect fool.'

'Now don't be silly,' I answered, smiling. 'How did you sleep?'

'So deeply, I—I don't really remember. That's thanks to your medicine, I suppose.'

'No bad dreams?'

'I don't think so.'

'Good. Now, first things first.' I gently took her hands in mine. 'May I look at your dressings?'

She turned her face from me, but meekly extended her arms. She had pulled down her cuffs to cover the bandages, and when I put them back I saw that the dressings were stained and ought to be changed. I went around the landing to the bathroom, and brought back a bowl of warm water; even with the water, however, the business of easing free the lint from the wounds was not very pleasant. Caroline stood to one side, looking on silently as I worked. Mrs Ayres herself bore the operation without a murmur, only catching her breath now and then as the bandage tugged.

The cuts, on the whole, were closing well. I carefully applied new dressings. Caroline moved forward to take away the bowl of tinted water and to roll up the soiled bandages, and while she was doing that I gently took her mother's pulse and blood-pressure, then listened at her chest. Her breaths were mildly laboured, but her heartbeat, I was pleased to find, was quick and very firm.

I closed the lapels of her dressing-gown and put my instruments away. Gently taking hold of her hands again, I said, 'I think you're doing very nicely. I'm relieved to see it. You gave the house quite a scare yesterday.'

She drew away her fingers. 'Don't let's talk about it. Please.'

'You had a very serious fright, Mrs Ayres.'

'I behaved like a foolish old woman, that's all!' Her voice, for the first time, lost some of its steadiness. She closed her eyes, then tried to smile. 'I'm afraid my mind ran away with itself. This house breeds fancies; such silly thoughts. We're too isolated out here. My husband always used to say that this Hall was the loneliest house in Warwickshire. Didn't your father used to say that, Caroline?'

Caroline was still tidying away the bandages. She said quietly, without looking up, 'He did.'

I turned from her back to her mother. 'Well, the house, in its present condition, is certainly partly to blame. But when I saw you yesterday, you said some very startling things.'

'I said a lot of nonsense! I'm ashamed to remember it. What Betty and Mrs Bazeley must think, I simply can't imagine . . . Oh, please don't let's talk about it, Doctor.'

I said carefully, 'It seems a serious matter to ignore.'

'We haven't ignored it. You've given me medicine. Caroline's been looking after me. I—I'm quite well now.'

'You haven't felt anxious? Afraid?'

'Afraid?' She laughed. 'Good heavens, of what?'

'Well, yesterday you seemed very afraid. You spoke of Susan—'

She moved in her chair. 'I told you, I spoke a lot of nonsense! I'd had—I'd had too much on my mind. I'd been spending too much time alone. I realise that now. I shall sit more with Caroline in future. In the evenings, and so on. Please don't nag at me. Please don't.'

She put her bandaged hand over mine, her eyes looking dark and large and still rather glassy in her drawn face. But her voice had levelled again, and her tone seemed very sincere. There was no trace of the staring, babbling woman who had greeted me yesterday.

I said at last, 'Very well. But I'd like you to rest now. I think you

ought to go back to bed. I shall give Caroline a prescription for you—
just a mild sedative, that's all. I want you sleeping eight dreamless hours
a night, until your strength returns. How does that sound?'

'As though I'm an invalid,' she answered, a hint of playfulness entering her tone.

'Well, I'm the doctor here. You must allow me to decide who the
invalids are.'

She rose, grumbling slightly, but allowed me to help her back to bed.
I gave her another Veronal—a lower dose, this time—and Caroline and
I sat beside her until, sighing and murmuring, she slept. When we were
sure she was slumbering properly, we slipped from the room.

We stood on the landing. I looked at the shut door, shaking
my head.

'She's so much better! It's incredible. Has she been like that all
morning?'

'She's been just like that,' Caroline answered, not quite meeting
my gaze.

'She seems almost her old self.'

'You think so?'

I looked at her. 'Don't you?'

'I'm not so sure. Mother's very good, you know, at hiding her real
feelings. All that generation are; especially the women.'

'Well, she seemed very much better than I expected to find her. If we
can just keep her quiet, now.'

She gave me a glance. 'Quiet? You really think we can do
that, here?'

The question struck me as a strange one, given that we were standing, talking in murmurs, at the centre of that hushed house. But before
I could answer, she had moved away from me. She said, 'Come downstairs for a moment, will you? To the library? I want to show you
something.'

I followed her uncertainly down to the hall. She opened the library
door, then stood aside for me to go on in ahead of her.

The room smelt mustier than ever after all the winter rains. The shelves were still draped with sheets, still looking faintly ghostly in the dimness. But she or Betty had opened up the single working window-shutter, and an ashy fire was smoking itself out in the grate. Two lamps were arranged beside an armchair. I looked at them in some surprise.

'You've been sitting in here?'

'I've been reading,' she said, 'while Mother's been asleep. I spoke to Betty yesterday, you see, after you left. And she set me thinking.'

She took a step back out into the hall, and called Betty's name. She must have put the girl to wait somewhere, for she called quite softly, but Betty appeared almost at once. She followed Caroline over the threshold, then caught sight of me in the gloom, and hesitated. Caroline said, 'Come right inside, and close the door behind you, please.'

The girl came forward, bowing her head.

'Now,' said Caroline. She had put her hands together, and was work-ing the fingers of one over the knuckles of the other, as if absently try-ing to smooth out the papery roughness of her own skin. 'I want you to tell Dr Faraday what you told me yesterday.'

Betty hesitated again, then mumbled, 'I don't like to, miss.'

'Come on, don't be silly. No one's cross with you. What did you come and tell me, yesterday afternoon, after the doctor had gone home?'

'Please, miss,' she said, with a glance at me, 'I told you this house's got summat bad in it.'

I must have made some sound or gesture of dismay. Betty lifted her head, and stuck out her chin. 'It does, too! And I knowed that, months ago! And I told Doctor, and he said I were only being daft. But I wan't being daft! I *knowed* there was summat! I *felt* 'm!'

Caroline was watching me. I looked over, and met her gaze, and said stiffly, 'It's perfectly true that I asked Betty not to mention this.'

'Tell Dr Faraday what you felt, exactly,' she said, as if she hadn't heard.

'I just felt 'm,' Betty said, more feebly, 'in the house. He's like a—a wicked servant.'

'A wicked servant!' I said.

She stamped her foot. 'He is! He used to move things about, up here; he never did nothing downstairs. But he used to push things over, and make stuff mucky—as though he touched it, with dirty hands. I nearly said summat, after that fire. But Mrs Bazeley said I oughtn't to, because Mr Roderick was to blame for that. But then all them queer things happened with Mrs Ayres—all them pops and flappings—and then I *did* say summat. I said summat to madam herself.'

Now I began to understand. I folded my arms. 'I see. Well, that explains a great deal. And what did Mrs Ayres say?'

'She said she knowed all about it. She said it was a ghost! She said she liked it! She said it was hers and my secret, and I wasn't to say. And I didn't say another word after that, not even to Mrs Bazeley. And I thought that must be all right, because Mrs Ayres seemed so happy. But now the ghost's turned wicked again, hasn't he? And I wish I *had* spoken! For then madam wouldn't have got hurt. And I'm sorry! But it in't my fault!'

She began to cry, putting up her hands to cover her face, her shoulders heaving. Caroline went across to her and said, 'All right, Betty. No one's blaming you for anything. You were very good and sensible yesterday, when the rest of us were so shaken. Wipe your eyes.'

Eventually the girl calmed down, and Caroline sent her back to the basement. She went meekly, but with a baleful look at me; and when she had gone I stood for a moment with my eyes on the shut door, very conscious of the silence and of Caroline's watchful gaze.

Turning at last, I said, 'She mentioned something to me, the morning I destroyed Gyp. You were all so unhappy, I didn't want to risk upsetting you further. When all that business started with Rod, I thought some of it might have come from her, that she might have put the idea into his head. She swore she hadn't.'

'I don't think she had,' said Caroline.

She had crossed to the armchair and now, from the table beside it, picked up two hefty books. She held them against her chest, and drew in her breath; and when she spoke again, it was with a quiet sort of dignity.

She said, 'I don't care that you didn't mention this to me before. I don't care that I had to hear it from Betty rather than from you. I know what you think about what's been happening in this house. But I want you to listen to me—just for a little while. You owe me that, I think?'

I took a step towards her, but her pose and manner were forbidding. I stopped, and said cautiously, 'All right.'

She drew another deep breath, and went on.

'After Betty spoke to me yesterday, I began to think things over. I suddenly remembered some books of my father's. I remembered the titles, and came looking for them last night. I half thought they might have been given away . . . But anyway, I found them.'

With a puzzling diffidence, she handed the two heavy books to me. I don't know what I expected them to be. From the look of them I thought they might be medical textbooks. Then I saw the titles: *Phantasms of the Living*, and *The Night Side of Nature*.

'Caroline,' I said, letting the books sink at my sides, 'I can't believe that these will help us.'

She saw that I didn't mean to open them, and took them back, and opened one herself. She did it fumblingly, as if not quite in command of her own movements; I looked again at the colour in her cheeks, and realised that what I had been taking for a blush of health was actually a sort of agitation. She found a page that she had marked with a slip of paper, and began to read aloud.

' "On the first day," ' she read, ' " the family were startled all at once by a mysterious movement among the things in the sitting-rooms and kitchen, and other parts of the house. At one time, without any visible agency, one of the jugs came off the hook over the dresser, and was broken; then followed another, and next day another. A china teapot, with the tea just made in it, and placed on the mantelpiece, whisked off on to the floor." '

She looked up at me, shyly but with a trace of defiance. Her colour was deeper than ever now. She said, 'That was in London, in the eighteen hundreds.' She turned a few pages, to another slip. 'This is in Edinburgh, in eighteen thirty-five. "Do what they would, the thing went on just the same: footsteps of invisible feet, knockings, and scratchings, and rustlings, first on one side, and then on the other, were heard daily and nightly."'

'Caroline,' I said.

She turned more pages—turned one so hastily, it tore. 'And here. Listen to this: "I meet with numerous extraordinary records of a preternatural ringing of all the bells in a house; sometimes occurring periodically for a considerable time, and continuing after precautions have been taken which precluded the possibility of trick or deception—"'

I took the book back from her hands. 'Very well,' I said. 'Let me look at it.'

I turned to the title page. The list of headings struck me, and, with a touch of distaste, I read them aloud. '"The Dweller in the Temple". "Double Dreaming and Trance". "Troubled Spirits". "Haunted Houses".' Again, I let the book sink. 'Didn't we discuss this yesterday? Do you really think your mother will recover if you encourage her in thinking that this house has a ghost in it?'

'But I don't think that,' she said quickly. 'I don't think that at all. I know it's what Mother believes; I know it's what Betty thinks, too. But these things the book talks about, they're not ghosts. If anything, they're . . . poltergeists.'

'Poltergeists!' I said. 'God! Why not vampires, or werewolves?'

She shook her head, frustrated. 'A year ago I might have said the same. But it's just a word, isn't it? A word for something we don't understand, some sort of energy, or collection of energies. Or something inside us. I don't know. These writers here: Gurney and Myers.' She opened the other book. 'They talk about "phantasms". They're not ghosts. They're parts of a person.'

'Parts of a person?'

'Unconscious parts, so strong or so troubled they can take on a life of their own.' She showed me a page. 'Look. Here's a man in England, anxious, wanting to speak to his friend—appearing to the woman and her companion, at exactly that moment, in an hotel room in Cairo!

Appearing as his own ghost! Here's a woman, at night, hearing a fluttering bird—just like Mother! Then she sees her husband, who's in
America, standing there before her; later she finds out he's dead! The
book says, with some sorts of people, when they're unhappy or troubled, or they want something badly— Sometimes they don't even know
it's happening. Something . . . breaks away from them. And what I can't
stop thinking is— I keep thinking back to those telephone calls. Suppose it's Roddie, all of it?'

I said in amazement, '*What?*'

'Well, if this book is right, then *someone*'s at the root of it. And suppose it's my brother, doing it all? Suppose he wants to come back to
us? You know how unhappy he could get, how frustrated. That ghost
of Betty's: it might have been *him*, the whole time.'

I said, 'It might have been Betty herself! Have you thought of that?
You've only had trouble, haven't you, since she's been in the house?'

She made a gesture of impatience, dismissing the idea.

'You might as well say we've only had trouble since *you've* been in
it! You aren't listening to me. The noises, the bells—they're all signals,
aren't they? Even the scribbles on the walls. The voice in the speaking-
tube yesterday—according to Mother it was faint, only really a breath.
Maybe she only supposed it was Susan's, because that's what she wanted
to hear. Maybe it was really *Rod*'s.'

'But there *was* no voice!' I said. 'There couldn't have been. As for
the bells—we've been over this. The faulty wires—'

'But here, in this book—'

I put my hands over hers, with the book between us. I said, 'Caroline, please. This is nonsense. You know it is. It's a fairy tale! For God's
sake. I had a patient once who tried to hit his wife over the head with
a hammer. He said she wasn't really his wife at all; another woman had
"swallowed her up", and he had to smash open the false wife's head to
let the real one out! No doubt this book would back him up. A nice
case of spirit-possession. Instead we got the man into hospital and gave
him a bromide, and in a week he was sane again. How would the book

account for that? They're giving your brother bromides, too. He's been a very ill young man. But to suggest that he might be haunting Hundreds like some sort of spook—'

I saw a flicker of doubt in her expression. But she said stubbornly, 'If you use words like that, then it's bound to sound foolish. But you don't live here. You don't know. Last night it all made sense to me. Listen.'

She opened the book again, and found another passage that seemed to her to demonstrate her point. After that she found another. I looked at her face, which was really flushed now, the blood beating almost hectically across it. I looked at her jerky, intent gaze. And I hardly knew her. I took hold of her hand. She didn't notice, she was still reading aloud from the book. I moved my fingers to her wrist, trying to feel for her pulse. I caught the rapid *tick-tick* of it.

She became aware of my purposeful grip. She pulled away from me, almost in horror. 'What are you doing? Stop it! Stop it!'

'Caroline,' I said.

'You're treating me like you treated my mother! Like you treated Rod! Is that all you can do?'

'Well, for God's sake,' I cried, my weariness and frustration catching up with me, 'I'm a doctor! What do you expect? You stand there, reading me that nonsense— You aren't some superstitious country girl. Look around you! Look what you've got! This house is falling down around your ears! Your brother brought the estate to the brink of ruin and blamed it all on an *infection*. Now you're finishing off the job— blaming spooks and poltergeists! I can't listen to any more of it! It's making me sick!'

I turned away, almost shaking, startled by the force of my own words. I heard her set aside the book, and with an effort I calmed myself down. I put my hand across my eyes and said, 'Forgive me, Caroline. I didn't mean any of that.'

'No,' she said quietly. 'I'm glad you said it. You're right. Even about Roddie. I shouldn't have shown you. It isn't your problem.'

I turned back to her, the anger flaring up again. 'Of course it's my problem! We're going to be married, aren't we? Though God knows when . . . Oh, don't look at me like that.' I caught hold of her hands. 'I can't bear to see you upset! But I can't bear to see you misled, either. You're just giving yourself more things to worry about. There are enough already, aren't there? Real things, I mean, in the real world, that we can do something about?'

Again I saw doubt in her eyes. Again she said, 'But last night it seemed to make such sense! Everything seemed to fall into place. I thought about Roddie so much, I could almost *feel* him here.'

'A few days ago,' I answered, 'listening at that damn speaking-tube, I convinced myself I could almost hear my mother!'

She frowned. 'You did?'

I lifted her hands, and kissed them. 'This house,' I said, 'is making us all crazy; but not in the way you think. Things have got . . . out of control here. But we can fix that, you and I. Meanwhile—well, it's perfectly understandable that you're worried about Rod. Let's—let's go and see him, if that will help.'

Her head had been lowered, but at my words she looked up, and for the first time in weeks I saw a little leap of brightness in her eyes. That gave me a different sort of pang. I wished the brightness were for me. She said, 'You mean it?'

'Of course I do. I don't advise it. I don't think, for Rod's sake, that we should. But that's a different matter. It's you I'm thinking of now. It's always you I'm thinking of, Caroline. You must know that.'

And, as it had once before, the last of my anger shifted, somehow transformed itself into desire. I drew her to me. She resisted for a moment, then her arms came around me, slender and hard.

'Yes,' she murmured, tiredly. 'Yes, I do.'

We drove to the clinic the following Sunday, leaving Mrs Ayres sleeping at home with Betty to watch her. The day was dry, but dark; the journey, inevitably, was a rather tense one. I had called ahead to arrange our visit, but, 'Suppose he won't see us?' Caroline asked me, a dozen times along the way. And, 'Suppose he's worse? Suppose he doesn't even recognise us?'

'Then at least we'll know,' I answered. 'That will be something, won't it?'

At last she fell silent, biting her nails. When I drew up in the court-yard she kept still for a moment, reluctant to get out. We went in through the clinic door and she gripped my arm, in real panic.

But then a nurse took us through to the day-room and we saw Roderick sitting waiting for us, alone, at one of the tables; and she left my side and went quickly over to him, laughing with nervousness and relief.

'Rod! Is it you? I hardly knew you! You look like a sea-captain!'

He had put on weight. His hair was shorter than when we had last seen it, and he'd grown a ruddy-coloured beard. The beard was uneven, because of his burns. His face, behind it, seemed to me to have lost its youth, to have settled in hard, humourless lines. He didn't return his sister's smiles. He let her lean to kiss his cheek and put her arms around him, but then he sat on the other side of the table—putting his hands on the table's surface, I noticed, in a deliberate kind of way, as if liking the solidity of it.

I took the chair beside Caroline's. 'It's good to see you, Rod.'

'It's wonderful to see you!' said Caroline, laughing again. 'How are you?'

He moved his tongue against his teeth, his mouth dry. He looked wary, suspicious. 'I'm all right.'

'You're fat as anything. They must be feeding you well, at least! Are they? Is the food OK?'

He frowned. 'I suppose so.'

'And are you pleased to see us?'

He didn't answer that. Instead, he glanced over at the window. 'How did you get here?'

'We came in Dr Faraday's car.'

He moved his tongue again. 'The little Ruby.'

'That's right,' I said.

He looked at me, still wary. 'They only told me this morning that you were coming.'

Caroline said, 'We only decided to, this week.'

'Isn't Mother with you?'

I saw her hesitate. I spoke instead.

'I'm sorry to say your mother has a touch of bronchitis, Rod. Just a touch. She'll be all right soon.'

'She sends her love,' said Caroline, brightly. 'She was . . . very sorry not to come.'

'They only told me this morning,' he said again. 'They're like that, here. They keep things secret so as not to frighten us. They don't want us to lose our heads, you see. It's just like the RAF, really.'

He shifted his hands. I saw then that they were shaking. Keeping them flat upon the table must have helped to still them.

I think Caroline saw the tremor, too. She put her own hands over his. 'We just wanted to see you, Rod,' she said. 'We haven't seen you for months. We wanted to be sure that you're . . . all right.'

He frowned down at her fingers, and for a moment we were silent. Then she exclaimed, again, over his beard, his extra weight. She asked after his daily routines, and he told us, in an uninvolved kind of way, how he passed his time now: the hours he spent in the 'craft room', making clay models; the meals, the spells of recreation, of singing, occasional gardening. He spoke lucidly enough, but with his features never breaking out of their stiff new mirthless lines, and his manner still very cautious. Then Caroline's questions became more hesitant—Was he really all right? Would he say if he wasn't? Was there anything he wanted? Did he think very often of home?—and he began to look at us both with cold suspicion.

'Doesn't Dr Warren tell you how I am?'

'Yes. He writes to us every week. But we wanted to *see* you. I had an idea—'

'What idea?' he said quickly.

'That you might be . . . unhappy.'

The tremor in his hands became more violent, and his mouth set tight. He sat stiffly for a moment, then jerked away from the table and folded his arms.

'I won't go back,' he said.

'What?' asked Caroline, bewildered. His sudden movement had made her start.

'If that's why you're here.'

'We just wanted to see you.'

'*Is* that why you're here? To take me back?'

'No, of course it isn't. At least, I hoped—'

'It isn't fair, if that's why you've come. You can't bring a chap to a place like this, and let him get used to it—let him get used to having no ties—and then send him back into that sort of danger.'

'Roddie, please!' said Caroline. 'I wish you'd come home. I wish it more than anything. I wish you'd come home with Dr Faraday and me right now. But if you'd rather stay here, if you're happier here—'

'It isn't a question of where I'm *happier*!' he said, with great contempt. 'It's a question of where it's safer for me to be. Don't you know anything?'

'Roddie—'

'You want to put me in charge again? Is that it? When any fool could see that if you give me something, I'll—I'll hurt it?'

'It wouldn't be like that,' I said, seeing Caroline shaken by his words. 'Hundreds is being well looked after now. Caroline is looking after it, and I'm helping. You wouldn't have to do anything you didn't care to do. We'd do it for you.'

'Oh, that's clever,' he said, as if talking, sneeringly, to a stranger. 'That's bloody good. You mean to trick me back like that. You just want to use me—to use me, and blame me. Well, I *won't* go back! I *won't* be blamed! Do you hear me?'

'Please,' said Caroline. 'Stop talking like this! No one wants to take you back. I had the idea, that's all, that you were unhappy. That you wanted to see me. I'm sorry. I—I made a mistake.'

'Do you think I'm an idiot?' he said.

'No.'

'Are *you* an idiot?'

She flinched. 'I just made a mistake.'

'Rod,' I began. But a nurse had been sitting near us all this time, discreetly overseeing the visit, and now, having registered the change in him, she came over.

'What's all this?' she asked him mildly. 'You're not upsetting your sister, surely?'

'I won't talk to bloody fools!' he said, looking rigidly away, his arms still folded.

'And I won't have language,' said the nurse, folding her own arms. 'Now, will you apologise? No?' She tapped her foot. 'We're waiting . . .'

Rod said nothing. She shook her head, and, with her face turned to him but her eyes on Caroline and me, she said, in over-clear nursery tones, 'Roderick's a mystery to the clinic, Miss Ayres, Dr Faraday. When he's in temper he's the nicest chap, and all we nurses love him. But when he's out of it—' She shook her head again, and drew in her breath, and tutted.

Caroline said, 'It's all right. He needn't apologise if he doesn't want to. I—I don't want to make him do anything he doesn't want to do.'

She gazed at her brother, then reached across the table again and spoke quietly and humbly. 'We miss you, Roddie, that's all. Mother and I, we miss you so much. We think about you all the time. Hundreds is horrible without you. I just thought you might be . . . thinking of us, too. I see now that you're doing fine. I'm—I'm so glad.'

Rod remained stubbornly silent. But his features tightened, and his breathing grew laboured, as if he were keeping in check some tremendous emotion. The nurse moved closer to us and spoke more confidentially.

'I'd let him alone now, if I were you. I should hate for you to see him in one of his rages.'

We had spent less than ten minutes with him. Caroline rose, reluctantly—unable to believe that her brother would let us go without a word or look. But he didn't turn, and at last we had to leave him. She went on ahead to the car while I spoke briefly with Dr Warren, and when I joined her, her eyes were red, but dry: she had been crying and had blotted the tears.

I took her hand. 'That was grim. I'm sorry.'

But she spoke tonelessly. 'No. We shouldn't have come. I should have listened to you, before. I've been stupid, thinking we'd find something here. There's nothing, is there? Nothing. It's all just how you said.'

We began the long trip back to Hundreds. I put my arm around her whenever the driving would allow. She kept her hands open in her lap, and her head moved slackly against my shoulder with the motion of the car—as if, disappointed, bewildered, she had lost all resistance and life.

None of this, of course, was particularly inspiring to romance; and our affair, for the moment, rather languished. Between the frustrations of that, and my anxiety about her and about Hundreds generally, I began to feel burdened and fretful, sleeping poorly, with muddled dreams. I thought several times of confiding in Graham and Anne. But it was many weeks since I had spent any proper time with them; I had the impression they were slightly hurt by my neglect, and I didn't like to go creeping back to them now in a spirit of failure. At last even my work started to suffer. On one of my evenings at the hospital I found myself assisting on some routine piece of minor surgery, and I did the job so badly, the physician in charge laughed at me and finished it off himself.

It happened to be Seeley. We stood together afterwards, washing our hands, and I apologised for my distraction. He answered with his usual affability.

'Not at all. You look done up! I know the feeling. Too many night calls, I suppose? This bad weather doesn't help.'

I said, 'No, it doesn't, does it?'

I turned away from him, but felt his eyes still on me. We went through to the common-room to retrieve our outdoor things, and as I lifted down my jacket from its hook it somehow slithered through my fingers, spilling the contents of its pockets to the floor. I swore, and bent to gather them up, and when I rose I found that Seeley was watching me again.

'You're in a bad way,' he said, smiling. He lowered his voice. 'What's the problem? Patient troubles, or your own?—Forgive my asking.'

'No, it's all right,' I said. 'It's patient business, I suppose. But then again mine too, in a way.'

I very nearly said more—badly wanting to get the thing off my chest, but thinking back to that unpleasant little moment at the January dance. Perhaps Seeley was also recalling it, and wanted to make up for his behaviour, or perhaps he could simply see from my manner how really troubled I was. He said, 'Look, I'm all finished here now, and I assume you are, too? How about coming back with me for a drink? Believe it or not, I've managed to put my hands on a bottle of Scotch. Gift from a grateful lady patient. Can I tempt you?'

'To your house?' I said, in some surprise.

'Why not? Come on. You'll be doing my liver a favour by taking a glass or two, for otherwise I'll only drink the whole damn bottle myself.'

It seemed months, suddenly, since I had done anything as ordinary as sitting down in another man's home with a glass of liquor, so I said I would. We wrapped ourselves up against the cold and headed out to our cars—he, in his slightly flamboyant way, in a thick brown coat and a pair of fur driving-mittens, which made him look something like a genial bear; I, more modestly, in my overcoat and muffler. I set off first, but he soon overtook me in his Packard, speeding recklessly along the frosty country lanes. When, twenty-five minutes later, I drew up at the gate of his house, he was already inside, already setting out the bottle and glasses and making up the fire.

His house was a rambling Edwardian place, full of bright, untidy rooms. He had married quite late in life, and he and his young wife, Christine, had four good-looking children. As I let myself in through the unlocked front door, two of the children were in the process of chasing each other up and down the staircase. Another was beating a tennis-ball against the drawing-room door.

'God damn you blasted kids!' Seeley bellowed, from the doorway of his study. He waved me into the room beyond him, apologising for the chaos. But he had an air, too, of being secretly pleased by it, and proud of it—as people often were, I'd noticed, when complaining of their large, noisy families to bachelors like me.

That thought put a distance between us. He and I had worked together as amiable rivals for nearly twenty years, but we had never exactly been friends. As he uncorked the bottle, I looked at my watch and said, 'You'd better make it a small one. I've a heap of prescriptions to do up tonight.'

But he let the whisky flow. 'All the more reason to pour it stiff. Give your patients some surprises! God, this smells good, doesn't it? Here's fun.'

We touched glasses and drank. He gestured with his tumbler to a couple of dilapidated armchairs, hooking a foot around one to draw it closer to the fire for me, then doing the same with the other for himself; rucking up the dusty rug in the process, and not caring. From out in the hall the thunder of children went on, and in another minute the door was flung open and one of the good-looking boys put in his head and said, 'Father.'

'Get out!' roared Seeley.

'But, sir—'

'Get out, or I'll cut off your ears! Where's your mother?'

'She's out in the kitchen with Rosie.'

'Well, go and pester her, you little sub!'

The door was closed with a bang. Seeley sipped violently at his whisky, at the same time fishing in his pocket for his case of Players. For once I beat him to it with my own case and lighter, and he sat back with the cigarette gripped between his lips.

'Scenes from Domestic Life,' he said, with a show of weariness. 'Do you envy me, Faraday? You shouldn't. A family man never makes a good family doctor; he has too many worries of his own. There ought to be a law making physicians single men, like Catholic priests. They'd be the better for it.'

'You don't believe that for a moment,' I said, after drawing on my own cigarette. 'Besides, if it were true, I'd be the proof of it.'

'Well, and so you are. You're a finer doctor than I am. You had a harder journey to get there, too.'

I raised a shoulder. 'I wasn't much of a shining example tonight.'

'Oh, routine work. You bring out the goods when the goods are needed. You said yourself, you've things on your mind . . . Want to talk about that? I'm not trying to pry, by the way. I know it helps sometimes, that's all, to chew over difficult cases with another medical man.'

He spoke lightly but sincerely, and the slight resistance I'd been feeling—a resistance to the charm of his manner, his untidy house, his handsome family—began to ebb. Perhaps it was simply the whisky doing its work, or the warmth of the fire. The room was such a contrast to my dreary bachelor home—a contrast, too, I realised suddenly, to Hundreds Hall. I had a vision of Caroline and her mother as they probably were at this time of night, hunched and chill and fretful at the heart of that dark, unhappy house.

I turned the glass of whisky in my hand. 'Perhaps you can guess my trouble, Seeley,' I said. 'Or part of it.'

I didn't look up, but saw him lift his own glass. He took a sip and said quietly, 'Caroline Ayres, you mean? I thought it must be something along those lines. You took my advice, did you, after that dance?'

I moved uncomfortably, and before I could answer he went on, 'I know, I know, I was filthy drunk that night, and bloody impertinent. But I meant what I said. What's gone wrong? Don't tell me the girl's turned you down. Too much on her mind, I suppose? Come on, you can trust me, I'm not drunk now. Besides—'

Now I did look up. 'What?'

'Well, one can't help but hear rumours.'

'About Caroline?'

'About the whole family.' He spoke more gravely. 'A Birmingham friend of mine does some part-time consulting for John Warren. He told me what a shocking state Roderick's in. A nasty business, isn't it? I'm not surprised if it's begun to get Caroline down. Now there's been some other sort of incident, I gather, out at the Hall?'

'There has,' I said, after a moment of silence. 'And I don't mind telling you, Seeley, the case is such a bloody queer one, I hardly know what to make of it . . .'

And I told him pretty much the whole story, beginning with Rod and his delusions, then describing the fire, the scribbles on the walls, the phantom rings on the call-bells, and baldly recounting Mrs Ayres's horrible experience up in the nurseries. He listened in silence, occasionally nodding, occasionally letting out a bark of grim laughter. But his laughter faded as the tale went on, and when I had finished he sat still for a moment, then leaned forward to flick ash from his cigarette. And what he said as he sat back was: 'Poor Mrs Ayres. A pretty elaborate way of cutting one's wrists, wouldn't you say?'

I looked at him. 'That's how you see the case, then?'

'My dear fellow, what else? Unless the wretched woman was simply the victim of someone's idea of a nasty joke. I suppose you've ruled that out?'

'I have,' I said. 'Of course.'

'Well, then. The footsteps in the passage, the heavy breathing in the tube: it seems a pretty plain case of psychoneurosis to me. She feels guilty about the loss of her children—Roderick, as well as the little girl. She's started punishing herself. It was up in the nurseries, you say, that the incident took place? Could she have chosen a more significant setting for the whole affair?'

I had to confess that the same idea had struck me—just as, three months before, I'd been impressed by the fact of the Hundreds fire having broken out in what was effectively the estate office—among the estate papers!—as if it were a concentration of all Roderick's frustration and dismay.

But something did not ring true to me. I said, 'I don't know. Even supposing this experience of Mrs Ayres's to be purely delusional, and assuming that, incident by incident, we can find a perfectly rational explanation for everything else that's happened out at the Hall—which, by the way, I think we can. Still, it's the *cumulative* nature of it all that troubles me.'

He took another sip of his whisky. 'What do you mean?'

'Well, put it like this. A child comes to you with a broken arm; all right, you set the bone and send him home. Two weeks later he returns, with broken ribs this time. Perhaps you patch him up and send him home again. A week later he's back, with another fracture . . . The individual broken bones are no longer the main problem, surely?'

'But we're not talking about bones,' said Seeley. 'We're talking about hysteria. And hysteria's altogether stranger—and unfortunately, unlike broken bones, contagious. I was medical officer to a girls' school years ago, and one term there was a fashion for fainting. You never saw anything like it: girls going down, in assembly, like skittles. In the end even the mistresses were doing it.'

I shook my head. 'This is a weirder thing even than hysteria. It's as if—well, as if something's slowly sucking the life out of the whole family.'

'Something is,' he said, with another bark of laughter. 'It's called a Labour Government. The Ayreses' problem—don't you think?—is that they can't, or won't, adapt. Don't get me wrong; I've a lot of sympathy for them. But what's left for an old family like that in England nowadays? Class-wise, they've had their chips. Nerve-wise, perhaps they've run their course.'

He sounded like Peter Baker-Hyde now, and I found his briskness rather repellent. After all, I thought, he had never become a friend to the family, as I had. I said, 'That might be true enough of Rod. Anyone who knew that boy well could have predicted that he was heading for some sort of breakdown. But Mrs Ayres, a suicide? I don't believe it.'

'Oh, but I'm not suggesting for a moment that in putting her hands through that window she was really meaning to end her life. I should say that, like most supposedly suicidal women, she was simply creating a nice little drama, with herself at its heart. She's used to attention, don't forget, and I can't imagine she's been getting too much of it lately . . . You'll want to be careful she doesn't try the same sort of trick again, once all the current fuss has died down. You're keeping an eye on her?'

'Of course I am. She seems to be making a full recovery. That baffles me, too.' I took a gulp of whisky. 'The whole bloody business baffles me! There are things that have happened, over at Hundreds, that I can't explain. It's as if the house is in the grip of some sort of *miasma*. Caroline—' I spoke reluctantly. 'Caroline's even had the idea in her head that there's been something almost supernatural going on—that Roderick's been haunting the house, or something, in his sleep. She's been reading some lurid books. Crank stuff. Frederic Myers, people like that.'

'Well,' said Seeley, stubbing out his cigarette, 'perhaps she's on to something.'

I stared at him. 'You're not serious?'

'Why not? Myers's ideas are the natural extension of psychology, surely?'

I said, 'Not as I understand psychology, no!'

'Are you sure? You subscribe, I suppose, to the general principle: a conscious personality, with a subliminal self—a sort of dream-self—attached?'

'Broadly, yes.'

'Well, then suppose that dream-self could, in certain circumstances, *break loose*: detach itself, cross space, become visible to others? Isn't that Myers's thesis?'

I said, 'As far as I know. And it makes for a good fireside story. But for God's sake, there isn't an ounce of science in it!'

'Not yet there isn't,' he said, smiling. 'And I wouldn't like to air the theory in front of the county medical board, certainly. But perhaps in fifty years' time medicine will have found a way to calibrate the phenomenon, and will have explained it all. Meanwhile, people will go on talking about ghoulies and ghosties and long-leggety beasties, simply missing the point . . .'

He sipped at his whisky, then went on in a different tone. 'My father saw a ghost once, you know. My grandmother appeared one night at his surgery door. She'd been dead ten years. She said, "Quickly, Jamie! Go home!" He didn't stop to think it over; he put on his coat and went straight to the family house. He found that his favourite brother, Henry, had injured his hand, and the wound was rapidly turning septic. He cut off a finger, and probably saved his brother's life. Now, how do you explain that?'

I said, 'I can't. But I'll tell you something. *My* father used to hang a bull's heart in the chimney, stuck with pins. He had it there to keep evil spirits away. I know how I'd explain *that*.'

Seeley laughed. 'Not a fair comparison.'

'Why not? Because your father was a gentleman, and mine a shop-keeper?'

'Don't be so touchy, man! Listen to me, now. I don't think for a moment that my father truly saw a ghost that night, any more than I think poor Mrs Ayres has been receiving calls from her dead daughter. The idea of one's deceased relations floating around in the ether, keeping their gimlet eyes on one's affairs, is really too much to stomach. But suppose the stress of my uncle's injury, combined with the bond be-tween him and my father—suppose all of that somehow released some sort of . . . psychic force? The force simply took the shape that would best get my father's attention. Very bright of it, too.'

'But what's been happening at Hundreds,' I said, 'there's nothing benign about that. Quite the reverse.'

'Is that so surprising, with things for that family so bleak? The sub-liminal mind has many dark, unhappy corners, after all. Imagine some-thing loosening itself from one of those corners. Let's call it a—a germ. And let's say conditions prove right for that germ to develop—to grow, like a child in the womb. What would this little stranger grow into? A sort of *shadow-self*, perhaps: a Caliban, a Mr Hyde. A creature motivated by all the nasty impulses and hungers the conscious mind had hoped to keep hidden away: things like envy, and malice, and frustration . . . Caroline suspects her brother. Well, as I said before, she might be right. Maybe it wasn't only bones that got fractured in that crash of his. Maybe it was something even deeper . . . Then again, it's generally women, you know, at the root of this sort of thing. There's Mrs Ayres, of course, the menopausal mother: that's a queer time, psychically. And don't they even have some teenage housemaid out there, too?'

I looked away from him. 'They do. She's the one who got them all thinking about spooks in the first place.'

'Is that right? And how old is she? Fourteen? Fifteen? Doesn't get much chance to flirt with the boys, I imagine, stuck out there.'

I said, 'Oh, she's a child still!'

'Well, the sexual impulse is the darkest of all, and has to emerge somewhere. It's like an electrical current; it has a tendency, you know, to find its own conductors. But if it goes untapped—well, then it's a rather dangerous energy.'

I was struck by the word. I said slowly, 'Caroline spoke of "energies".'

'Caroline's a clever girl. I always thought she got the thick end of things in that family. Kept at home with a second-rate governess while the boy was packed off to public school. And then, just when she'd got out, to be dragged back again by her mother, so that she could wheel Roderick up and down the terrace in his Bath chair! Next I suppose she'll be wheeling Mrs Ayres. What she needs, of course—' He smiled again, and the smile was sly. 'Well, it's hardly my place. But the girl isn't getting any younger; and, my dear fellow, neither are you! You've put this whole case before me and haven't mentioned your own situation once. What exactly is it? You and she have some sort of . . . understanding, is that it? Nothing firmer than that?'

I felt the whisky inside me. Raising my glass for another gulp I said quietly, 'The firmness is all on my side. Rather too much of it, to be honest with you.'

He looked surprised. 'Like that?'

I nodded.

'Well, well. I'd never have guessed it. Of Caroline, I mean . . . Though there, perhaps, you have the root of your *miasma*.'

His expression was slyer than ever now, and I took a second to understand him. I said at last, 'You aren't suggesting—?'

He held my gaze, then started to laugh. He was enjoying himself enormously, I realised suddenly. He polished off the rest of his whisky, then generously refilled our glasses and lit a second cigarette. He began to tell me another ghost story, this one more fantastic than the last.

But I barely heard it. He'd started me thinking, and the beat of my thoughts, like the ticking arm of a metronome, would not be stilled. It was all nonsense; I knew it was nonsense. Every ordinary thing around me worked against it. The fire was crackling in the grate. The children still thundered on the staircase. The whisky was fragrant in the glass . . . But the night was dark at the window, too, and a few miles away through the wintry darkness stood Hundreds Hall, where things were different. *Could* what he had suggested have any truth to it? *Could* there be something loose in that house, some sort of ravenous frustrated energy, with Caroline at its heart?

I thought back, to the start of it all—to the night of that unlucky party, when Caroline had been so humiliated, and the Baker-Hyde child had ended up hurt. What if some process had begun that night, some queer seed been sown? I remembered, in the weeks that followed, Caroline's mounting hostility towards her brother, her impatience with her mother. Both her brother and her mother had become injured, just like Gillian Baker-Hyde. And it was Caroline who had first brought those injuries to my attention—Caroline who had noticed the burns in Roderick's room, who had discovered the fire, who had heard the taps and felt 'the little rapping hand' behind the wall.

Then I thought of something else. The thing that had started with Gyp, perhaps as a 'nip' or a 'whisper'—as Betty, I suddenly recalled, had put it—that thing had been slowly gathering strength. It had moved objects about, lit fires, put scribbles on a wainscot. Now it could run on pattering feet. It could be heard, as a struggling voice. It was growing, it was developing . . .

What would it be next?

Unnerved, I moved forward. Seeley offered the bottle again, but I shook my head.

'I've wasted enough of your time. I really must go. It's been good of you to listen.'

He said, 'I'm not sure I've done much to reassure you. You look worse than you did when you arrived! Why not stay longer?'

But he was interrupted by the noisy re-entrance of his good-looking son. Loosened up by the whisky, he leapt from his chair and chased the child back out into the hall, and by the time he had returned to me I had finished my drink and had my hat and coat on, ready to leave.

He had a better head for alcohol than I did. He saw me breezily to the door, but I made my way out into the night not quite steady on my feet, and feeling the liquor, hot and sour, in my unlined stomach. I drove the short distance home, then stood in my cold dispensary, the nausea rising like a wave inside me—and, rising with it, something worse than nausea; almost a dread. My heart was beating unpleasantly hard. I took off my coat, and found I was sweating. After a moment of indecision I went through to my consulting-room. I picked up the telephone and, with clumsy fingers, dialled the Hundreds number.

It was after eleven. The phone rang and rang. Then came Caroline's cautious voice. 'Yes? Hello?'

'Caroline! It's me.'

Her tone at once grew anxious. 'Is something the matter? We'd gone to bed. I thought—'

I said, 'Nothing's the matter. Nothing. I—I just wanted to hear your voice.'

I spoke simply, I suppose. There was a silence, and then she laughed. The laughter was tired, ordinary. The dread and the nausea began to dwindle, as if punctured by a pin.

She said, 'I think you must be a little drunk.'

I wiped my face. 'I think I am. I've been with Seeley, and he's been plying me with whisky. God, what a brute that man is! He's had me thinking . . . ridiculous things. It's so good to hear you, Caroline! Say something else.'

She tutted. 'How silly you are! What on earth will the operator think? What should I say?'

'Say anything. Say a poem.'

'A poem! All right.' And she went on, in a prompt, perfunctory way: ' "The frost performs its secret ministry, Unhelped by any wind." Now go to bed, will you?'

'I will, in a second. I just want to think of you there. Everything's all right, isn't it?'

She sighed. 'Yes, everything's all right. The house is behaving itself for once. Mother's asleep, unless you've woken her.'

I said, 'I'm sorry. I'm sorry, Caroline. Good night.'

'Good night,' she said, laughing tiredly again.

She put up the receiver, and I heard the laughter fade. Then came the click of the broken connection, followed by the vague hiss and muddle of other people's voices, trapped in the wire.

TWELVE

The next time I called in at Hundreds I found Barrett there: Caroline had brought him in to rip out that troublesome speaking-tube. I saw the tube as he took it away, and, just as I'd guessed, its braiding in places was loose and torn, the rubber beneath quite perished; it looked as harmless and pathetic, coiled in his arms, as a mummified snake. Mrs Bazeley and Betty, however, were reassured by its removal, and began to lose the air of tension and dread that had possessed them both since the day of what we all now referred to as Mrs Ayres's 'accident'. Mrs Ayres herself also continued to recover well. Her cuts healed cleanly. She spent her days down in the little parlour, reading, or dozing in her chair. There was just a slight trace of glassiness or remoteness to her, to hint at the ordeal she had been through—and most of that I put down to the effects of the Veronal, which she was continuing to take to help her sleep at nights, and which in the short term, I thought, could do her no harm. I rather regretted that Caroline was kept so much indoors now, sitting with her mother, for it meant that she and I had even fewer opportunities to be alone together. But I was glad to see that she, too, was less preoccupied and fretful. She seemed to have become reconciled to the loss of her brother, for instance, since our visit to the clinic; and, to my very great relief, there was no more talk of poltergeists and spooks.

But then, there were no more mysterious occurrences, either—no rings on the bells, no raps, no footsteps, no more curious incidents of any kind. The house continued to, as Caroline had put it, 'behave itself'. And as March drew to a close and one uneventful day gave way to another, I really began to think that the strange spell of nervousness that had been cast over Hundreds in the past few weeks must somehow, like a fever, have reached its crisis and worn itself out.

Then, at the end of the month, there came changes in the weather. The skies darkened, the temperature plummeted, and we had snow. The snow was a novelty—nothing at all like the impossible blizzards and drifts of the previous winter—but it was a nuisance to me and my fellow GPs, and even with chains on its tyres my Ruby struggled with the roads. My round became something of a slog, and for more than a week the park at Hundreds was quite impassable, the drive too treacherous to be risked. Still, I managed to get out to the Hall quite often, leaving the car at the east gates and going the rest of the way on foot. I went mainly to see Caroline, not liking to think of her out there, cut off from the world. I went to keep an eye on Mrs Ayres, too. But I also liked those journeys for their own sake. Breaking free of the snowy drive, I never got my first glimpse of the house without a thrill of awe and pleasure, for against the white, white ground it looked marvellous, the red of its brick and the green of its ivy more vivid, and all its imperfections softened by a lace-work of ice. There would be no hum from the generator, no snarl of machinery from the farm, no clash of building-work: the building-work had been suspended because of the snow. Only my own quiet footsteps would disturb the silence, and I would move on, almost abashed, trying to muffle them further, as if the place were enchanted—as if it were the castle of the *Belle au Bois Dormant* I remembered Caroline envisaging a few weeks before—and I feared to break the spell. Even the interior of the house was subtly transformed by the weather, the glass dome above the stairwell now translucent with snow, making the hall dimmer than ever, and the windows letting in a chill reflected light from the whitened ground, so that shadows fell puzzlingly.

The stillest of those snowbound days was a Tuesday, the sixth of April. I went out to the house in the afternoon, expecting to find Caroline, as usual, sitting downstairs with her mother; but it was Betty, it seemed, who had been keeping Mrs Ayres company that day. They had a table between them, and were playing draughts, with chipped wooden pieces. A good fire was crackling in the grate, and the room was warm and stuffy. Caroline had gone over to the farm, her mother told me; she was expected back within the hour. Would I stay, and wait for her? I was disappointed not to see her, and it was the quiet period before my evening surgery, so I said I would. Betty went off to make our tea, and I took her place at the draught-board for a couple of games.

But Mrs Ayres played absently, losing piece after piece. And when the board had been put aside to make way for the tea-tray we sat together in near silence; there seemed little to say. She had lost her taste for county gossip over the past few weeks. I brought out a few stories and she listened politely enough, but her responses, when they came, were distracted or oddly delayed, as if she were straining her ears to catch the words of a more compelling conversation going on in a neighbouring room. At last my small fund of anecdotes was completely used up. I rose and walked to the French window, and stood gazing out over the dazzling landscape. When I turned back to Mrs Ayres, she was rubbing her arm as if cold.

Catching my eye, she said, 'I'm afraid I'm dull for you, Doctor! I do apologise. That's what comes of sitting so long indoors. Shall we go out, into the garden? We might meet Caroline that way.'

I was surprised by the suggestion, but happy to leave the airless room. I fetched her outdoor things myself, making sure she was properly dressed for the cold; I put on my overcoat and hat, and we went out by the front door. We had to pause a moment to let our eyes grow accustomed to the whiteness of the day, but then she linked her arm with mine and we moved off, going around the house, then making our way, slowly and idly, across the west lawn.

The snow lay smooth as foam there, almost silky to the eye, but crisp and powdery underfoot. In places it was broken by the cartoonish tracks of birds, and soon we found more substantial prints, the dog-like pads and claws of creeping foxes. We followed those for a minute or two; they led us over to the old outbuildings. There the air of general enchantment was even more pronounced, the stable clock still fixed at twenty to nine in that grim Dickensian joke, the stables themselves with their fittings all in place, their doors neatly bolted, but everything thick with cobwebs and dust, so that one half expected, on peeping inside, to find a line of slumbering horses, all thick with cobwebs too. Beside the stables was the garage, with the bonnet of the family Rolls-Royce just showing at its half-open door. Beyond that was a chaos of bushes, and the fox tracks were lost to us. But our walk had taken us almost as far as the old kitchen gardens, so, still idly, we moved on, passing through the arch in the high brick wall to the plots beyond.

Caroline had given me a tour of these gardens, back in the summer. They were barely in use now that life at the house was so diminished, and I thought them the loneliest and most melancholy section of the park. One or two beds were still relatively well tended by Barrett, but other areas, which must once have been lovely, had been dug over for vegetables by the soldiers during the war, and since then, without the hands to manage them, they had run wild. Brambles rose through the glassless roofs of the greenhouses. The cinder paths were choked with nettles. Here and there were great lead pots, giant saucers on slender stems, the saucers tilting tipsily where the lead had buckled from the heat of too many summers.

We made our way from one untidy walled space to the next.

'Isn't it a shame!' Mrs Ayres said softly, now and then pausing to brush aside a frill of snow and examine the plant beneath, or simply to stand and gaze around her, almost as if wanting to memorise the scene. 'The Colonel, my husband, used to love these gardens. They're arranged as a sort of spiral, each one smaller than the last, and he used to say they were like the chambers of a sea shell. Such a fanciful man sometimes.'

We moved on, and soon passed through a narrow gateless opening into the smallest garden there, the old herb garden. At its centre was a sundial, set in an ornamental pond. Mrs Ayres said she believed the pond still had fish in it, and we wandered over to look. We found the water frozen, but the ice was thin, quite flexible, so that we could press it and watch silvery bubbles racing about underneath, like the steel balls in a child's puzzle. Then there came a flash of colour, a darting of gold in the murk, and, 'There goes one,' said Mrs Ayres. She sounded pleased, but unexcited. 'There's another, do you see it? Poor things. Won't they be stifled? Isn't one supposed to break the ice? Caroline would know. I can't remember.'

Retrieving a scrap of knowledge from my Boy Scouting days, I said perhaps I ought to melt it a little. I squatted at the side of the pond, breathed into my ungloved hands, and put my palms to the ice. Mrs Ayres watched me, and then, with an elegant tucking in of her skirts, she lowered herself at my side. The ice stung. My wet hands, when I lifted them back to my mouth to warm them, felt numb and almost rubbery. I shook my fingers, pulling a face.

Mrs Ayres smiled. 'Oh, what babies you men are.'

I answered, laughing, 'That's just something women say. Why *do* women say it?'

'Because it's perfectly true. Women are built for pain. Now, if you men had to go through childbirth . . .'

She didn't finish, and her smile faded. I had my hands at my mouth again, and my falling sleeve had uncovered my wrist-watch. She glanced at that and said, in a different tone, 'Caroline might be at home now. You'll want to see her, of course.'

I said politely, 'I'm happy to stay here.'

'I don't want to keep you from her.'

There was something to the way she said it. I met her gaze, and saw that, for all that Caroline and I had been so careful, she knew perfectly well how matters stood between us. Slightly self-conscious, I turned back to the pond. I put my palms to the ice again, then lifted and warmed them, several times, until at last I felt the ice give way, and I saw that I had made two irregular openings into the tea-coloured water beneath.

'There,' I said, pleased with myself. 'Now the fish can do what Eskimos do, in reverse: catch flies and whatnot. Shall we go on?'

I offered my hand, but she didn't answer, and didn't rise. She watched me shake the water from my fingers, and then she said quietly, 'I'm glad, Dr Faraday, about you and Caroline. I'll admit that I wasn't, at first. When you began to come to the house, and I saw that you and my daughter might form an attachment, I didn't like it. I'm an old-fashioned woman, and you weren't quite the match I'd planned for her . . . I hope you never suspected it.'

I said, after a moment, 'I think I did.'

'Then, I'm sorry.'

I gave a shrug. 'Well, what does it matter now?'

'You do mean to marry her?'

'Yes, I do.'

'You think a great deal of her?'

'A very great deal. I think a great deal of you all. I hope you know that. You spoke to me once of your fear of being . . . abandoned. Well, in marrying Caroline, I mean not only to care for her, but for you, and the house; for Roderick, too. You've been through some desperate times lately. But, now that you're better, Mrs Ayres, now that you're calmer, more yourself—'

She looked at me, saying nothing. I decided to risk it, and pressed on.

'That time in the nursery,' I said. 'Well, that was a strange thing, wasn't it? A horrible thing! I'm so glad it's all over.'

She smiled—an odd smile, patient and secret. Her high cheeks rose, narrowing her eyes. She straightened up, carefully brushing the snow from her wash-leather gloves.

'Oh, Dr Faraday,' she said, as she did it. 'What a perfect innocent you are.'

She said it so mildly, and with such a touch of indulgence, I almost laughed. But her expression was still an odd one, and I began, without quite knowing why, to be frightened. I rose, hastily and not very gracefully, catching the tail of my overcoat beneath my heels and tipping myself off balance. She had begun to walk away. I caught up with her and touched her arm.

'Wait,' I said. 'What do you mean?'

Her face was turned from mine, and she didn't answer.

I said, 'There haven't been . . . other things? You don't still imagine that—that Susan—?'

'Susan,' she murmured, her face still half hidden from me. 'Susan is with me all the time. She follows me wherever I go. Why, she's here in this garden with us.'

For a second I managed to persuade myself that she was speaking figuratively, that all she meant was that she carried her daughter around with her in her thoughts, in her heart. But then she turned her face back to mine, and her expression had something terrible in it, a mixture of absolute loneliness, huntedness, and fear.

I said, 'For God's sake, why haven't you spoken of this?'

'And have you test me and treat me,' she said, 'and tell me I'm dreaming?'

'But oh, Mrs Ayres, my dear Mrs Ayres, you *are* dreaming. Don't you see?' I took her two gloved hands in mine. 'Look around you! There's no one here. This is all in your mind! Susan *died*. You know that, don't you?'

'Of course I know it!' she said, almost loftily. 'How could I not? My darling died . . . But now she has come back.'

I squeezed her fingers. 'But, how *could* she? How can you think this?

Mrs Ayres, you're a sensible woman. *How* does she come? Tell me. Do you *see* her?'

'Oh, no, I haven't seen her yet. I feel her.'

'You feel her.'

'I feel her, watching. I feel her eyes. They must be her eyes, mustn't they? Her gaze is so strong, her eyes are like fingers; they can touch. They can press and pinch.'

'Mrs Ayres, please stop this.'

'I hear her voice. I don't need tubes and telephones to hear it now. She talks to me.'

'She talks—!'

'She whispers.' She tilted her head, as if listening, then raised her hand. 'She's whispering now.'

There was something horribly uncanny about the intentness of her pose. I said, not quite steadily, 'What is she whispering?'

Her look grew bleak again. 'She says the same things, every time. She says, *Where are you?* She says, *Why won't you come?* She says, *I am waiting.*'

She spoke these words in a whisper of her own; they seemed to hang for a moment in the air, along with the cloudy breath that made them. Then they vanished, eaten up by the silence.

I stood frozen for a moment, not knowing what to do. A few minutes before, the little garden had appeared almost snug to me. Now the small walled patch, with its single narrow exit leading only to another choked and isolated space, seemed filled with menace. The day, as I have said, was a peculiarly still one. No wind disturbed the branches of the trees, no bird rose, even, in the thin, chill air, and if any sound had come, any movement been made, I would have caught it. Nothing changed, nothing at all—and yet, it began to seem to me that something was there in the garden with us, creeping or edging towards us across the crisp, white snow. Worse than that, I had the bizarre impression that this thing, whatever it was, was in some way *familiar*: as if its bashful advance towards us was more properly a *return*. I felt the flesh of my back rise, anticipating a touch—as in a childish game of tig. I drew my hands from hers, and twisted round, looking wildly all about.

The garden was empty, the snow unmarked except by our own foot-prints. But my heart was lurching, my hands trembling. I took off my hat and wiped my face. My brow and lip were sweating, and where the cold air met my flushed wet skin it seemed to burn.

I was just putting my hat back on when I heard Mrs Ayres sharply draw in her breath. I turned back to her, and found her with her gloved hand at her collar, her face creased, her colour rising. I said, 'What is it? What's the matter?' She shook her head and wouldn't answer. But she looked so distressed, I thought of her heart: I plucked her hand back, drew open her scarves and coat. Beneath the coat she had on a cardigan; beneath that, a silk blouse. The blouse was pale, the colour of ivory, and as I watched, incredulous, three small drops of crimson seemed to spring from nowhere to the surface of the silk, and then, like ink on blotting-paper, rapidly to spread. I tugged down the blouse's collar and saw beneath it, on her bare skin, a scratch, quite deep, evi-dently freshly made, still rising, still beading red.

'What have you done?' I said in horror. 'How did you do this?' I looked over her gown, for a pin or a brooch. I caught up her hands, examined her gloves. There was nothing. 'What did you use?'

She dropped her gaze. 'My little girl,' she murmured. 'She's so eager for me to join her. I'm afraid she . . . isn't always kind.'

When I realised what she was saying, I felt sick. I stepped back, away from her. Then, with a further surge of understanding, I caught hold of her hands again and pulled the gloves from them, and roughly pushed up her sleeves. Where the broken window had cut her a few weeks before, the wounds had healed, pink and healthy against the paler skin. Here and there among the scars, however, it seemed to me that I could see new scratches. And one of her arms bore a faint bruise, curiously shaped, as if the flesh had been pinched and twisted by a small, determined hand.

Her gloves had fallen to the ground. Trembling, I picked them up and helped her put them back on. I caught hold of her by the elbow.

'I'm taking you back to the house, Mrs Ayres.'

She said, 'Are you trying to take me away from her? It isn't any use, you know.'

I turned, and shook her. 'Stop it! You hear me? For God's sake, stop saying these things!'

She moved loosely in my arms, and after that I found I didn't quite want to look at her face again. I felt a curious shame about it. I took her wrist, and led her out of the tangled gardens, and she came quite readily. We went past the frozen stable clock, back over the lawns and into the house; I took her straight upstairs, not pausing to remove her outdoor things. Only once we were in the warmth of her own room did I take her coat and hat and snowy shoes, and I put her to sit in her chair beside the fire.

But then I gazed at the things that were near her, the coals in the hearth, the pokers, the tongs, the glass tumblers, the mirrors, the ornaments . . . Everything seemed brutal or brittle, suddenly, and capable of harm. I rang the bell for Betty. The lever moved uselessly in my hand, and I remembered that Caroline had cut the wire. So I went out to the top of the staircase and called and called into the silence, and eventually Betty came.

'Don't be frightened,' I said, before she could speak. 'I want you to keep Mrs Ayres company, that's all.' I set down a chair and led her to it. 'I want you to sit right here and make sure she has everything she needs, while I—'

But the fact is, having got Mrs Ayres this far I didn't know what to do with her. I kept thinking of the snow on the ground outside; of the isolation of the house. If even Mrs Bazeley had been there, I think I should have felt calmer. But with only Betty to help me—! I hadn't even brought my doctor's bag from the car. I had no instruments, no drugs. I stood dithering, almost panicking, while the two women watched.

Then I heard footsteps on the marble floor of the hall downstairs. I went to the door and looked out, and with a rush of relief I saw Caroline, just beginning to mount the stairs. She was unwinding her scarf and drawing off her hat, her brown hair falling down untidily around her shoulders. I called out to her. Startled, she looked up, then came on more hastily.

'What's the matter?'

I said, 'It's your mother. I— Just a moment.'

I hurried back into the bedroom, to Mrs Ayres's side. I took her hand, and spoke as I would to a child or an invalid.

'I'm just going to talk with Caroline for a minute or two, Mrs Ayres. I shall leave the door open, and you must call me—you must call me at once, if anything frightens you. You understand?'

She seemed weary now, and didn't answer. I looked meaningfully at Betty, then went out, and caught hold of Caroline, and took her around the landing to her own room. I left her door ajar, too, and stood with her just inside it.

She said, 'What's happened?'

I put my finger to my lips. 'Speak softly . . . Caroline, my dear, it's your mother. God help me, but I fear I've misjudged her case, misjudged it badly. I'd supposed her showing signs of real improvement. Hadn't you? But what she's just told me— Oh, Caroline. You haven't noticed any changes in her, since I was last here? She hasn't seemed especially troubled, or nervous or afraid?'

She looked bewildered. She saw me moving back to the door to gaze across the landing to her mother's room, and said, 'What is it? Can't I go to her?'

I put my hands on her shoulders. 'Listen,' I said. 'I think she's hurt.'

'Hurt, how?'

'I think she's . . . hurting herself.'

And I told her, as briefly as I could, what had passed between her mother and me out in the walled garden. I said, 'She thinks your sister is with her all the time, Caroline. She sounded terrified! Tormented! She said—she said your sister harms her. I saw a scratch,' I gestured, 'just here, on her collarbone. I don't know how she did it, what she used. But then I looked at her arms, and saw what might have been other cuts and bruises. Have you noticed anything? You must have seen something. Haven't you?'

'Cuts and bruises,' she said, struggling to take the idea in. 'I'm not sure. Mother has always bruised rather easily, I think. And I know the Veronal makes her clumsy.'

'This isn't clumsiness. This is— I'm sorry, my darling. Her mind has gone.'

She looked at me, and her face seemed to close. She turned away. 'Let me see her.'

'Wait,' I said, drawing her back.

She shook me off, suddenly angry. 'You promised me! I told you, weeks ago. I *warned* you that there was something in this house. You laughed at me! And you said that if I did what you told me to do, she'd be all right. Well, I've watched and watched her. I've sat with her, day after day. I've made her take those hateful pills. You promised.'

'I'm sorry, Caroline. I did my best. Her condition was worse than I knew. If we can just watch her a little longer, just for tonight.'

'And what about tomorrow? And the days after that?'

'Your mother has moved beyond ordinary help now. I'll make all the arrangements myself, I promise you that. I'll do it this evening. And tomorrow I'll take her.'

She didn't understand. She shook her head, impatient. 'Take her where? What do you mean?'

'She can't stay here.'

'You mean, like Roddie?'

'I'm afraid it's the only way.'

She put a hand to her forehead and her face convulsed. I thought she was crying. But she'd she started to laugh. The laughter was mirthless, terrible. She said, 'Dear God! How long till it's my turn?'

I took her hand. 'Don't say things like that!'

She moved my fingers to the pulse in her wrist. She said, 'I mean it. Go on, tell me. You're the doctor, aren't you? How long do I have?'

I shook her off. 'Well, not long at all, perhaps, if your mother stays here and something terrible happens! And that's exactly what I'm worried about. Look at the state of you now! How can you possibly cope, you and Betty? It's the only solution.'

'The only solution. Another clinic.'

'Yes.'

'We can't afford it.'

'I'll help with that. I'll find a way. Once we are married—'

'We aren't married yet. God!' She put her hands together. 'Aren't you afraid?'

'Afraid of what?'

'Of the Ayres family taint.'

'Caroline.'

'That's the sort of thing people will say, isn't it? I know there's already talk about Roddie.'

'We're past the point, surely, of minding what people will say!'

'Oh, it can't matter, of course, to someone like *you*.'

She spoke almost savagely. I said, in surprise, 'What do you mean?'

She turned away, confused. 'I just mean that what you're planning, what you want to do to my mother—she would *hate* it. If she were herself again, I mean. Don't you see? When we were children, whenever we were ill, she'd barely let us make a murmur. She said families like ours, they had a—a responsibility, they had to set an example. She said, if we couldn't do that, if we couldn't be better and braver than ordinary people, then what was the point of us? The shame of your taking my brother was bad enough. If you try and take her, too— I don't think she'll let you.'

I said grimly, 'Well, I'm sorry to say she won't have much choice. I'll bring Graham in again. If she acts with him in the way she's acted with me this afternoon, there'll be no question.'

'She'd rather *die*.'

'Well, it may kill her, to leave her here! And on top of that— which worries me more, if I'm brutal about it—it might kill you. I won't put you through it. I hesitated over Roderick and I've always regretted it. I won't make the same mistake again. If I could, I'd take her right now.'

And as I spoke, I gazed over at the windows. The white ground had kept the day light, but the sky was now a darkening zinc grey. Still, I thought seriously of taking her, right there and then. I said, talking it through, 'It could be done, I suppose. I could sedate her. We could manage her, you and I. The snow would hold us up, but we need only get her as far as Hatton, in the first place—'

She said, appalled, 'The county asylum?'

'Just for tonight. Just while I make the arrangements. There are one or two private clinics I think will take her, but they'll want a day's notice at least. She needs to be kept under close observation now. That will complicate things.'

She was looking at me in horror, understanding at last how serious I was. She said, 'You're talking as if she were dangerous.'

'I think she's a danger to herself.'

'If you had let *me* take her away when I wanted to, weeks ago, none of this would have happened. Now you want to bundle her off to the madhouse, like a lunatic on the street!'

'I'm sorry, Caroline. But I know what she told me. I know what I saw. You can't expect me to leave her untreated, surely? You don't actually think I should abandon her to her delusions, purely for the sake of keeping intact some sort of . . . class pride?'

She had put her hands to her face again, her fingers were steepled over her mouth and nose, the tips of them pressing into the inner corners of her eyes. For a moment she gazed at me without speaking. I saw her draw in her breath, and as she released it she seemed to come to some decision. She dropped her hands.

'No,' she said. 'I don't think that. But I won't let you take her to Hatton, for everyone to see. She would never forgive me. You may take her tomorrow, privately. I'll—I'll be used to the idea then.'

I hadn't seen her so certain and determined since the days before Gyp's death. Slightly abashed, I said, 'Very well. But in that case, I'll stay here with you tonight.'

'You needn't do that.'

'I'll be easier in my mind. I'm due on the wards at eight, but for once

I'll cancel. I'll say an emergency's come up. For God's sake, this *is* an emergency.' I looked at my watch. 'I can make my evening surgery and then come back, spend the night here.'

She shook her head. 'I'd rather you didn't.'

'Your mother needs watching, Caroline. Right through the night.'

'I can watch her, can't I? Won't she be safest, with me?'

I opened my mouth to reply, but her question had rung some sort of alarm bell in me, and I realised with a shock that I was thinking of that conversation I'd had with Seeley. I felt a touch of the sick suspicion that had risen in me then. The idea was impossible, grotesque . . . But other grotesque and impossible things had happened, there at Hundreds; and suppose Caroline *was* somehow to blame for them? Suppose, unconsciously, she had given birth to some violent shadowy creature, that was effectively haunting the house? Ought I to leave Mrs Ayres unprotected there, for even one more night?

She was looking at me, waiting, confused by my hesitation. I saw a suspicion begin to creep into her clear, brown eyes.

I shook the madness away. 'All right,' I said. 'She can stay here with you. But don't leave her alone—that's all I ask. And you must telephone me at once if anything happens. Anything at all.'

She said she would. I put my arms around her for a second, then took her across the landing to her mother's room. Mrs Ayres and Betty were sitting exactly as I'd left them, in the thickening gloom. I tried a light-switch, then remembered the silent generator, so took a flame from the fire to a couple of oil-lamps, and drew the curtains. The room at once grew cheerier. Caroline went to her mother's side.

'Dr Faraday tells me you're not very well, Mother,' she said, almost awkwardly. She reached, and tucked back a lock of her mother's greying hair. '*Are* you unwell?'

Mrs Ayres turned up her tired face. 'I suppose I must be,' she said, 'if Doctor says I am.'

'Well, I've come to keep you company. What shall we do? Shall I read to you?'

She caught my eye, and gave me a nod. I left her taking Betty's place in the second armchair. Betty herself I took downstairs. I asked her, as I had asked Caroline, if she hadn't noticed any recent changes in Mrs Ayres's behaviour, and if she hadn't seen any small injuries, scratches, or cuts?

She shook her head, looking frightened. She said, 'Is Mrs Ayres took bad again? Is it—is it starting off again?'

'Nothing's "starting again",' I said. 'I know what you're thinking, and I don't want you saying those things in this house. And you needn't be frit—' I used the Warwickshire word, almost unconsciously. 'This is nothing like what happened before. I just need you to be a good girl for Mrs Ayres, and keep your head, and do everything you're told. And, Betty—' She'd begun to move away. I touched her arm and added quietly, 'Look after Miss Caroline too, won't you? I'm relying on you now. Call me, if things don't seem quite right?'

She nodded, her lips pressed tight, some of her childishness fallen away.

Outside, the snow had lost its dazzle with the darkening of the sky, and the day was even colder; only the energetic trek back up the drive kept the warmth in my limbs, and once I was in my car the chill began to tell on me and I started to shake. The engine, thank God, turned at the first try, and the journey back to Lidcote was slow but uneventful. But I was still shaking as I let myself into my house, still shaking as I stood at the stove, hearing my evening patients gather on the other side of the wall. Only by holding my hands in a stream of what felt like nearly boiling water at the dispensary sink could I draw the cold from them at last and make them steady.

Dealing with a string of routine winter ailments brought me back to myself. As soon as the surgery was over I put through a telephone call to the Hall; and hearing Caroline's clear, strong voice assuring me that all was well calmed me further.

After that I made two more calls.

The first was to a woman I knew up at Rugby, a retired district nurse to whom I occasionally sent private patients as paying guests. She was more used to physical cases than to nervous ones, but she was a capable woman and, after listening to my guarded account of Mrs Ayres's case, said she'd be very willing to take her for the day or two I would need to set up more appropriate care. I told her that, assuming the roads were clear, I would bring the lady to her tomorrow, and we made the appropriate arrangements.

The second call I hesitated over, for I wanted simply to talk the thing through, and by rights I should have turned to Graham for that. But it was Seeley I rang in the end. He was the only man who knew all the details of the case. And it was a great relief to me now to tell him what had happened, mentioning no names on the open line, but making everything clear enough, and hearing his usual genial tone grow very much graver as he took in what I was saying.

'That's bad news,' he said. 'And just as you supposed the whole thing blown over.'

'And you don't,' I asked, 'think I'm acting too hastily?'

'Not at all! Haste is what's needed, by the sound of it.'

'I didn't see much actual evidence that physical harm's been taking place.'

'Did you really need to? The mental aspect is clearly worrying enough. Let's face it, no one wants to take this sort of step with people like that, least of all when there are—well, other involvements. But what's the alternative? Let the delusions run on, get an even stronger hold? Want me to come and back you up in the morning? I will, if you like.'

'No, no,' I said. 'Graham will do it. I just wanted reassurance . . . But Seeley, listen.' He'd been about to ring off. 'There's one more thing. The last time we met. You remember what we talked about?'

He was silent for a second, then said, 'You mean, that guff about Myers?'

'*Was* it guff? You don't think— I have this feeling, Seeley, of danger. I—'

He was waiting. And when I didn't finish, he said firmly, 'You've done everything you can. Don't go troubling yourself now with crazy ideas. Remember what I said to you once before: what's being asked for here, essentially, is attention. It's as simple as that. Our patient may dig in her heels tomorrow when it comes to the crunch. But you'll be giving her what, in her heart, she craves. Get a good night's sleep now, and don't brood on it.'

Had our situations been reversed, I would have said exactly the same to him. But I went upstairs, not quite convinced, and had a drink and a cigarette. I ate my supper without appetite, then headed gloomily off to Leamington.

I got through my hours at the hospital in a state of distraction, and when I drove home, at just before midnight, I was still unhappy. As if the thought of Caroline and her mother were exerting some sort of magnetic pull over me, I inadvertently took the turning away from Lidcote, and was a mile along the Hundreds road before I saw what I had done. The weird pallor of the snowy landscape only added to my unease. I felt odd and conspicuous in my black car. For a moment I actually considered carrying on, going out to the Hall; then I realised that to upset the house by arriving late like that would do no good to anyone. So I turned the car around—looking across the bleached fields as I did it, as if searching for a light or some other impossible signal from Hundreds that all was well.

The telephone call came through next morning, just as I was sitting down to my breakfast after a broken night's sleep. There was nothing at all unusual in my being called at that sort of time; patients often rang me then, wanting to be added to my round. But I was already in a keyed-up state, thinking of the difficult day ahead of me, and I sat tensely, straining to hear, as my housekeeper answered. She came back through to me almost at once, looking puzzled and anxious.

'Excuse me, Doctor,' she said, 'but it's someone wanting to speak to you. I can hardly make her out. But I *think* she said she was calling from over at Hundreds—'

I threw down my knife and fork and ran into the hall.

'Caroline,' I said breathlessly, as I picked up the receiver. 'Caroline, is it you?'

'Doctor?' The line was bad because of the snow, but I could tell at once that the voice was not hers. It was high as a child's, and pinched, with weeping and with panic. 'Oh, Doctor, can you come? I'm to say, will you come? I'm to tell you—'

It was Betty, I realised at last. But her voice reached me as if from an impossible distance, broken up by puffs and squeals. I heard her say again, 'I'm to tell you . . . an accident . . .'

'An accident?' My heart contracted. 'Who's hurt? Is it Caroline? What's happened?'

'Oh, Doctor, it's—'

'For God's sake,' I cried. 'I can hardly hear you! What's the matter?'

Then, in a sudden burst of clarity: 'Oh, Dr Faraday, she told me I wasn't to say!'

And by that, I knew it must be bad.

'All right,' I said. 'I'll come. I'll come, as quickly as I can!'

I went racing down the stairs to my dispensary, to get my bag, and to throw on my hat and overcoat. Mrs Rush followed me anxiously down. She was used to me racing off to bad confinements and other emergencies, but she had never, I suppose, seen me quite as demented as this. The first of my surgery patients would be arriving soon; I called hastily to her that she must tell them to wait, to come back in the evening, to go elsewhere, do anything. She said, 'I will. But, Doctor'— holding out a cup—'you've eaten nothing! Drink your tea, at least.' So I stood for a second longer, gulping the hot tea down, before bowling out of the house and into my car.

It had snowed again in the night, not heavily, but enough to make the drive out to Hundreds a newly treacherous one. Naturally I went too fast, and several times, despite the chains on my tyres, felt the car slip and slide. Had I met another vehicle at those moments I might have added another disaster to that already disastrous day, but as it was, the snow kept other drivers off the roads and I saw almost no one. I looked at my watch as I drove, fretting over the racing minutes. I don't think I ever felt a journey as keenly as I felt that one; I seemed to sweat out the miles as I covered them, yard by yard. And then, at the gates of the park I had to leave the car altogether and go slithering along the drive. In my haste I'd put on my ordinary shoes, and within a minute my feet were soaked and freezing. Half-way along the drive I caught my ankle and turned it, badly, and had to go running on over the pain.

Betty was at the door of the house as, limping and panting, I arrived at it, and I could see at once from her expression that things were quite as bad as I'd feared. When I joined her at the top of the steps she put her hard little hands across her face and burst into tears.

Her helplessness was no use to me. I said impatiently, 'Where do you need me?' She shook her head and couldn't answer. Beyond her, the house was silent. I peered up the staircase. 'Up there? Tell me!' I caught her by the shoulders. 'Where's Caroline? Where's Mrs Ayres?'

She gestured back into the body of the house. I went rapidly along the passage to the door of the little parlour and, finding it ajar, pushed it open, my heart like a hammering fist in my throat.

Caroline was sitting alone on the sofa. I saw her and said, in sick relief, 'Oh, Caroline, thank God! I thought— I don't know what I thought.'

Then I saw how strangely she sat there. She wasn't pale, so much as greyish; but she didn't tremble, she seemed quite calm. She saw me in the doorway and lifted her head, as if mildly interested—no more—by the sight of me.

I went across to her and took her hand and said, 'What is it? What's happened? Where's your mother?'

She said, 'Mother's upstairs.'

'Upstairs, alone?'

I turned. She drew me back. 'It's too late,' she said.

And then, bit by bit, the whole frightful story came out.

She had sat with her mother the day before, it seemed, just as I'd instructed. First she had read aloud to her; then, when Mrs Ayres had begun to doze, she'd put the book aside and had Betty bring her

her sewing. They had sat together like that, companionably, until seven o'clock, when Mrs Ayres went alone to the bathroom. Caroline didn't think she could very well accompany her there, and in fact her mother reappeared, having washed her hands and face, looking 'rather brighter' than before; she even insisted on changing her clothes, putting on a smarter gown for dinner. They took the meal in the little parlour, as they usually did these days. Mrs Ayres's appetite seemed good. Made wary and anxious by me, Caroline watched her very closely, but she seemed 'just her ordinary self'—just the ordinary self, in other words, that she had lately become, 'quite quiet, and tired; distracted but not at all nervous'. When the dinner was cleared away, the two women stayed in the little parlour, listening to a crackling music programme on the house's portable wireless. Betty brought them cocoa at nine o'clock; they read, or sewed, until half past ten. Only then, Caroline said, did her mother grow restless. She went to one of the windows and put back the curtain, and stood looking out at the snow-covered lawn. Once she tilted her head and said, 'Do you hear that, Caroline?' Caroline, however, could hear nothing. Mrs Ayres remained at the window until the draught drove her back to the fire. The fit of restlessness, apparently, had passed; she spoke of ordinary things and her voice was steady, again she seemed 'just herself'.

So calm did she appear, in fact, that at bedtime Caroline was almost embarrassed to insist on sitting with her in her room. She said it made her mother unhappy, too, to see her settling down with a blanket in the not very comfortable armchair, while she herself lay alone in the bed. But, 'Dr Faraday says I must,' she told her mother, and her mother smiled.

'You might be married already.'

'Hush, Mother,' said Caroline, self-conscious. 'How silly you are.'

She had given her mother a Veronal to take, and the drug acts swiftly; Mrs Ayres was asleep within minutes. Caroline tiptoed over to her once, to make sure she was warmly covered by her blankets, then she settled down again as best she could on the uncomfortable chair. She'd brought up a flask of tea with her, and kept a dim lamp burning, and was content enough, for the first couple of hours, with her novel. But when her eyes began to smart she closed the book, and smoked a cigarette, and simply watched her mother sleep; and then, with nothing to check them, her thoughts became gloomy. She pictured all that was to happen the following day, all I planned to do, bringing in David Graham, taking her mother away . . . My anxiety and sense of urgency had impressed and frightened her, before. Now she began to doubt me. Those old ideas rose up in her, about the house—about there being something in it, or something that came to it, that wished her family harm. She looked through the shadows at her mother, lying slackly in her bed, and she said to herself: 'Surely he's wrong. He has to be wrong. In the morning I'll tell him. I won't let him take her, not like that. It's too cruel. I'll—I'll take her myself. I'll go away with her, right away. It's this house that's hurting her. I'll take her away, and she'll recover. I'll take Roddie, too—!'

Her thoughts ran wildly like that, until her head began to feel like an engine, churning and hot. By now, several hours had passed: she looked at her watch and found that it was almost five, well past the dead point of the night, but still an hour or two from daybreak. She needed the lavatory, and she wanted to wash and cool her face. Her mother was apparently still deeply asleep, so she went around the landing, past the shut door of Betty's room, to the bathroom. Then, her flask of tea finished and her eyes still sore, she thought to calm herself down and keep herself awake by smoking another cigarette. The packet in her cardigan pocket was empty, but she knew there was another in the drawer of her bedside table; and since she could see very clearly across the well of the staircase into her mother's room, she went into her own room, sat on her bed, got a cigarette out, and lit it. To make herself more comfortable she just kicked off her shoes and raised her legs, so that she was sitting against her pillow with the ashtray in her lap. Her bedroom door was wide open, and the view across the landing was a very clear one. She kept impressing this fact on me, when we talked about it later. By turning her head, she said, she could actually see, through the dimness, the footboard of her mother's bed. The house was so still, she could even hear the steady gentle push and draw of her mother's breaths . . .

The next thing she knew, Betty was at her side with the breakfast tray. There was a tray for Mrs Ayres, too, sitting out on the landing. Betty wanted to know what she ought to do with it.

'What?' asked Caroline thickly. She had woken from the deepest phase of sleep, unable to understand why she was on her bed rather than in it, fully dressed, very chilled, with a spilling ashtray in her lap. She propped herself up, and rubbed her face. 'Take the tray in to my mother, can't you? But if she's asleep, don't wake her. Leave it for her beside her bed.'

'That's just it, miss,' said Betty. 'I think madam must still be asleep, for I've knocked and I've got no answer. And I can't take it in; the door's locked.'

At that, Caroline woke properly. Glancing at the clock, she saw that it was just after eight. The day was bright beyond the curtain—unnaturally bright, because of the snowy ground. Alarmed, queasy, trembling with lack of sleep, she rose and went rapidly around the landing to her mother's room. Just as Betty had claimed, its door was closed and locked, and when she tapped on the door—lightly at first, but then more firmly, as her anxiety mounted—she received no answer.

'Mother!' she called. 'Mother, are you awake?'

Still no reply. She beckoned to Betty. Could she hear anything? Betty listened, then shook her head. Caroline said, 'She might, I suppose, be sleeping too deeply. But then, the door— It was closed when you got up?'

'Yes, miss.'

'But I know I remember—I'm *sure* I remember—that both the doors were open. We don't have a spare key for this, do we?'

'I don't think so, miss.'

'No, neither do I. Oh, God! Why the hell did I leave her?'

Trembling harder, she knocked on the door again, louder than before. Again no answer. But then she thought to do what Mrs Ayres herself had recently done when faced with an inexplicably locked door:

she stooped, and put her eye to the keyhole. And she was reassured
to see that the keyhole was empty, and the room beyond it quite light.
For, not unnaturally, she took this to mean that her mother was not in
the room at all. She must have locked the door when she left it, and
taken the key away with her. Why would she have done that? Caroline couldn't imagine. She got to her feet and, with more confidence
than she felt, she said, 'I don't think my mother's in there, Betty. She
must be somewhere in the house. I suppose you've been in the little
parlour?'

'Oh, yes, miss. I've been and laid the fire in there.'

'She couldn't be down in the library, I suppose. And she wouldn't
have gone upstairs—would she?'

She and Betty gazed at each other, both thinking back to that horrible incident of a few weeks before.

'I'd better go up and take a look,' said Caroline at last. 'Wait here
for me.—No, on second thoughts, don't wait here. Check all the rooms
on this floor, and then check downstairs. My mother might have had
some accident.'

They went off in separate directions, Caroline running upstairs, then
laboriously trying every door, and calling out. The shady corridors
didn't frighten her. She found the nurseries, as I had, bleak but lifeless,
and quite empty. Defeated, she returned to the door of her mother's
room. A moment later Betty joined her. She had also found nothing.
She had tried every room—and she had looked from the windows, too,
in case Mrs Ayres had gone outside. There were no new footprints in
the snow, she said; and madam's coat, she added, was still on its peg in
the porch, and her boots were dry on the rack.

Caroline began to bite nervously at the tips of her fingers. Again she
rattled the handle of her mother's door, and knocked and called. Again,
nothing.

'God!' she said. 'This is no good. My mother *must* have gone outside. She must have gone before this latest fall of snow covered up her
footprints.'

'Without her coat and her boots?' asked Betty, in horror.

Again they looked at each other; then they turned, and hurried down the stairs, and drew back the bolts of the front door. The whiteness of the day almost blinded them, but they went, as quickly as they could, across the gravel, then right along the south terrace to the steps that led down to the lawn. Here, dazzled and frustrated by the unbroken blanket of snow with which the lawn was covered, Caroline came to a halt, and peered across the garden. She cupped her hands to her mouth, calling, 'Mother! Mother, are you there?'

'Mrs Ayres!' called Betty. 'Madam! Mrs Ayres!'

They listened, and heard nothing.

'We might try the old gardens,' said Caroline then, moving forward again. 'My mother was there yesterday with Dr Faraday. I don't know, perhaps she took it into her head to go back.'

But as she spoke, her eye was caught by a small imperfection in the snow ahead of her; and warily, she moved towards it. Something had fallen there, some small metal object: she thought at first that it must be a coin, then realised as she drew closer that what she'd mistaken for a tilted shilling was actually the glittering oval end of a long-stemmed key. It was the key—she knew it had to be—to her mother's locked room, but how it had dropped or tumbled there, into that unmarked stretch of snow, she couldn't imagine. She could only think, for one wild moment, that it had slipped from the beak of a bird, and she lifted her eyes and turned her head, in search of a magpie or a crow. What her gaze met instead were the windows of her mother's bedroom. One was closed, its curtains shut. The other was open—wide open to the frosty air. And her heart, at the sight of it, seemed to die in her breast. For suddenly she knew that the key was here because her mother herself, after locking her door from the inside, had thrown it out. She knew that her mother was still in her room, and did not want to be easily found; and she guessed why.

She ran, then—just as, soon, I myself would be running—ran awkwardly back through the powdery snow, catching hold of a startled Betty and taking her with her, pulling her into the house and up the stairs. The key was as cold as an icicle in her fingers as she fitted it into the lock. Her hand was trembling so violently that, for a second, the metal wouldn't catch, and her leaden heart gave a desperate kick: she thought that, after all, she had made a mistake, the key was the wrong one, not her mother's at all . . . But then the lock shifted. She caught hold of the handle and pushed at the door. She felt it open an inch or two and then stop, as something behind it, something heavy and resisting, got in its path.

'For God's sake, help me!' she cried, in a terribly broken voice, and Betty moved forward to push the door with her, until it had opened just far enough for them to be able to put in their heads and look behind it. What they saw made them both cry out. It was Mrs Ayres, slumped and ungainly, her head lolling, her pose queer, as if she had sunk to her knees in a sort of half-faint just inside the threshold. Her face was hidden by her loose greying hair, but as they pushed the door further, her head moved slackly to the side. Then they could see what she had done.

She had hanged herself, with the cord of her dressing-gown, from an old brass hook on the back of the door.

There followed several ghastly minutes as they tried to release her, to warm and revive her. The cord was drawn so tightly by her weight they couldn't unknot it. Betty had to run for scissors, and when she returned, with kitchen shears, they found the blades of them so dull they could only saw away at the thickly braided silk until it frayed, and then they had literally to prise the cord away from the swollen flesh of her throat. There is a particular horror to the appearance of a hanged person, and Mrs Ayres looked dreadful, bloated and dark. She'd clearly been dead for some time—her body was already cool—and yet, according to Betty when I spoke to her later that day, Caroline bent over her, shaking and chiding her—not speaking gently or sorrowfully but telling her, almost playfully, that she must wake up, must pull herself together.

'She didn't know what she were saying, sir,' Betty said, sitting at the kitchen table and wiping her eyes. 'She went on shaking and shaking her, until I said perhaps we ought to get her up on to the bed. So between us we lifted madam up—' She covered her face. 'Oh, my God, it were awful! She kept slipping out of our arms, and every time she did Miss Caroline told her not to be silly, speaking just as she would've if madam had done some ordinary thing like—like losing her glasses. We got her lying down, and she looked worse than ever with the white pillow by her head, but still Miss Caroline was acting like she couldn't see it. So I said, "Oughtn't we to send for someone, miss? Oughtn't we to send for Dr Faraday?" And she said, "Yes, go and telephone for Doctor! He'll see my mother's all right." Then, as I was going out the door, she calls after me in a different voice: "Don't you tell him, mind, what's been done! Not over the telephone! Mother wouldn't want everyone hearing that! Say there's been an accident!"

'And after that, you see, Doctor, she must have thought about what she'd said. When I went back in she were sitting down quietly at the side of the bed, and she just looked at me and she said, "She's dead, Betty"—as if I might not've knowed it. I said, "Yes, miss, I know, and I'm ever so sorry." And we just stopped there, the two of us, not knowing what else we should do . . . But then I got frit. I got frit terrible. I pulled on Miss Caroline's arm, and she rose to her feet like she were dreaming. We went out together, and I shut the door and turned the key. And it seems an awful thing to have done, to have left Mrs Ayres lying in there all on her own. She were such a kind lady, she were always nice to me . . . And then it come to me how, just a bit before, we had been standing there in front of her door, wondering where she could be, not thinking anything of it, and peeping through the keyhole, when all the time— Oh!' She began to cry again. 'Why would she have done such a horrible thing to herself, Dr Faraday? Why would she?'

It was a good hour or so after I'd arrived at the house that she told me all this, and by then I had been up to Mrs Ayres's room myself. I had to nerve myself to go in there, standing at the door with my hand on the key. I, too, kept thinking of Caroline having been there before me, pushing the door and finding it blocked . . . My first sight of Mrs Ayres's swollen, darkened face made me shudder; but worse was to come, for when I opened up her nightgown in order to examine her body, I found a score of little cuts and bruises, apparently all over her torso and limbs. Some were new, some almost faded. Most were simple scratches and nips. But one or two, I saw with horror, had the appearance almost of *bites*. The freshest, still smeared with blood, had clearly been made very shortly before her death—in other words, in that relatively brief space of time between Caroline's having left her at five o'clock and Betty's appearance with the breakfast tray at eight. What terror and despair must have gripped her in those three dark hours, I couldn't imagine. The Veronal should have kept her sleeping long past the point of Caroline's departure; instead, somehow, she had woken, had risen, had calculatedly closed and locked her bedroom door and disposed of the key, and begun the systematic business of torturing herself to death.

Then I found myself recalling our conversation in the walled garden. I remembered those three springing drops of blood. *My little girl, she isn't always kind . . .* Was it possible? Was it? Or was it even worse than that? Suppose, in willing her daughter to come, she had only given strength and purpose to some other, darker thing?

I couldn't bear to think of it. I drew up the blanket, to put her from my sight. Like Betty, I found myself overcome by a strong, almost guilty desire to get away from the room and the horrors it suggested.

I locked the door and went back down to the little parlour. I found Caroline still sitting blankly on the sofa; Betty had brought in tea, but the tea was cold in its cups, and the girl herself was moving between that room and the kitchen as if sleepwalking through the motions of her ordinary chores. I put her to make coffee, and when I had drunk a strong cup of that, I went slowly out to the hall to use the telephone.

It was like a nightmarish echo of the previous evening. First I called the district hospital, to arrange for a mortuary van to be sent for Mrs Ayres's body. Then, with more reluctance, I rang the local police sergeant, to report the death. I gave the man the barest details, and arranged for him to come and take statements. And then I made my third and final call.

It was to Seeley. I caught him just at the end of his morning surgery.

The line was bad, but I was glad of the crackles. I'd heard his voice and for a moment my own had faltered.

I said, 'It's Faraday. I'm out at the house. Our patient, Seeley. I'm afraid she's beaten us.'

'Beaten us?' He couldn't hear, or didn't understand. Then he caught his breath. 'Hell! I don't believe it. How was it done?'

'A bad way. I can't say.'

'Of course you can't . . . God, this is terrible. After everything else!'

'Yes, I know. But, look here, the reason I'm calling: that Rugby woman I told you about; the nurse. Do me a favour, will you? Call her for me, and explain what's happened? I can't do it.'

'Yes, of course.'

I gave him the number; we spoke for another minute or two. He said again, 'A bloody awful business for the family—what's left of it. And for you, Faraday! I'm so sorry.'

'It's my fault,' I said. The line was still crackling and he thought he'd misheard me. I said it again. I said, 'I should have taken her. I had my chance.'

'What? You're not seriously blaming yourself! Come on, now. We've all seen this. When a patient has made up their mind to it, there's very little one can do to stop them. They become devious, you know that. Come on, man.'

'Yes,' I said. 'I suppose so.'

But I was unconvinced by my own words. And when I had returned the ear-piece to the stand, I glanced up through the curve of the staircase to Mrs Ayres's door, and I found I had almost to creep abjectly away with my eyes lowered and my head bowed.

I rejoined Caroline in the little parlour and sat beside her, holding her hand. Her fingers were as chill and anonymous in mine as those of a wax mannequin; I gently raised them to my lips, and she made no response. She only tilted her head as if listening for something. That made me listen, too. We sat with frozen gestures—she with her inclined head, me with her hand still raised to my mouth—but the Hall was soundless. There wasn't so much as the ticking of a clock. Life seemed held, arrested inside it.

She caught my eye and said quietly, 'You feel it? The house is still at last. Whatever it was that was here, it has taken everything it wanted. And do you know what the worst thing is? The thing I shan't forgive it for? It made me help it.'

THIRTEEN

B ut that was all she would say on the matter. The police and the
mortuary men arrived, and while the body was removed from
the house, our statements—hers, mine, and Betty's—were taken
down. When the men had left, she stood blankly again for a moment,
but then, like a puppet being twitched into life, she seated herself at the
writing-table and began to make a list of all the things that must be
done in the days ahead; on a separate sheet she wrote the names of the
friends and relations who ought to be notified of her mother's death. I
wanted her to leave it all until later; she shook her head, working dog-
gedly on, and I realised at last that the chores were protecting her from
the worst of her own shock, and were perhaps the best thing for her. I
made her promise she would rest soon, take a sedative and go to bed,
and I took a tartan blanket from the sofa and tucked it round her to
keep her warm. I left the house to the thud of closing shutters and the
rattle of curtain-rings: she had sent Betty to darken the rooms, in an
old-fashioned gesture of grief and respect. As I crossed the gravel I
heard the last of the shutters being closed, and when I looked back at

the Hall from the mouth of the drive it appeared to be gazing, sightless with grief, across the hushed white landscape.

I didn't want to leave the house at all, but I had some dreary duties of my own now, and I drove, not home, but into Leamington, to discuss Mrs Ayres's death with the borough coroner. I'd realised already that there was no concealing the facts of the case, no way of passing the death off, as I'd now and then done for other grieving families, as a natural one; but since I had effectively been treating Mrs Ayres for mental instability, and had already seen evidence of self-violence, I had an ill-formed hope that I could save Caroline from the ordeal of an inquest. The coroner, however, though sympathetic, was a scrupulous man. The death had been sudden and violent; he would do his best to keep it a muted affair, but an inquest had to be held.

'That means a post-mortem, too, of course,' he said to me. 'And since you're the notifying doctor, ordinarily I'd instruct you to carry it out yourself. Think you're up to it, though?' He knew about my connection with the family. 'There'd be no shame at all in your handing the task on.'

For a second or two I considered it. I have never relished post-mortems, and they are especially hard to perform when the patient in question has been a personal friend. At the same time, I thought of giving Mrs Ayres's poor marked body over to Graham, or to Seeley, and my mind revolted from it. It seemed to me that I had let her down badly already; if there was no way of sparing her this final indignity, then the least I could do was to see the thing through myself, and see it done gently. So I shook my head and told him I would manage. And as it was now well past noon, with my morning surgery irrecoverable and the afternoon stretching blankly before me, when I left the coroner's office I went straight to the mortuary, to get the examination over with as quickly as I could.

It was a horrible business all the same, and I stood in the freezing white-tiled room with the covered body before me, the instruments waiting in the tray, wondering if I could really go through with it. Only once I had put back the sheet did I start to regain my nerve. The injuries were less shocking now that I knew what to expect; those nips and cuts, which had so unnerved me out at Hundreds, began, on inspection, to lose some of their horror. I had supposed them to have covered almost Mrs Ayres's entire body; now I saw that most were located on areas that had been well within her own reach—her back, for example, being unmarked. What harm she had suffered, she had plainly caused herself: that was a relief to me, though I didn't quite know why. I pressed on, and began the incisions . . . I expected secrets, I think; but no secrets came. There were no signs of illness, only the mundane deteriorations of age. There was no evidence that any sort of force had been used against Mrs Ayres in her final days or hours; no damaged bones or internal bruising. Death was plainly the result of asphyxiation by hanging, completely compatible with the facts as Caroline and Betty had described them to me.

Once again, I found myself relieved; this time the feeling was unmistakable. And I realised I had had a darker reason for wanting to perform the post-mortem myself. I had been afraid of some detail emerging that would throw suspicion—I didn't know what, I didn't know how exactly—on Caroline. I had still had that niggling doubt about her. Now, finally, the doubt was dispelled. I was ashamed I'd ever entertained it.

I restored the body as best I could, and passed my report on to the coroner. The inquest was held three days later, but with the evidence so pointed, it was a very summary affair. The verdict returned was 'suicide whilst the balance of mind was disturbed', and the whole process took less than thirty minutes. The worst thing was the public nature of it all, for though the crowd was kept quite small, several newspaper-men were present and they made rather a nuisance of themselves as I took Caroline and Betty away from the court. The story appeared that week in all the Midland papers, and was swiftly taken up by a couple of nationals. One reporter came up from London and drove out to the Hall, wanting to interview Caroline, and passing himself off as a policeman in order to do it. She and Betty managed to get rid of him without too much trouble, but the thought of that kind of thing happening again appalled me. Remembering the time when the park had been briefly barricaded against the Baker-Hydes, I resurrected those chains and padlocks and refastened the gates. I left one of the keys at the Hall, and kept the other on my own key-chain; I had a duplicate cut from the key to the garden door, too. After that, I felt happier, and could come and go from the house as I needed.

Not surprisingly, Mrs Ayres's suicide shocked and stunned the whole district. She had rarely been seen outside of Hundreds in recent years, but she was still a very well-known and well-liked figure, and for many days I couldn't walk through any of the villages without someone stopping me, keen to hear my side of the story, but also wanting to say how upset and sorry and disbelieving they were, that 'such a lovely lady', 'such a real old-fashioned lady', 'so handsome and kind', should have done a dreadful thing like that—'leaving those two poor children, too'. Many people asked where Roderick was and when he would be coming home. I said he was holidaying with friends, and his sister was trying to get hold of him. Only to the Rossiters and the Desmonds did I give a truer account, for I didn't want them bothering Caroline with difficult questions. I told them frankly that Rod was in a nursing home, being treated for a breakdown.

Helen Desmond said at once, 'But this is terrible! I can't believe it! Why didn't Caroline come to us sooner? We guessed the family was in trouble, but they seemed bent on managing things by themselves. Bill offered them help many times, you know, and they always refused. We thought it simply a question of money. If we had known things were so bad—'

I said, 'I don't think any of us could have predicted this.'

'But what's to be done? Caroline can't possibly stay out there now, in that great big unhappy house. She should be with friends. She should come here, to Bill and me. Oh, that poor, poor girl. Bill, we must go and get her.'

'Of course we must,' said Bill.

They were ready to leave for the Hall at once. The Rossiters were exactly the same. But I wasn't sure Caroline would welcome the inter-ference, however well meant. I asked them to let me speak to her about it first; and, as I'd suspected, when I told her what they wanted for her, she shuddered.

'It's very kind of them,' she said. 'But the idea of being in someone else's house, with people watching, every minute, to see how I am— I just couldn't. I should be afraid of seeming too unhappy; or else of not seeming unhappy enough. I'd rather stay here, at least for now.'

'Are you sure, Caroline?'

Like everyone else, I felt terribly uneasy at the thought of her there, alone in that house, with only poor, sad Betty for company. But she seemed very resolved to stay, so I went back to the Desmonds and the Rossiters, and this time when I spoke to them I made it plainer that Caroline was not quite as lonely and unsupported as they feared; that she was being pretty well cared for, in fact, by me. After a moment of misunderstanding, they took the hint, looking surprised. The Desmonds were quickest to congratulate me; they said it was by far the best thing that could happen to Caroline now, and 'a huge weight off their minds'. The Rossiters, though polite, were more wary. Mr Rossiter shook my hand amiably enough, but I could see his wife rapidly thinking the whole thing through, and I learned later that as soon as I left their house she called Caroline up, to have the story confirmed. Caught off guard, distracted, tired, Caroline had little to say. Yes, I was being a great help to her. Yes, a wedding was planned. No, we had no date for it. She couldn't give it much thought yet. Everything was 'too un-settled'.

But after that, at least, there were no more attempts to persuade her from the house, and the Desmonds and the Rossiters must have quietly passed on news of our engagement to one or two of their neighbours, who must just as discreetly have passed it on to their own friends. Over the next few days I sensed the slightest of shifts in the district's attitude towards me; I began to be treated less as the Ayres family physician, who might be companionably pumped for information about that dreadful business out at Hundreds, and more almost as a member of the family itself, worthy of respect and commiseration. The only person I spoke to directly about it was David Graham, and he was absolutely delighted by the news. He had 'known there was something afoot', he said, for months. Anne had 'scented it out', but they hadn't liked to press me. He only wished it hadn't taken such a tragedy to bring it all into the open . . . He insisted that Caroline be my priority for a while, arranging for the easing of my case-load, taking some of the patients himself. So in that first week after the death I spent a good part of each day at the Hall, helping Caroline with her various chores; sometimes going for gentle walks with her in the gardens or the park, sometimes simply sitting with her in silence, holding her hand. She still gave the impression of being slightly insulated from her own grief, but I think my visits provided a structure for her patternless days. She never spoke about the house; but the house, oddly enough, continued to feel strikingly calm. Over the past few months I had watched life in it dwindle to what had felt like almost impossible proportions; now, astonishingly, it dwindled further, became a matter of murmurs and quiet footsteps in two or three dim rooms.

With the inquest out of the way, the next ordeal was the funeral. Caroline and I arranged it together, and it took place on the Friday of the following week. Given the nature of her mother's death, we both agreed that the event should be a subdued one; our biggest dilemma at first was whether or not to involve Rod. It seemed out of the question that he should miss it, and we gave much serious thought as to how his presence could be managed—wondering, for example, if he mightn't come down from Birmingham in the company of a male attendant, who could be passed off as a friend. But we might have saved ourselves the debate: I myself drove up to the clinic to break the news of his mother's suicide, and his reaction horrified me. The loss itself he seemed hardly to register. It was the fact of her death that impressed him. For he saw it as evidence that she, too, had finally fallen victim to that diabolical 'infection' he had struggled so hard to contain.

'It must have been waiting,' he said to me, 'all this time; breeding, in the quiet of the house. I thought I'd beaten it! But you see what it's doing?' He reached across the table to grip my arm. 'No one's safe there now! Caroline— My God! You mustn't leave her there alone. She's in danger! You must get her away! You must get her right away, from Hundreds!'

Just for a moment, I was unnerved; the warning almost rang true to me. Then I caught the wildness in his eye, and saw how far beyond the reach of reason he had strayed—and realised that I was at risk of following him. I spoke calmly and rationally to him. That made his manner grow even wilder. A couple of nurses came running to restrain him, and I left him struggling and shouting in their arms. To Caroline I said only that he was 'no better'. She could see from my expression what that meant. We gave up as hopeless our idea of his returning to Hundreds even for a day, and, with the Desmonds' and Rossiters' help, we put out the story that he was abroad, and unwell, and unable to make the journey home. How much anyone was really deceived by that, I don't know. I think rumours as to the real nature of his absence had been circulating for some time.

Anyway, the funeral went ahead without him, and it went about as well, I suppose, as such a thing could. The coffin left from the Hall, Caroline and I followed the hearse in the undertaker's car, and in the three or four cars that came after us there rode the closest family friends, and those relations who had been able to make the difficult journey up to Hundreds from Sussex and Kent. The weather had lifted properly now, but the last of the snow was still on the ground; the black cars looked grimly impressive in the leafless white lanes, and all our attempts to keep the affair a low-key one came to nothing, after all. The family was too well known, and the local feudal spirit too resilient; on top of that, there had always been more than a touch of tragic mystery to Hundreds Hall, and the newspaper coverage of Mrs Ayres's death had only intensified it. At the gates of farms and cottages people had gathered in solemn curiosity to see the coffin go by, and once we turned into Lidcote High Street we found the pavements crowded with watchers, falling silent as we approached, the men removing their hats and caps, a few of the women crying, but all of them craning for a better view. I thought of the time, nearly thirty years before, when I had stood beside my parents in my College blazer to watch another Ayres funeral, its coffin half the size of this one; I thought it with an almost giddy feeling, as if my life were twisting round its head to snap at its own tail. As we approached the church the crowd grew thicker, and I felt Caroline tense. I took her black-gloved hand and said quietly, 'They want to show their respect, that's all.'

She raised her other hand to her face, trying to escape from their gazes.

'They're all looking at me. What are they looking for?'

I squeezed her fingers. 'Be brave.'

'I don't know if I can be.'

'Yes, you can. Look at me. I'm here. I shan't leave you.'

'No, don't leave me!' she said, turning her face to me, gripping my hand as if the idea startled her.

The church bell was tolling as we crossed the churchyard, unnaturally loud and plaintive in the crisp, windless air. Caroline kept her head lowered, her arm linked heavily with mine, but once we had entered the church itself she grew calmer, for then it was simply a question of getting through the service, making the correct responses and so on, and she did that in the efficient, perfunctory way she had done all the other tasks and duties of the past few days. She even joined in with the hymns. I had never heard her sing before. She sang as she spoke, tunefully, the words coming clean and whole from her well-shaped mouth.

The service was not a long one, but the vicar, Mr Spender, had known Mrs Ayres for many years, and gave a feeling little speech about her. He called her 'an old-fashioned lady'—just the phrase I'd heard other people use. He said she was 'part of a different, more gracious age', as if she'd been rather older than she was, almost the last of her generation. He remembered the death of her daughter, Susan; he was sure, he said, that most of us remembered it, too. Mrs Ayres, he reminded us, had walked behind her child's coffin that day, and it seemed to him that, in her heart, she must have continued to walk behind it every day of her life. Our consolation now, in the tragedy of her death, was to know that she had joined it.

I glanced across the congregation as he spoke, and saw many people nodding sadly at his words. None of them, of course, had seen Mrs Ayres in her final few weeks, when she had been in the grip of a delusion so powerful, so grotesque, it had seemed almost to cast a spell of gloom and torment over the solid inanimate objects around her. But as we made our way out to the churchyard, to the opened family plot, it seemed to me that perhaps Spender was right. There was no spell, there was no shadow, there was no kind of mystery. Things were very simple. Caroline stood beside me, blameless; Hundreds, a thing of brick and mortar, was blameless too; and Mrs Ayres, unhappy Mrs Ayres, was to be reunited with her lost little girl at last.

The prayers were said, the coffin was lowered, and we moved away from the grave. People began to approach Caroline, wanting to exchange a few words of condolence with her. Jim Seeley and his wife shook her hand. They were followed by Maurice Babb, the builder, and then by Graham and Anne. They stayed with her for several minutes, and while they spoke I saw that Seeley had hung back and was looking my way. After a slight hesitation I stepped aside to join him.

'A grim day,' he murmured. 'How's Caroline holding up?'

I said, 'All things considered, pretty well. A bit withdrawn, that's all.'

He gazed over at her. 'Bound to be. I expect it's now she'll start to feel it. But you're looking after her.'

'I am.'

'Yes, other people have commented on that. I think I'm to congratulate you, in fact?'

I said, 'It hardly feels like a day for congratulation, but'—inclining my head, pleased and self-conscious—'yes.'

He tapped my arm. 'I'm glad for you.'

'Thanks, Seeley.'

'Caroline, too. God knows, she deserves her bit of happiness. If you take my advice, you won't hang about, the pair of you, once this is all out of the way. Get her away, give her a nice honeymoon. A fresh start and so on.'

'I intend to,' I said.

'Good man.'

His wife called to him. Caroline turned as if looking for me, and I went back to her side. Her arm moved heavily through mine again, and I wished with all my heart that I could simply take her home to Hundreds and see her safely to her bed. But a party of people had been invited to the Hall for the obligatory drinks, and there followed a trying few minutes as we worked out who could travel with whom, who might be squeezed into the undertakers' vehicles and who could share a private car. Seeing Caroline growing anxious about it, I sent her off in the care of her Sussex uncle and aunt, and I ran to fetch my own Ruby, which had room for myself and three passengers. I was joined by the Desmonds, and by a stray young man with a slight look of Roderick about him, who turned out to be Caroline's cousin on her father's side. He was a nice boy, sympathetic, but clearly not overly affected by Mrs Ayres's death, for he kept up a light flow of conversation with us all the way to Hundreds. He hadn't visited the Hall in more than ten years, and seemed naively pleased to have this chance to see the place again. He had used to come up here with his parents, he said, and had many happy memories of the house, the gardens, the park . . . He only fell silent as we started to bump our way along the tangled drive. When we broke free of the laurel and nettle and drew up on the sweep of gravel, I saw him looking at the blind-eyed house as if he couldn't believe it.

'You find it changed, I'm afraid?' Bill Desmond said to him, as the four of us climbed out.

'Changed!' the boy said. 'I wouldn't have known it as the same place! It looks like something from a horror film. No wonder my aunt—' He bit off the words, embarrassed, his young cheek flaring.

But as we joined the small crowd of mourners making their way to

the little parlour, I could see other people looking around, clearly thinking the same thing. There were about twenty-five of us: too many, really,
for the room, but there was simply nowhere else we could have gathered,
and Caroline had made extra space by pushing back the furniture—
unfortunately, in the process, exposing the worst of the threadbare carpets and the rips and wear in the furniture itself. To some of the guests I
suppose this looked no worse than eccentric, but to anyone who had
known the Hall in its grander days the house's decline must have been
shocking. Caroline's Sussex aunt and uncle, in particular, had already had
a good look round. They had seen the saloon, with its sagging ceiling and
its torn wallpaper, and the blackened ruin that had once been Roderick's
room; and they had gazed across the unkempt park at the breach in the
wall and at the red council houses that seemed to have sprung up inside
it like so many toadstools. They still looked stunned. Like the Desmonds
and the Rossiters, they thought it out of the question that Caroline should
remain at the Hall alone. When I went in, they had drawn her aside and
were trying to persuade her to return with them to Sussex that afternoon.
She was shaking her head.

'I can't think about leaving just yet,' I heard her say. 'I can't think
about anything yet.'

'Well, all the more reason for us to look after you, surely?'

'Please—'

She tucked back her hair, her fingers clumsy, the hair separating into
strands across her cheek. She was dressed in a plain black gown and
her throat was exposed, so pale one could see the veins in it, blue as
bruises. 'Please don't go on about it,' she was saying, as I went over to
her side. 'I know you're only trying to be kind.'

I touched her arm, and she turned to me, grateful. She said in a
softer voice, 'You're here. Has everyone arrived?'

'Yes,' I said gently, 'everyone's here, you mustn't worry. Everything's
fine. Would you like a drink, something to eat?'

The table had a spread of sandwiches on it. Betty was beside it, filling plates, pouring drinks, her cheek almost as white as Caroline's and

her eyes red. She hadn't come to the funeral; she had stayed here, getting things ready.

Caroline shook her head as if the idea of food made her queasy. 'I'm not hungry.'

'I think a glass of sherry would do you good.'

'No, not even that. But perhaps, my aunt and uncle—?'

The aunt and uncle, for the moment, seemed relieved that I had arrived. I had been introduced to them before the funeral as the family doctor; we had spoken a little about Mrs Ayres's illness, and about Roderick's, and I think they had been glad to see how closely I was keeping at Caroline's side—for, not unnaturally, they supposed my presence to be a mainly professional one, and Caroline looked so desperately tired and pale. Now the aunt said, 'Doctor, do back us up. It would be different if Roderick were here. But Caroline can't stay on in this great house all by herself. We want her to come to Sussex with us.'

'And what does Caroline want?' I said.

The woman drew in her chin. She resembled her sister, Mrs Ayres, but was built on a larger, less charming scale. She said, 'All things considered, I don't think Caroline is in much of a position to know what she wants! She's dropping on her feet. Surely a change of scene can only be good for her. As her doctor, you must agree.'

'As her doctor,' I said, 'I probably do. In other respects—well, I'm afraid I shouldn't be at all happy to see Caroline leave Warwickshire just now.'

I smiled as I said this, and returned my hand to Caroline's arm. Caroline shifted, conscious of the pressure of my fingers, but I think most of what had been said had passed her by; she was gazing around the room, anxious that all was as it should be. I saw her aunt's expression change. There was a pause. Then she said, in a slightly crisper tone, 'I'm afraid I've forgotten your name, Doctor.'

I repeated it. She said, 'Faraday . . . No, I don't believe my sister ever mentioned you.'

I said, 'I don't imagine she did. But we were talking about Caroline, I think?'

'Caroline's in a rather vulnerable state.'

'I quite agree with you.'

'When I think of her here, alone and friendless—'

'But she's hardly that. Look about you: she has many friends. More, I think, than she would have in Sussex.'

The woman gazed at me, frustrated. She turned to her niece.

'Caroline, do you truly want to stay here? I shan't be easy about it, you know. If anything should happen to you, your uncle and I would never forgive ourselves.'

'Happen to me?' said Caroline, puzzled, her attention drawn back to us. 'What do you mean?'

'I mean if something should happen to you here, while you're alone in this house.'

'But nothing can happen to me now, Aunt Cissie,' Caroline said. 'There's nothing left to happen.'

She was speaking seriously, I think. But the older woman looked at her, and perhaps imagined that she was making a grim attempt at humour. I saw, in her expression, the faintest stirring of distaste. 'Well, of course you aren't a child,' she said, 'and your uncle and I can't force you—'

At that point the discussion was broken up by the arrival of another guest. Caroline excused herself, and moved dutifully to greet him; and I also moved on.

The gathering, understandably, was a very subdued one. There were no speeches, no attempts to follow the vicar's example and find some touches of comfort in the gloom. It seemed harder to do that here, with the obvious derangement of the house and landscape so brutally recalling that of Mrs Ayres herself; and it was impossible not to remember that the suicide had happened in a room just a few feet over our heads. People stood about, talking awkwardly, in murmurs, not as if simply unhappy, but as if unsettled, unnerved. Now and then they would glance at Caroline, as her aunt had, with a touch of disquiet. As

I moved from group to group I heard several people quietly speculating on what would happen to the Hall now—confident, apparently, that Caroline would have to give it up, that the place could have no future.

I began to resent them all. It seemed to me that they had come here, knowing nothing about the house, and nothing about Caroline and what was best for her, yet were making judgements and assumptions as if that were their right. I was relieved when, after an hour or so, people began to apologise and slip away. Because so many had shared vehicles, the crowd thinned very quickly. Soon, too, the visitors from Sussex and Kent began to look at their watches, thinking of the long, uncomfortable car rides or train journeys ahead of them. One by one they went to Caroline to say their emotional goodbyes, to kiss and embrace her; the aunt and uncle made one last fruitless attempt to persuade her to leave. I saw her growing tireder with every farewell: she was like a flower, being passed from hand to hand, wilting and bruising. When the final guests left she and I went with them to the front door, to stand on the cracked steps and watch their cars rasp away across the gravel. Then she closed her eyes and covered her face; her shoulders sank, and it was all I could do to catch her in my arms and lead her, stumbling, back to the warmth of the little parlour. I put her to sit in one of the wing-backed chairs—her mother's chair, it had used to be—beside the fire.

She rubbed her forehead. 'Is it really over? This has been the longest day of my life. I think my head is about to burst.'

'I'm surprised you haven't fainted,' I said. 'You've eaten nothing.'

'I can't. I can't.'

'Just a little something? Please?'

But she wouldn't take food, no matter what I offered. So finally I mixed her up a glass of sherry, sugar, and hot water, and she drank that, with a couple of aspirins, while I stood and watched. When Betty began to clear the table and rearrange the room, she automatically rose to help; I gently but firmly pushed her back down, and brought her extra cushions and a blanket, and I took the shoes from her feet and briefly rubbed her stockinged toes. She looked on unhappily as Betty gathered plates, but soon her weariness overtook her. She drew up her legs, rested her cheek against the worn velvet nap of the chair, and closed her eyes.

I looked at Betty, touching my finger to my lips. We worked quietly together, gently loading trays, tiptoeing with them from the room, and down in the kitchen I took off my jacket and stood at the girl's side, drying the crockery and glasses as she passed them, soapy, from the sink. She didn't seem to find it odd. I didn't find it odd, either. The Hall had been knocked out of its routines, and there was a comfort to be had—I'd seen it, in other bereaved houses—in little ordinary chores, conscientiously done.

But when the washing up was finished, her narrow shoulders drooped; and partly because I'd begun to realise how hungry I was, but also simply to keep her occupied, I had her heat up a pan of soup, and we took a bowlful each to the table. And as I set down my bowl and spoon on the table's scrubbed deal top, I found myself growing thoughtful.

I said, 'The last time I sat down to eat at this table, Betty, I was ten years old. My mother was with me—sitting just where you are.'

She turned up her tear-reddened eyes to me, uncertainly. 'Is it a funny thought, sir?'

I smiled. 'It is, a bit. I certainly never guessed then that I'd be back here one day, quite like this. I dare say my mother never guessed it, either. A pity she didn't live to see it . . . I wish I'd been kinder to my mother, Betty. My father, too. I hope you're nicer to your parents!'

She put an elbow on the table and rested her cheek on her hand. 'They get on me nerves,' she said, with a sigh. 'Me dad made all that fuss about me coming out here. Now he's on at me to leave.'

I said, alarmed, 'He isn't, is he?'

'He is. He's been reading all the papers, and he says the house is turned too queer. Mrs Bazeley says the same. She came in this morning, but when she went she took her apron. She says she in't going to come back again. She says what happened with madam was too much; her nerves in't up to it. She says she'd sooner take in laundry, like a washing-woman . . . I don't think she's told Miss Caroline yet.'

I said, 'Well, I'm very sorry to hear it. You're not going to give your notice, are you?'

She ate her soup, not looking at me. 'I don't know. It in't the same without madam.'

'Oh, Betty, please don't. I know the house is an unhappy one just now. But we're all Miss Caroline has left, you and I. I can't be here all the time to keep an eye on her; but you can. If you were to leave—'

'I don't want to leave, not really. I don't want to go back home, anyway! It's just, me dad.'

She sounded genuinely torn, and I found her loyalty to the house, after everything that had happened, rather touching. I watched her eat a little more, thinking over what she'd told me, then I said cautiously, 'How about if you were able to tell your father, well, that things might soon be changing here at Hundreds?' I hesitated. 'If you were able to tell him, say, that Miss Caroline was going to be married—'

'Married!' She looked amazed. 'Who to?'

I smiled. 'Well, who do you think?'

She understood, and blushed; and, stupidly, I blushed, too. I said, 'Now, you're not to go talking about it. Some people know; most people don't.'

She had straightened up, growing excited. 'Oh, when is it to be?'

'I don't know yet. It hasn't been fixed.'

'And what will Miss Caroline wear? Will it have to be black, because of madam?'

I said, 'Good heavens, I don't think so! This isn't the eighteen nineties. Come on now, eat your soup.'

But her eyes were filling with tears. She said, 'Oh, but in't it a shame that madam won't be here to see it! And who's to give Miss Caroline away? It ought to be Mr Roderick, oughtn't it?'

'Well, I fear Mr Roderick will still be too poorly.'

'Who will it be, then?'

'I don't know. Mr Desmond, perhaps. Or perhaps nobody. Miss Caroline can give herself away, can't she?'

She looked horrified. 'She can't do that!'

We talked it over for a few more minutes—both of us glad of the lightness of the subject, after that hard day. When we had finished our dinners she wiped her eyes and blew her nose, then took the bowls and spoons to the sink. I put my jacket back on, then ladled out another portion of soup, and set it, covered, on a tray, to take upstairs to the little parlour.

I found Caroline still sleeping, but as I drew near her she woke with a start, putting down her legs and half rising. Her cheek was marked, like creased linen, where it had rested against the chair.

She said, still partly in her dream, 'What time is it?'

'It's half past six. I've brought you some soup, look.'

'Oh.' Her expression cleared. She rubbed her face. 'I really don't think I can eat.'

But I put the tray across the arms of her chair, effectively pinning her behind it. Laying a napkin in her lap, I said, 'Just try a little, will you? I'm afraid of you growing ill.'

'I don't want it, truly.'

'Come on. Or you'll hurt Betty's feelings. You'll hurt mine, too . . . Good girl.'

For she had picked up her spoon and begun half-heartedly to stir the soup. I brought across a footstool and sat at her side, putting my chin on my fist and solemnly watching her, and she started to eat, very slowly, one small mouthful at a time. She did it quite without relish, plainly forcing the morsels of meat and vegetable down, but when she had finished she looked better, with colour in her cheeks. Her head, she said, was aching less; she felt only so desperately weary. I moved aside the tray and took her hand, but she drew it from me, putting it instead across her mouth while she yawned and yawned, her eyes watering.

Then she wiped her face and sat forward in the chair, moving closer to the fire.

'God,' she said, gazing into the flames. 'Today has been just like a horrible dream. But it wasn't a dream, was it? My mother's dead. Dead, and buried, and now she'll be dead and buried for ever. I can't believe it. It seems to me that she must be just upstairs—just upstairs, resting. And when I was dozing, before, I could nearly imagine that Roddie was out there, in his room, and that Gyp was here, beside my chair . . .' She raised her eyes to me, bewildered. 'How did it happen, any of it?'

I shook my head. 'I don't know. I wish I did.'

'I heard a woman say, today, that this house must be cursed.'

'Who said that? Who was she?'

'I didn't know her. A newcomer, I think. It was in the churchyard. I heard her say it to somebody else. She looked at me as if I were cursed, too. As if I were Dracula's daughter . . .' She yawned again. 'Oh, why am I so tired? All I want to do is sleep.'

'Well, that's probably about the best thing you can do. I only wish you didn't have to do it here, all on your own.'

She rubbed her eyes. 'You sound like Aunt Cissie. Betty will look after me.'

'Betty's exhausted, too. Let me put you into your bed.' Then, seeing something in her expression, I added, 'Not like that! What kind of a brute do you take me for? You're forgetting I'm a doctor. I see young women into their beds all the time.'

'But I'm not your patient, am I? You must go home.'

'I don't like to leave you.'

'I'm Dracula's daughter, remember? I'll be all right.'

She got to her feet. She almost swayed as she did it, and I caught hold of her shoulders to steady her, then stroked the brown hair away from her forehead and cupped her face with my hands. She closed her eyes. As they often did when she was tired, her eyelids looked nude, moist, swollen. I kissed them, lightly. Her arms hung loose as a jointed doll's. She opened her eyes and said, more firmly than before, 'You must go home. But, thank you. For everything you've done. You've been so good to us today.' She checked herself. 'So good to me, I mean . . .'

I found my coat and hat, and took her hand, and we went out to the hall. It was chill there, and I saw her shiver. I didn't want to keep her standing in the cold, but when we had kissed and moved apart and her hand was tugging away from mine, I glanced over her shoulder to the staircase, thinking of the dark, empty rooms above; and the sight of her moving off alone like that, after the day she had had, was dreadful.

I tightened my grip on her fingers and pulled her back.

'Caroline,' I said.

She came slackly, protesting. 'Please. I'm so tired.'

I drew her close, and spoke quietly, into her ear. 'Tell me just one thing. When may we be married?'

Her face moved against mine. 'I must go to bed.'

'When, Caroline?'

'Soon.'

'I want to be here with you.'

'I know. I know you do.'

'I've been patient, haven't I?'

'Yes. But not right away. Not so soon after Mother—'

'No, no . . . But, perhaps, in a month?'

She shook her head. 'We can talk tomorrow.'

'A month will be just long enough, I think. I mean, for sorting out the licence, things like that. But I shall need to plan, you see. If we could just settle on a date.'

'There are so many things still to discuss.'

'Not the important things, surely. Can we say a month? Or at most, six weeks? Six weeks from today?'

She hesitated, struggling with weariness. Then, 'Yes,' she said, pulling away. 'Yes, if you like. Only let me go to bed! I'm so, so tired.'

It seems an odd thing to say, given all the terrible things that had happened, but I remember the period following the funeral as one of the brightest of my life. I left the house bursting with plans; the very next day I went into Leamington to put in the application for the wedding licence, and a few days later the date was fixed: Thursday, the twenty-seventh of May. As if in anticipation of the event, over the next couple of weeks the weather grew finer, and the days visibly lengthened; the leafless trees and flowerless landscape seemed suddenly tense with colour and life. The Hall had stayed shuttered since the morning of Mrs Ayres's death, and in contrast with the stir of the season and the clear blue skies the gloom and the hush began to feel oppressive. I asked Caroline's permission to open up the house, and on the last day of April I went through all the ground-floor rooms, carefully drawing back the shutters. Some had been closed for months: they groaned on their hinges, the dust clouding, the paint-work crackling and flaking. But the sounds, to me, were those of a creature gratefully surfacing from a long slumber, and the wooden floors creaked almost luxuriously as the warm day met them, like cats extending themselves in the sun.

I wanted to see Caroline herself returning to life like that. I wanted gently to kindle and rouse her. For now that the first phase of grief had passed, her spirits had sunk a little; with no more letters to write, and no funeral arrangements absorbing her, she grew aimless, and listless. I'd had to resume my surgeries and rounds, which meant leaving her alone for long stretches of time; with Mrs Bazeley gone, there were many chores she might have seen to, but Betty told me that she did nothing with her days but sit, or gaze blankly from the windows, sighing, yawning, smoking cigarettes, biting her nails. She seemed unable to plan for the wedding, or for any of the changes that would follow; she took no interest in the estate, the garden, the farm. She had lost, even, her ability to read: the books bored and frustrated her, she said; the words seemed to glance against her brain as if it were made of glass . . .

Remembering Seeley's words at the funeral—'get her away, a fresh start'—I started to think about our honeymoon. I imagined all the good it would do her to be taken out of the county—right out, to a completely different landscape, to mountains, or beaches and cliffs. For a time I considered Scotland; then I thought, perhaps the Lakes. Then, quite by chance, one of my private patients mentioned Cornwall to me, describing an hotel he had recently stayed at in one of the coves: a wonderful place, he said it was, quiet, romantic, picturesque . . . It seemed like fate. Without saying anything to Caroline, I found out the hotel's address, made enquiries, and reserved a room for a week, for 'Dr and Mrs Faraday'. The wedding-night itself I thought we could spend on the sleeper train out of London; it had a silly sort of glamour to it I suspected Caroline would like. And in the many lonely hours when I was separated from her, I thought often of the journey: the narrow British Railways bunk, the sliver of moonlight at the blind, the guard going delicately past the door; the gentle jog and rumble of the train on the shining track.

M eanwhile the wedding itself crept nearer, and I tried to encourage her to plan for the ceremony.

'I'd like to have David Graham, you know, as my best man,' I told her, as we strolled in the park one Sunday afternoon in early May. 'He's been a good friend to me. Anne must come too, of course. And you had better choose your bridesmaid, Caroline.'

We were walking through bluebells. Almost overnight, the rough ground at Hundreds had been transformed with them, through acre after acre. She stooped to pick one, and rolled the stem of it between her fingers, frowning down at the flowers as they whirled.

'A bridesmaid,' she repeated dully, as we moved on. 'Must I, though?'

I laughed. 'You must have a bridesmaid, darling! Someone to hold your bouquet.'

'I hadn't thought. There's no one I quite like to ask.'

'There must be someone. What about that friend of yours, from the hospital dance? Brenda, was it?'

She blinked. 'Brenda? Oh, no. I shouldn't like— No.'

'Then how about Helen Desmond, as—what d'you call it? Matron of honour? She'd be touched, I think.'

She had begun to pick apart the blue flowers, clumsily separating the petals with her bitten-down nails.

'I suppose she would.'

'All right. I'll call in, shall I, and mention it to her?'

She frowned again. 'You needn't do that. I can speak to her my-self.'

'I don't want you to be bothered with all the little details.'

'A bride is supposed to be bothered with them, isn't she?'

'Not a bride,' I said, 'who's been through all the things that you have.' I put my arm through hers. 'I want to make this easy for you, darling.'

'Easy for me?' she said, resisting the pull of my hand. 'Or—?' She didn't finish.

I stopped, and stared at her. 'What do you mean?'

Her head was still lowered; she was still working at the petals. She said, without looking up, 'All I mean is, must things really move so quickly?'

'Well, what have we to wait for?'

'I don't know. Nothing, I suppose . . . I just wish people wouldn't keep going on about it to me. Yesterday, Paget's man congratulated me, when he brought the meat! Betty can talk of nothing else.'

I smiled. 'What harm can it do? People are pleased.'

'Are they? More likely they're laughing. People always do, when a spinster marries. I expect they think it's funny that I'm . . . coming off the shelf. As if I've been brought from the back of the display, had the dust blown off me.'

I said, 'Is that what you think I've done? Blown the dust off you?'

She threw away the mangled flower and said, tiredly and almost crossly, 'Oh, I don't know what you've done.'

Catching hold of her hands, I drew her round to face me.

'I happen,' I said, 'to have fallen in love with you! If people want to laugh at that, they must have a bloody silly sense of humour.'

I had never spoken to her in quite those terms before, and for a second she looked startled. Then she closed her eyes, and turned her head from me. The sun caught her hair; I saw a thread of grey in the brown.

'I'm sorry,' she murmured. 'You're always so good, aren't you? And I'm always so beastly. It's hard, that's all. So much has changed. But in other ways, nothing seems to be changing at all.'

I put my arms around her and pulled her close. 'We can make all the changes we want, once Hundreds is our own.'

Her cheek was resting on my shoulder, but I could tell from the intentness of her pose that she had opened her eyes and was gazing back across the park at the house.

She said, 'We've never talked about how it will be. I'll be a doctor's wife.'

I said, 'You'll be marvellous at it. You'll see.'

She drew back, to look at me. 'But how will it work, with you, with Hundreds? You keep talking about the estate as though you'll have time and money to fix it. How will it work?'

I gazed into her face, wanting only to reassure her, but the truth is, I didn't quite know how it would work. I had recently told Graham about my plan to move into the Hall after the wedding, and he had seemed taken aback. He had been supposing, he said, that Caroline would give Hundreds up, that she and I would live at Gill's, or find a nicer house together. I told him in the end that 'nothing was settled', that Caroline and I were still 'playing with ideas'.

I said something similar now.

'Things will sort themselves out. You'll see. It will all become clear to us. I promise.'

She looked frustrated, but didn't answer. She let me pull her back into my arms, but again I could feel her gazing tensely at the Hall. And after a moment she broke the embrace, and moved away from me in silence.

Perhaps a man with more experience of women would have acted differently; I don't know. I imagined that things would come right once we were married. I pinned a great deal on that one day. Caroline herself, however, continued to speak of the wedding, when she spoke

of it at all, with a disconcerting vagueness. She failed to contact Helen
Desmond: I had to do that for her after all. Helen was delighted, but
the lively questions she asked me about our plans made me realise all
the preparations that were still to be made, and when I spoke to Caroline next I saw with a shock that she had given no thought to them—no
thought, even, to what she would wear to be married in. I said she must
let Helen advise her; she answered that she 'didn't want to be fussed'.
I offered to take her into Leamington—as I'd once planned, anyway, to
do—and buy her a new set of clothes; she said I 'mustn't waste my
money', that she would 'put something together from the things she
had upstairs'. I pictured her unbecoming gowns and hats, and inwardly
rather shuddered. So I spoke to Betty, secretly, and asked her to bring
me a sample of Caroline's dresses, and, picking out what we thought
was the best of them, I took it quietly off to Leamington one day, to a
ladies' tailors, and asked the shop-girl if I might have a costume made
up in a matching size.

I told her the dress was for a lady who was soon to be married but
was currently unwell. The girl called over a couple of colleagues and
the three of them had a very excited time, producing pattern-books,
unrolling bolts of cloth, sifting through buttons. I could tell they had
formed a picture of the bride as a sort of romantic invalid. 'Will the
lady be able to walk?' they asked me delicately, and, 'Will her hands
bear gloves?' I thought of Caroline's thick strong legs, her well-shaped,
work-spoiled fingers . . . We settled on a plain, slim-belted dress, in
some light, fawn material I hoped would suit her brown hair and hazel
eyes; and for her head and hands I ordered simple sprays of pale silk
flowers. The whole ensemble cost just over eleven pounds, and took all
my clothing coupons. Once I'd started to spend, however, I found a
queasy sort of pleasure in keeping going. A few doors down from the
ladies' outfitters was Leamington's best jeweller. I went in, and asked
to see their selection of wedding-rings. They didn't have many, and
most were utility rings: nine-carat, light and brassy, looking to me like
something from Woolworth's. From a more expensive tray I picked out
a simple gold band, slender but heavy, at fifteen guineas. My first motor

car had cost me less. I wrote the cheque with a nervous flourish, trying to give the impression that I dispensed such sums every day.

I had to leave the ring at the jeweller's, to be slightly expanded to what I had calculated as Caroline's size. So I drove home with nothing to show for the money I had spent, my bravado failing with every mile, my knuckles paling on the steering-wheel as I thought over what I'd done. I passed the next few days in the grip of a bachelor's panic, going wildly through my accounts, asking myself how the hell I meant to support a wife anyway; worrying again about the Health Service. In despair I went to see Graham—who laughed at me and gave me a whisky, and finally managed to calm me down.

A few days later I returned to Leamington to collect the ring and the gown. The ring was weightier than I had remembered, which reassured me no end; it sat snugly in a ruffled silk mount, inside an expensive-looking little shagreen box. The gown and flowers came in boxes, too, which also cheered me up. The dress was exactly what I'd wanted: pure, crisp, unfussy, and seeming to shine with newness.

The shop-girls hoped the lady was better. They grew quite emotional about it, wishing her 'good luck, and good health, and a long and happy marriage'.

This was on a Tuesday, two weeks and two days before the wedding itself. That night I worked at the hospital, with the ring in my pocket and the gown in its box in the boot of my car. The next day I was frustratingly busy, with no chance to call in at the Hall. But on the Thursday afternoon I did get out there—letting myself into the padlocked park with my own key as usual, then going, whistling, along the drive, with my car window lowered, for the day was glorious. I put the boxes under my arm and went quietly into the house by the garden way. At the turn of the basement stairs I called softly down.

'Betty! Are you there?'

She emerged from the kitchen and stood blinking up at me.

I said, 'Where's Miss Caroline? The little parlour?'

She nodded. 'Yes, Doctor. She's been in there all day.'

I lifted the boxes. 'What do you think I've got in here?'

She peered, puzzled. 'I don't know.' Then her face changed. 'Things for Miss Caroline's wedding!'

'Perhaps.'

'Oh! Can I see?'

'Not yet. Maybe later. Bring us some tea in half an hour. Miss Caroline might show you then.'

She gave a funny skip of pleasure and returned to the kitchen. I went through to the front of the house, manoeuvring my boxes carefully around the green baize curtain, then taking them on to the little parlour. I found Caroline sitting on the sofa, smoking a cigarette.

The room was stuffy, the smoke hanging as viscidly in the warm still air as the white of an egg hangs in water, as if she'd been sitting there for some time. I put my boxes on the seat beside her, kissed her, and said, 'This lovely day! My dear, you'll be kippered. May I open the French window?'

She didn't look at the boxes. Instead she sat tensely, gazing at me, biting the inside of her mouth. She said, 'Yes, if you like.'

I don't think the window had been properly opened since she and I had left the house by it to go and look at the building-work, back in January. The handles were stiff to turn, and the door-frames grated as they moved; the steps beyond were thick with creeper, just beginning to stir with life. But once the doors were ajar, the air came straight in from the garden, moist and fragrant, tinged with green.

I went back to Caroline's side. She was stubbing out her cigarette and had moved forward, as if to rise.

I said, 'Now, don't get up. I've something to show you.'

'I have to talk to you,' she said.

'I have to talk to you, too. I've been busy, on your behalf. Our behalf, I ought to say. Look here.'

'I've been thinking,' she began, as if she hadn't heard me and meant to say more. But I had brought forward the largest of the boxes, and she looked at it at last and saw its label. Suddenly wary, she said, 'What's that?'

Her tone made me nervous. I said, 'I told you. I've been busy on

your behalf.' I licked my lips; my mouth had dried, and as I held the
box out to her my confidence wavered. So I spoke in a rush.

'Look, I know this is flying in the face of convention, rather, but I
didn't think you'd mind. There hasn't been much of the conventional—
well, about us. I do so want the day to be special.'

I put the box across her lap. Now she looked almost frightened of
it. When she lifted off the lid and parted the folds of tissue paper and
saw the simple gown beneath, she sat in silence. Her hair fell forward,
obscuring her face.

'Do you like it?' I asked her.

She didn't answer.

I said, 'I hope to God it fits. I had it made to match one of your
others. Betty helped me. We've been quite the secret agents, she and I.
There's plenty of time to fix it, though, if it isn't right.'

She hadn't moved. My heart gave a lurch, then beat on, faster than
before. I said, '*Do* you like it?'

She answered quietly, 'Yes, very much.'

'I bought something for your head and hands, too.'

I passed her the second box, and she slowly opened it up. She saw
the sprays of silk flowers inside it but, as before, she didn't draw them
from the paper; she simply sat looking down at them, her face still hidden from me by her own drooping hair. Like an idiot I pressed on,
putting my hand to my jacket pocket and bringing out the little shagreen case.

When she turned and saw that, the sight seemed to galvanise her.
She got to her feet, the boxes sliding and spilling from her lap.

She walked to the open window and stood with her back to me. Her
shoulders moved; she was twisting her hands. She said, 'I'm sorry, I
can't do this.'

I had scrambled to catch the gown and the flowers. I said, as I folded
the dress back up, 'Forgive me, darling. I shouldn't have sprung it all
on you. We can look at these later.'

She half turned to me. Her voice flattened. 'I don't mean the dress.
I mean everything. I can't do any of it. I can't marry you. I just can't.'

I was still folding the dress as she spoke, and my fingers faltered for a moment. But I returned the gown neatly to its box, and set the box on the sofa, before going across to her. She watched me approach, her pose stiff, her expression almost fearful. I placed a hand upon her shoulder, and said, 'Caroline.'

'I'm sorry,' she said again. 'I do so like you, so very much. I always have. But I think I must have been confusing liking with . . . something else. For a time I wasn't sure. That's what's made it so hard. You've been such a good friend, and I've been so grateful. You've helped me so much, with Rod, with Mother. But I don't think one should marry out of gratitude, do you? Please say something.'

I said, 'My darling, I—I think you're tired.'

A look of dismay came into her face. She moved her shoulder to shrug off my grip. My hand slid down her arm and caught at her wrist instead. I said, 'With everything that's happened, it's not surprising you're confused. Your mother's death—'

'But I'm not a bit confused,' she said. 'My mother's death was what made me begin to see things clearly. To think about what I wanted, and didn't want. To think about what you want, too.'

I tugged at her hand. 'Come back to the sofa, will you? You're tired.'

She pulled herself free, and her voice hardened. 'Stop saying that! It's all you ever say to me! Sometimes—sometimes I think you want to *keep* me tired, that you *like* me to be tired.'

I looked at her, amazed and appalled. 'How can you say that? I want you to be well. I want you to be happy.'

'But don't you see? I shan't be either of those things if I marry you.'

I must have flinched. Her expression grew kinder. She said, 'I'm sorry, but it's the truth. I wish it wasn't. I don't want to hurt you. I care about you too much for that. But I think you'd prefer me to be honest with you now, wouldn't you? Than to become your wife, knowing in my heart that I didn't—well, that I didn't love you?'

Her voice dipped on those last few words, but she kept her eyes on mine and her gaze was so unwavering I began to be frightened. I reached for her hand again.

'Caroline, please. Think about what you're saying, will you?'

She shook her head, her face creasing. 'I've done nothing but think since Mother's funeral. I've thought so hard, my thoughts have been tangled up, like strings. They've only just begun to come straight.'

I said, 'I know I've rushed you. That was stupid of me. But we can . . . begin again. We don't have to be like husband and wife. Not at first. Not until you're ready. Is that the problem?'

'There isn't a problem, not like that. Not really.'

'We can take our time.'

She pulled her hand away. 'I've wasted too much time already. Can't you see? This whole thing between us, it's never been real. After Rod went, I was so unhappy, and you were always so kind. I thought that you were unhappy, too; that you wanted to break away as much as I did. I thought that in marrying you I'd be able to . . . change my life. But you'll never leave, will you? And my life wouldn't change like that, anyway. I'd just be swapping one set of duties for another. I'm tired of duties! I can't do it. I can't be a doctor's wife. I can't be anybody's wife. And most of all, I can't stay here.'

She spoke these last words with something like loathing, and when I stared at her, not understanding, she said, 'I'm going away. That's what I'm telling you. I'm leaving Hundreds.'

I said, 'You can't.'

'I have to.'

'You can't! Where the hell do you think you're going to go?'

'I haven't decided. London, at first. But after that, perhaps America, or Canada.'

She might as well have said 'the moon'. Catching my look of disbelief, she said again, 'I have to! Don't you see? I need to . . . get out. Get right away. England's no good any more for someone like me. It doesn't want me.'

'For God's sake,' I said, 'I want you! Doesn't that mean anything to you?'

'Do you, really?' she asked me. 'Or is it the house you want?'

The question stunned me, and I couldn't answer. She went on quietly, 'A week ago you told me you were in love with me. Can you truly say you would feel the same, if Hundreds weren't my home? You've had the idea, haven't you, that you and I could live here as husband and wife. The squire and his lady . . . But this house doesn't want me. I don't want it. I hate this house!'

'That's not true.'

'Of course it's true! How could I do anything but hate it? My mother was killed here, Gyp was killed here; Rod might as well have been killed here. I don't know why nothing's ever tried to kill me. Instead, I'm being given this chance to get away.—No, don't look like that.' I'd moved towards her. 'I'm not going crazy, if that's what you're thinking. Though I'm not sure you wouldn't quite like that, too. You could keep me upstairs in the nursery. The bars are already on the windows, after all.'

She was like a stranger to me. I said, 'How can you say these terrible things? After all I've done, for you, for your family?'

'You think I should repay you, by marrying you? Is that what you think marriage is—a kind of payment?'

'You know I don't think that. For Christ's sake! I just— Our life together, Caroline. You're going to throw it all away?'

'I'm sorry. But I told you: none of it was real.'

My voice broke. '*I'm* real. *You're* real. *Hundreds* is real, isn't it? What the hell do you think's going to happen to this house if you leave it? It'll fall apart!'

She turned away from me, saying wearily, 'Well, someone else can worry about that.'

'What do you mean?'

She turned back, frowning. 'I shall be putting the estate up for sale, of course. The house, the farm—everything. I shall need the money.'

I thought I had understood her; I hadn't understood at all. I said, in absolute horror, 'You're not serious. The estate could get broken up; anything could happen. You can't possibly mean it! For one thing, it isn't yours to sell. It belongs to your brother.'

Her eyelids fluttered a little. She said, 'I've spoken to Dr Warren. And the day before yesterday I went to see Mr Hepton, our solicitor. When Rod was first ill, at the end of the war, he drew up a power of attorney, in case Mother and I should ever have to make decisions about the estate on his behalf. The document still holds, Mr Hepton says. I can put the sale through. I'll only be doing what Rod himself would do, if he were well. And I think he *will* start to get well, once the house has gone. And when he's really better—well, wherever I am, I'll send for him, he can come and join me.'

She spoke levelly, reasonably, and I saw that she meant it, every word. A kind of panic closed my throat and I began to cough. The cough rose up in me like a convulsion, sudden, violent, and dry. I had to move away from her to lean against the frame of the open French window, shuddering and almost retching over the creeper-choked steps outside.

She put out her hand to me. I said, as the cough subsided, 'Don't touch me, I'm all right.' I wiped my mouth. 'I saw Hepton the day before yesterday, too. I ran into him in Leamington. We had a pleasant little chat.'

She knew what I meant, and for the first time looked ashamed. 'I'm so sorry.'

'So you keep saying.'

'I should have told you sooner. I shouldn't have let things go so far. I . . . wanted to be sure. I've been rather a coward, I know that.'

'And I've been rather a fool, haven't I?'

'Please don't say that. You've been so awfully decent and kind.'

'Well, what fun they'll have with me now, in Lidcote! Serve me right, I suppose, for looking outside my class.'

'Please don't.'

'Isn't that what people will say?'

'Not nice people, no.'

'No,' I said, straightening up. 'You're right. What they'll say is this. They'll say, "Poor, plain Caroline Ayres. Doesn't she realise that even in Canada she'll never find another man who wants her?"'

I said the words deliberately, straight into her face. Then I went back across the room to the sofa and caught up the dress.

'You'd better keep this,' I said, bundling it up and throwing it at her. 'God knows, you need it. Keep these, as well.' I threw the flowers. They landed, quivering, at her feet.

Then I saw the little shagreen box, which I had set down, without thinking, when she'd first begun to speak. I opened it up, and took out the heavy gold ring; and I threw that at her, too. I'm ashamed to say that I threw it hard, meaning to hit her. She dodged away, and the ring went out through the open window. I thought it went out cleanly, but it must have glanced against one of the glass doors as it went. There came a sound like an air-pistol firing, astonishingly loud in the Hundreds silence, and a crack appeared, as if from nowhere, in one of the handsome old panes.

The sight and the sound of it frightened me. I looked at Caroline's face and saw that she was frightened, too. I said, 'Oh, Caroline, forgive me,' taking a step towards her with my arms outstretched. But she stepped hastily back, almost scuttling, and to see her moving away from me like that made me sick with myself. I turned and left her, going out into the passage—almost colliding with Betty as I did it. She had come up, with the laden tea-tray—come up with excitement in her eyes, hoping for the look that I had promised her at Miss Caroline's fine new wedding things.

FOURTEEN

I can hardly describe the state of my feelings over the next few hours. Even the journey back into Lidcote was somehow a torment, my thoughts seeming to be whipped up, by the motion of the car, like furiously spinning tops. As bad luck would have it, too, on my way into the village I saw Helen Desmond: she raised her hand excitedly to me, and it was impossible not to stop and wind down my window and exchange a few words with her. She had something to ask me about the wedding; I couldn't bear to tell her what had just passed between Caroline and me, so had to listen, nodding and smiling, making a pretence of thinking the matter through, saying I would check with Caroline and would be sure to let her know. What she made of my manner, God knows. My face felt taut as a mask to me, and my voice sounded half strangled. I managed to get away from her at last by saying I had an urgent call to make; arriving home, I found that there was, in fact, a message waiting for me, a request that I look in on a bad case in a house a couple of miles away. But the thought of climbing back into my car absolutely appalled me. I didn't trust myself not to run it off the road. After a minute of rather agonised indecision I wrote a note to David

Graham, telling him I'd been struck down with a violent stomach upset and asking him to take the case, and to take my evening surgery patients too, if he could manage them. I told my housekeeper the same story, and once she had carried off the message and brought back Graham's sympathetic reply, I gave her the rest of the day off. The moment she had gone I pinned a notice to my surgery door, shot the bolt, and drew the curtains. I got out the bottle of brown sherry I kept in my desk, and, there in my dimmed dispensary, with people going busily by on the other side of the window, I drank glass after choking glass of it.

It was all I could think of to do. My mind, sober, felt as though it would burst. The simple loss of Caroline was hard enough to bear, but the loss of her was the loss of so much more. Everything I'd planned and hoped for, I could see it—I could see it, melting away from me! I was like a thirsty man reaching after a mirage of water—putting out my hands to the vision and watching it turn to dust. And then there was all the stab and humiliation of having supposed it to be mine. I thought of the people who must now be told: Seeley, Graham, the Desmonds, the Rossiters—everyone. I saw their sympathetic or pitying faces, and I imagined the sympathy and pity turning, behind my back, to scandal and satisfaction . . . I couldn't bear it. I got to my feet and paced about—just as I'd often seen very ill patients attempting to pace away pain. I drank as I walked, giving up on the glass, supping straight from the bottle, the sherry spilling over my chin. And when the bottle was finished I went upstairs and started turning out the cupboards in the parlour, looking for another. I found a flask of brandy, and some dusty sloe gin, and a small sealed keg of pre-war Polish spirit I had once won at a charity raffle and had never had the courage to try. I put them together to make one vile mixture and swallowed it down, coughing and spluttering as I drank. I would have done better to take a tranquilliser; I wanted the squalor of drunkenness, I suppose. I remember lying on my bed in my shirt-sleeves, still drinking, until I slept or passed out. I remember waking in darkness, hours later, and being violently sick. Then I slept again, and next time I woke I was shivering;

the night had cooled. I crept under the blankets, ill and ashamed. And after that I didn't sleep again. I watched the window lighten, and my thoughts, like icy water, ran brutally clear. I said to myself, *Of course you've lost her. How could you think you ever had her? Look at you! Look at the state of you! You don't deserve her.*

B ut by one of those tricks of self-protection, once I'd risen, and washed, and queasily made myself a pot of coffee, my mood began slightly to lift. The day was fine and mild and spring-like, just as the previous day had been, and it seemed impossible suddenly that between the dawning of one and the dawning of the other things could have changed so disastrously. My mind ran over the scene with Caroline, and now that the first sting of her words and manner had worn itself out I began to feel amazed that I had taken her so seriously. I reminded myself that she was exhausted, depressed, still in shock from her mother's death and from all the dark events that had led to it. She had been behaving erratically for weeks, succumbing to one outlandish idea after another, and I had managed to talk her into behaving sensibly every time. Surely this was just a final piece of wildness, the culmination of so much anxiety and strain? Surely I could talk sense into her again? I began to be certain that I could. I began to think that, in fact, she might be longing for it. She might have been almost testing my reactions, wanting something from me that I'd so far failed to give.

The thought buoyed me up, and drove away the worst of my hangover. My housekeeper arrived, and was reassured to see me so recovered; she said she'd been worried about me all night. My morning surgery began, and I applied myself with extra care to my patients' complaints, wanting to make up for my disgraceful lapse of the evening before. I rang David Graham to tell him that my spell of sickness was past. Relieved, he passed on a list of cases, and I spent the rest of the morning diligently making calls.

And then I went back out to Hundreds. I let myself in through the garden door again and went straight to the little parlour. The house looked so exactly as it had on my last visit, and on every visit before that, that I grew more confident with every step. When I found Caroline at the writing table, going through a heap of papers, I half expected her to rise and greet me with a sheepish sort of smile. I even took a few steps towards her, beginning to lift up my arms. Then I saw her expression, and the dismay in it was unmistakable. She screwed on the lid of her pen and got slowly to her feet.

My arms sank. I said, 'Caroline, what nonsense this all is. I've had a miserable, miserable night. I've been so worried about you.'

She frowned, as if troubled and sorry.

'You mustn't worry about me now. You mustn't come out here any more.'

'Not come out here? Are you mad? How can I not come out here, knowing you're here, in this kind of state—'

'But I'm not in any kind of "state".'

'It's only a month since your mother died! You're grieving. You're in shock. These things you say you're doing, these decisions you're making, about Hundreds, about Rod—you're going to regret them. I've seen this sort of thing before. My darling—'

'Please don't call me your darling now,' she said.

She said it, half pleading, but half with a touch of disapproval; as if I'd spoken a dirty word. I had taken another few steps towards her, but again I came to a halt. And after a silence I changed my tone, became more urgent.

'Caroline, listen. I understand if you're having doubts. You and I, we're not giddy youngsters. Marriage is a big step for us. I worked myself into a panic last week, just as you're doing now. David Graham had to calm me down with whisky! I think, if you could just calm down, too—'

She shook her head. 'I feel calmer now than I've felt in months. From the moment I agreed to marry you, I knew it wasn't right, and last night was the first time I felt easy. I'm so sorry that I wasn't more honest with you—and with myself—right at the start.'

Her tone wasn't disapproving now so much simply as cool, remote, contained. She was wearing one of her homespun outfits, a ragged cardigan, a darned skirt, her hair tied back with a bit of black ribbon, but she looked oddly handsome and poised, with an air of purposefulness I hadn't seen about her for weeks. All of the morning's bright confidence began to crumble away from me. I could feel, just beyond it, the fear and humiliation of the night. For the first time I glanced properly around, and the room looked subtly different to me, tidier and more anonymous, with a heap of ash in the grate as though she'd been burning papers. I saw the cracked window-pane, and remembered with shame some of the things I'd said to her the day before. Then I noticed that on one of the room's low tables she had made a neat pile of the boxes I had brought her: the dress-box, the flower-box, and the shagreen case.

Seeing me looking at them, she went across to pick them up.

'You must have these back,' she said quietly.

I said, 'Don't be absurd. What the hell would I do with them?'

'You could return them to the shop.'

'A nice idiot I should look doing that! No, I want you to keep them, Caroline. You're to wear them at our wedding.'

She didn't answer that, but held them out to me until it became clear that I simply wouldn't take them. So she put down the two card boxes, but kept the shagreen case in her hand.

She said firmly, 'You really must take this. If you don't take it now, I shall just post it to you. I found the ring on the terrace. It's a lovely ring. I hope—I hope you might give it to somebody else one day.'

I made a sound of disgust. 'It was made to fit you. Don't you understand? There won't *be* anybody else.'

She held it out to me. 'Have it. Please.'

Reluctantly, I took the box from her hand. But as I dropped it into my pocket I said, with an attempt at bravado, 'I'm only taking it back for now. This is a temporary thing. I'm keeping it until I can put it upon your finger. Don't forget that.'

She looked uncomfortable, but still spoke calmly.

'Please don't. I know this is hard, but please don't make it any harder. Don't think I'm ill, or afraid, or being foolish. Don't think I'm doing—I don't know, one of those things that women are supposed to do sometimes—creating a drama, making their man put up a fight . . .' She pulled a face. 'I hope you know me better than to think I would ever do anything like that.'

I didn't answer. I'd begun to grow panicked again: panicked and frustrated, at the simple idea that I wanted her and couldn't have her. She had come close, to give me the ring. All that separated us was a yard or so of cool clear air. My flesh seemed tugged through it towards her. It was tugged so plainly and so urgently, I couldn't believe that there was no answering tug in her. But when I reached to her, she stepped back. She said again, apologetically, 'Please don't.' Then I reached again, and she moved more quickly. I was reminded of the way she had scuttled from me almost in fear on my last visit. But this time she didn't look afraid; and when she spoke, even the note of apology had gone from her voice. She sounded rather as I remembered her sounding in the days when I'd first known her and had sometimes thought her hard.

She said, 'If you care even slightly for me, you won't ever try and do that again. I think of you with great fondness, and should be sorry for that to change.'

I went back to Lidcote in almost as wretched a state as I had been in the day before. But this time I struggled on through the afternoon, and it was only when my evening surgery had finished and the night loomed ahead of me that my nerve began to fail. I started to pace about again, unable to sit, unable to work, perplexed and tormented by the thought that, in a single moment—in the uttering of a handful of words—I had lost my claim on Caroline, on the Hall, and on our bright future. It made no sense to me. I simply couldn't let it happen. I put on my hat, and got back into my car, and headed out to Hundreds again. I wanted to catch hold of Caroline, and shake and shake her, until she saw reason.

But then I had what seemed to be a better idea. At the Hundreds crossroads I turned north, on to the Leamington Road, and I drove to the house of Harold Hepton, the Ayres's solicitor.

I'd lost sense of the time. When the Heptons' maid let me in I heard voices and the chink of cutlery: I saw from the hall clock that it was just after half past eight, and realised with dismay that the family were gathered in the dining-room for their supper. Hepton himself came out to greet me with a napkin in his hand, still dabbing gravy from his mouth.

I said, 'I'm sorry. I've disturbed you. I'll come back another time.'

But he put the napkin aside good-humouredly.

'Nonsense! We've almost finished, and I shall be glad of a pause before my pudding. Does me good to see a man's face, too. I'm surrounded by women in this house . . . Come through here, where it's quieter, will you?'

He took me into his study, overlooking the twilit garden at the back of the house. The house was a fine one. He and his wife had money behind them, and had managed to hang on to it. They were both big people in the local fox-hunting set, and the walls of the room were hung with various bits of hunting memorabilia, crops and trophies and photographs of meets.

He closed the door and gave me a cigarette, taking one for himself. He perched on the edge of his desk while I sat tensely in one of the chairs.

I said, 'I won't mess about. I dare say you know why I'm here.'

He was busy lighting his cigarette, and made a noncommittal gesture.

I said, 'It's this business with Caroline, and Hundreds.'

He closed his lighter. 'You know, of course, that I can't possibly discuss the family's financial affairs.'

'You realise,' I said, 'that *I* was soon to be a member of that family?'

'Yes, I'd heard that.'

'Caroline's called off the wedding.'

'I'm sorry.'

'But you knew that, too. You knew it before I did, as it happens. And you know what she's planning to do, I believe, with the house, and the estate. She says Roderick's made some sort of power of attorney. Is that right?'

He shook his head. 'I can't discuss it, Faraday.'

I said, 'You mustn't let her go ahead with it! Roderick's ill, but he isn't so ill that he should have his property snatched away from under his nose like this! It isn't ethical.'

He said, 'Naturally, I wouldn't proceed in such a case without seeing a proper medical report.'

'For God's sake,' I cried, 'I'm his doctor! I'm Caroline's doctor, come to that!'

'Keep your voice down, would you, old man?' he said crisply. 'You yourself, you might remember, signed a paper putting Roderick into the care of Dr Warren. I made sure to see it. Warren is satisfied that the poor boy's in no condition to manage his own affairs; nor is he likely to be, apparently, for some time. I'm only telling you what Warren himself would tell you, if he were here.'

'Well, then perhaps I should speak to Warren.'

'Speak to him, by all means. But I don't take my instructions from him. I take them from Caroline.'

His obtuseness exasperated me. I said, 'You must have an opinion on this. A personal opinion, I mean. You must see the absolute folly of it.'

He studied the tip of his cigarette. 'I'm not sure that I do. It's a very great shame for the district, certainly, to lose another of its old families. But that house is falling down around Caroline's ears. The whole estate needs proper management. How can she possibly hope to maintain it? And what does the place hold for her now but so many unhappy memories? Without her parents, without her brother, without a husband—'

'*I* was to be her husband.'

'That I really can't comment on . . . I'm sorry. I don't quite see what I can do for you.'

I said, 'You can keep this thing from going any further, until Caroline begins to see sense! You've talked about her brother's illness, but isn't it obvious? Caroline herself is far from well.'

'You think so? She seemed very well indeed when I saw her last.'

'I'm not talking about a physical illness. I'm thinking of her nerves, her mental state. I'm thinking of everything she's been through in the past few months. The strain of it's affecting her judgement.'

He looked embarrassed, but also faintly amused.

'My dear Faraday,' he said, 'if every time a fellow was jilted he tried to get his girl certified . . .'

He spread his hands, and didn't finish. In his expression I saw what a fool I was making of myself, and just for a second I felt the reality of my situation, and the absolute hopelessness of it. But the knowledge was too hard. I shrank from it. I told myself bitterly that I was wasting my time with him; that he had never liked me; that I wasn't a part of his 'set'. I rose and moved away from him. I found an ashtray—a pewter thing, with a fox-hunting motif—and ground out my cigarette.

I said, 'I must let you get back to your family. I'm sorry to have bothered you.'

He rose, too. 'Not at all. I wish I had some way of putting your mind at rest.'

But we both spoke blandly now. I followed him out into the hall, and shook his hand and thanked him for his time. At the open door he looked up at the luminous evening sky, and we exchanged some pleasantry about the lengthening days. As I went back to my car I glanced through the uncurtained dining-room window and saw him returning to his table: he was explaining my visit to his wife and daughters—shaking his head, shrugging me off, settling back down to his dinner.

I passed a second bad night, followed by another fretful day; the week ground miserably on, until I began to feel almost suffocated by my own grief. I'd confided in no one so far; on the contrary, I'd been keeping up a pretence of jolliness, for by now most of my patients had heard about the forthcoming wedding and wanted to congratulate me and talk over all the details. By the Saturday evening I couldn't take any more. I went to see David and Anne Graham and confessed the whole story, sitting on the sofa in their happy little house with my head in my hands.

They were very kind to me. Graham said at once, 'But this is crazy! Caroline can't be in her right mind. Oh, this is pre-wedding jitters, that's all. Anne was exactly the same. I lost count of how many times she gave me back her engagement ring. We used to call it "the boomerang". Do you remember, darling?'

Anne smiled, but looked anxious. In telling them what had happened I had repeated some of Caroline's own words, and they had clearly made more of an impression on her than they had on her husband.

She said slowly, 'I'm sure you're right. Caroline's never really struck me as the jittery type, of course. But then, things have been so miserable for her lately; and now she's out there, without a mother . . . I do wish I'd made more of an effort to be friends with her. She just doesn't seem to want friends, somehow. But I wish I'd tried harder.'

'Well, is it too late?' asked Graham. 'Why not go and have a word with her, tomorrow, on Faraday's behalf?'

She looked at me. 'Would you like me to?'

She spoke, I thought, without enthusiasm. But by now I was desperate.

I said, 'Oh, Anne, I'd be so grateful. Would you really do it? I'm at my wits' end.'

She put her hand on mine, and said she'd be happy to help. Graham said, 'There you are, Faraday. My wife could sweet-talk Stalin. This'll sort things out, you wait and see.'

He spoke so comfortably, I felt almost a fool for having made such a fuss, and for the first time since the thing had started I slept well, and I woke on the Sunday morning feeling slightly less oppressed. I drove Anne out to Hundreds later that day. I didn't go into the house myself, but watched nervously from the car as she went up the front steps and rang the doorbell. The door was opened by Betty, who let her in without a word; once it had closed I half expected her to return almost at once, but in fact she was in there for twenty minutes—long enough for me to pass through all the stages of anxiety and begin to feel almost optimistic.

But when she came back—let out by an unsmiling Caroline, who glanced blankly over at the car before moving back into the pinkish gloom of the hall and closing the door—my heart sank.

She climbed in, saying nothing at first. Then she shook her head.

'I'm so sorry. Caroline seems quite to have made up her mind. She clearly feels dreadful about the whole business. She feels she has shamefully strung you along. But she's quite decided.'

I said, 'You're sure?' I glanced over at the shut front door. 'You don't think she might have resented your coming out here, and spoken more harshly as a result?'

'I don't think so. She was perfectly kind; pleased to see me, in fact. She's been worried about you.'

'She has?'

'Yes. She was very glad to know that you've confided in David and me.'

She said this as if it would bring me some sort of comfort. But the thought that Caroline was *glad* that I'd begun to share the news that our affair was over—that she was *glad* to have, as it were, passed on the responsibility for me to other friends—made me sick with fear.

The fear must have shown in my face. Anne said, 'I wish things were different. Truly I do. I said all I could on your behalf. Caroline actually spoke very warmly of you! She clearly likes you, a great deal. But she also spoke of what was, well, missing from her feelings for you. I don't think a woman ever makes a mistake about that sort of thing . . . And then, all this other business: leaving the house, putting Hundreds up for sale. She clearly means that, too. She's begun to pack things up, did you know that?'

I said, 'What?'

'It looks as though she's been busy for days. A dealer's already been out here, she said, to make her an offer on the contents of the house. All those lovely things! It's such a shame.'

I sat tensely, in silence, for a second. Then, 'I can't stand this,' I said. I plucked at the catch of the door and got out.

I think Anne called after me. I didn't look back. I strode in an absolute fury over the gravel and went running up the steps, and when I shouldered open the front door I found Caroline almost right behind it, with Betty at her side: they were setting down a tea-chest on the marble floor. Other chests and crates lay scattered in the well of the staircase. The hall itself looked stripped, its walls bare and marked, the ornaments gone, the tables and cabinets standing about at odd angles, like awkward guests at a failed party.

Caroline was dressed in her old drill slacks. Her hair was tucked into a turban. Her sleeves were rolled up and her hands were filthy. But once again, even through my anger, I felt the desperate, diabolical straining of my blood, my nerves, my everything, towards her.

But her expression was cold. She said, 'I've nothing to say to you. I said it all to Anne.'

I said, 'I can't give you up, Caroline.'

She almost rolled her eyes. 'You must! That's all there is to it.'

'Caroline, please.'

She didn't answer. I looked at Betty, standing self-consciously by.

'Betty,' I said, 'will you leave us, for a minute or two?'

But as Betty began to move off, Caroline said to her, 'No, you needn't go. Dr Faraday and I have nothing to say to each other that you can't hear. Get on with packing that case.'

The girl looked torn for a moment, then put down her head and half turned away from us. I stood in silence, frustrated; then dropped my voice.

'Caroline,' I said, 'I'm begging you. Please think again. I don't care if you don't feel . . . quite enough for me. You feel something, I know you do. Don't pretend there's nothing. That time, at the dance—or, when we stood outside, on the terrace—'

She said wearily, 'I made a mistake.'

'There was no mistake.'

'There was. It was all a mistake, from start to finish. I made a mistake, and I'm sorry.'

'I can't let you go.'

'God! Do you want to make me hate you? Please don't keep coming out here like this. It's over. All of it.'

I grabbed at her wrist, suddenly furious again.

'How can you talk like that? How can you do what you're doing? For Christ's sake, look at you! Destroying this house. Abandoning Hundreds! How *can* you? How—how *dare* you? Didn't you tell me once that living here was a sort of bargain? You had to keep up your side of it? Is that what you're doing now?'

Her wrist twisted out of my hand. She said, 'That bargain was killing me! You know it was. I wish I'd left a year ago, and taken my mother and my brother with me.'

She'd started to move away from me, wanting to get on with her work. Watching her go, I said levelly, 'Are you sure about that?'

I'd been struck, once again, by her air of competence and purpose. As she turned back to me, frowning, I said, 'A year ago, what did you have? A house you claimed drained all your time. An ageing mother, a sick brother. What was your future? And yet, look at you now. You're free, Caroline. You'll have money, I suppose, once Hundreds is sold. It seems to me, you know, that you've done really rather nicely.'

She stared at me for a second, and then the blood flew into her face. I realised what a terrible thing I had suggested, and grew flustered.

'Caroline, forgive me.'

'Get out,' she said.

'Please—'

'Get out. Get out of my house.'

I didn't look at Betty, but somehow saw her expression anyway, embarrassed and startled and shaded with pity. I turned and fumbled for the door, and went blindly down the steps and across the gravel to the car. Anne saw my face and said gently, 'No good? I'm so very sorry.'

. . .

I drove us back to Lidcote in silence, defeated at last—defeated not so much by the knowledge that I had lost Caroline, as by the thought that I had had a chance to win her back, and had thrown that chance away. When I remembered what I had said to her, what I'd implied, I felt ill with shame. But I knew in my heart that the shame would pass, and my misery rise, and that then I would go to Hundreds again, and finish by saying something worse. So, in order to put the business utterly beyond recovery, when I had dropped Anne off I drove straight to the Desmonds, to tell them that Caroline and I had parted and that the wedding had been called off.

It was the first time I had said the words, and they came more easily than I'd been expecting. Bill and Helen were concerned, sympathetic. They gave me a glass of wine and a cigarette. They asked who else had heard the news; I told them they were more or less the first, but that as far as I was concerned they could pass it on to whoever they liked. The sooner everyone knew, I said, the better.

'Is there really no hope at all?' Helen asked me, as she saw me out.

I said, 'None at all, I'm afraid,'—smiling ruefully as I said it, managing to suggest, I think, that I was reconciled to the separation; possibly even giving the impression that Caroline and I had arrived at the decision together.

Lidcote has three public houses. I left the Desmonds just on opening-up time, and stopped for a drink at each of them. At the last I bought a bottle of gin—the only spirit they had—to take away with me; and once again I stood in my dispensary, squalidly knocking back the liquor. This time, however, for all that I drank, I remained obstinately sober, and when I summoned up Caroline's image, I did it with an oddly clear head. It was just as though my ravings of the past few days had worn out my capacity for violent feeling. I left the dispensary and went upstairs, and my house, which recently had begun to seem flimsy as a stage-set to me, now, with every step I took, seemed to harden, to reassert itself in all its dreary colours and lines. But even that failed to depress me, somehow. Almost in an effort to stoke up some misery I carried on up to my attic bedroom, and I got out everything I could find that I had ever had from Hundreds, or that connected me to the house. There was the Empire Day medal, of course, and the sepia photograph that Mrs Ayres had given me on my first visit, that might or might not contain a portrait of my mother. But there was also the ivory whistle I had drawn from the kitchen end of the speaking-tube, that time in March: I had put it in my waistcoat pocket that day, and had inadvertently brought it home with me. I had kept it in a drawer with my studs and cuff-links since then, but now I fished it out and set it down, on my bedside table, beside the photograph and medal. I added the keys to the park and the house itself, and next to them I put the shagreen box that held Caroline's ring.

A medal, a photograph, a whistle, a pair of keys, an unworn wedding-ring. They formed the spoil of my time at Hundreds: a queer little collection, it seemed to me. A week before, they would have told a story, with myself as the hero of the tale. Now they were so many unhappy fragments. I looked to them for a meaning, and was defeated.

The keys I returned to my own key-chain; I couldn't quite give them up, not yet. But the other things I hid away as if ashamed of them. I went to bed early, and next morning I began the joyless task of picking up the threads of my old routines—the routines I'd had, I mean, before life at Hundreds so absorbed me. That afternoon I learned that the Hall and its lands had been put up for sale with a local agent. Makins, the dairyman, had been given the option of leaving the farm or buying it up for himself, and was choosing to leave: he hadn't the money to go into business on his own; the sudden sale had put him in a difficult spot and he was said to be very bitter about it. More pieces of information filtered through as the week progressed; vans were seen coming and going from the Hall, slowly emptying it of its contents. Most people naturally assumed that this was some plan of Caroline's and mine, and I had a trying few days, repeatedly explaining that the wedding had been cancelled and that Caroline was leaving the district alone. Then the news must have spread, for the questions abruptly died down, and the subsequent awkwardness was almost harder to bear than anything. I threw myself back into hospital work. There was, at that time, a great deal to do. I made no more visits to Hundreds; I'd already given up my short-cut across the park. I saw nothing of Caroline, though I thought about her, and dreamt about her, unnervingly often. I heard at last from Helen Desmond that she was due to leave the county, with the minimum of fuss, on the last day of May.

After that, there was only one desire in my heart, and that was for the rest of that month to pass as quickly and as painlessly as possible. I had a calendar on my consulting-room wall, and when the date of the wedding had first been decided I had taken it down and added jolly ink doodles to the square representing the twenty-seventh. Now a pride or a stubbornness prevented me from putting the calendar away. I wanted to see the day out: four days after it, Caroline would disappear properly from my life, and I had a superstitious feeling that once I could turn the page to June, I should be a new man. Meanwhile I watched the inked square approaching with a queasy mixture of longing and dread. In the final week of the month I grew increasingly distracted, unable to concentrate much on my work, and sleeping badly again.

As a result, the day itself passed off rather flatly. At one o'clock— the hour fixed for our wedding—I was sitting at the bedside of an elderly patient, concentrating on the case before me. When I left the patient's house and heard the half-hour struck, I felt almost unmoved— wondering vaguely which other couple had taken our slot at the registry office, that was all. I saw a few more cases; evening surgery was quiet, and I spent the rest of the evening at home. By half past ten I was weary, and was actually thinking of my bed; in fact, I had got as far as kicking off my shoes and was heading upstairs in my bedroom slippers, when there was a furious knocking and ringing at my surgery door. I found a boy of about seventeen there, so breathless he could hardly speak. He'd run five and a half miles to fetch me out for his sister's husband, who was in terrible trouble, he said, with pains in his belly. I gathered up my things and drove him back to his sister's house: it turned out to be the worst sort of place imaginable—an abandoned hut, with holes in its roof and gaps in its windows, and without light or water. The family were squatters, Oxfordshire people who had moved north looking for work. The husband had been ill 'on and off' for days, they told me, with vomiting, fever, and stomach pain; they had been treating him with castor oil, but over the past few hours he had grown so poorly they'd become frightened. Having no regular doctor, they hadn't known who to send out for. They had come to me in the end because they could remember having seen my name in the local paper.

The poor man was lying in the candle-lit parlour on a sort of truckle-bed, fully clothed and with an old army greatcoat across him. His temperature was high, his abdomen swollen, and so painful that when I started to examine him he screamed and swore and drew up his knees and feebly tried to kick me off. It was the plainest case of acute appendix I had ever seen, and I knew I had to get him to hospital at once, or risk the appendix bursting. The family were horrified at the thought of the expense that would be involved in submitting him for an operation. 'Can't you do nothing for him here?' the wife kept asking me, tugging at my sleeve. She and her mother knew of a girl who'd had her stomach washed after swallowing a bottle of pills; they wanted me to do the same for him. The man himself, even, had fastened on to this one idea: if I would 'just wash the poison out of him' he would be fine; that was all he wanted, and all he'd stand for. He hadn't let them fetch me, he said, to have me send him off to be cut up and pulled about by a lot of f—g doctors.

Then he was seized by a dreadful fit of vomiting, and passed beyond the point of speech. The family grew more frightened than ever. I managed to persuade them at last of the seriousness of his condition, and the issue then became how to get him to the hospital without delay. Ideally he should have gone by ambulance. But the hut was an isolated one, and the nearest telephone was at a post-office two miles away. I could see nothing for it but to take him myself, so the brother-in-law and I, between us, carried him outside on his truckle-bed, then carefully laid him on the back seat of my car. The wife squeezed herself in beside him, the boy sat in the front, and the couple's children were left in the care of the elderly mother. It was a pretty frightful journey we made, seven or eight miles mostly on lanes and back roads, the man groaning or screaming with every jolt of the car, now and then vomiting into a bowl; the woman weeping so much she was more or less useless; the boy scared out of his wits. The only thing in our favour was the moon, which was full, and bright as a lamp. Once we joined the Leamington road I could go faster; by half past twelve we were pulling up at the hospital doors, and twenty minutes later the man was taken off to the operating theatre—looking so ill by then, I really feared for his chances. I sat with the woman and the boy, not wanting to leave them until I had seen how the case turned out. At last the surgeon, Andrews, came to tell us that all had gone well. He had caught the appendix before perforation could take place, so there was now no threat of peritonitis; the man was weak but, apart from that, recovering nicely.

Andrews had the worst kind of public-school accent, and the wife was so dazed with worry I could see that she hardly understood him. When I explained that her husband had been saved, she almost fainted with relief. She wanted to see him; there was no chance of that. Nor would they let her and the boy stay in the waiting-room overnight. I offered to drive them home again on my way back to Lidcote, but they didn't want to stray so far from the hospital—possibly they were thinking of the bus-fares they would have to pay in coming back the next day. They said they had friends just outside Leamington who would let them have the use of a pony and cart; the boy would go back in it to let the old mother know that all was well, the woman would spend the night in town and return to see her husband in the morning. They seemed as fixated on the pony and cart idea as they had previously been on the stomach-washing, and I secretly wondered if they weren't simply going to go and sleep in some ditch until daylight. But again I offered them a lift, and this time they accepted; the place they led me to was another squatters' hut, just as dismal as their own, with a couple of dogs and horses tethered outside. The dogs set up a crazy barking as we arrived, and the door of the hut was opened by a man with a shotgun in his hands. But when he recognised his visitors he put the gun down and welcomed them in. They asked me to join them—they had 'plenty of tea and cider', they told me, warmly. For a second I was almost tempted. In the end I thanked them, but said good night. Before the door closed again I caught a glimpse of the room beyond, its floor a chaos of mattresses and sleeping bodies: adults, children, babies, dogs, and squirming blind-eyed puppies.

After the race to the hospital, followed by the dread of waiting and the subsequent relief, there was something mildly hallucinatory about the whole encounter, and my car, as I drew away, seemed by contrast very hushed and lonely. It's a queer thing, being plunged in and out of the dramas of one's patients—especially at night. The experience can leave one feeling drained, but also oddly wakeful and edgy, and now my mind, with nothing to anchor it, began to run over the details of the past few hours like a film on a loop. I remembered the boy, speechless and panting at my surgery door; the man, drawing up his knees and weakly kicking out at me; the woman's tears, the vomiting and yelling; Andrews, with his surgeon's manner and voice; the impossible cottage; the bodies and the puppies— On and on it went, over and over, compelling and exhausting, until, to break the spell of it, I wound down my window and lit a cigarette. And something about doing that, in the darkness of the car, with the soft white glare of the moon and the headlamps lighting my hands—something made me realise that the journey I was making was the journey I had made back in January, after the hospital dance. I looked at my watch: it was two a.m., on what should have been my wedding-night. I was meant to have been lying in a train now, with Caroline in my arms.

The loss and the grief rose up and swamped me, all over again. It was just as bad as it had ever been. I didn't want to go home to the empty bedroom in my cramped and cheerless house. I wanted Caroline;

I wanted Caroline and couldn't have her—that was all I knew. I had joined the Hundreds road by now, and the thought that she was so near, and yet so lost to me, made me shake. I had to throw away my cigarette and stop the car until the worst of the sensations had passed. But still I couldn't face going home. I drove on, slowly; and soon I reached the turning into the lane that led to that shady overgrown pond. I took it, and bumped along the track, and parked where Caroline and I had parked that time—the time I had reached to kiss her and she had first pushed me away.

The moon was so bright, the trees cast shadows, and the water seemed white as milk. The whole scene was like a photograph of itself, oddly developed and slightly unreal: I gazed at it, and it seemed to absorb me, I began to feel out of time and out of place, an absolute stranger. I think I smoked another cigarette. I know that presently I grew cold, and groped about on the back seat for the old red blanket I kept in the car—the blanket I had once tucked around Caroline—and wrapped myself up in it. I felt not at all weary, in the ordinary sense. I think I expected to sit there, wakeful, for the rest of the night. But I turned, and drew up my legs, and lowered my cheek to the back of the seat; and I sank into a fretful sort of slumber almost at once. And in the slumber I seemed to leave the car, and to press on to Hundreds: I saw myself doing it, with all the hectic, unnatural clarity with which I'd been recalling the dash to the hospital a little while before. I saw myself cross the silvered landscape and pass like smoke through the Hundreds gate. I saw myself start along the Hundreds drive.

But there I grew panicked and confused—for the drive was changed, was queer and wrong, was impossibly lengthy and tangled with, at the end of it, nothing but darkness.

I woke in daylight, chastened and cramped. It was just after six. The windows of the car were running with condensation and my head was bare: my hat had worked its way down between my shoulder and the seat, to be crushed beyond recovery, and the blanket was lumped around my waist as if I'd been wrestling with it. I opened the door to the fresh air, and climbed awkwardly out. There was a scuffling at my feet—I thought of rats, but it was hedgehogs, a pair of them, they had been nosing at the tyres of the car and now disappeared into the long grass. They left dark trails behind them: the grass was pale with dew. The pond had a faint mist across it—the water was grey now instead of white; the place had lost the air of unreality it had had in the early hours. I felt rather as I could remember feeling after a bad air raid in the city: coming blinking out of the shelter, seeing the houses marked but still standing, when in the midst of the worst of the bombing it had seemed as though the world were being blasted to bits.

But I felt, not dazed, so much simply as washed-out. The passion was gone from me. I wanted coffee, and a shave; and I needed the lavatory, badly. I moved to one side, and saw to that; then I combed my hair and did my best to straighten my crumpled clothes. I tried the car. It was damp, and cold, and wouldn't start at once, but after I'd lifted the bonnet and wiped the spark-plugs I got it going—the engine hammering open the country silence, frightening the birds from the trees. I drove back along the lane, briefly rejoined the Hundreds road, then turned off towards Lidcote. I met no one on the way, but the village was just coming to life, the labouring families already stirring, the bakery with a smoking chimney; the sun was low and shadows were long, and all the little details on the cobbled church, the red-brick houses and the shops, the empty pavements and the carless road—all looked crisp and clean and handsome.

My own house sits at the top of the High Street, and as I approached it I saw, at the surgery door, a man: he was ringing the night-bell, then cupping his hands around his eyes to gaze in through the pane of frosted glass beside the door. He had on a hat and a coat with the collar up, and I couldn't see his face; I supposed him a patient, and my heart sank. But hearing my car, he turned—and then I recognised David Graham. There was something about his pose that made me guess he had brought bad news. When I drew up, and saw his expression, I knew it must be very bad. I parked, and got out, and he came wearily over.

He said, 'I've been trying to find you. Oh, Faraday—' He passed his hand across his mouth. The morning was so silent, I heard the rasp of his unshaved chin against his palm.

I said, 'What is it? Is it Anne?' It was all I could think of.

'Anne?' He blinked his tired-looking eyes. 'No. It's— Faraday, I'm afraid it's Caroline. There's been an accident, at Hundreds. I'm so sorry.'

A telephone call had come out from the Hall, some time around three. It was Betty, in a dreadful state, wanting me; I, of course, was not at home, so the exchange had passed the message on to Graham. He was given no details, told only that he must get out to Hundreds as quickly as he could. He had pulled on his clothes and driven straight there—only to find his way blocked by the chained park gates. Betty had forgotten about the padlock. He tried one gate, then drove around and tried the other, but both were very securely fastened, and far too high to climb. He was just on the point of heading home and calling Betty by telephone when he thought of the new council houses and the breach in the park wall. The houses now had rudimentary gardens, with chain-link fences at the back; he was able to clamber over one of these fences and make his way up to the Hall on foot.

Betty answered the door to him, an oil-lamp trembling in her hand. She was, he said, 'beyond hysteria', almost dumb with shock and fear, and as soon as she had let him into the house he could see why. Behind her, in the moonlight, on the pink and liver–coloured marble floor, lay Caroline. She was dressed in her nightgown, the hem of it flung up and twisted. Her legs were bare, her hair seemed spread out like a halo around her head, and for a second, with the shadows so thick, he thought she might simply be lying there in some kind of fit or faint. Then he took the lamp from Betty and went over and, with horror, saw

that what he had taken for the spread of Caroline's hair was actually
darkening blood; he realised that she must have fallen from one of the
upstairs landings. Automatically he looked up, as if for broken banis-
ters; there was nothing amiss. He lit another couple of lamps and briefly
examined the body, but it was clear that Caroline was well beyond help.
She would have died, he thought, the moment her head had struck the
marble. He fetched a blanket and covered her over, then he took Betty
downstairs, and brewed some tea.

He hoped for an account of what had happened. But Betty, frustratingly, had nothing much to tell him. She had heard Caroline's step on
the landing, in the middle of the night. Coming out of her room to see
what the matter was, she had actually seen Caroline's falling body, then
heard the dreadful thump and crack of it hitting the marble below. That
was more or less all that she could say. She 'couldn't bear to think about
it'. The sight of Caroline plunging down in the moonlight was the most
horrible thing she'd ever seen. When she closed her eyes, she could still
see it. She thought she'd 'never be right again'.

Graham gave her a sedative, and then, just as I had recently done,
he picked up the old-fashioned Hundreds telephone and called for the
police and the mortuary van. He also called me, wanting to let me
know what had happened; again, of course, there was no answer. He
thought of the vehicles that would soon be coming, and remembered
the fastened park gates; he got the key to the padlocks from Betty and
went back across the moonlit park to his own car. He said he was glad
to leave the house, and reluctant to enter it again. He felt, irrationally,
as if the place had a sickness in it, a sort of lingering infection in its
floors and walls. But he stayed through all of the ensuing business: the
arrival of the sergeant, and the loading of Caroline's body into the van.
It was all finished by five o'clock; after that, there was only Betty to
deal with. She looked so shaken and pathetic, he considered taking her
home with him; again, though, he found himself oddly unwilling to
prolong his contact with the Hall. But it was out of the question to
leave her alone in that frightful setting, so he waited while she put her
things together, then drove her the nine-and-a-half miles to her parents'

house; he said she shivered all the way. After that he had returned to Lidcote, to tell Anne what had happened; and then he'd come looking for me.

He said, 'There was nothing you could have done, Faraday. And to be honest, I think it's a blessing the call came to me. There would have been no pain, I promise you. But Caroline's injuries—well, they were mostly to the head. It wasn't something you should have seen. I just didn't want you to hear about it from someone else. You were out with a patient, I suppose?'

We were upstairs by now, in my sitting-room. He had taken me up there and given me a cigarette. But the cigarette was burning beside me, unsmoked: I was leaning forward in my armchair, my elbows on my knees and my head in my hands. Without lifting my head, I said dimly, 'Yes. An acute appendix. It looked bad for a while. I took the man to Leamington myself. Andrews sorted him out.'

Graham said again, 'Well, there was absolutely nothing you could have done. I wish I'd known you were at the hospital, though. I could have reached you sooner there.'

I was having trouble piecing things together, and it took me a moment to understand him. But finally I realised that he assumed I had been at Leamington all night. I opened my mouth to tell him that, by a wretched coincidence, I'd actually been asleep in my car, only a couple of miles from Hundreds, when Caroline's fall must have taken place. But as I drew my hands from my face, I remembered the queer state I had worked myself into the night before, and I felt a curious shame about it. So I hesitated, and the moment passed; and then it was too late to speak. He saw my confusion, and misinterpreted it as grief. He said again how desperately sorry he was. He offered to make me tea, cook me up a breakfast. He said he didn't like to leave me on my own. He wanted me to go home with him, so that he and Anne could look after me. But to every suggestion, I shook my head.

When he saw that he couldn't persuade me, he slowly got to his feet. I rose too, to see him out, and we went downstairs to the surgery door.

He said, 'You look terrible, Faraday. I do wish you'd come back with me. Anne will never forgive me for not bringing you. Will you really be all right?'

I said, 'Yes. Yes, I'll be fine.'

'You're not going to sit here brooding? I know it's a lot to take in. But,' he grew awkward, 'don't go torturing yourself with all sorts of useless speculation, will you?'

I peered at him. 'Speculation?'

'I mean, as to how exactly Caroline died. The post-mortem might shed some light on it. There might have been some kind of seizure, who knows? People are bound to assume the worst, but it was probably an ordinary accident, and we'll simply never know for sure what happened . . . Poor Caroline. After all she'd been through. She deserved better, didn't she?'

I realised I hadn't even begun to wonder what had caused her to fall; as if her death had a sort of inevitability to it, that could overpower logic. Then, muddily thinking over Graham's words, I realised something else.

I said, 'You're not suggesting she did it deliberately? You can't think it was . . . suicide?'

He said hastily, 'Oh, I don't think anything. I only mean, because of what happened with her mother, people are bound to wonder. Look, what the hell does it matter? Forget about it, will you?'

'But it can't have been suicide,' I said. 'She must have slipped, or lost her balance. That house, at night, with the generator off—'

But I thought of the moonlight, that would have come streaming into the stairwell through the dome of glass in the roof. I pictured the solid Hundreds banister. I saw Caroline making her sturdy, sure-footed way along those familiar landings and stairs.

I stared at Graham, and he must have seen the bewildered churning of my ideas. He put his hand on my shoulder and said firmly again, 'Don't think about it. Not now. It's a ghastly thing, but it's finished. It was no fault of yours. There was nothing anyone could have done. You hear me?'

. . .

And perhaps there is a limit to the grieving that the human heart can do. As when one adds salt to a tumbler of water, there comes a point where simply no more will be absorbed. My thoughts chased themselves in uneasy circles for a time, then wore themselves out. I passed the next few days almost calmly, almost as if nothing much had changed; in a sense, for me nothing *had* changed. My neighbours and patients were very kind, but even they appeared to struggle to respond properly to Caroline's death: it had come too soon after her mother's, and was too much of a piece with all the other recent Hundreds mysteries and tragedies. There was a certain amount of muted debate about how the fall might have occurred, with most people, as Graham had predicted, favouring suicide, and many—thinking of Roderick, I suppose—mentioning madness. It was hoped that the post-mortem would reveal something; the results of the examination, however, did nothing to clear things up. For they revealed only that Caroline was fit and perfectly healthy. There had been no stroke, no seizure, no heart attack, and no struggle.

I would have been bleakly content for the matter to be left there. No amount of debate or speculation would return Caroline to life; nothing would bring her back to me. But from an official point of view, cause of death had to be determined. As he had after Mrs Ayres's suicide six weeks before, the borough coroner called for an inquest. And since I was the Ayres family doctor, to my very great dismay I was subpoenaed to attend.

I went along with Graham, and sat at his side. The day was Monday the fourteenth of June. The court was not crowded, but the weather was fine; we were all of us dressed as if for a funeral, in heavy blacks and greys, and the room quickly grew warm. Glancing around me as I sat, I made out the various spectators: the newspaper-men, the family friends, Bill Desmond and the Rossiters. Even Seeley, I saw, was there: he caught my eye, and inclined his head. Then I spotted Caroline's Sussex uncle and aunt, sitting with Harold Hepton. I had heard that they had been to see Roderick, and had been shaken by how they'd found him. News of his sister's death, apparently, had tipped him into absolute mania. They were staying out at Hundreds, doing what they could to sort out the estate's tangled finances on his behalf.

The aunt, I thought, looked ill. She seemed to want to avoid my eye. She and her husband would have heard from Hepton what had happened about the wedding.

Proceedings began. The members of the jury were sworn in; the coroner, Cedric Riddell, outlined the case, then started to call forward the witnesses. There were not many of us. The first to go up was Graham, to give a formal account of his attendance at the Hall on the night in question, and to offer his conclusions as to the circumstances of Caroline's death. He repeated the post-mortem results, which in his opinion ruled out the possibility of any physical crisis. He thought it much more likely, he said, that Caroline had simply fallen, through—as he put it—'accident or design'.

The local sergeant went up next. He confirmed that the house had given no sign of having been broken into, with its doors and windows all quite fast. He then produced photographs of Caroline's body, which were passed to the jury, and to one or two other people. I didn't see them, and was glad not to; I could tell from the jurors' reactions that the images were grim ones. But the man also had photographs of the Hall's second-floor landing, with its sturdy banister rail; Riddell looked closely at those, and requested details of the banister's dimensions—its width, its height from the floor. He then asked Graham for Caroline's measurements, and when Graham had hastily looked through his notes and provided them, he had one of his clerks improvise a mock-up of the banister, and invited the court secretary, a woman about the same height as Caroline, to stand beside it. The rail came to just above her hip. He asked her how easily she felt she might be tipped—say, after stumbling— over a rail at that height. She answered: 'Not very easily at all.'

He asked the sergeant to step down, and then he called Betty to the stand. She, of course, was the chief witness.

This was the first time I had seen her since my last, disastrous visit to the Hall, a fortnight before Caroline's death. She had come to the inquest with her father, and had been sitting with him at the side of the room; she made her way forward, a small, slight figure, looking more girlish than ever against that crowd of dark-suited men, her face pale, her colourless fringe pinned up at the side with a crooked grip, just as I remembered seeing it on my first trip to Hundreds nearly a year before. Only her clothes were a surprise to me, used as I was to her parlourmaid's costume. She wore a neat skirt and jacket, with a white blouse beneath. Her shoes had little tapping heels to them, and her stockings were dark, with seams.

She kissed the Testament with a nervous ducking of her head, but repeated the oath, and answered Riddell's preliminary questions in a strong, clear voice. I knew that her words would basically be an elaboration of what she'd already told Graham, and I dreaded having to hear the story again in more detail. I rested my elbows on the table before me, and sat with my hand across my eyes.

On the evening of the twenty-seventh of May, I heard her say, she and Miss Ayres had gone to bed early. The house was in 'a funny way' at that time, because virtually all of its carpets, curtains, and furniture had gone. Miss Ayres was due to leave the county on the thirty-first, and on the same day Betty herself had arranged to return to her parents. They were spending their final few days seeing to all the last jobs that had to be done before the house could be handed over to the agents. They had passed that particular day in sweeping and cleaning the empty rooms, and were very tired. No, Miss Ayres had not appeared to be in low spirits, was not dejected in any way. She had worked just as hard as Betty—if anything, she had worked harder. She had seemed to Betty to be looking forward to leaving, though she had not spoken much about her plans. She had said more than once that she 'wanted the house to be left tidy, for whoever should live in it next'.

Betty had gone to bed at ten o'clock. She had heard Miss Ayres go into her own room about half an hour later. She had heard it very clearly, because Miss Ayres's room was just around the landing from her own. Yes, that was the first landing. There was a second landing above, both of them overlooking the hall by the same stairwell, both lit by a glass dome in the roof.

At about half past two she had been woken by the creak of footsteps out on the stairs. At first she had been frightened. Why was that, Riddell asked her? She didn't quite know. Possibly the house, being large and lonely, was an unnerving one at night? Yes, she supposed that was it. The fear, anyway, had soon passed. She'd realised the steps were Miss Ayres's. She guessed that she had got up, perhaps to go to the lavatory, perhaps to make herself a warm drink in the kitchen downstairs. Then she heard more creaks, and realised with surprise that Miss Ayres was heading, not down, but up, to the house's second floor. Why did she think Miss Ayres had done that? She couldn't say. Was there anything up there but empty rooms? No, nothing at all. She had heard Miss Ayres go very slowly along the upstairs passage, as if she was feeling her way through the dark. Then she heard her stop, and make a sound.

Miss Ayres had made a sound? What sort of sound?

She had called something out.

Well, what had she called?

She had called out: 'You.'

I heard the word, and looked up. I saw Riddell pause. Gazing hard at Betty through the lenses of his spectacles he said, 'You heard Miss Ayres call out the single word, "You."'

Betty nodded unhappily. 'Yes, sir.'

'You are quite positive about that? She couldn't simply have been crying out? Exclaiming, or groaning?'

'Oh no, sir. I heard it very clear.'

'You did? And how exactly did she call it?'

'She called it as if she had seen someone she knew, sir, but as though she was afraid of them. Mortal afraid. And after that I heard her running. She came running back towards the stairs. I got out of bed, and went over to the door, and quickly opened it. And that's when I saw her falling.'

'You saw the fall clearly?'

'Yes, sir, because the moon was so bright.'

'And did Miss Ayres make any sound as she fell? I know it's a hard thing for you to recall. But did she seem to you to be struggling? Or did she drop straight, with her arms at her sides?'

'She didn't make any sound; only her breath was sort of rushing. And no, she didn't drop straight. Her arms and legs were waving about. They were waving like—like when you pick up a cat and it wants to be set down.'

Her voice had begun to falter on these last words, and now failed her completely. Riddell had one of the court clerks pour her a glass of water; he told her she was being very brave. But I heard all this, rather than saw it. I was leaning forward again with my hand across my eyes. For if the memory had proved too much for Betty, it had very nearly proved too much for me. I felt Graham touch my shoulder.

'All right?' he murmured.

I nodded.

'You're sure? You look ghastly.'

I straightened up. 'Yes, I'm all right.'

Reluctantly, he drew his hand away.

Betty had also recovered by now. Riddell, anyway, was almost finished. He was sorry to have to keep her there, he said; there was one last puzzling point he needed to clear up. She had said a moment ago that, in the seconds before she fell, Miss Ayres had called out in fear, as if to someone she knew, and that then she had been running. Had there been the sound of any other footsteps, or a voice—any other sound at all—either before the fall, or after it?

'No, sir,' said Betty.

'There was definitely no other person in the house, apart from you and Miss Ayres.'

Betty shook her head. 'No, sir. That is—'

She hesitated, and the hesitation made Riddell study her more closely. As I've said, he was a scrupulous man. A moment before, he had been ready to ask her to step down. Now he said, 'What is it? Do you have something to say?'

She said, 'I don't know, sir. I don't like to.'

'You don't like to? What do you mean? You mustn't be bashful or fearful, here. We are here to ascertain the facts. You must tell the truth, as the truth strikes you. Now, what is it?'

Biting at the inside of her mouth, she said, 'There wasn't a person in the house, sir. But I think there was something else. Something that didn't want Miss Caroline to leave it.'

Riddell looked puzzled. 'Something else?'

'Please sir,' she said, 'the ghost.'

She spoke fairly quietly, but the room was hushed; the words carried clearly across it, making a great impression on the gathering. There were murmurs; one person even laughed. Riddell glared around the court, then asked Betty what on earth she meant. And, rather to my horror, she began earnestly to tell him.

She told him about the house having been, in her expression, 'jumpy'. She said 'a ghost lived in it'; that it was this ghost that had made Gyp bite Gillian Baker-Hyde. She said that then the ghost had started fires, and the fires had driven Mr Roderick mad; and after that the ghost had 'spoken to Mrs Ayres, and said awful things, that made her kill herself'. And now the ghost had killed Miss Caroline too, by drawing her up to the second landing and pushing or scaring her off it. The ghost 'hadn't wanted her in the house, but it hadn't wanted her to go, either'. It was 'a spiteful ghost, and wanted the house all for its own'.

I suppose that, having been repeatedly denied an audience at Hundreds itself, she was innocently determined to make the most of the one before her now. When there were murmurs from the crowd again, she raised her voice and her tone grew stubborn. I glanced around the room, and saw several people openly smiling; most, however, were gazing at her in fascinated disbelief. Caroline's aunt and uncle looked outraged. The newspaper-men, of course, were busily writing the whole thing down.

Graham bent his head to me, frowning. 'You knew about all this?'

I didn't answer. The grotesque little story had come to its end, and Riddell was calling for order.

'Well,' he said to Betty when the room was silent. 'You have told us a most extraordinary tale. Not being an expert on ghost-hunting and so on, I hardly feel qualified to comment on it.'

Betty flushed. 'It's true, sir. I in't lying!'

'Yes, all right. Let me just ask you this: Did Miss Ayres herself believe in the Hundreds "ghost"? Did she think it had done all those terrible things you've mentioned?'

'Oh, yes, sir. She believed it more than anyone.'

Riddell looked grave. 'Thank you. We are very grateful to you. You have thrown a good deal of light, I think, on Miss Ayres's state of mind.'

He waved her down. She hesitated, confused by his words and gesture. He dismissed her more plainly, and she went back to join her father.

And then it was my turn. Riddell called me to the stand, and I rose and took my place, with a feeling almost of dread—almost as if this were some sort of criminal trial, with myself as the accused. The clerk swore me in, and when I spoke I had to clear my throat and say the oath over again. I asked for water, and Riddell waited, patiently, while I drank it.

Then he began his examination. He began it by briefly reminding the court of the evidence we had heard so far.

Our task, he said, was to determine the circumstances surrounding Miss Ayres's fatal fall, and as far as he could see it, there were several possibilities still before us. Foul play, he thought, was not one of them; none of the pieces of evidence pointed that way. It seemed unlikely, too, given the report of Dr Graham, that Miss Ayres had become physically ill—though it was perfectly possible that she had, for whatever reason, *believed* herself to be ill, and that belief might have startled or weakened her to the extent of causing her to fall. Or, if we kept in mind what the family maid claimed to have heard her cry out, we might conclude that she had been startled by something else, something she had seen or fancied she had seen, and had lost her footing as a result. Working against those theories, however, was the height and obvious solidity of the Hundreds banister rail.

But there were two further possibilities. Both were forms of suicide. Miss Ayres might have flung herself from the landing as a way of taking her own life, in a premeditated act, planned in the full clarity of mind—in other words, a *felo de se*. Or she might have jumped deliberately, but in response to some delusion.

He glanced over his notes, then turned to me. I was, he knew, the Ayres family doctor. Miss Ayres and I had also—he was sorry to have to raise this, but he understood that Miss Ayres and I had recently been engaged to be married. He would attempt, he said, to keep his questions as delicate as possible, but he was anxious to establish all he could about Miss Ayres's emotional state on the night of her death; and he hoped I would help him.

Clearing my throat again, I said I would do my best.

He asked me when I had last seen Caroline. I answered that I had last seen her in the afternoon of the sixteenth of May, when I had visited the Hall with Mrs Graham, my partner's wife.

He asked about Caroline's state of mind at that time. She and I had only very recently broken off our engagement—was that correct?

'Yes,' I said.

Had the decision been a mutual one?

'You'll forgive my asking, I hope,' he added, perhaps in response to my expression. 'What I'm trying to ascertain for the court is whether the separation might have left Miss Ayres unduly distressed.'

I glanced over at the jury, and thought how much Caroline herself would have hated all this; how she would have loathed to think of us here, in our black suits, picking over the last days of her life like crows in a cornfield.

I said quietly, 'No, I don't think it had left her in undue distress. She had had a—a change of heart, that's all.'

'A change of heart, I see . . . And one of the effects of this change of heart, I believe, was that Miss Ayres had decided to sell her family home and leave the county. What did you make of that decision?'

'Well, it surprised me. I thought it drastic.'

'Drastic?'

'Unrealistic. Caroline had spoken of emigrating, to America or Canada. She had spoken of possibly taking her brother with her.'

'Her brother, Mr Roderick Ayres, who is currently a patient at a private institution for mental cases.'

'Yes.'

'His condition, I understand, is a grave one. Was Miss Ayres upset by his illness?'

'Naturally she was.'

'Overly upset?'

I thought about it. 'No, I wouldn't say that.'

'Did she show you tickets, or reservations, or anything like that, relating to this trip to America or Canada?'

'No.'

'But you think she meant it, sincerely?'

'Well, as far as I know. She had the idea'—I paused—'well, that England didn't want her. That there was no place for her here now.'

A couple of the gentry spectators nodded grimly at that. Riddell himself looked thoughtful, and was silent for a moment, adding a note to the papers before him. Then he turned to the jury.

'I'm very interested in these plans of Miss Ayres's,' he told them. 'I'm wondering how seriously we ought to take them. On the one hand, you see, we've heard that she was about to begin a new life, and was full of excitement about it. On the other, the plans might have struck you, as they struck Dr Faraday and, I must confess, they've struck me, as rather "unrealistic". No evidence exists to support them; all the evidence, in fact, suggests that Miss Ayres was far more concerned with *ending* a life than with beginning one. She had recently broken off an engagement of marriage; she had disposed of the bulk of her family's possessions; and she was taking care to leave her empty home in good order. All this *might* speak to us of a suicide, carefully planned and reasoned.'

He turned back to me.

'Dr Faraday, did Miss Ayres ever strike you as the sort or person who might be capable of suicide?'

I said after a second that I supposed any person might be capable of suicide, given the right conditions.

'Did she ever mention suicide to you?'

'No.'

'Her mother, of course, had recently and most tragically taken her own life. That must have affected her?'

'It had affected her,' I said, 'in all the ways one would expect. It had put her in low spirits.'

'Would you say it had made her feel hopeless about life?'

'No, I— No, I wouldn't say that.'

He tilted his head. 'Would you say it had affected the balance of her mind?'

I hesitated. 'The balance of a person's mind,' I started at last, 'is sometimes a difficult thing to gauge.'

'I'm certain it is. That is why I am taking such pains to try and gauge the balance of Miss Ayres's. Did you ever have any doubts about it, Dr Faraday? Any doubts at all? This "change of heart", for example, over your wedding. Did that seem in character to you?'

After another hesitation I admitted that Caroline had, in fact, seemed to me to have been behaving erratically, in the final weeks of her life.

He said, 'What do you mean by "erratically"?'

I said, 'She was distant, not herself. She had . . . odd ideas.'

'Odd ideas?'

'About her family, and about her house.'

My voice sank on these words. Peering at me rather as he had peered at Betty, he said, 'Did Miss Ayres ever mention ghosts or phantoms to you, things like that?'

I didn't answer.

He went on, 'We have all just heard a quite extraordinary account of life at Hundreds Hall from the family's maid, that is why I am asking. You'll appreciate, I think, that this is an important point. Did Miss Ayres ever at any time speak to you about ghosts or phantoms?'

I said finally, 'Yes, she did.'

There were more murmurs. This time Riddell ignored them. Looking fixedly at me, he said, 'Miss Ayres seriously believed her home to be haunted?'

I said, with reluctance, that Caroline had believed that the Hall was in the grip of some sort of influence. A supernatural influence. 'I don't think she ever believed in an actual ghost.'

'But she believed she had seen evidence of this . . . supernatural influence?'

'Yes.'

'What form did the evidence take?'

I took a breath. 'She believed that her brother had more or less been driven mad by it. She believed that her mother had been affected by it, too.'

'She believed, like the family maid, that the influence was responsible for her mother's suicide?'

'Broadly, yes.'

'Did you encourage her in that belief?'

'Of course I didn't. I deplored it. I thought it morbid. I tried my very best to *dis*courage it.'

'But the belief persisted?'

'Yes.'

'How do you account for that?'

I said miserably, 'I can't. I wish I could.'

'You don't think it was evidence of mental derangement?'

'I don't know. Caroline herself spoke to me of a—a family taint. She was afraid, I know that. But you have to understand, there were things that happened at the house— I don't know.'

Riddell looked troubled, removing his spectacles to pinch at the bridge of his nose. And as he worked the wire arms back around his ears he said, 'I have to tell you, Dr Faraday, I met Miss Ayres, more than once; many people in this room knew her far better than I did. All of us, I think, would agree that she was the most level-headed of young women. That the Hundreds parlourmaid should have given way to supernatural fancies is one thing. But for an intelligent, healthy, well-bred girl like Caroline Ayres to have come to suppose herself haunted—well, surely some quite serious deterioration must have taken place? This is a terribly sad case, and I realise it may be difficult for you to admit that someone for whom you once cared very deeply was of an unbalanced state of mind. But it seems pretty clear to me that what we are dealing with here is a case of inherited family madness—a family "taint", in Miss Ayres's own expression. Could it be that when, in the seconds before she died, she called out "You!", it was in response to some hallucination? That the madness already had her in its grip? We will never know. I am strongly inclined, however, to instruct the jury to return a verdict of "suicide whilst of unsound mind".

'But I am not a doctor,' he continued. 'You are the family physician, and I would like your support on that verdict. If you do not feel able to give me that support, you must say so, very plainly; in which case, my instruction to the jury may have to be different. Can you offer me that support, or not?'

I gazed down at my hands; they were shaking slightly. The room was warmer than ever, and I was horribly aware of the jurors' eyes. Again I had the sense that something was on trial here, something in which I was personally and guiltily involved.

Was there a taint? Is that what had terrorised the family, day after day, month by month, and finally destroyed it? That was what Riddell believed, clearly, and once I would have agreed with him. I would have set out the evidence just as he had, until it told the story I wanted it to tell. But my confidence in that story was shaken now. It seemed to me that the calamity that had overtaken Hundreds Hall was a far stranger thing; not a thing to be decided on, neatly, in a small plain room in a court of law.

But then, what *was* it?

I looked up, into the sea of watchful faces. I caught sight of Graham, and Hepton, and Seeley. I think Seeley nodded slightly—though whether he was urging me to speech, or to silence, I don't know. I saw Betty, gazing at me with her light, bewildered eyes . . . Then across that image there came another: the Hundreds landing, lit bright by the moon. And once again I seemed to see Caroline, making her sure-footed way along it. I saw her doubtfully mounting the stairs, as if drawn upwards by a familiar voice; I saw her advance into the darkness, not quite certain of what was before her. Then I saw her face—saw it as vividly as the faces all around me. I saw recognition, and understanding, and horror, in her expression. Just for a moment—as if it were there, in the silvered surface of her moonlit eye—I even seemed to catch the outline of some shadowy, dreadful thing—

I seized the wooden rail in front of me, and heard Riddell say my name. The clerk hastily brought more water; there were more murmurs from the court. But the moment of giddiness had already passed, and the fragment of Hundreds nightmare that I had glimpsed had retreated into darkness. And what did it matter now, anyway? Everything was finished, now; wasted and gone. I wiped my face, and stood more steadily, and turned to Riddell to say in a toneless voice that, yes, I would support him. I believed Caroline's mind, in the last few weeks of her life, to have become clouded, and her death to have been a suicide.

He thanked me, and stood me down, then gave his summing up of the case. The jury retired, but with such a clear direction, they had little to debate: they soon returned, with the expected verdict and, after the usual formalities, the inquest was closed. People stood, chairs scraped and grated. The voices rose up. I said to Graham, 'For God's sake, let's go quickly, can we?'

He put his hand under my elbow and steered me from the room.

I didn't look at any of the newspapers that came out later that week, but I gather they made a great deal of Betty's account of Hundreds being 'haunted'. I understand that a few ghoulish people even contacted the house-agent, posing as prospective buyers in an attempt to be given a tour of the Hall; and once or twice when I was out on the Hundreds road at that time I saw cars or bicycles drawn up at the park gates, and people peering through the ironwork—as if the house had become an attraction for trippers, like a castle or a stately home. Caroline's funeral drew spectators, for the same sort of reason, though it was kept as modest as possible by her uncle and aunt, with no pealing of the church bell, no display of flowers, and no wake. The crowd of actual mourners was small, and I stayed well to the back of it. I took along the unworn wedding-ring, and held it in my pocket, and turned and turned it between my fingers as the coffin was lowered.

FIFTEEN

T hat was just over three years ago. Since then, I have kept very busy. When the new Health Service arrived I didn't, as I'd feared I would, lose patients; in fact I gained them, probably partly as a result of my connection with the Ayreses, for, like those Oxfordshire squatters, many people had come across my name in the local papers and seemed to see me as a sort of 'coming man'. I am told now that I am popular, that my manner is down-to-earth. I still practise out of Dr Gill's old place at the top of Lidcote High Street; it still suits a bachelor, well enough. But the village is rapidly expanding, there are many new young families, and the consulting-room and dispensary look increasingly out-of-date. Graham, Seeley, and I have begun to talk of combining practices in a brand-new health centre, with Maurice Babb to build it.

Roderick's condition, unfortunately, has failed to improve. I had hoped that the loss of his sister might finally release him from his delusion: for what, I thought, could he possibly still have to fear from Hundreds, after that? But Caroline's death, if anything, has had the opposite effect. He blames himself for all the tragedies, and seems bent on self-punishment. He has burnt and bruised and scalded himself so many times he's now kept almost permanently sedated, and is the shadow of the boy he once was. I go to see him when I can. That is easier than it used to be, because with the final drying up of the family income it became impossible for him to remain at Dr Warren's rather costly private clinic. These days he is a patient at the county mental hospital, sharing a ward with eleven other men.

The council houses on the edge of Hundreds Park have been a great success—so much so that last year a dozen more were added, and others are planned. Many of the families are on my list, so I am out there quite often. The houses are cosy enough, with neat flower and vegetable gardens, and swings and slides set up for the children. Only one real change has been made, and that is that the chain-link fences at the rear of the estate have been replaced by a fence of wood. The families themselves requested this: it seems that none of them much enjoyed gazing out from their back windows at the Hall; they said the house 'gave them the creeps'. Stories about the Hundreds ghost continue to circulate, mainly among the younger people and the newcomers, people with no real knowledge of the Ayreses themselves. The most popular tale, I gather, is that the Hall is haunted by the spirit of a servant-girl who was badly treated by a cruel master, and who jumped or was pushed to her death from one of the upstairs windows. She's regularly seen in the park, apparently, weeping and weeping as though her heart will break.

I bumped into Betty once, on the road in front of the houses. One of the families living out there is related to hers. It was a few months after Caroline's death. I saw a young woman and a young man coming out through a garden gate as I was parking my car; a minute later I drew in my door to let them pass, and the young woman paused and said, 'Don't you know me, Dr Faraday?' I looked into her face, and saw those wide grey eyes of hers, and her little crooked teeth; I wouldn't have recognised her otherwise. She was wearing a cheap summer frock with a fashionable swing to its skirt. Her colourless hair had been lightened and permed, her lips and cheeks were red with rouge; she was still small, but her slightness had gone, or else she'd found some artificial way to improve her figure. I suppose she was almost sixteen. She told me she was still living with her parents, and her mother was still 'carrying on', but she'd at last got the sort of job she wanted, in a bicycle factory. The work was dull enough, but the other girls were 'a laugh'; she had her evenings and her weekends to herself, and often went dancing up in Coventry. She kept her arm through that of her young man all the time she spoke. He looked about twenty-two or -three: almost the same age as Roderick.

She made no reference to the inquest, or to Caroline's death, and I began to think, as she chattered on, that she wasn't going to mention Hundreds at all—as if the whole dark interlude had left no mark on her. But then the people she had been visiting looked out of their house and called to the young man, and once he had moved off her bright manner seemed slightly to fade.

I said quietly, 'You don't mind coming so close to Hundreds then, Betty?'

She blushed, and shook her head.

'I wouldn't go back in the house, though. Not for a thousand pounds! I have dreams about it, all the time.'

'Do you?' I never dreamt about it now.

'Not bad dreams,' she said. She wrinkled up her nose. 'Funny dreams. I dream most about Mrs Ayres. I dream she tries to give me things, jewels and brooches and things like that. And I never want to take them, I don't know why; and in the end it makes her cry . . . Poor Mrs Ayres. She were such a nice lady. Miss Caroline, too. It wasn't fair, was it, what happened to them?'

I agreed that it wasn't. We stood sadly for a moment, with nothing more to say. I thought what a very unremarkable pair we must have made to anybody watching; and yet, out of the wreckage of that terrible year, she and I were the only survivors.

Then her young man ambled back to us, and she grew pert again. She gave me her hand in farewell, put her arm through his, and they headed off towards the bus-stop. I saw them still there, twenty minutes later, when I returned to my car: they were larking about on the bench, he had pulled her into his lap and she was kicking up her legs and laughing.

Hundreds Hall is still unsold. No one has the money or the inclination to take it on. For a while there was talk of the county council making a teacher-training centre of it. Then a Birmingham businessman apparently considered it for an hotel. But the rumours surface, and come to nothing; and recently they've begun to surface less often. Probably the look of the place has begun to put people off—for of course, the gardens are hopelessly overgrown now, and the terrace has been lost to the weeds; children have chalked on the walls and thrown stones at the windows, and the house seems to sit in the chaos like some wounded, blighted beast.

I go out there whenever my busy days will allow. None of the locks has been changed, and I still have my keys. Very occasionally I'll find that someone has been there in my absence—a tramp or a squatter—and has tried to force the door; the doors are solid ones, however, and on the whole the Hall's reputation keeps outsiders away. And there is nothing to steal, for what Caroline failed to sell in the weeks before she died, her uncle and aunt disposed of.

The downstairs rooms I tend to keep shuttered. The second floor has been giving me some anxiety lately: there are holes appearing in the roof, where slates have been lost in bad weather; a family of swallows has come right into the old day-nursery and built a nest there. I put down pails to catch the rainwater, and have boarded up the worst of the broken windows. Every so often I go right through the house, sweeping up the dust and the mouse-dirt. The saloon ceiling still holds, though it can only be a matter of time before the bloated stucco tumbles. Caroline's bedroom continues to fade. Roderick's room, even now, smells faintly of burning . . . Despite all this, the house retains its beauty. In some ways it is handsomer than ever, for without the carpets and the furniture and the clutter of occupation, one appreciates the lines and Georgian symmetries, the lovely shifts between shadow and light, the gentle progression of the rooms. Wandering softly through the twilit spaces, I can even seem to see the house as its architect must have done when it was new, with its plaster detail fresh and unchipped, its surfaces unblemished. In those moments there is no trace of the Ayreses at all. It is as if the house has thrown the family off, like springing turf throwing off a footprint.

I am no nearer now to understanding just what happened at the Hall than I was three years ago. Once or twice I've spoken about it to Seeley. He has come down firmly in favour of his old, rational view that Hundreds was, in effect, defeated by history, destroyed by its own failure to keep pace with a rapidly changing world. In his opinion, the Ayreses, unable to advance with the times, simply opted for retreat—for suicide, and madness. Right across England, he says, other old gentry families are probably disappearing in exactly the same way.

The theory is convincing enough; and yet, sometimes I am troubled. I remember poor, good-tempered Gyp; I recall those mysterious black smudges on the walls and ceiling of Roderick's room; I picture the three little drops of blood that I once saw springing to the surface of Mrs Ayres's silk blouse. And I think of Caroline. I think of Caroline, in the moments before she died, advancing across that moonlit landing. I think of her crying out: *You!*

I've never attempted to remind Seeley of his other, odder theory: that Hundreds was consumed by some dark germ, some ravenous shadow-creature, some 'little stranger', spawned from the troubled unconscious of someone connected with the house itself. But on my solitary visits, I find myself growing watchful. Every so often I'll sense a presence, or catch a movement at the corner of my eye, and my heart will give a jolt of fear and expectation: I'll imagine that the secret is about to be revealed to me at last; that I will see what Caroline saw, and recognise it, as she did.

If Hundreds Hall is haunted, however, its ghost doesn't show itself to me. For I'll turn, and am disappointed—realising that what I am looking at is only a cracked window-pane, and that the face gazing distortedly from it, baffled and longing, is my own.

ACKNOWLEDGEMENTS

Thanks to all my supportive and generous early readers: Alison Oram, Sally O-J, Antony Topping, Hirāni Himona, Jennifer Vaughan, Terry Vaughan, and Ceri Williams. Thanks to my agent, Judith Murray; and to my editors in the U.K., the U.S., and Canada: Lennie Goodings, Megan Lynch, and Lara Hinchberger. Thanks to the staff at Greene & Heaton Ltd; Little, Brown; Riverhead; and McClelland & Stewart who read and commented on the manuscript. Thanks to Hilda Walsh for advice on muscles. Special thanks to Angela Hewins for her patient answers to my fumbling queries on Warwickshire life. Extra special thanks to Lucy Vaughan.

Part of *The Little Stranger* was written during an inspiring month at Hedgebrook women writers' retreat on Whidbey Island, and I am hugely grateful both to the staff of Hedgebrook for facilitating that visit, and to the authors I met while I was there.

I am also indebted to various works of nonfiction. These include: Edmund Gurney, Frederic W. H. Myers, and Frank Podmore, *Phantasms of the Living* (London, 1886); Catherine Crowe, *The Night Side of Nature* (London, 1848); Harry Price, *Poltergeist Over England* (London, 1945); Hereward Carrington and Nandor Fodor, *Haunted People* (New York, 1951); Nandor Fodor, *On the Trail of the Poltergeist* (New York, 1958); A. R. G. Owen, *Can We Explain the Poltergeist?* (New York, 1964); Kenneth Lane, *Diary of a Medical Nobody* (London, 1982) and *West Country Doctor* (London,

1984); John Pemberton, *Will Pickles of Wensleydale* (London, 1970); Dawn Robertson, *A Country Doctor* (Kirkby Stephen, 1999); Geoffrey Barber, *Country Doctor* (Ipswich, 1974); Geoffrey Tyack, *Warwickshire Country Houses* (Chichester, 1994); George Hewins, *The Dillen*, edited by Angela Hewins (London, 1981); and Angela Hewins, *Mary, After the Queen* (Oxford, 1985).